JUDGE LYNCH!

by

James M. Redwine

authorHOUSE®

AuthorHouse™
1663 Liberty Drive, Suite 200
Bloomington, IN 47403
www.authorhouse.com
Phone: 1-800-839-8640

First published by AuthorHouse 7/9/2008

ISBN: 978-1-4343-9402-6 (sc)
ISBN: 978-1-4343-9403-3 (hc)

Library of Congress Control Number: 2008906172

Printed in the United States of America
Bloomington, Indiana

This book is printed on acid-free paper.

Taken from The Police Gazette (1878),
edited by Gene Smith and Jayne Barry Smith

Acknowledgements

Research for this book began in 1990. From 1990 to December 2007, I wrote several published newspaper columns on the lynchings and continued to search and research court records and other sources such as microfilmed newspapers and state archives.

My wife, Peg, suffered through this entire period without demur as factual information remained buried. I did not wish to have hiatuses. Interpretation was acceptable; interpolation was not, as long as the work was one of pure history.

However, when I announced to Peg during Christmas of 2007 that I needed just a few more pieces of hard evidence, she broke. The options she gave were simple: finish the book or never mention it again. In May 2008, four hundred plus pages were sent to the publisher as historical fiction, not historical fact. As Peg has tried for years to explain to me, an imperfect justice for the actors involved is still better than none at all.

As Peg has typed and retyped every word, she is justified in demanding either completion or abandonment, not of me, of course, just the book. Thank you, Peg, you made it happen.

Many thanks are also due to Rodney Fetcher, for his generous help and expertise with photographs, graphics and computerization of the manuscript. Rodney and RAF Productions helped bring this project to print. Thank you, Rodney. Thanks also to Denny Schwindel and Schwindel Graphics for expertise in enhancing the illustrations.

My sister, Associate Professor Jane (Redwine) Bartlett, ret., made important suggestions about the manuscript and encouraged Peg and me over these many years. She is the world's best sister and our parents' favorite; at least that has always been my position and the position of our brothers, C.E. and Philip Redwine, who also helped bring this book to print.

Judge D. Neil Harris of Pascagoula, Mississippi gave important encouragement and support. His comments on the manuscript were most helpful. Thank you, Neil.

Shawnna Newton Rigsby provided insight and constructive criticism. Dr. John Emhuff made valuable suggestions and Ed Mc Cutchen shared his research on the lynchings. Thank you, Shawnna, John and Ed.

Gene Smith and Jayne Barry Smith compiled and edited an October 1878 report on the lynchings as carried in *The Police Gazette*. Gene also made helpful suggestions concerning the publication of this book. Thank you, Gene.

Becky Boggs generously allowed her photographs to be used as did Anne Doane her sketches. Thank you, Becky and Anne.

Ilse Horacek, about whom more will be written in the Preface, guided me to the newspaper accounts of the events that are the focus of this story. Thank you, Ilse.

Richard Simmons was the maintenance supervisor at our old courthouse for over ten years. He is solely responsible for finding and preserving numerous irreplaceable artifacts of Posey County history. His vision, hard work and personal sacrifice should be appreciated by all residents of Posey County. Thank you, Dick.

Posey County's officially designated Historian, Glenn Curtis, and his brother, Kenneth Curtis, saw a photograph of the 1878 lynchings. Each brother was shown the photograph by Oscar Weckesser while in the Noble Ford Barbershop that used to be across Fourth Street from the old Weckesser Tavern in Mt. Vernon, Indiana. Glenn saw the sepia toned picture in 1952, and Kenny saw it about 1956 after he returned from his service with the Marines. Thank you, Glenn and Kenny, for sharing your observations of the photograph with me.

Each brother vividly remembers, even after fifty years, the elongated necks, swollen tongues and "cue ball size" eyes of the four young Negro men hanging from the locust trees on the courthouse campus, strange fruit indeed.

CONTENTS

PREFACE

On March 14, 1990, I spoke to the Posey County Coterie Literary
Society in the courtroom of the Posey Circuit Court in Mt. Vernon,
Indiana. As a thank you, the Society presented me with William P.
Leonard's *History and Directory of Posey County* (1882). The presenta-
tion was made by the Society's President, Ilse Horacek.

I read the book the following weekend and was struck by three
brief paragraphs found at page 101:

cs

"Annie McCool, a white prostitute, was murdered at Mt.
Vernon, by some unknown person, in September, 1878. Her
murderer was supposed to have been a negro paramour.

Daniel Harris, a negro, on October 11, 1878, shot and
killed Cyrus Oscar Thomas, a son of Geo. W. Thomas, Esq.,
of Mt. Vernon, while the latter was in discharge of his duty as
Deputy Sheriff. Harris was indicted by the grand jury at the
October term of the Circuit Court in 1878, and at the August
term of that court in 1881, the prosecutor, William H. Gudgel,
entered a *nolle prosequi*. It is supposed by some and denied by
others that Harris was murdered by the friends of his victim
who disposed of his body by means which will forever leave its
whereabouts a mystery.

James Good, Jeff Hopkins, Wm. Chambers and Edward Warner, all colored, were hanged October 12, 1878, by a body of unknown men, from trees in the Public Square, at Mt. Vernon for murders and other heinous acts committed by them during that year."

CŖ

I could not find any further description of these events that had occurred right outside my court chambers so I contacted Ilse who brought me a copy of the *Western Star* newspaper of October 17, 1878, that she had pieced together from the microfilm records stored at the Alexandrian Public Library in Mt. Vernon.

As a German child during World War II, Ilse observed firsthand the denial of civil rights by those in power. After marrying a soldier from Posey County whom she met in Germany, Ilse made her home in Mt. Vernon and has always been vigilant in the cause of equal justice for all. Ilse pointed me to other sources for more information.

One thing that I personally observed was the four old hangman's nooses that are still on display at the Posey County Jail. On May 21, 1992, I took those nooses to be props for a speech I had been asked to give on the 1991 Rodney King police brutality case to our local Kiwanis Club. The reaction of the crowd of business and professional leaders to my comparison of the 1991 case in Los Angeles to the 1878 lynchings in Posey County was a surprise to me. That is when I began in earnest to search through the old court records in the courthouse catacombs and the Indiana State Archives.

I have also written about the events of October 1878 several times over the last few years in my weekly column, "Gavel Gamut". The column appears in our three Posey County newspapers, *The Mt. Vernon Democrat, The Posey County News,* and the recently revived *Western Star* as well as *The Carmi Times* in Illinois.

Each October for the past three years I have reprised the murders and the cover-up. On numerous occasions I have solicited family diaries or records, such as a copy of the photograph Glenn and Kenneth Curtis saw in the 1950's. Perhaps this book may help bring out more facts.

The Harrison family is often referred to in news accounts and even court records as Harris. For the sake of consistency, Harrison is used throughout this book.

Much of this novel is rooted in fact. But, because many in the white community of 1878 had good reason to avoid exposure and many in the black community were driven out, I have taken poetic license to tell the story and call for such atonement as may be possible.

Jim Redwine, May 2008

FOREWORD

IF WE STAND IN THE shadows cast by those who have touched our lives, as a respected friend has said, then the shadows of our parents dwarf the efforts of my brothers and me to be egalitarian. Tolerance and acceptance were not simply ideals to A. C. and Clarice Redwine but were concepts which fueled their daily speech and behaviors.

Oklahoma, including the small town in which we were raised in the 1940's into the 1960's, was segregated by race, skin color, culture and religion. To say the citizens of our community were actively prejudiced would be basically untrue. The truth was that separation and prejudice were the reality of life in our culture at that time and in that place, ingrained to the point of invisibility, except to those most affected.

Our hometown housed the Osage Indian Agency on the hill and Indian Camp at the north edge of town where some Osages lived and many Osage students attended school. At the south edge of town were the homes for our Black residents and the school for Black students.

Many of the Osage families lived throughout the town; however, all of the Black families lived across the tracks and on the other side of Bird Creek. The varying segments of our community lived apart yet were interdependent in ways that probably only a citizen from that era would recognize.

We Redwine siblings are grateful that in a time of prejudice and segregation, in a small Oklahoma town, we came under the shadow cast by and the influence of our parents. Dad's business took him into the homes of all—Blacks, Indians and Caucasians; and he counted all friends and equals. Any behavior on his children's part to not emulate him met with firm but kind disapproval.

Dad and Mom visited the Black churches, taking us with them and inviting a choir they had heard in those churches to sing in our home church—Dad along with a friend and colleague resigning from our church board in the aftermath of the response to that invitation. The resignations were not accepted, and the choir did eventually sing, to a standing room only crowd.

Conversations in our home focused often on the inequalities, prejudices and segregated policies with which we lived, and we were expected to be actively involved in seeking to end these where we encountered them. A poignant memory is of the anger and helplessness expressed by Dad and Mom when a Black friend's son drowned in Bird Creek. The city swimming pool was not open to the Black community.

Dad and Mom followed the Civil Rights bill debates and shared their hopes for enlightened action by our political leaders, believing such laws could be a beginning to the end of segregation and prejudice. Dad died before that legislation was passed.

Atypical of that era was the presence of our Black friends at Dad's funeral—typical was the felt need for a Black spokesperson to call and ask if the Black community would be welcome in our church. Mom responded positively, and privately said that when I talked to our pastor, if the Black community would not be welcome, Dad's services would be held elsewhere.

Readers who recall parents similar to ours know that the shadow of such character strengths demand similar actions and behaviors. Beyond all of that, the ability to perceive, to recognize, to realize, to investigate, to attempt to remedy injustice may be such a parent's greatest gift.

I believe this is the impetus that drives my brother, Jim, to tell the story of these seven men. That the events must be fictionalized says much about the culture in which they occurred and the difficulty of uncovering the truth.

D. Jane Redwine Bartlett,
Associate Professor of Psychology,
Retired

This work is offered as an elegy to:

<u>Daniel Harrison, Sr.</u>

Who was, "butchered like a hog",
then dumped into the jailhouse privy on October 12, 1878;

<u>Daniel Harrison, Jr.</u>

Who was burned to death in the fire box of a steam locomotive on
October 10, 1878;

<u>John Harrison</u>

Who was shot then stuffed into the hollow trunk of a tree
on October 11, 1878; and

<u>Jim Good, William Chambers,</u>
<u>Edward Warner & Jeff Hopkins</u>

Who were lynched on the courthouse campus in Posey County, Indiana on October 12, 1878.

THE FOLLOWING SPEECH/POEM WAS WRITTEN by the author and given February 2, 2003 at the Alexandrian Public Library in Mt. Vernon, Indiana to commemorate Black History week.

In-Egalité

All people are created equal
Each person's death diminishes me
Challenger people, Columbia people
Our whole country mourns for thee

Oklahoma and New York cities
Sack cloth, ashes and eulogies
Presidential/Congressional sorrow and pity
Heartfelt compensation and sympathy

Thousands of people hanged from trees
No one to care but their families
No trial, no appeal, no one set free
No blame, no shame, no apologies

Fruit from the Trees of Knowledge
Knowledge from the strange fruit
By our fruits they will know us
Whirlwinds reaped from the dangling fruit

Courtrooms ringed with a blue phalanx
A modern lynching by law and pomp
A modern version of walking the plank
The last best hope but an idle romp

Amendments 13, 14, 15 and 8
The promise of freedom, the sword of justice
The goddess' blindfold not on straight
Hollow words and a tarnished cutlass

Yes, mourn for the deaths of the unfortunate few
But mourn, also, for the loss of our soul
And strive to right State's ship askew
Act and believe we are all of one whole

One world, one country, one people, one home
Treat everyone as we want to be treated
Each person's worth the same as our own
One Law for all, all deaths equally grievous.

(James M. Redwine, February 2, 2003)

Chapter One

THE BOOK

"Judge, what is this old thing? As far as I can tell it's all whores and murders."

Judge John Eagleson winced when his bailiff dropped a heavy dusty tome on his beautiful oak judge's bench that was nearly as old as his Romanesque courthouse.

The judge knew much of the history of the Posey Circuit Court with its full balcony where Eagleson could almost hear the old black man from *To Kill a Mockingbird* say, "Stan up, Scout, Yo' Daddy's passing."

He, also, knew of the mystery of the missing Order Book from 1878 and the local legal folklore surrounding it. Eagleson had assumed for years that its absence from the court archives was neither sinister nor apocryphal, but merely another misfiling and eventual loss by some underpaid clerk.

He had heard the rumors about the prominent people who had somehow hidden their nefarious deeds, but Eagleson was personally aware that the public prefers its leaders to have egregious flaws, even if they have to manufacture them.

As Eagleson carefully lifted the thick pages filled with holographic orders by one of Posey County, Indiana's most honored judges, William F. Parrett, Jr., he had to agree with Tom Hanson's crude assessment; fighting and fornicating were quite well represented.

Judge Parrett's style of clear, parsimonious and legible docket entries was familiar to Eagleson who had studied Parrett's order books from before and after 1878.

Eagleson knew that just after the Civil War there were twenty thousand people in Posey County to support its numerous churches and Belleville girls. Thirty five hundred of these mainly German, English immigrants lived in the county seat, Mt. Vernon, with three hundred Negroes whose restriction to "Belleville" was de facto but absolute.

Belleville was pent up on the south by the Ohio River, the west by Main Street, the north by First Street, often called Water Street due to flooding, and, on the east by Mc Fadin Creek.

Belleville was "colored" except for the two rival houses whose working girls appeared so regularly in the old court records that Eagleson knew their careers about as well as those of the miscreants who came before him.

One house was run by Rosa Hughes and Ida Davis. Davis worked herself and, also, collected a portion of the earnings of her two daughters.

Rosa's and Ida's best girls, at least the ones who appeared most often in court, were Jennie Summers and young Emma Davis. Rosa was of an age where she could only hope for the occasional drunken boatman. That is why, according to the gossip columns in the newspapers of that era, she desperately tried to hold on to her long time arrangement with William Combs who was an owner of a large farm implement company. Apparently his proclivity for extra-marital relief was an open secret.

Jennie Bell ran the other prominent establishment in Belleville, a sobriquet first applied to the area by Ohio River boatmen who often sought comfort there.

Annie Mc Cool was one of Jennie's belles and must have been quite popular if her numerous five dollar fine payments were a barometer.

Under the subject of fighting and killing the old Order Book had numerous entries that mentioned the death of Duffy the Dyer at the hands of two Negroes, the murder of Annie Mc Cool by her "colored paramour", and the sexual assault on the widow Watson by the Negro, Jim Good, who was both beaten and jailed.

Judge Eagleson suddenly realized he had gotten lost in 1878 while Tom shifted and waited for instructions.

"Where'd you get this, Tom?"

"The maintenance man, Dick Simmons, found it in the catacombs behind the old gas furnace. He didn't know what to do with it so, like everything else in this courthouse, he asked me to ask you. I guess they figure since you're the judge you'll either know or what you say's the law anyway. He found it and this rotting old leather valise when he decided to tear out the old boiler and install our new furnace. What is it, Judge? What's them gold letters 'I.C.' on that old case mean?"

Eagleson thought he knew what the old book was and maybe why it had been missing for over 100 years.

These names of the belles and the Negroes were even now sometimes coupled in teenage type conversations among the old guys around the *stumpftisch* at The Posey County Grill in the early morning.

Usually the topic of Mt. Vernon's ribald past was bandied about with an appreciation and envy.

No one seemed to know why or how the county seat's forefathers had urban renewed Belleville out of existence in 1880, but most everyone in Mt. Vernon today had an ancestor involved in the "cleansing" according to their family folklore.

He also knew that Mt. Vernon had at least two thriving Belleville whorehouses in 1878 and none in 1881 or now, although a number of barflies in the still numerous cheap taverns freelanced with alacrity.

It was also curious that while the white population had grown by two thousand, blacks were down to two hundred between 1870 and 1880, a post-War decade that saw the migration of many blacks into other Indiana counties in spite of Indiana's constitutional prohibition to their settlement there.

"Just leave it, Tom. I'll decide what to do with it." Judge Eagleson was excited by the possibilities the old volume presented, but he felt a slight unease when he touched the musty cover and read the oversized, thick pages. It was as if he felt compelled to study the contents while a vague foreboding accompanied the smell of over one and a quarter centuries of mystery.

Each of the entries from January through October 11 of 1878 were succinct accounts of daily court activity written clearly in Judge Parrett's firm style, vignettes from the 19th century, which Judge Eagleson easily recognized as the same parade of human foibles he saw daily.

The Order Book entry for Tuesday, October 8, 1878 contained charges against William Chambers, Ed Warner, Jim Good, and Jeff Hopkins for the October 7 rape of Jennie Summers. Ed Hill, alias Ed Johnson, and "other unnamed Negroes" were charged with raping Emma Davis. Ed Warner and "three other Negroes" were alleged to have raped Rosa Hughes while Jeff Hopkins threatened to kill her if she did not submit.

Just as Judge Eagleson recognized Jennie Summers, Emma Davis, and Rosa Hughes from their numerous appearances in the order books for prostitution, he recognized the names of their attackers as being involved in several incidents in the years following the Civil War. They were usually identified as "col" in the court records of those years, something Eagleson noticed had not often occurred before the War, and, of course, would never happen, officially, today.

Eagleson carefully turned the huge, dry pages impressed by both the legibility and beauty of the languid script. He felt the pace of the small Ohio River community of the 1870's in the form and vernacular of the entries. The patriarchal nature of the descriptions was evident. Prostitutes were boldly identified for the edification of the populace, but those who engaged their services were charged with "Disturbing a Meeting". Eagleson noticed that, at least, both vendor and vendee were penalized the same five dollar fine.

Eagleson found numerous well preserved newspaper articles from the autumn of 1878 pressed between the thick pages of the Order Book. No articles had appeared until the entries of October 8, and there were none after the end of November, 1878 even though the Order Book covered the period from 1878 to 1881.

The *Mt. Vernon Democrat*, the *Mt. Vernon Dollar Democrat*, the *Mt. Vernon Western Star*, the *New Harmony Register*, the *New Harmony Times*, the *Evansville Courier* and the *Evansville Journal* were all represented.

He, also, was impressed that in those days the editors appeared to have no fear of libel suits as quite often a prominent man's name was boldly set forth in a coupling with the name of a soiled dove and the notation that they had been caught *flagrante delicto*!

Much of the flavor of those times was reflected in the accounts of contemporary flotsam Eagleson read every week in the *Mt. Vernon Democrat*, the newspaper that had its origin in 1869 and continued publishing local stories.

The tales of those times were now published each week in Ilse Horacek's *One Hundred Years Ago* column. Eagleson read these stories with bemusement and the both comforting and disquieting feeling that, except for the names, not much had changed.

In fact, just before Tom dropped the Order Book on the Bench, Eagleson had been reading about the young African American boxer who had hit a white policeman who had intervened during a domestic dispute.

The Evansville Courier & Press of February 22, 2002 reported that thirty uniformed police officers packed the courtroom as the prosecutor called for the judge to imprison the young black man. The case made Eagleson wonder what Judge Parrett thought when he read *The Western Star* article of October 17, 1878 with its banner headline, "Judge Lynch Holds Court!"

Eagleson was shocked and sickened by the graphic eyewitness account of lynchings right on the courthouse lawn. In his thirty years as judge in Posey County he had never heard of these events. But Judge William Parrett, Jr., must have known about them.

CHAPTER TWO

"JUDGE LYNCH!"

"JUDGE LYNCH HOLDS COURT!" My god, what an oxymoron, how could we let this happen? No, how could we have done it? We just killed a half million men, for what, to give the lie to our lives?

Judge William F. Parrett, Jr., stared incredulously at the huge headline in the Mt. Vernon, Indiana, *Western Star* weekly newspaper of Thursday, October 17, 1878.

Could it be true that in the early morning of Saturday, October 12, "two to three hundred of Mt. Vernon's best men," right outside his beautiful new courthouse, had broken into the old jail and desecrated the huge locust trees outside his courtroom windows?

The next day the four young Negroes were still hanging there to be seen by all. If Parrett had walked his family their normal route by the Posey Circuit Courthouse on their way to church October 13th, they would have passed within a few feet of the bodies. The judge had kept his family home that morning by claiming he was expecting William Gudgel, the prosecuting attorney, to come by and ask the judge to impanel an emergency grand jury. "A reminder to others", the news article said in reference to the "strange fruit" left hanging on the courthouse campus.

A reminder to whom of what, Parrett wondered. Was the irony lost on "others" or on himself?

And what of these "best men" who allegedly overpowered Deputy Sheriff Ed Hayes and his deputies then butchered old Dan Harrison with the knives and swords they had carried not long ago in the great struggle for Harrison's civil rights?

In the jailhouse privy, they stuffed his body parts in the privy. Sweet Jesus, how could the Harrison family maintain any other memory? And what of young Dan Harrison who allegedly started this debacle by joining in the rape of those white women on Monday, October 7? What's left for his widowed mother and his seven siblings to mourn over?

Editor John Leffel's account obliquely referred to young Dan's "escape", but Leffel knew Dan had been hunted down trying to hide in the coal car of the Evansville & Crawfordsville Railroad.

Leffel had told Judge Parrett how several of their mutual friends led by one of Posey County's wealthiest businessmen had flushed young Dan Harrison out of the false cistern under Robin Hill Manor near the railroad tracks.

Dan then ran towards the crossing at the Lower New Harmony Plank Road where the train had to slow down to watch for carriage traffic.

The vigilantes saw him hop the train. They boarded the train and ordered the frightened engineer at gunpoint to hold the train while they searched for Harrison.

When they found him trying to hide under the coal, they ordered the coal stoker to open the fire door to the engine. The men then threw the struggling young Daniel Harrison into the fire. One wag opined that, "Harrison was black as coal anyhow and this would just be an early taste of where he was going."

Parrett still had his copy of the Thursday, October 10, 1878 edition of the paper which had reported on Old Dan's claim that, "Five or six boys, on Wednesday night, went to the residence of Dan Harrison, colored, on First Street and carried off his boy. Dan was out hunting our Marshall this morning saying that they had lynched his son."

Also, since the vigilantes had allowed Leffel to speak with Old Dan just before he was butchered, Leffel was able to publish Dan's account of the shooting of Deputy Sheriff O.C. Thomas at Dan's home on the night of Friday, October 11, 1878.

CHAPTER THREE

OLD DANIEL HARRISON

ON THE EVENING OF OCTOBER 11 while lying wounded on a pallet in the jail, Old Dan told Leffel that after his son, Dan, Jr., had been chased from his home on Wednesday, October 9, 1878 that, "My house was visited on the previous night (Thursday, October 10, 1878) by Henry Jones, William Combs, and George Daniels. I was at the table at the time eating supper; they asked me where my boy John was at, and I told them he had just gone downtown. Jones said, 'I'm going to kill you tonight,' and after pointing his pistol at my head, and searching the house, they left. I went downtown next morning (Friday, October 11) and asked Mr. Caborn (James L. Caborn, Mt. Vernon constable) to protect me. Several parties told me the white people were going to kill me and as nobody helped me, I went to Mr. Schieber's (August Schieber, store owner) and bought some shot. I did not tell Bill Topper (co-owner with Enoch Thomas of Pittsburgh Coal Company in Mt. Vernon) or anybody else that I was buying the shot to kill some white son-of-a-bitch. I went home, loaded my gun and went to bed. I left my pants on. I heard the men coming before they got to my house; got up and went to the next room with my gun.

"Seen a man passing the window, run gun through lower left-hand window light and fired. Don't know who the white man was, thought it was same crowd that came to my house night before. I believe I shot through window twice; believe I put the third load in my gun before I ran out back door; don't know where I lost caps and ramrod; don't know that I killed Thomas; This is all I know about it and if you want to hang me take me out and hang me. Did not send my wife and children away; don't know whether they left or not. I was the only man in the house for two nights; John and Robert (two of Harrison's eight children) were out on the farm. I laid in my bed watching. I don't know whether my boys ravished the girls. I had nothing to do with it. When I heard the noise made by the mob outside of the jail this morning (a smaller mob had been dispersed earlier that day), I asked Mr. Musselman (Town Marshall for Mt. Vernon) for his pistol to defend myself, as I was not able to get up. I am married, have eight children, and am 51 years old. Take me out and hang me I have no more to say."

Because Parrett, as Judge, had received the Coroner's Verdict on the Thomas killing, Parrett knew that Old Dan had been shot during the O.C. Thomas incident and that his claim was that the man outside his window shot Dan before Dan fired back.

Chapter Four

CORONER'S INQUEST

THE CORONER'S INQUEST HAD BEEN held in Cyrus O. Thomas' home October 11, 1878 and took testimony from eyewitnesses Charles C. Baker, Edward Hayes, William Russell, and medical doctors Edwin V. Spencer and Simon H. Pearse.

<u>CHARLES C. BAKER</u>

Baker testified that the four men went to Old Dan's house about 3:00 o'clock a.m. October 11. He said he and Hayes went to the back of the house while Thomas and Russell were to go in the front door and make the arrest of Ed Hill, one of the indicted rapists who was supposed to be hiding there. Baker stated that about a minute or so after the men separated he heard a shot and very shortly Thomas came around to the northeast corner of the house and said, "boys I am shot." Baker stated he and Hayes ran to Thomas. According to Baker, Hayes said, "I guess not much", as Thomas said, "Yes, I am killed", as he sank back on the ground and said, "Boys, watch the negro, don't let him get away." Baker said he then left Thomas and went for the front of the house. When he got to about midway between the rear and the front he heard a shot from the direction he had just left Hayes. He turned and saw a man running across the back fence. Baker then returned to Thomas who was still breathing. He went to search for Dr. John B. Weaver. He returned about one half hour later. By then, Thomas was dead.

DRS. EDWIN V. SPENCER AND SIMON H. PEARSE

Weaver was not called before the Coroner's Jury but Drs. Edwin V. Spencer and Simon H. Pearse were. These two examined Thomas' body and determined that, "one ball entered the top of the right lung, one entered the chest two inches above the left nipple. One entered near the center of Scarpia's Triangle severing the jugular vein and probably the carotid artery of the left side. One entered the left orbit immediately beneath the globe of the eye passing inwards and backwards lodging in the base of the brain. One passed through the left ear. One through the left arm entering anterior middle and internal aspect and emerging on the posterior surface. A large number entered the left shoulder over the middle portion of the clavicle and passing backwards and emerging over the superior portion of the scapula. The combined effect of these wounds produced almost instant death."

WILLIAM B. RUSSELL

William B. Russell testified that he, Oscar Thomas, Edward Hayes and Charles Baker started from the jail about 2:00 o'clock a.m., October 11, 1878.

They were looking for Ed Hill who supposedly was at Daniel Harrison's house. They planned to arrest Hill on the Grand Jury indictment for the rape of the white girls.

Russell said, "When we got there we went in to the yard, when we were about halfway between the gate and the house someone stuck a gun out of the window and fired. Thomas said, 'Bill, I am shot, they have killed me. Don't let the negro get away.'

"I then went around to the east end of the house with Thomas. Thomas then sank down on the ground. I then went round to the west end of the house when someone came out of the house by the back way and ran. We then shot at him.

"We stayed at the house about an hour guarding it when several persons came and we went into the house and searched it. We found no one there but two negro children. Thomas died in about thirty minutes after he was shot.

"I then started in the direction that the person ran. When I was about one and one half mile from town on the Ditch Road I met a man with a wagon and team with Daniel Harrison in the wagon coming to town.

"I told Harrison I was an officer and would take charge of him. He said, 'there is a mob after me; don't let them kill me.'

"I then asked him what he shot that man for? He said, 'They shot at me first.' I said, 'you have killed Oscar Thomas.' He said, 'Is that so?'

"I then said he'd better tell the whole matter. He said, 'I am clogged up in my throat and can't tell now, but will tell you all about it after a while.' I then took him to the jail yard and delivered him up to Edward Hayes."

EDWARD HAYES

Edward I. Hayes testified that Deputy Sheriff O.C. Thomas had asked him to wake Thomas up at 1:00 o'clock a.m., October 11, 1878 because he wanted to make an arrest in Belleville. Hayes stated that

Thomas had asked him to go along on the arrest. William Russell and Charles Baker were going too.

When they got to Daniel Harrison's house it was agreed that Hayes and Baker would go to the rear of the house and Thomas and Russell would go to the front.

Hayes testified, "We had scarcely got to the rear of the house when I heard the report of a gun on the front side of the house. Knowing that Thomas and Russell did not have any gun I was surprised. I then ran round the end of the house toward the front and met Thomas. He said, 'that negro has killed me.' I then went to the front and got opposite the middle window on the south side of the house where I discovered the muzzle of a gun with about six inches of the end sticking out through the sash where the glass was broken out in one of the lower lights of the window.

"As soon as I discovered that I jumped back and as soon as I jumped back the gun went off. Then I passed around to the rear of the building and saw a man crossing the partition fence between the two lots. I then met Thomas who had just fallen to the ground and never spoke after he fell. He was dead in about thirty minutes from the time he fell."

CHAPTER FIVE

ONE-SIDED COINS

WHEN HE FIRST TOOK THE bench, Judge Parrett had no difficulty deciding cases quickly. Usually the right outcome was clear to him after the pleadings were read, the opening statements of the attorneys were given and the main witnesses or even one important witness testified.

But after about five years of watching his first impressions wither before the whole weight of the evidence, Parrett understood why lay people serving as jurors were told to keep an open mind throughout a trial.

Now Parrett sometimes was not sure decisions were rightly made by juries and even himself long after cases were closed.

The Coroner's Inquest had no trouble finding Cyrus Oscar Thomas, Parrett was surprised at O.C.'s real name, age 39, five feet seven inches tall, was killed by Daniel Harrison.

Probably so, but did others not wonder why this group of four men supposedly made an appointment for 2:00 o'clock a.m. to serve a warrant?

Why look for Ed Hill at old Dan Harrison's? Why were Daniel's wife, Elizabeth, and all but two of their children out at the Harrison farm? Did Dan expect more trouble after Henry Jones, William Combs and George Daniels had taken young Dan on Wednesday and then had come back Thursday asking where another of Harrison's sons, John, was?

Did it make sense for Ed Hayes and Charles Baker to have guns at the back, but for Deputy Sheriff O.C. Thomas and William Russell, both unarmed according to Hayes, to go to the front to effect the arrest? Why did William Russell say, "We shot at him," if he had no gun? And why did Russell not say that he had shot at Harrison?

How could a man who had died "almost instantly" go around the house, talk twice about his wounds, live for half an hour and see in the dark that "the negro" had shot him? Yet Charles Baker quoted Thomas as saying "boys, I'm shot" and Bill Russell reported that Thomas said "Bill, I am shot, they have killed me. Don't let the Negro get away."

Why would not Thomas say that the Negro had killed him?

And why did Ed Hayes comment that Thomas was shot, "I guess not much"?

Was Thomas trying to protect Harrison from just what eventually happened when he told them not to let him get away or was he hoping that Harrison would know who truly shot Thomas and could bring "them" to justice?

What medical attention did his three companions give Thomas? Where was Dr. Weaver? Why did the men hang around the house with Thomas for half an hour instead of carrying him a few blocks to a doctor?

Parrett had often been amused at jury members who let such chimeras obscure the obvious guilt of defendants or the unfounded claims of plaintiffs. One can easily lose one's way if subsidiary facts are allowed to cloud the process of deliberation.

This comparison of his own weak analysis to similar lay frailties startled Parrett back to the obvious: old Dan ended up killing O.C. Thomas as an unfortunate attenuated consequence of young Dan's crossing of the great taboo, miscegenation.

Thomas dead, old Dan dead, both young Dan and John Harrison "missing" but actually dead, and William Chambers, Ed Warner, Jim Good and Jeff Hopkins lynched with many of Posey County's leading citizens standing by.

Parrett knew these were the issues that should occupy him. But he just could not quiet the questions he had about O.C.'s murder when it was reported on the front page of the October 17, 1878, *Mt. Vernon Western Star* that, "Mr. Baker, also, emptied both barrels of his gun at the Negro." Baker testified before the Coroner's Jury and never claimed that he fired a gun at anybody.

Ed Hayes, who was the source of most of the accounts about Thomas' death, had lost the Democratic nomination for sheriff to Thomas in the May 1878 primary by twenty votes. Now the Republican candidate, John Wheeler, would easily win the November election and he had already offered the Chief Deputy Sheriff's job to Hayes if he would support Wheeler over Thomas. The race between Thomas and Hayes had been so bitter Hayes had no trouble crossing party lines to get back at Thomas. But Posey County was strongly Democratic so Thomas, who was a popular Civil War hero, was heavily favored to win.

Parrett tried to tell Leffel he did not want to hear anything about the incident as it might end up in his court. He already knew too many of the facts even though he had managed to prevent Leffel from naming the members of the mob.

According to Leffel, that Saturday night the individuals outside the courthouse had turned their coats inside out, covered their faces with handkerchiefs and the new gaslights were still not working. This was the explanation for no one being able to identify any of the men who actively participated. In spite of his effort to remain neutral, Parrett suspected he could reliably guess the names of several of the prime movers and many of the hangers-on. He, also, could predict that the county would be quickly dividing into two camps. One camp would be demanding an investigation and the other would want the whole matter ignored.

After all, there were only about twenty thousand people in the whole county and Parrett had served sixteen years as Posey County's only judge. He knew more about most people and they him than he or they wanted. Parrett was confident that he would soon be receiving a visit from one white man who was not involved.

Morita Maier, the German immigrant who had built Robin Hill in 1838 for William Lowry and his wife, was not only one of the area's best carpenters and woodworkers, but also one of its most ardent antebellum abolitionists and he, also, was Parrett's best friend. Morita would be looking to Parrett for justice. Parrett was already torn between his sense of duty and his need to protect his political and social survival.

CHAPTER SIX

STEERAGE CLASS

MORITA MEIER AND EIGHTEEN YEAR old Hagar Heckler met aboard the sailing vessel, The Brunswick, that departed the port at Bremen, Germany September 2, 1831 and arrived in Philadelphia on October 17, 1831. Morita was a young carpenter from Bamburg in Bavaria and Hagar was a Berlin native. Hagar was drawn to the fiery Morita who stood up to the ship's officers on behalf of the steerage deck passengers. The steerage deck had been oversold. The ship's captain had ordered reduced rations for the poorer passengers so that the wealthy upper deck passengers would not have to suffer any shortages. Morita refused to accept this treatment and organized his fellow passengers.

Meier's Bavarian German tongue was difficult for some to understand and Hagar whose family had originated in Bavaria helped Morita communicate. Together they managed to meld the steerage deck passengers into a unified group. To avoid any uprising, the captain ordered a fair allocation of food and water to all passengers.

Morita and Hagar then asked the captain to marry them aboard ship. Upon their eventual arrival in Indiana where Morita started his carpentry business, they were both surprised to find a prevalence of anti-Negro feeling. They had been determined to choose a free state to live in and the topography of southwestern Indiana reminded Morita of Bavaria. There was, also, an abundance of hardwood trees for furniture and cabinet making.

But the young Germans saw it as their Christian duty to oppose the "blackbirding" and discrimination that occurred in Posey County. They became the most important southern Indiana contacts for escaped slaves. Such activity might well have resulted in disaster for the Meiers if Morita had not formed friendships with two up and coming young lawyers, Alvin Hovey and William Parrett. Hovey and Parrett looked to their mentor, the well respected Judge John Pitcher, for public support in their efforts against blackbirding. Pitcher did not care for Negroes, but he detested slavery. His influence prevented the southern sympathizers in the community from ostracizing the new immigrants and the young lawyers.

Over the years Pitcher and Meier had occasionally clashed over Negro civil rights. But before the Civil War, Pitcher had always stood with Meier on the general issues of humane treatment for Negroes. After Negroes were made citizens under federal law, Pitcher's attitude hardened against them and anyone who sided with them. Hovey and Parrett, however, remained close to the Meiers as did Christian Willis who often turned to Morita for help in building the cabins at Brewery Hills where Willis attempted to bring Negroes to Jesus.

CHAPTER SEVEN

ROBIN HILL

WILLIAM LOWRY HAD PURPOSEFULLY LOCATED his large home near the railroad and on the banks of Mill Creek. Little Mill Creek fed into the Ohio River within three miles of its confluence with the Wabash River. More importantly, its mouth was close to the west edge of Mt. Vernon and the creek was obscured by many trees.

Robin Hill had been Posey County's most prolific station on the Underground Railroad until the end of the War and Morita Maier knew all about Robin Hill. A mutual friend of Maier and Parrett, Joseph P. Welborn, had bought Robin Hill just a few months before October, 1878 from its next most recent owner, Charles Haas. After young Dan was murdered, Mr. Welborn had notified Morita that both Dans had been at his home and Old Dan still was. Welborn did not think he could protect old Dan from the mob so he turned him over to Morita.

That Robin Hill's sanctuary had been defiled by other friends of Parrett, some of whom had aided Maier's efforts before the War, was just another nonsequitur Parrett could not explain.

Judge Parrett knew that after old Dan Harrison had allegedly shot and killed Deputy Sheriff O.C. Thomas on Friday, October 11th, between one and two a.m., he had fled to Robin Hill. Morita had later prevented a vigilante posse from lynching old Dan after Joseph Welborn turned Harrison over to Maier.

Morita had turned Harrison over to William Russell who had been with Thomas when he was shot at old Dan's home. Russell turned Harrison over to Deputy Sheriff Ed Hayes who was, also, at Harrison's house when Thomas was shot.

What Parrett knew from the Coroner's Jury proceeding of Saturday, October 12th, that the mob who killed old Dan may not have known, was that O.C., Deputy Sheriff Ed Hayes, and Deputies Bill Russell and Charles Baker had gone to old Dan Harrison's home on Second Street looking for Ed Hill on the rape claim.

When old Dan heard noises in the dark outside his home and saw four men with guns and torches, it is possible he would not have known that the men were law officers. He might well have thought they were the same men who had come to his home each of the two previous nights. At least this was old Dan's version to Morita as the judge perceived it filtered through excited Bavarian English when Morita Meier pounded on Parrett's door at about 3:00 o'clock a.m. on October 11th with old Dan hidden under a canvas in his wagon. Maier's birthplace of Bamberg spoke a German even most other Germans had difficulty deciphering.

Maier's English still made both men laugh, especially when Morita was excited and searching for words. So not only did the judge fail to remain unaware, he even aided and was bemused by the agitated German before he realized the gravity of his plea.

Harrison told Maier someone shot through his window first, then Harrison fired his shotgun twice. Harrison told Maier he did not know the men were law officers. He then fled from his home so that whoever the men were would chase him and not try to enter his home where two of his children were. The baby girl, Hattie, his wife, Elizabeth, and his other children were at the farm.

Young Dan and John Harrison had already been murdered before the Thomas shooting, although Old Dan may not have known for sure that his sons were dead.

Judge Parrett knew much of what old Dan had told Maier even though Parrett had tried to not know. Parrett did firmly staunch Maier's excited exposition as to anyone's identity. He did hear what he had already assumed: just as in the Great War, many of their friends had acted on both sides.

CHAPTER EIGHT

THE JUDGE

WILLIAM PARRETT NO LONGER HAD a name in Posey County. After so many years on the Bench he was simply "Judge" to everyone but his family.

And to most people, Parrett not only was called Judge, he was the personification of the Law. People assumed he could and would resolve their legal dilemmas.

Parrett had long ago given up trying to dispel this myth of omniscience and the uncomfortable elevation based on the vagaries of a partisan election or appointment – Parrett had been robed both ways.

The Judge knew of his inability to alleviate all the problems and conflicts people brought to him.

He tried hard to remember the title had been applied to many before and would be to many after. He felt keenly both the power and impotence of his position.

Over the years he knew he had sometimes been wrong and even unfair in his rulings, but never intentionally so or because of the identity or status of the litigant.

Socrates had it right: a judge's duty is to do justice, not make a present of it.

He considered it the highest honor that people who had no personal dealings with him, and his friends and neighbors who knew him well, brought their conflicts to him for resolution.

Sometimes people would try for years to settle disputes among themselves. Then, when they were unable to do so they would seek help from their clergymen or some mutual friend. After that failed, each would retain an attorney for advice. Then the parties and the attorneys would try to alleviate the conflicts.

Finally, when everyone agreed there was no hope of resolution, someone would file a lawsuit and ask the Judge to make everything right. It was an honor, but often it just meant the Judge drew the animosity from both sides. At least that allowed the parties to move on.

Morita had asked Judge Parrett what he should do with old Dan and Parrett had advised him to turn him over to the sheriff.

Old Dan agreed to submit his fate to the law. But young Dan, who had suffered some bitter experiences with Lady Justice, had opted to run from Robin Hill on Wednesday evening.

Judge Parrett marveled at the similar ultimate outcomes from his legal advice and young Dan's panicked *ultra vires* approach. Parrett had often noted and tried to deny the *de minimis* differences in results from a lawful and unreasoned approach to the same problem. It was as if some mischievous force delighted in seeing lawful behavior mocked. He sometimes feared Gloucester in *King Lear* was correct about the gods – "they kill us for their sport".

Parrett realized that his small county was roiling with emotion even before O.C. Thomas was killed. Soon after the War, some of the Indiana whites, who had long moralized about their northwestern Kentucky and southeastern Illinois neighbors directly across the Ohio and the Wabash rivers, began to categorize Posey County's Negroes collectively as shiftless or worse.

No longer were allowances made for lack of education or job opportunities. Now that there were no southern whites to be better than, these good people began to set the Negroes apart for criticism and blame.

Of course, Parrett remembered that some of these same arbiters of morality had supported their families by "blackbirding".

On Sundays they would rail against slavery in church then kidnap escaped Negroes and return them across the Ohio and Wabash rivers for rewards under the aegis of the Fugitive Slave Act of 1850.

Parrett despised these hypocrites more than the original slaveholders. The fact that several of these good people had later fought along with Posey County's favorite son, General Alvin Peterson Hovey, in the Twenty-Fourth Indiana Volunteers in the War only increased his disdain.

On the other hand, there were several Posey County leaders who had stood with Parrett in his efforts to protect Negroes from mistreatment.

Isaac Blackford, one of Parrett's mentors, had been Posey County's first circuit court judge in 1816. Blackford was appointed to the Indiana Supreme Court in 1817 where in 1820 he joined the majority in a blackbirding type of case, STATE V. LASSELLE, which declared, "...(S)lavery can have no existence in Indiana."

And old Judge John Pitcher, one of Posey County's common pleas judges who had lived near Abraham Lincoln in Spencer County, Indiana, and loaned him law books, was a friend of Parrett. Pitcher had not hesitated to condemn the blackbirders publicly while privately he disdained Negroes as not worthy of citizenship. Pitcher, also, owned a large lot close to the Ohio River dock and close to old Dan's home on Second and Elm Streets. Though John Pitcher changed from the Republican to the Democratic Party when Negroes were enfranchised, Pitcher's son, Thomas Pitcher, served the Union as a General in the Civil War and later as Superintendent of West Point in 1866.

Parrett had learned to admire Judge Pitcher's call for the abolition of slavery and to make no demur to Mr. Pitcher's patrician self-image. Parrett had often been bemused by Pitcher's and others' convoluted thinking about Negroes. And he had learned that pointing out these inconsistencies was not suffered gladly by the beneficiaries of his wisdom.

Hovey, Blackford, Parrett and a few others had tried to discover and keep track of these blackbirding incidents, but the War had interrupted their efforts. Still, Parrett remembered some of the good men who pedaled flesh back to the flesh peddlers.

These friends and acquaintances of Parrett seemed to have little difficulty wrapping their human business dealings in economic, moral, even Biblical righteousness.

Parrett had not forgotten the Reverend Mr. John Scammahorn of the Mt. Vernon Methodist Church castigating the congregation for offering a resolution against blackbirding just before the War.

Scammahorn cited Exodus 21, he felt it necessary to intone the entire chapter, and noted that God told Moses that anyone who has another's slave should be put to death.

Reliance on slave holding by ancient Hebrews and citation of Biblical authority by people who usually had never read more than the Christmas story was particularly galling.

Parrett knew that many religions had been used to justify the manifest destinies of many chosen peoples. What often caused him pause was the frequency and zealousness with which conquered people embraced the religions which were used to help destroy their cultures.

When Parrett would talk with colored acquaintances, such as the ex-slave and minister Absolom Brewery, or the Shawnee Indian Chief Tecumseh's descendant, Christian Willis, he was often saddened by their need to thank the white man's god for their fate.

The diabolical method of controlling victims by forcing an exchange of one set of myths for another was not so difficult to analyze. However, the re-naming by the victims of themselves and their children in honor of the people who brought about the demise of their culture perplexed Parrett.

But Parrett was most angered by the blackbirders' reliance on law.

Explanations that the escaped slaves were the duly acquired and paid for property and economic assets of American freeholders had a certain logic among these civic leaders before the War.

Returning thieves, who had stolen themselves, usually with the complicity of people like Morita Maier, was the right thing to do.

The monetary rewards were no different than any other economic incentive and were just compensation for the dangerous and time consuming business.

Parrett put such self-righteous behavior in the same class with the good men who denounced sin in general and found their own special arrangements with Belleville a deserved convenience.

CHAPTER NINE

THE BELLES

JENNIE BELL GAZED OUT HER bedroom window at the beautiful Ohio River as the setting sun turned its gentle waves into diamonds.

She felt a part of the current of the sparkling water as it slowly but unrelentingly worked and wandered its course from Pittsburgh, Pennsylvania to Cairo, Illinois where it joined the Mississippi on its way to New Orleans.

Having been to its beginning, its end, and places in between during her thirty some years, Jennie felt she could chart her life by the undulating rhythms of the Ohio.

Her earliest memories were of the smells and sounds of the river. While she might not know when, where, or to whom she was born, she knew the river and especially its men well, although she found her own sex much more complex and interesting. While a man's behavior was usually one dimensional, a woman's motivations were often intriguingly layered.

Jennie had wasted many hours trying to explain some of her own actions to herself in the hope of heading off future mistakes. She finally had accepted the futility of trying to understand herself and her sisters and restricted her business dealings to men. Her personal life was not so easily compartmentalized.

But if women were perplexing to her, Jennie knew the only men who could not be beguiled by an experienced woman were ones who were uninterested in sex or preferred it with other men.

That was why she laughed aloud when she read the front page of the special addition of the *Mt. Vernon Dollar Democrat* from October 17, 1878: "White Girls Outraged by Negroes"

Only a man would portray the victims as, "…(T)hree white girls living very quietly in a retired and lonely part of the city".

Jennie knew from the vicissitudes of her own life that white men's egos required that no white woman could ever willingly bed a Negro, even for money.

The best hope Jennie had of living a life at least a little like other white women were born into had been lost when her wealthy white businessman had found her in bed with Jim Good this past Fourth of July.

Jennie had screamed and cried that Good had assaulted her, which the elderly white man readily used to have Good jailed. Unfortunately, that son-of-a-bitch, Judge Parrett, had thrown out the charges when Good's court appointed attorney, Alvin P. Hovey, had produced Rosa Hughes who testified that Jennie had bragged about her colored clientele.

The old fool knew, of course, that Jennie was a willing participant and ended their relationship. Jennie figured his wife was as upset as Jennie was about the situation since for three years he had not challenged his wife's claims of physical incapacity.

To Jennie the absurdity was that neither the old white man whose sexual attempts were anemic nor the young Negro whose preference for sex from the rear was disgusting excited her at all. If the white man had not steadily promised more money and given her less, she would not have subjected herself to earning the premium amounts she charged Good and his colored friends.

Now she had lost not only the easy white money, but the Negroes shifted their business to Rosa Hughes' house.

According to the newspaper, Jim Good, Jeff Hopkins, Bill Chambers, Ed Warner, Dan Harrison, Jr., Ed Hill and John Harrison had used the excuse that a white gentleman had given them a note for Rosa. When the door was opened the Negroes forced their way in and ravished Rosa, Jennie Summers, and Emma Davis at knife point.

Jennie Bell had no trouble believing the Negroes had carnal relations with all three as the paper quoted Rosa as saying the men took the women from behind. Whether force was involved was another matter in Jennie Bell's mind.

Jennie knew that Annie Mc Cool, who had been one of her best girls until she was murdered in September of 1878, always complained that her Negro paramour never wanted normal sex. He had demanded that she service him first then several of his colored friends, all from behind as he watched, and all for free.

Most people believed that William Chambers, her lover, had murdered Annie when she tried to break off their arrangement so that she could cultivate a promising situation with the owner of the new dry goods store. However, the white man had started to back away just before she was found strangled with one of her own stockings.

Jennie knew that the white man's wife had begun to question Mr. U.G. Damron about her husband's frequent visits to the hotel which was just south and west of the dry goods store.

Jennie had enjoyed charging the young Negroes for what Annie was giving away. But her carelessness with Jim Good ended all that.

What perturbed Jennie the most was that the brouhaha over Annie McCool's murder had resulted in the good white men of Posey County gaining knowledge that the white working girls were not culling Negro men and money from white.

Rage had been growing among the white male community since Jennie's businessman had caught her in July. White wives were organizing informally and in the forty churches in the county to oust the girls from Belleville.

And Jennie longed for the touch and companionship of the first person she had ever really needed, Emma Davis.

After nearly twenty years of searching for closeness among men of all ages and descriptions, she had found something in Emma she had not even known she needed.

Emma was only sixteen but had been put to work by her mother, Ida Davis, when she was barely into puberty. They both lived at Rosa Hughes' who provided room and board for half of their earnings.

Emma was Rosa's most popular girl especially among the older, wealthy white men who gladly paid exorbitant rates to spend time with her.

Jennie had tried many times to convince Emma to leave Ida and Rosa and come live with Jennie. But the qualities that made Jennie love Emma kept Emma loyal to her mother. And her mother would not forsake Rosa.

Jennie hated it that Emma was subjected to the grunts, filth and fluids of men who had no imagination that this boorish behavior was repugnant to Emma. Jennie could have relieved Emma of these duties and cared for her for nothing but her company.

The awakening in Jennie the first time she and Emma touched remained constantly fresh and exciting to her. Surprise was her first reaction followed by a desire she had always feigned with men but assumed was not meant to be hers.

Jennie remembered the day in December, 1877 when she had been negotiating with Rosa Hughes over how they might both benefit from a truce or even some kind of cooperative division of business.

Rosa had brought Ida with her to help with the talks and Ida had brought then fifteen year old Emma to see how the other house in Belleville looked.

Jennie had known about Emma for some time and had seen her at a distance. She thought of her just as a competitor who would lose her special drawing power quickly, much as Jennie herself had, when she could no longer re-sell her virginity to gullible men.

But on that December afternoon she saw something in Emma's eyes that stirred an uncomfortable quickening inside her. Jennie had tried hundreds of times to be interested and excited by the male body. She had sought guidance from other women who claimed to actually enjoy sex with the men they charged. Some often gave their favors away because, or so they told Jennie, a man had made them extremely happy in the few minutes the acts took. Such rewards had never been visited on Jennie until she encountered Emma.

As the candles in her parlor caught the depth in Emma's eyes and Jennie's eyes were drawn to Emma's gently lifted breasts each time Emma laughed her soft girlish response to some witty remark Jennie made, new emotions had begun to warm within Jennie.

The negotiations did not produce any fruit except for the agreement to meet again the following afternoon. Jennie had offered Rosa and Ida her best brandy, but they were too savvy for that. Emma also declined but with the warmest smile from the prettiest mouth Jennie had ever seen.

On the following day Jennie and Rosa met at Rosa's with Ida in attendance. Jennie was amazed at the disappointment she experienced when Ida told her Emma had a tryst with one of the prominent local businessmen whose wife was visiting her relatives in nearby Evansville. Ida bragged about the old fool's fawning over Emma and how he often told her she reminded him of his wife when she could still get him aroused.

Jennie's resentment of this normal business transaction caused her to re-examine her powers of concentration. Usually she knew what she wanted from a deal, what she would accept and how to try for the former until she had accomplished the latter. On that day she found herself thinking about Emma when she needed to think about business.

At the end of the session Jennie felt desperate to see Emma. She asked Ida if she would send Emma over the next Sunday morning, the last Sunday before Christmas, as Jennie wanted to have her pick up a wreath Jennie was making for Rosa's house. When Ida told her she would be pleased to do so, Jennie knew she had to make one.

Jennie still did not understand what was compelling her to see Emma. She had never been attracted to another woman and, in fact, had always refused the money she could have made from men who suggested they were titillated by watching such aberrant activities. It was more of an undefined longing than a pulsating excitement she felt when she thought of Emma. After a succession of imitation mothers and part time sisters, perhaps, she thought, Emma aroused in her the yearnings for the female love she had never received. Or maybe the two self-induced abortions had not extinguished her need to have a daughter of her own.

When Emma arrived that Sunday morning, Jennie invited her into her kitchen and offered her the German crumb cake she had learned to bake from the wife of Morita Meier. Hagar Meier was one of the few good Christian folk who would deign to recognize her existence. Jennie occasionally visited Mrs. Meier on her back porch at Hagar's home where the two women would exchange recipes and laugh good naturedly at Hagar's husband's attempts to enter into their English conversations. Morita Meier was one of the few white men who neither leered nor sneered at Jennie.

In Jennie's kitchen Emma sat on one of the high stools by the sink. She was wearing a long woolen coat which she began to unbutton as the warmth from the new gas fired cook stove pervaded the room.

Jennie caught herself staring at Emma's small, delicate fingers as they nimbly opened the coat revealing a one piece cotton dress which followed the contour of her lithe body. Emma's thick golden hair cascaded down over her shoulders and framed her smooth skin that glowed from her exposure to the frigid December air.

Emma seemed unaware of Jennie's voice changing to a higher pitch as her breathing accelerated. Jennie tried to draw her eyes away from Emma's chest which barely moved as Emma reached over and pumped some water into the sink so that Jennie could heat water for tea.

No matter what Emma did Jennie found herself interested in watching her.

When Emma turned from the sink towards Jennie, their eyes met for an instant before both quickly looked out the window towards the Ohio. Emma's eyes were clear and her pupils widened rapidly as they looked into each other's faces when they exchanged the tea kettle.

What was it that Jennie saw? What was it that she felt? Although she was more than twice Emma's age, Jennie felt off balance and shy. She knew she was getting closer to Emma and was almost against her hips when Emma smiled that warm invitation and nervously laughed at the tea kettle poised between them forgotten in the moment.

Jennie took the kettle and placed it on the stove. The wreath that she had made was lying on the butcher block. Jennie turned her attention to it and asked Emma if she had plans for Christmas dinner as that might be a good reason to get the two houses and all the girls together in a relaxed atmosphere.

It made Jennie wince when Emma told her that she thought Rosa and Ida and the other girls might enjoy getting together with Jennie's house, but her main gentleman wanted her to spend Christmas Eve and Christmas Day at his farm house because his wife and grown children were spending those days in Evansville.

Jennie had no desire to spend Christmas with Rosa. Christmas alone would be far more jolly, but to withdraw the invitation immediately after suggesting it felt awkward. Perhaps she could extricate herself later.

As Emma stood up and reached for her coat Jennie said she had not had any tea and she should drink something hot before going back out. Emma hesitated but reminded herself that her mother had told her to be home to help clean up after the normal Saturday night run of business. She thanked Jennie who took her long coat and helped her on with it. Jennie nervously lifted Emma's hair over her coat collar. The feel of Emma's hair in her fingers caused a reaction within Jennie she could not hide.

Emma turned so that the two were only inches apart and face to face. Jennie noticed her eyes were not blue but gray and that her lips were pink and full. Jennie, who made her living making advances to men, felt helpless as Emma started towards the door with the wreath. Jennie's voice cracked as she asked if Emma could stop by the next day. Emma smiled that ingénue smile and without a trace of any promise that Jennie could discern said she would like that if her Monday appointments would allow.

Jennie could not function after Emma left. She could not believe the feelings she was having. She did not want to desire anyone, especially a woman. She did not want to make a fool of herself and be rejected by this girl who could hurt her business if she approached her and was laughed at or scorned. But mainly she did not want to lose control over her emotions. Years of being fooled by pseudo families and lovers had taught her that love was just another name for pain. She guarded her soul against the Satan of vulnerability. Only those you cared about could truly hurt you.

That cold December night Jennie told her working girls to open up without her if any men came calling. She went to her room overlooking the Ohio and resolved to never again allow herself to be alone with Emma until she had conquered her passion.

As she looked out the bedroom window she saw the light drizzle begin to fall against the glass. She awoke to a hard cold rain.

CHAPTER TEN

GOLDEN RAIN

ABOUT 9:00 O'CLOCK A.M. ON Monday, Jennie's working girl, Mary Harker, told her that she and the other girls were going to brave the rain and take the train to Evansville for the day. Mary told Jennie they would all be back on the evening run in case any Ohio River boatmen came through. Mary asked Jennie to go, but Jennie told her "no" as she needed to go over the books. She just did not feel like going out and knew the books would have to wait for her mood to change.

Jennie made herself some tea and sat in the kitchen staring out at the gray day. She felt empty but knew she had somehow avoided doing something that might have caused her long term difficulty.

As Jennie thought about nothing and stared vacantly towards the river with its muddy waters and rising whitecaps, a movement by the back door caught her eye. She turned towards the door and saw a small dark figure in a long coat approaching the door.

Jennie's chest began to pound and her fingers lost control of the tea cup which crashed to the floor. She thought how she must look wrapped in an old housecoat with her hair still in its pillow position.

Emma's knock on the door was barely audible. Jennie thought that such a shy and timid knock would have not gotten a response if she had not been close to the door.

She quickly grabbed the three large pieces the cup had broken into and threw them into the trash basket as she hastily mopped up the tea and small pieces of the cup with a towel.

Jennie opened the door and pulled Emma in by her wet coat. Her hair was hanging in clumps and Jennie thought her eyes were red. Her right cheek looked as if it was darkened with makeup.

Jennie got Emma a cup of hot tea and helped her off with her coat. She shivered as her wet dress shifted against her body.

After a few minutes of silence Jennie asked if anything was wrong and Emma said her main benefactor had complained about her seeing another customer with whom she had spent the night. He had sent for her unexpectedly because his wife had been called by their Methodist minister to help with a church member's illness.

When she had to delay their meeting until 10:00 o'clock a.m. that Monday morning he was angry and slapped her. He said they did not have enough time before his wife might return and he sent her off in the rain with no money. His main residence was on Walnut Street in Mt. Vernon about four blocks from Belleville. He owned a farm in addition to his farm implement business, but usually stayed in town. Emma was upset and worried that Rosa and her mother might blame her for not making any money. She also feared the gentleman might not continue to patronize her.

Jennie tried to hide her pleasure at this last prospect and placed her arm around Emma's thin body. She was surprised to find herself staring at Emma's nipples which were erect under the thin cotton blouse.

Jennie told Emma she needed to get out of her wet clothes and get a hot bath, "before she caught her death." She led her to her upstairs bedroom, gave her a robe to wear and told Emma to remove her wet clothing. Jennie stepped out of the bedroom and closed the door.

The house had just been furnished with a gas fired water heater, one of the first in Posey County. Even the one installed in the new courthouse was not yet fully operational. Jennie thought the expenditure was well worth it as she and her girls refused to bed any man until they had scrubbed him with soap and hot water.

Now she was doubly glad to have hot water readily available.

As she filled the large tub with steaming water she sprinkled lavender oil on the water. When she looked up Emma was standing in the bathroom door with the robe covering her from her ankles to her neck. Her blond hair was beginning to dry but still clung to the nape of her graceful neck. Jennie thought she was the most beautiful human she had ever seen.

Jennie tested the water with her hand and motioned for Emma to step into the tub. Jennie had planned to leave the bathroom before Emma took off her robe, but Emma loosened the belt and handed the robe to Jennie who could not move. She had never felt the rushing excitement she now tried to contain.

Emma's body was perfect in Jennie's view. Her firm breasts reminded Jennie of how her own had looked twenty years before and the tiny area of blond hair that drew Jennie's furtive glance was like a small softly curling flower.

Emma seemed completely devoid of self-consciousness in front of Jennie and unaware of her own beauty. When she cautiously stepped into the tub holding onto Jennie's hand she let out a delighted laugh and splashed water on her breasts and face and across her flat stomach that had some barely visible white lines running down it.

Jennie felt as though she had found a treasure for which she had looked a lifetime. She still was afraid of her own feelings and of being made to look like a fool, but her passion was driving out her caution. She longed to touch that glorious young body and see where her excitement would lead.

Trying to control her quaking voice, Jennie told Emma that her hair was cold and wet and probably should be washed. Emma immediately agreed and asked if Jennie would mind loaning her some shampoo. Jennie smiled and told Emma if she wanted her to she would wash Emma's hair. Emma gaily laughed and ducked her head under the hot water.

With trembling fingers Jennie slowly and carefully caressed the shampoo into Emma's hair. As the shampoo began to foam, Jennie gently used her fingernails to massage Emma's scalp.

Emma tilted her head back and closed her eyes in pleasure. Jennie's lips were within inches of Emma's but fear held her in check.

Just as Jennie was about to back away Emma opened those wide gray eyes and looked directly into Jennie's. Jennie leaned closer and placed her lips on Emma's.

The shudder that Jennie experienced was almost too much to bear. She let out a gasp and stood up. Emma smiled and rose to touch Jennie's cheek with the back of her hand.

Now Jennie was alone again because three hundred white men had used the events of October 12, 1878 to defend the honor of white women and avenge the death of Deputy Sheriff O.C. Thomas.

Jennie did not give a damn about any of that; she just missed Emma.

CHAPTER ELEVEN

ABRAHAM AND ALVIN

ALVIN PETERSON HOVEY WAS EXCITED to be chosen by his fellow citizens to represent them in the 1850-1852 Indiana Constitutional Convention in Indianapolis. Hovey had raised himself from age fifteen and struggled for acceptance from the hoi polloi all of his adult life. He despised this aspect of his character, but knew from many attempts to excise it that he simply could not withstand his need to be accepted, respected, and envied.

His father's financial mismanagement then death when Hovey was two and his mother's death when Hovey was fifteen, his brother Charles' irresponsible behavior, and Hovey's lack of formal education were the factors Hovey usually cited to himself in his dark periods of self-pity.

But in his more lucid self-analysis he accepted that, somehow, he was encumbered with an inexorable need to be admired by others, even others whom he detested or who mistreated him.

Judge John Pitcher who had moved to Posey County from Rockport in Spencer County, Indiana after his first wife's death, had recognized this weakness in Hovey and repeatedly used it to Pitcher's advantage.

Pitcher had known Abraham Lincoln who had lived in Spencer County from the age of seven to twenty-one. And Pitcher had loaned Lincoln the same copies of *Blackstone's Commentaries* that Hovey later used to "read for the law".

When Hovey met Lincoln, Hovey was struck by the similarities in the views of Pitcher and Lincoln on slavery and their differing views on Negroes.

It was clear to Hovey that Pitcher abhorred the institution of slavery but had nothing but disdain for any nonAnglo-Saxon.

Lincoln had told Hovey that when Indiana became a state in 1816, Tom Lincoln had moved his family from Kentucky across the Ohio River because of slavery. Tom was without any formal education but was a skilled carpenter who resented losing work to unpaid craftsmen.

Tom Lincoln, also, had lost legal title to all three of his Hardin County, Kentucky farms in the courts. And while in Kentucky, the family's Baptist church had split over the slavery issue.

In Indiana, the Spencer County Baptists divided over slavery as did the local Methodists. Abraham told Alvin that he believed his life was defined by these early events. Slavery, organized religion and law occupied much of Lincoln's thinking.

Each man had lost his mother while young. Lincoln was a carpenter; Hovey trained himself to be a stone mason. Each saw much hypocrisy in religion and politics. Each believed that law and government were the best instruments to achieve public good. And while each had been influenced by Judge John Pitcher, each differed from Pitcher's position that abolition of slavery was all that society owed to Negroes, although neither would chance making a public stance on this volatile issue.

A common crotchet of Lincoln and Hovey that early on helped meld their friendship was the irritation each felt when people addressed them by nicknames. Lincoln found "Abe" and Hovey found "Al" disconcerting. While neither man took issue with others who addressed them so familiarly, both men found such appellations off-putting. Early on, Abraham's use of "Alvin" and Alvin's use of "Abraham" on a consistent basis helped ease the formation of their friendship. Later, Lincoln recognized that "Honest Abraham" had no zing. A rail splitter needed a nickname.

Another similarity in the men was their willingness to subjugate their true beliefs in order to succeed. When Hovey and Lincoln would discuss this aspect of their characters they refused to ignore their weakness except to note that the only man they would confess this to was the other.

Hovey often recalled the first truly personal conversation he had with Lincoln. It occurred at the stage coach depot in Warrenton, Indiana in the summer of 1849. Lincoln planned to visit his mother's grave in Spencer County, Indiana and he had written to Hovey from Springfield, Illinois and suggested they meet at Warrenton to celebrate Hovey's selection to represent Posey County at the Indiana Constitutional Convention of 1850. Lincoln wryly commented that, "Hovey's training as a lawyer should only slightly impinge on the process of making law." Hovey had taken the attorney's oath in the Posey Circuit Court in 1842 and Lincoln in Illinois in 1836.

Although Lincoln and Hovey had spoken twice in person and had exchanged an occasional letter, usually with some interesting news item enclosed, their relationship had remained more of a polite extension of their mutual connections to Judge Pitcher than a personal friendship. Later their relationship became an important vehicle for each of them to test their ideas with complete faith in the good will, sound judgment and discretion of the other.

Hovey marked the beginning of this loss of fear and hubris to their meeting at Warrenton. His own defense of formality and Lincoln's mask of self-deprecating humor were penetrated by mutual fatigue and unfamiliarity with the station master's spirits.

Their conversation began with their mutual respect for Judge Pitcher and for Pitcher's son, Thomas, who had been appointed to West Point in 1841. While neither Lincoln nor Hovey had any formal military training, each had studied strategy and tactics for several years. And while Lincoln did not live to enjoy General Thomas Pitcher's appointment as Superintendent of West Point in 1866, President Lincoln had already assured that it would occur.

Lincoln had volunteered in the 1832 Black Hawk War in Illinois and Hovey in the 1846 Mexican War, but neither saw any action.

Each later confided to the other what they were ashamed to express to anyone else; the exhilaration from the anticipation of battle was the most intense and passionate emotion either had ever experienced. When Lincoln became Commander in Chief and Hovey led men in the Great War, each knew the dark side of the other's soul.

War was terrible in its results but, also, one of life's greatest gifts.

Hovey remembered how easily he and Lincoln discussed their admiration for Napoleon's military genius and the necessary evil of war for national defense. Victory by full measure for a just cause was both militarily and morally sound.

Hovey understood Lincoln's later choices of West Point graduates to command the Union forces and especially his choice of Ulysses Grant.

Hovey served under Grant at the siege of Vicksburg and was struck by his military brilliance and tenacity. Hovey secretly believed that he himself had a mystical connection to Napoleon and that Grant somehow recognized the similarities.

When Grant in a communiqué to Lincoln commended then Major General Hovey for winning the pivotal battle of Champion Hill at Vicksburg, Grant was unaware that his commander of the Indiana 24th Division, "Hovey's Babies", was a personal friend of the President.

However, Lincoln's response to Grant included his gratitude for the victory, a wish for his "old friend's continued good health", and the cryptic, "Tell General Hovey that we knew even less than we thought at Warrenton".

Hovey knew that Lincoln's encouragement of Hovey's political career had led to his election as judge of the Posey Circuit Court in 1851 and to his selection as one of Posey County's representatives to the Indiana Constitutional Convention of 1850-52.

Robert Dale Owen of New Harmony, Posey County, Indiana was the other representative from the "pocket area" where the Wabash and Ohio rivers meet. Owen had beaten Judge John Pitcher in a runoff election for the slot and Pitcher never forgave him.

Indiana had decided to replace its 1816 Constitution due in part to the financial debacle caused by the State's investment in the ill-fated Wabash and Erie Canal. However, the unwritten impetus was to deal with Hoosier fears of the influx of escaped and freed Negroes.

In the summer of 1849, the forty year old Lincoln had just completed his Congressional term and the twenty-nine year old Hovey was preparing for the Constitutional Convention.

When they met at Warrenton about thirty miles northeast of Mt. Vernon and between Mt. Vernon and Lincoln's old home place in Spencer County, Indiana, they were well established lawyers and influential in their own communities.

Hovey was a handsome young man of five feet eight inches who was much better known in southern Indiana than the six foot four inch homely Lincoln. The station master greeted Hovey as Mr. and ignored Lincoln until Hovey introduced him as a friend of Judge Pitcher.

Lincoln had already heard that at age twenty-two Thomas Pitcher had been severely wounded in the leg during the Mexican War. Hovey told Lincoln that Pitcher's bravery and leadership as a second lieutenant had been recognized by the army with a battlefield promotion to First Lieutenant.

After the home brewed beer began to take effect on the tired and hungry men, Lincoln remarked that the last time he had seen Thomas, Judge Pitcher was ordering the five year old to sit still while the judge explained the value of reading about great men. On that occasion in Rockport, Judge Pitcher had loaned Lincoln his volume of Weems' *Life of Washington* which recounted battles of the Revolutionary War.

Young Thomas was hanging on the twenty year old Lincoln's leg and challenging him to wrestle.

Lincoln told Hovey how proud he was of Thomas. "I know the fear and pain must have been severe, but oh how I wish I could have been in the cauldron with him".

Hovey was surprised by the window Lincoln left open by this remark. Hovey surprised himself by his response. "Abraham, ever since I read *To Lucasta on Going to War* I have dearly wished to test myself in combat. My mother had not yet died, so I must have been about fourteen."

Lincoln leaned his spare body towards Hovey and said, "Lovelace, 'I could not love thee dear so much loved I not honor more.'" His boney face was animated and his speech lost its laconic demeanor. "Alvin, do you know *Henry the Fifth*? It has what has long been one of my favorite soliloquies. 'We few, we happy few. We band of brothers...'" Hovey broke in with, "'...for he who fights with me this day will surely be my brother.'"

Each man was less surprised by the other's enthusiasm than his own. Neither was accustomed to such closeness and usually guarded against such vulnerability. Experience had too often taught the folly of allowing intimacy.

"Abraham, I was crestfallen that I missed the chance to test myself in the Mexican War. Each generation gets but one chance to go to war and we missed ours, although not from lack of trying."

"We both know that we must publicly proclaim our abhorrence of war, Alvin. But now with law careers, families and our positions in our communities, even if the gods should grant us another opportunity, how could we justify our young man's fantasies?"

As the men discussed Alexander the Great's genius at Gaugamela, King Philip II's misfortune with the weather in 1588, and George Washington's leadership style of inapproachability, vanities and fears each had seldom admitted to themselves began to be carefully deployed.

"Alvin, you are going to a different kind of battle next year. What would you say is the salient issue for Indiana at the Constitutional Convention?"

Hovey would have normally seen such a gambit as an attempt to discover any secret agenda he might have. But with this unusual man he perceived genuine interest in what Hovey's contribution might be.

So when Hovey answered it was with passion, not prudence. "Something must be done to protect the Negro from bondage and northern states from freed Negroes. This country is too young to be sacrificed on the altar of state's rights, yet it must not founder on its own ideals."

Hovey could scarce believe he had spoken so rashly. The people of Posey County had elected him because he was seen as a believer in Indiana first without regard to national issues.

"Alvin, I hear you echoing my deepest concerns. Indiana may be a free state, but many Negroes in northwestern Kentucky are still considered property. What happens when slaves grow old, get injured or are manumitted and encouraged to migrate to free states? The evil of slavery remains but its damaged results become the problem of Illinois and Indiana. I assume that you will be called upon to perform that most difficult of tasks, to advocate for a necessary short term solution that violates your true beliefs but which has the best chance of leading to the end result you believe is just."

Hovey knew that Lincoln had seen into his heart. He feared that such knowledge might be used against him somehow. But the Rubicon had been crossed. Lincoln might betray him but Hovey desperately needed a friend on his perilous journey between the Scylla of public service and the Charybdis of personal success.

And there was Hovey's faith in the rule of law versus his fear of the majority's tyranny. He plunged ahead.

"Abraham, have you ever heard the origin of the term, 'lynching'?"

Lincoln was taken aback by what appeared to be an oblique turn in Hovey's thoughts. "As I recall, a justice of the peace in Virginia saw fit to run his own court by his own rules which often included hanging; am I correct?"

"Yes. From a lawyer's perspective what could be worse than serious sanctions without standards, precedents and equal treatment? But on a personal note, how would you like your name to be used as the metonymy for injustice? Lynch probably believed his actions were justified by necessity. Most of us can rationalize any desired result. But look what history has done to Lynch. Will this be our fate if our fear of the moment defeats our true passions? If history takes note of our deeds at all, will it be for fame or infamy? I confess, I have a burning desire to be both right and liked; the Furies often require a choice."

"Ah, the gods, Alvin, my experience with gods is they are no better or worse than the people who create them. The terms 'lynch law' or 'Judge Lynch' are oxymoronic. On the other hand, democracy is often defined by one's situation. For example, my view of Indians is probably skewed by my grandfather's death at the hand of an Indian in 1786. And my wife's youngest brother allows as how my view of state's rights is less a matter of conscience than geography. He says I rail for democracy when I am in the majority but that I would most likely call for secession if still in Kentucky; I hope he has not completely captured my character.

"When I retreat into my soul and make my best effort to face my demons, I keep coming to the same place. Yes, slavery is an abomination, but this great experiment in which we are such minor actors overrules all else. Can people, common people, govern themselves? If we pass laws to outlaw slavery in all states and the union is rent, will Negroes be better off? The answer is, 'yes', because it is always better to reign in one's own hell than to be forced to serve in another's heaven.

"However, will the country be better off? I think not. There will be at least two countries and maybe several, one for each state, one for the untamed wilderness, etc. Each nation will pass its own parochial laws which will not be the will of the majority but only that of the local aristocracy. Kings, interminable warfare over natural resources and rivers, who knows what would result. The Holy Grail is the Union. At least, I think so at the moment. What say you, Alvin?"

He sees me for what I am and he is the same, thought Hovey. He knows what is right but is willing to accept what is practical. "Abraham, you were last in Indiana in 1844 you said. Do you know when you might return?"

Lincoln recognized Hovey's unspoken agreement with his advice. Lincoln thought, he is a good and courageous man who knows positive change must come slowly by careful means or, perhaps, not at all. If men such as Adams and Madison could assuage their guilt with the legerdemain of three fifths of a man, who were he and Hovey to gainsay their efforts? They accepted that an imperfect democracy was far better than none and that time must abide such a divisive issue as universal abolition.

"Alvin, I have no plans to return soon. When I was here in '44 I was electioneering for the Great Compromiser; we lost, of course. Perhaps when my boys are older I can show them their grandmother's grave and where I grew to manhood. There's, also, the Baptist church at Pigeon Creek my father helped build and I joined at fourteen. My son, Todd, is now six and keeps asking me why I don't attend church much. He might be interested in seeing that at one time I was about as pious as other youngsters. I suppose the battle between faith and fact kept raging in my young mind and faith usually lost out. Also, it seemed that the Baptists and Methodists spent more time trying to expiate each other than the Devil."

"It has been the law based on fact and human experience versus religion based on faith which has interfered with my reverie, Abraham. I used to engage with others in their debate but too often found that I hurt their feelings or angered them rather than enlightened them or myself. Now, I regularly attend the Methodist church in Mt. Vernon and try to not ask questions. The last time I queried the Reverend Mr. Scrammahorn about his definition of God he gave an entire sermon on why such predilections were heresy. At least he only stared at me for the whole hour and did not damn me with attribution."

"Alvin, bring me up to date on Mt. Vernon. How are the good wives currently marshaling their forces against the boatmen and brothels?"

"If they ever get rid of the fallen angels, our little bucolic county will die of ennui. Then we'd have to actually address real issues such as blackbirding. We need our licentious ladies. In fact, Madam Jennie Bell not only provides basic services she is one of our best businessmen. I just wish some of our local politicians were as public spirited as she is. They certainly rival her in being for sale. But let me go back to the Constitutional Convention.

"Abraham, do you remember Robert Dale Owen? He was at Judge Pitcher's home when you and I were there about five years ago. You and he were talking about our two Utopian experiments in Posey County. You may recall that our small community of New Harmony was the site of two attempts at communal living. One from 1817 to 1825 based on religion and one from 1825 to 1827 based on the Enlightenment. I don't know what it means that scientific discovery produced less than religious epiphany.

"Anyway, Robert Dale, as he is known, is the eldest son of the wealthy Scotsman, Robert Owen, who bought the community of Harmonie from Father George Rapp and his German-Lutheran flock after Rapp got his vision revision from Michael the Archangel and moved everyone back to Pennsylvania. If you take the road through New Harmony on your way back to Illinois, you can even see the angel's footprint in a stone there. I'll leave up to you if it looks like God's work or erosion.

"Robert Dale and I quite often find ourselves on the same side of the negra issue. We sometimes waffle between some kind of integration and a return to Africa or removal to the frontier or some other land such as Haiti. He is a good man and, I believe, has a great deal of our common interests. Of course, his financial status and fine education insulate him from our pedestrian worries. If it's alright, the next time you come to Indiana, I will have him, Judge Pitcher and you down to my law office near the Ohio so that Robert Dale and I can get a feel for what our new constitution should look like.

"If his former companion, Frances "Fanny" Wright, is back from her freed slave community in Haiti, I might see if Robert Dale can bring her also. She is one of the most intelligent women I have ever known. Her ideas on slavery, women's rights, marriage and religion are subjects a new Constitution should probably address. Fanny is controversial. Her position on religion and marriage is that their main purpose is to allow men to keep women in their place. But her view on the negra problem is absolutely dangerous. Fanny says interbreeding is the only real solution. You will find her fascinating and a welcome addition to the repartee."

"Well, my friend, since my public service is at an end now, I may be able to work that out occasionally if my wife and family can spare me from Springfield. Practicing law greatly appeals to me after a term in Congress. And nothing would give me more pleasure than to exchange ideas with you on how to form a new government.

"We missed our chance for war, but bare knuckle politics might suffice. I do remember Mr. Owen. In fact, our paths crossed briefly in Congress when he represented Indiana. His second term was ending as my term was beginning in 1847. We found a commonality of philosophies in several areas, especially the Negro issue. He told of the community in Tennessee that he and Miss Wright founded. It is a beau geste, I fear, but only because we humans seem incapable of doing the right thing the easy way. I would enjoy watching the sparks fly when Judge Pitcher and he discuss the merits of manumission and integration. And I have heard of Miss Wright and her ideas on free love and slavery. As to the Negro problem, I see no hope. We must not sacrifice everyone for some, and we lose our souls when we deny others the existence of theirs."

"Abraham, in Mt. Vernon other than the economic impact of hoards of freed Negroes coming to Indiana, my friends appear most fearful of inter-breeding. We have had a few nasty incidents. Now, I don't mean white men with coloreds, for some reason that almost never seems to happen. No, the problems we have had are white women being put upon. So far the county has been satisfied with beating the bucks or jailing them for a time. I fear the good citizens of Posey County may require a much higher price soon, especially if some respectable woman is subjected to more than inappropriate comments.

"While we have not had a great deal of difficulty, we have had an incident or two of some prostitute taking up willingly with coloreds. Of course, the whore is then shunned by white men and the Negro is driven off.

"Abraham, we both know the delicate balance upon which the Negro problem teeters. Black craftsmen taking white jobs, tax monies used to pay for problems caused by migrating Negroes who do not pay taxes and valuable real estate damaged by the proximity of blacks are just some of the volatile issues.

"But all of these pale next to miscegenation. White men will not countenance it. Frankly, I see this as one of the recurring themes of human folly. There's always some group in power telling others how to live. Be that as it may, Mt. Vernon could well erupt if some white woman is taken advantage of and white men let their hatred obscure their reasoning. It does seem that Negro men with white women must be guarded for. Fanny Wright may believe the only long term solution is interbreeding, but then she openly cavorted with the great Marquis de LaFayette and Robert Dale too."

"Now, Alvin, I don't know about Mt. Vernon, but in slave states it is all the other way. Some slave owners see their coloreds as chattels for all purposes. And the consequences for both the colored male and white woman from some tryst would be too horrible to endure. Did you have any particular matter in mind in your town? Ah, there it is. My weakness for salacious rumor has escaped my best efforts at containment. Unless there is some situation you wish to get a foreigner's view on, just forget that my frailty occurred."

"In fact, there are some complications involving coloreds and a few influential members of our community. My concern is not titillation, but impact on the town. However, through my law practice, I have heard rumor of a very dangerous liaison involving the wife of one of our richest men that may have occurred not long ago. And true or not, whites may exact a terrible price on the black community if this becomes a public matter. Fortunately, the Negro has now fled and the husband is more concerned with his reputation than his wife's frailty. He has convinced himself her honor is intact. But this rumor has not waned in three years. One of our madams despises the wife and keeps stirring the pot.

"This is where your advice as a lawyer, outsider and friend might be most valuable. Let me swear you to secrecy and tell you what little I know. Remember, my information is innuendo based on rumor via hearsay. And, like you, I confess my interest is not merely out of public concern."

CHAPTER TWELVE

HATTIE

SARAH JONES CAREFULLY OPENED HER etui and gently caressed the large ivory button carved into the shape of a baby's face. Sarah traced the lines of the girl's brow and jaw with her right index finger. "Hattie", she moaned.

It was Easter Sunday in 1878. Sarah had gone to church with her husband, Henry, who had walked her back to their home on Locust Street. Henry left her alone while he went to the Pittsburgh Coal Company on Mill Street to work on the books of account with his business associates, E.E. Thomas and Bill Topper.

Sarah sat in her drawing room in her new white Easter outfit and wondered what Henry knew about the past year that had at first pulled her back from suicide then had her in ever deeper despair. There was no reason to go on, yet her life belonged to God; it was not hers to take. The Bible, or so she had been told, made suicide a mortal sin. But could eternal damnation be worse than the torment she now suffered? Two years ago she thought being barren was worse than death. Now that she had known the joy of motherhood and had to disavow her child, she believed that tree of knowledge surely bore the bitterest fruit.

Yet, Hattie was her child. Hattie was but ten blocks away at Elizabeth Harrison's house at Second and Elm. Hattie would be loved. She would be cared for. Sarah did get to hold her when Elizabeth occasionally brought Hattie with her as she came to clean Sarah's large home. They both knew the danger of this proximity of mother and child in their small town, but Sarah had to have some relief and Elizabeth understood.

This was more than the forty years old Sarah ever thought possible when Hattie was born. Was not this enough when compared to years of anguish over being childless? God had apparently forgiven her for whatever sins that had kept her and Henry wealthy but lonely. She and Henry had made their accommodations. He was respectful but without passion. She was dutiful without joy. The twenty year difference in their ages seemed irrelevant at twenty and forty but omnipresent at thirty-eight and fifty-eight.

Their dreams of children faded with each year and were mocked by the constant reminders of church and social gatherings. The cruelest times were family holidays, especially Christmas and Easter. They both called for rebirth, hope, salvation and continuity of life.

Sarah loved Henry and knew he loved her. But Sarah believed Henry silently blamed her for their fate and this seeped into all aspects of their lives. Sarah would have been amazed if she could have known Henry's mind instead of his words. She, also, would be devastated to know that in his private sanctuary Henry would have accepted a child by any means if public ridicule could be avoided.

CHAPTER THIRTEEN

SOARING BIRD

HENRY KNEW FROM HIS FIRST love that he was probably the source of his and Sarah's childlessness. Henry had never told Sarah about Soaring Bird, the Indian girl he had met through Christian Willis when they were camping with Christian's Shawnee people near Vincennes, Indiana, in 1841. He and Christian planned to trap fox and beaver until they had saved enough money to open a trading post in which they would employ Indians. They believed that the only realistic hope for the survival of the Shawnee was their successful integration into the white man's culture, especially its business practices and Christian religion. Willis had made these transitions and Jones believed he had received a calling to bring the indigenous people of this new state of Indiana to Jesus.

Henry Jones was the son of Tom Jones, the first white man to settle in what later became Posey County, Indiana, in 1795. Henry was raised by Tom's white wife in the wilderness above the Ohio River. Henry's mother had died of smallpox in 1820 before his stepmother arrived from Pennsylvania to marry Tom. Henry's mother's identity was a taboo subject until Tom's death in 1826. Henry then learned from his stepmother of his Indian blood. While his father had often spoken with disparagement of Indians and Negroes, his stepmother concentrated on Henry's religious training and Jesus' command to "suffer the little children", which is what she called the dark peoples.

Although Henry kept his Indian heritage to himself, he felt a curiosity about his mother's Shawnee tribe. However, he was thankful that his father's hair and complexion had trumped.

Henry lived in fear that white people would discern his true make-up. Yet he identified with those less fortunate than he, especially Indians. Only his step-mother who died when he was twenty, and Christian Willis whom Henry had told, knew of his Indian blood. Christian and Henry knew their mission was to save the Shawnee from themselves and their pagan beliefs.

A trading post and a church were what the Indians needed for deliverance. Henry and Christian were God's instruments of Shawnee salvation. Henry's father had begun and operated a trading post in Posey County until his death in 1826. Henry had spent the first eight years of his life at the post on Bone Bank Road in Posey County. His father began to teach Henry how to keep the accounts before Henry started going to school.

When Henry met Soaring Bird she was fourteen summers and he was but twenty-three. Henry had never known a woman at less than polite distance. Bird, as Henry called her, was small and bronze with bright brown eyes and straight black hair. She knew the best spots to set traps. She made her own clothing. She was fascinated by Henry's golden hair and mustache. She loved him without conditions. He knew not what he had.

Henry knew he could not marry Bird and be accepted by Mt. Vernon. He wanted wealth but he needed respect, both might be jeopardized by Bird. Henry had seen the stares of disapproval when he and Bird were together in Vincennes. He could not overcome his shame.

Christian and Henry had spent part of each week trying to explain to the Shawnee that Jesus was saddened and angered for them to put credence in the transcendentalism of their environment. Such ignorance would cause them to lose their souls.

As part of their plan Henry would try to explain the benefits of permanent structures and education in English so that they could learn of God's plan for them.

Christian revised Shawnee legends about the Shawnee being "The People" and the myth of the Shawnee having been created from the stars, to bring the stories of *Genesis* home to the Indians.

The Indians enjoyed the stories and accepted Henry and Christian into their village. They tried to share their own stories and ways of commerce with them, but this always seemed to frustrate Henry and Christian. After a while the Shawnee quit talking and just pretended to listen.

When Henry was seen in Vincennes with Bird by Judge John Pitcher, Henry explained she was his guide for trapping. The look from Pitcher began the death of the trading post, the church, and Henry's happiness.

Henry broke with Christian and left Bird without explanation. Christian turned his zeal to saving Negroes.

Henry had lived with Bird for two years and amassed enough money to invest in some farm land when he returned to Mt. Vernon to do the books for the Pittsburgh Coal Company. Christian decided to start a school for Negro children with his share. The Indians were not ready to be saved. He and the Negro minister, Reverend Ben Wilson, opened and financed the Brewery Hills Community just north and west of Mt. Vernon. The white community kept an eye on the project.

When Henry left Bird he gave her ten percent of his earnings. The sixteen year old Bird did not die from losing Henry as he feared she might. Bird moved in with a French trapper and had a child by him within a year.

CHAPTER FOURTEEN

THE APPRENTICE

HENRY EXPECTED TO REMAIN A bachelor, but the twenty years old Sarah erased Bird from his mind, at least until he connected Bird's child bearing with Sarah's childlessness.

Sarah and Henry had so desperately wanted children and had made many plans for their arrival. But as the years flew by, Henry protected himself from his yearnings with success in business and involvement in politics. Sarah had nowhere to turn but within. Fortunately, she had Elizabeth and her eight children to keep her from total introspection. Elizabeth's husband, Daniel Harrison, Sr., was much like Henry when he was starting out. He farmed and did any odd job he could to make money. He had managed to accumulate forty acres of farmland just south and west of Mt. Vernon near the slough. Daniel's parents, Nicy and Fredunes Harrison, had deeded him a three room house with two lots at Second and Elm. Daniel divided the lots and put one in Elizabeth's sole name as insurance against the changing attitudes of whites. He, also, occasionally gave small amounts of gold coins to his younger brother, Charles, and his wife, Eliza, to hold in case there was trouble. Charles was a restaurant cook and he and Eliza had several children of their own. They lived in the house Daniel had built on the lot he deeded to Elizabeth.

Daniel had a secret passion that sometimes bubbled to the surface. He desperately wanted his children to have the opportunities he had been denied. He knew that education was the key that could unlock those doors, but Posey County would not allow Negro children to attend school with whites. Over the years, Eppie Daniels along with Sarah Jones had worked with all of the Harrison family privately to teach them to read and write.

Still, Daniel silently seethed with anger when his daughter, Jane, and his son, John, were denied entrance into Posey County's only high school. The Harrisons were resolved to push harder when Daniel, Jr., was ready for a secondary education.

Daniel Jr., was already eleven years old when Elizabeth came to work for Sarah. By the age of seventeen young Dan was five feet ten inches tall and light complexioned. Before Elizabeth had been brought to Indiana by her white mistress in 1838, her mother had been the head negress for a white slave owner in Tennessee. Elizabeth was sent away when she was less than four years old.

Elizabeth's oldest daughter, Jane, was even lighter than young Dan and cleaned for a local law officer and his wife. She was born in 1852 and appeared to have no interest in marriage although she longed for children of her own.

Young Dan was his mother's favorite and his father's concern. He was powerfully built and sometimes unwilling to keep his place. He had the disturbing habit of looking white men and even white women in the eye. His skill as a brawler kept fellow Negroes at bay and white men somewhat off guard.

Young Dan did not see why he should have to pretend to lose a fight to a white man who had caused the problem. Therefore, he rarely was bothered even though the white men of Mt. Vernon seethed with resentment at his uppity attitude.

In addition to his physical abilities, young Dan was born with Elizabeth's artistic bent. He often carved items for his younger siblings and always made Elizabeth some special object for her birthday.

Young Dan was called Da by his family because his brother, John, who was four when Da was born, could not say Daniel. Sarah called him Da and he called her Miss Sarah.

Da was not well treated by Henry. He reminded Henry of the son he did not have, yet Henry could not overcome his fear of public disapproval should he allow Daniel to approach. Daniel at eleven had no fear of Henry and repeatedly tried to engage him with childish banter. There was a time when Henry had dropped his public persona with Daniel and began to enjoy the boy's unusual bearing and skill.

But when he allowed the thirteen year old Daniel to accompany him to the coal company one day, his business associates ridiculed him about his nigger shadow whose curiosity and brazen questions about the business annoyed his partners.

When Bill Topper referred to Da as Henry's nigger apprentice, Daniel saw the denial in Henry's eyes and felt Henry's flush of embarrassment.

But what caused Henry to finally sever personal contact with Da was the public outcry when Sarah and Eppie Daniels had taken Elizabeth and Daniel, Sr., before the county school board and asked that Da be admitted to the county's only high school when he turned fourteen.

Eppie and Sarah had brought John and Jane Harrison with them to remind the school board that for years Negro children had been denied a public education. All that **was** accomplished was that the businesses of both George Daniels and Henry were informally boycotted until white resentment subsided.

To protect his pride and his business, Henry began to build the barriers between himself and Daniel. Daniel's resentment and hurt from the rejection turned to defiance. As young Daniel began to feel the awakenings of manhood, he realized that the ultimate revenge was that greatest of taboos. He had his first girl when he was fourteen; she was the daughter of a poor white farmer who lived next to the Harrison forty acres.

Daniel would not have made it to 1878 had white men known of his conquest. Even the lowest caste of white woman was forbidden to any Negro. Of course, Daniel was subject to the girl's ability to cry rape if he mentioned their relationship, although she would have been ostracized or worse if the white community had any suspicion of her story. He and she kept their bargains and went their separate ways.

What this first experience taught Daniel was how good he felt taking what white men most feared he would get. He, also, learned that not only did some white women gladly give of their favors if they could taste forbidden fruit, but the worse he treated them the more he got from them. However, he soon realized that even when a white woman was desperate for his sexual services, she still would avoid any public acknowledgement of him other than as a generic "boy". He learned that what he most longed for was beyond his grasp. He was good enough to split their wood or their legs but not good enough to come in the front door.

But by age seventeen Daniel had begun to realize that the only white women who would commerce with him were ones most white men did not pursue, at least publicly. He came to wonder if he was stealing forbidden treasures or simply collecting refuse. These thoughts caused an even greater anger within him.

CHAPTER FIFTEEN

FULFILLMENT
AND DAMNATION

THE ONLY WHITE WOMAN DANIEL knew personally who was part of respectable society was Miss Sarah. Daniel had always thought of her as an old woman. She was about the same age as his mother. She seemed like some sexless saint who was pious and passionless.

When he was eleven Miss Sarah had not even touched him when his mother introduced them. It made Daniel kind of queasy to even think of what might be under her clothes. He liked her very much and she was kind and generous with him. But Miss Sarah was more like one of the statues in the Catholic Church his mother cleaned than a woman.

And what would his mother say if she had any idea Daniel might have an inappropriate thought about Miss Sarah. Also, his whole family might be destroyed if he should have any unacceptable contact with her.

These were Daniel's thoughts when he was chopping wood for Miss Sarah that unusually warm spring day in 1877. Daniel had his shirt off and was perspiring heavily. Mr. Henry was at the coal company and Daniel's mother had already gone home.

Sarah brought a pitcher filled with water and two glasses out the kitchen door and into the backyard where Da was working. The yard was shaded and fenced for privacy.

"Da, come over here and get yourself a drink. You are getting too hot."

Sarah had never seen Da without his shirt. She was surprised at how mature he looked with his veins popping out on his arms. Da's thin cotton pants were clinging to his legs and hips. Sarah was embarrassed when she caught herself deciding he could not have on any underwear since his manhood was outlined so prominently.

"Thank ya, Miss Sarah. It shore be hot."

Da took one of the glasses and thought how Miss Sarah, unlike other white folks, did not seem to keep track of which dishes he used. She poured it full and then refilled it.

"Da, just sit a minute, I'm going to get a towel for you. I don't see how you can keep that sweat out of your eyes."

Sarah entered the kitchen and steadied herself on the counter. What was wrong? She felt uneasy and she noticed she was unusually warm. She managed to get a towel from the closet and return to Da.

"Here you are, Da. Dry yourself off. You'll have to put either your axe or your water down to do it you silly boy. Oh, just turn around and drink your water and I'll do it."

Sarah did not know why she said this. She had never touched a Negro man; Da seemed like a man now. She had always cringed at the thought of any man's touch but Henry's. He was the only man she had ever known Biblically. Why was she so nervous? Sarah took the towel and began to rub Da's back with it.

Da was surprised at the pleasure this gave him. His thoughts were confused and troubling. He could not speak.

"Turn around, Da, and I'll dab your forehead."

When Da turned around he tried to bend over and cover his front with the axe handle. He was embarrassed and frightened at his condition. Sarah wanted to avert her eyes but could not. She slowly patted Da's forehead then his face with the towel. Da raised his eyes to see if she had noticed.

Afterwards Sarah often tried to recall exactly what happened next. She tried to remember the smell of the sweat, the throbbing of Da's body. After the passing of years she was not sure what she remembered and what she created. That is, she tried to remember these details when she thought of Hattie.

When she thought of Henry and God and eternal damnation and the lynchings she felt debilitating guilt and shame. Sarah's ambivalence about the catastrophe she had helped create was her knowledge that the horror came after and, in part because of, the creation of Hattie. The moments of creation could sometimes assuage her guilt.

As Da's eyes met Sarah's, Da dropped the axe and bent down to place the glass on the ground. When he arose his fullness was no longer hidden. Sarah took Da's hand and led him to her and Henry's bedroom.

Sarah removed Da's pants. She had been correct. She then removed her clothing as Da stood naked with his eyes downcast. Sarah raised his head with her hand and kissed him on the mouth.

She was surprised that Da's lips felt like Henry's and that she was not repulsed by the contact.

Da looked at Sarah and was amazed that her breasts were small but firm and that her body filled him with desire. Surely this had to be wrong. Miss Sarah was not an object for defiance.

What Daniel did not realize was that Sarah was about to give him the gift of humanity. What Sarah somehow knew even before they lost themselves in this improbable moment of absolution and creation was that Da was about to give Sarah what she had longed for since her wedding. All fears and needs were absolved for the moment by this exchange.

They would soon have to deal with the beauty and danger resulting from their unspeakable forbidden acts.

Chapter Sixteen

SHAWNEETOWN

Moses Rawlings believed in fortune. After several attempts at business in that backwater of Chicago, he realized it had no future. He had relocated to the fledgling but pulsating community of Shawneetown after reading an edition of *The Illinois Emigrant* from 1818.

His friends Henry Eddy and Allen Kimmel had started their newspaper there that year and had sent Rawlings one of their first printings. Eddy and Kimmel had the same experiences with Chicago as Rawlings and had gone searching for a new El Dorado. They had decided that following the Lewis and Clark Expedition's river landing sites would be a good way to predict future growth such as had already occurred at the Mississippi River port of St. Louis.

Eddy and Kimmel's research drew them to Shawneetown at the opposite end of Illinois from Chicago and on the banks of the Ohio River just south of its confluence with the Wabash and just north of its confluence with the Mississippi. Rivers were the great constant highways of America where land travel was unpredictable and dangerous. While struggling for survival in Chicago, Rawlings, Eddy and Kimmel clearly saw the fortunes to be made elsewhere, especially on the frontier. The lodestone was commerce and the key to commerce was travel.

Along with the newspaper extolling Shawneetown's fortuitous location, Eddy and Kimmel sent a note reminding Rawlings of a conversation they had just before Eddy and Kimmel decided to seek more options than Chicago provided. It had been Rawlings who could see clearly the possibility of interlocking waterways from New York to New Orleans. As Rawlings had excitedly said, America had been selected by God as a land of infinite opportunities and given to European immigrants as a sacred trust. To leave it undeveloped would be a blasphemy.

Eddy and Kimmel had stopped first at Grayville, Illinois on the banks of the Wabash River about ten miles north of its mouth into the Ohio River. Grayville was a vibrant ganglia of energy and speculation that put Chicago to shame. But Eddy and Kimmel were concerned they might be a little too late to Grayville as land and building material prices were rising too quickly for them to get in on the ground floor of the rush. They feared they might end up as the last fools. Also, Grayville was just across the Wabash from the new State of Indiana which was solidly anti-slavery and had joined the Union in 1816, two years before Illinois.

And even less appealing was Grayville's juxtaposition to the new religious commune started by George Rapp whose followers called him Father. Rapp had brought his band of German-Lutherans from Pennsylvania to the erstwhile Northwest Territory to purify themselves and wait for the Second Coming which God had told Father Rapp was imminent.

Harmonie, Indiana, although slightly south, was almost directly across the Wabash from Grayville. A community founded on the New Testament which looked to *Isaiah* of the Old Testament for its *raison d'etre* did not mesh with the entrepreneurial visions of Eddy and Kimmel.

How surprised they were less than ten years later when the Harmonists sold their onetime worthless low lands to Robert Owen for a quarter of a million dollars.

But in 1817, Eddy and Kimmel were searching for just the right combination of location, budding speculation and cheap labor. Meriwether Lewis and William Clark's 1803 landing at Shawneetown drew them.

Shawneetown was about as close to being in slave friendly Kentucky and Tennessee as one could get and still be in Illinois. It was raw and the frontier spirited inhabitants of the region tended to eschew the legal niceties of borders and federalism. Laying up for themselves the wages of this world was more likely in Shawneetown.

Moses Rawlings arrived in Shawneetown, Illinois in 1820. There were countless massive hardwood trees still lying uprooted from the 1811 New Madrid Fault earthquake. Rawlings organized a logging operation with the help of Henry Eddy and Allen Kimmel and they used this manna to erect Rawlings' first small inn and a new office for *The Illinois Emigrant*.

From this base Moses began a small brick factory using the hard clay from where the Ohio River bed had shifted over the years. Soon a small city of solid brick buildings was a beacon to travelers from the banks of the Ohio.

With the *Emigrant* touting Shawneetown's virtues and contributions by Rawlings to selected politicians, Shawneetown began to rival Grayville.

Moses decided that a "front door" for the city would be the large three story brick hotel he planned facing the Ohio with a grand walkway down to the river landing. He had to borrow heavily, but he was certain Shawneetown's growth in population and regional importance justified the gamble.

In 1822, the three friends and business associates were rewarded for their risky ventures when Edward Coles was elected as the second governor of Illinois. Coles had been born in Virginia in 1786 to an influential plantation owner who served as a colonel in the Revolutionary War.

Coles was personally acquainted with Thomas Jefferson and James Monroe and had served in President James Madison's administration. He was wealthy and respected, and he had visited Shawneetown in 1815. More significantly for Moses Rawlings' aspirations, Coles knew the great Marquis de LaFayette who had been invited by Congress to make a triumphant return to America in 1824 and 25. The Mississippi and Ohio rivers were the only available means of traversing America's interior.

Coles was an avid abolitionist who had freed his own slaves in 1819. He was familiar with the reality that pro-slavery forces were quite strong in Illinois in general and in southern Illinois in particular. In fact, hundreds of slaves and indentured Negroes were publicly laboring in the vicinity of Shawneetown in the 1820's. Governor Coles was eager for an opportunity to expose this situation and decided to use his friendships with LaFayette and Jefferson to do so.

This fortuitous conjunction of time and circumstance boded well for Moses Rawlings and Shawneetown too he thought. Rawlings had supported Coles in his first election of 1822 and had corresponded regularly with him since. Therefore, when Coles wrote to Rawlings about a possible reception for LaFayette in Shawneetown, the details were all that remained.

The Marquis and his entourage, who would be traveling by steamboat, should arrive at Shawneetown in April or May of 1825. In a series of letters, Governor Coles and the Marquis decided that they could meet in Shawneetown May 7, 1825 and have a gala reception that evening.

Coles sent a formal invitation to LaFayette April 25, 1825. By separate letter, he invited his fellow abolitionists Robert Owen and his sons, as well as William MacClure, Thomas Say, Charles-Alexandre Lesueur and Mr. and Mrs. Josiah Warren from the New Harmony commune in Indiana. Another letter bearing the fine details would be waiting for LaFayette's party when they made their landing at Mt. Vernon, Indiana about the first of May.

Moses Rawlings could scarcely believe these developments. He carefully planned the accommodations for each guest. Coles was a bachelor as were Owen's sons, Robert Dale and David Dale. The famous naturalists Say and Lesueur could share a room without complaint. Of course, the Warrens would be housed together but LaFayette was bringing his son, George, as well as Miss Frances Wright, the Marquis' mistress, and Camilla Wright, her sister. Rawlings would have to give the place names at dinner and the room locations discreet attention.

Moses was further excited because, as he had speculated, intra-America water travel by Robert Fulton's newly perfected steamboat was integral to achieving this gathering of famous and wealthy personages at his new hotel.

Moses had studied Robert Fulton's writings on the feasibility of connecting the states of New York and Pennsylvania then the whole country via river travel by steamboat. Canals were all that was needed and, surely, America would soon build them.

Shawneetown was on its way to becoming Illinois' leading city. The reception for the great LaFayette was the spark that would light the future.

CHAPTER SEVENTEEN

FREE ILLINOIS

THE MORNING OF MAY 7, 1825 broke across the Ohio River into the front windows of the Rawlings Hotel as though drawn by Apollo for Moses' sole benefit. Gleaming, mist penetrating and glorious, the sunshine was a harbinger of important people doing extraordinary things.

As Moses nervously paced the portico and willed the steamboat to appear he tried to force his large expenditures for food, wine, new linens and extra servants from his reverie. At least, several of the added staff were slaves loaned by public minded citizens for the great occasion.

The businessmen of Shawneetown were banking on this event to bring attention and investment, especially government contracts, to the area. The whole community was contributing, but Rawlings was going deeply in debt for the honor of hosting the Marquis. And Moses had already told Governor Coles and the other personages that all would be his guests. Of course, Moses knew that gentlemen of such rank would insist on favoring him with some honorarium in return for which Moses had already commissioned a gold medallion commemorating the great event as a lagniappe.

Moses knew that the New Harmony party had planned to join LaFayette when his steamboat tied up at the Ohio River landing at Mt. Vernon, Indiana on May 5th or 6th, 1825. The two groups would then leave for Shawneetown at first light on May 7 for the thirty mile trip.

Governor Coles had scheduled his travel overland from the state capital at Vandalia so that he could greet the steamboat about 9:00 a.m. Moses had stationed a mounted lookout five miles from the hotel on the only road into Shawneetown from the northwest. Rawlings kept his glass trained up the Ohio River to the northeast until he heard the excited shouts of the young slave as he came riding bareback down the road on the struggling, unshod and slavering nag that stumbled into the courtyard of the hotel.

"Master Rawlings, de Gubner coming, de Gubner coming!" Moses did not have a name for the slave but the generic "boy" was ubiquitous and serviceable.

"Boy, you're going to kill that horse. How far out did you see Governor Coles, how long ago?"

"Oh, Master Moses, I seed 'em just coming o'ber de big hill comin' down de valley." Moses knew the Negro was referring to the rim of the old river bed which meant Coles would be at the hotel within half an hour. The plans of half a year and the hopes of Shawneetown were rapidly closing in on Moses Rawlings who felt the call of an early morning fortification. Alas, he could not afford to waste the expensive imported spirits he had laid in store for his guests, so he fell back on a brief meeting with Mr. John Barleycorn from his own still.

When Governor Coles' party reached the clearing which opened onto Shawneetown, Moses greeted the Governor and led him along the walkway from the hotel to the landing on the Ohio River. From there, they and other dignitaries, including Henry Eddy and Allen Kimmel, watched for LaFayette's steam packet.

The nervous Rawlings mistook distant flying herons and even floating timbers in the roiling muddy water as smokestacks. Between extolling Shawneetown's potential to Governor Coles and barking orders to attendants and slaves, he failed to sense the Governor's displeasure with the presence of slaves in free Illinois.

CHAPTER EIGHTEEN

GOLDEN RAINTREES

WHEN THE COURIER HANDED LaFAYETTE's letter to Robert Owen he was sitting on a small bench left by the Rappites. The sturdy golden poplar wood had been shaped by some talented German-Lutheran craftsman into an unadorned homage to God.

Thomas Saye had placed the bench at the center of a copse of young golden rain trees which he had planted on the bank of the Wabash River near the spot their "Boatload of Knowledge" had landed.

Saye had noticed the unique flowering tree in the fall of 1824 as the Owenites were finalizing their purchase of Father Rapp's commune.

The golden blossoms were dropping in a shower which Father Rapp had told his followers was a sign from God that Harmonie was the new Eden and that they would be His new chosen people to meet Jesus as soon as they had purified themselves.

These small lush trees grew wild in the area of the Northwest Territory and were perceived by Rapp to be God speaking to him as He had to Moses.

And while Owen saw such stated beliefs as so much legerdemain, the Tree of Knowledge analogy well fit his vision of a paradise based on scientific discovery.

Robert Owen read the letter from LaFayette for the second time more deliberately. His excitement and pride which obscured the important nuances at first blush were sternly restrained as he parsed the elegant formal language of his friend's good wishes on the New Harmony endeavor.

Owen had supported Congress' plan to honor LaFayette and had pushed for the inclusion of an inland journey. Owen had finalized his and William MacClure's purchase of the Harmonie religious commune from Father George Rapp during the buildup to LaFayette's return. He hoped to publicize his Enlightenment vision for America, especially its scientific basis and egalitarian philosophy, with the great Revolutionary's help.

The letter had finally reached Owen on April 19, 1825. While Owen was free of superstition, the coincidence of a Patriot's Day arrival was noted. LaFayette wrote that the reality of the Ohio River tour leg had already been confirmed but the details were enmeshed in the competing interests of many individuals, pressure groups and territories. However, a short stop to meet their mutual friend, Edward Coles, at Shawneetown had already been arranged for May the Seventh.

LaFayette wrote of their friendship and his gratitude to America. He mentioned the unfinished business of the Peculiar Institution and his regret at not being able to eliminate it as part of the Nation's great struggle to be born. But what Owen discerned from his synthesis of the long explication of the Marquis' personal situation was that LaFayette's memory of his Adrienne had finally wearied him of his relationship with Frances Wright. Also, the Marquis' son, George, was voicing his concerns that the beautiful young Scottish woman with her original thinking was not just another of his father's peccadilloes but that La-Fayette might be tottering towards that saddest of caricatures, a great hero turned old fool.

The Marquis described the twenty-nine year old Miss Wright and her younger sister as his wards who had much to offer to the great experiment in New Harmony. The already famous "Boatload of Knowledge" which Owen had led to this erstwhile promised-land would be complimented by the well known writings of "Mad Fanny" and her total commitment to equality for the genders and races.

LaFayette informed Owen that the Wright sisters had their own fortune, were unmarried and childless. They would join, if accepted, as equals, not mere hangers-on.

LaFayette suggested that if Owen was amenable to the sisters joining the commune, the Marquis' entourage would be passing just south of New Harmony sometime during the first week in May on their way to Shawneetown.

Owen responded that he planned to attend the reception at Shawneetown and offered to meet LaFayette's steamboat at Mt. Vernon, Indiana on May 5th or 6th and travel with LaFayette. Owen wrote that he and his party would stay in Mt. Vernon from May the Fourth and watch for LaFayette to land. They would make their own way back to New Harmony after the reception in Shawneetown with the sisters as full working members if they so desired.

Chapter Nineteen

THE LOCUST TREES

MAY THE SIXTH, 1825 WAS a cold, rainy day in Mt. Vernon. The Ohio River was rising, causing MacFadden Creek to back up into the residential area of the town to within a quarter of a mile of the new courthouse built at the center of the village square.

When LaFayette's steamboat came into view for twenty-three year old Robert Dale Owen he ran the four blocks from McFadin's Bluff on the river bank to the courthouse to ring the cupola bell.

Indiana had just reorganized its counties and their county seats. Posey County's county seat at Springfield had been moved to McFadin's Bluff which the townsmen had voted to re-name Mt. Vernon. They did this ostensibly to honor George Washington, but, also, because the several McFadin/McFaddin/MacFadden clans were feuding over the spelling of the new county seat. The Revolutionary War veterans living in Posey County seized the opportunity to perpetuate their glory and poke a finger in the eyes of one of the first families of Posey County.

From the cupola atop the two story brick courthouse Robert Dale could watch the boat negotiating the passage between Kentucky and Diamond Island up past the inlet to MacFadden Creek to the landing at the south end of Main Street. As the steamboat was tying up, the town emptied onto the landing.

Although the sun had only been up a few hours, the drinking had started at the Pilot House Tavern, also at the south end of Main Street, as soon as the pealing of the courthouse bell turned excited anticipation to jubilation.

Posey County's War of Liberation Detachment was composed of veterans who had served under Colonel George Rogers Clark at the Battle of Fort Vincennes in 1779 and a few other men whose military exploits were more of the Baron Munchausen variety.

Regardless of their bona fides, it was remarkable how many of these aging warriors remembered serving directly under George Washington and his protégé, LaFayette, in the Great War. And now the great general was landing in their town with both his son and mistress; forming up on the landing to salute the Marquis with volleys from their aging muskets was to reprise their youth and add to its glory.

The Detachment formed a single line of fifteen men in various remnants of ill-fitting uniforms. They faced the Ohio River and when LaFayette started down the gangplank they fired and reloaded until the command to stop was shouted over the cheers of the townspeople.

Robert Owen greeted LaFayette and led him and his company up Main Street to the campus of the courthouse where Owen presented four golden raintree and four flowering locust tree seedlings to the General to plant.

LaFayette planted the raintrees on the north side of the courthouse and Robert Owen helped him plant the locusts between the courthouse and the river on the south side. The locusts were placed beside the new one room log jail that had been erected on the southeast side of the courthouse.

Robert Owen thanked LaFayette for his great service to America and to the cause of liberty everywhere. Owen stated that the raintrees would be a living reminder of LaFayette's commitment to progress and the locust trees would grow tall and strong and stand as a memorial to the General's struggle for equality for all people.

Robert Dale Owen's role in the ceremony was to stand with his father and younger brother David and help Thomas Saye plant the trees after LaFayette's and Robert Owen's initial spades were turned. Fortunately, he had no other part as he could not have spoken after he had met the eyes of the beautiful woman who so boldly stared at him from behind the General.

At twenty-three, Robert Dale had spent most of the last ten years wondering about girls but none of them discovering anything personally. However, he was accustomed to the demure downcast eyes of young women and the deferential attitude of most women of any age. He was usually able to steal a glance at a girl's face or bosom without knowing he had been caught.

CHAPTER TWENTY

HARMONIE

AT THE GALA IN SHAWNEETOTWN on May 7, 1825, Robert Dale Owen could only mumble his admiration when his father, Robert Owen, introduced him to Marie Joseph Paul Yves Roche Gilbert du Motier, Marquis de LaFayette, the hero of the American Revolution.

LaFayette was sixty-eight years old at the time but was without time or plane to Robert Dale. To touch LaFayette was to touch Washington. Without LaFayette there would be no United States but only divided colonies of England, France and Spain.

The night of the gala Robert Dale could not make an audible response when the Marquis inquired of the social experiment of the Owenites. The beautiful woman across the table from LaFayette answered the inquiry. She had been introduced to him as the Miss Frances Wright who was interested in joining their commune. Unlike any other woman Owen had known, Wright spoke first and directly to Owen.

"As I understand it, the Owenites of New Harmony, Indiana are believers in equality of the races and sexes and that accomplishments not status at birth, are how people should be valued."

"Thank you, Miss Wright. I would say that is an excellent capsule of our goals which include universal education, also."

"Mr. Owen, you obviously, as yet, have not received Fanny's ideas on religion, marriage, slavery and the rights of 'woe man'. I predict you soon will be deluged if you have the time and inclination. Fanny has that look about her which tells me she is in a proselytizing frame. You will not readily escape her spell."

"Ah, Marquis, she will have a ready acolyte if she adheres to your *Rights of Man*, especially your views on law. If I may be so bold as to attempt to recite your statement about the separation of powers, 'A society that does not obey its own laws and which does not well define and clearly separate its powers has no viable Constitution.'"

"Very good, Mr. Owen, I see that my conversion of you has already been well begun by the General's ideals. Perhaps you will allow my sister, Camilla, and me to join your noble experiment after the Marquis continues his grand tour?"

"If General LaFayette does not object, my father and I and my brothers would be honored to introduce you and your sister to New Harmony."

"Mr. Owen, you will soon find that Fanny brooks no man telling her her mind. She will do as she pleases and that has always pleased me. She is prepared to leave with you tomorrow as your father and I discussed by previous correspondence."

"It will be an honor to escort Miss Fanny and Miss Camilla to our community that we strive to organize on principles of the Enlightenment. I am sure the young ladies will greatly enlighten us with their wit and beauty. If it is agreeable with them and you, they will reside at the home of Mr. and Mrs. Josiah Warren who are affable hosts but are especially fond of brilliant women. You may know of Mr. Warren's writings on the rights of the working class and the political philosophy of anarchism. I assure you that the ladies will be welcome and well cared for."

"What say you, Fanny? Do you believe the Owens can enlighten you and Camilla or do you secretly hope you will usurp their great endeavor to your causes?"

"With your blessing and endorsement, Marquis, we will see if our journey is an odyssey of discovery or diversion. Tomorrow New Harmony, thereafter is to be determined. Oh, and, Mr. Owen, I am familiar with Mr. Warren's so-called radical thinking. However, it may be mundane compared to the great LaFayette's penchant for revolution."

CHAPTER TWENTY-ONE

BEL ESPRIT

"WHEN YOU INVITED ME TO La Grange I was but a girl of twenty-five and you were the greatest hero in the world. And your recently departed wife, Adrienne, was justly venerated for her fierce loyalty to both you and your ideals. I had read your *Declaration of the Rights of Man and of the Citizen* and had heard men whom I admired, such as my surrogate father, James Mylne, extol your greatness in war and letters. Were it not for this conjunction of purpose and opportunity which has occurred, I almost said miraculously before I remembered that I do not believe in miracles, I would never leave your side.

"My sister, Camilla, and I have strived to be ever discreet in our arrangement with you. I hope we have caused no consternation among those legions who admire you and honor Adrienne's memory. And your introduction of me to Mr. Owen in New Harmony I now understand was your way of continuing me on my quest for the abolition of slavery for which we both have given much already. To have the great LaFayette present me to the Owenites as a friend and equal affirmed my reason for falling in love with you. Robert Owen and his sons as well as such men as the brilliant Josiah Warren all in one small commune and all working for liberty and equality of the races and sexes must surely be my destiny.

"I will be eternally in your debt for including me and Camilla in your triumphant and glorious return to America. But your words to Mr. Owen and his son Robert Dale at the dinner party last evening about our noble purpose and theirs to free the Negro have lighted my way. I now see clearly both my calling and the means to fulfill it. Camilla and I will make our home in New Harmony as we work with the Owenites to implement our plan for the Negroes. It is my fondest hope to see you again and walk with you once more along the Seine. However, if the fates do not allow us to rejoin, we have already shared more than I could have ever dreamed."

"That I have been granted this marvelous gift at the twilight of my life is miraculous; I do believe in them. But to deny your great passion to the cause of liberty would gainsay my life's work. When we stayed with Thomas Jefferson at Monticello last month he and I had the opportunity to reflect on what we and General Washington and so many others had achieved in the Revolution. Jefferson told me that all we had sacrificed for would be lost if America did not atone for the great sin of slavery. It will be but a matter of time before the United States divide along this issue. He quoted the book of *Job* to me: 'Those who plow inequity and sow trouble reap the same.'

"Mr. Jefferson and I know that our struggle is but half over. If all men are not equal in peace, then they may be equaled by war. The great and good men of the Revolution accepted the half loaf sincerely believing slavery would soon after collapse of its own evil weight. It has not, and the cause of liberty and union has great need of your youth's passion and energy. For, 'Better is a poor and wise youth than an old and foolish king, who will not take advice.' I am at that age where there is more past than future and less energy than aching.

"You must help complete the Revolution we started. Thank you for loving me. These four years have been as important to me as my four years in the great struggle for America's independence. But there is, 'a time to embrace and a time to refrain from embracing.' I must return to La Grange alone. To cling to you longer would deny to you your opportunity to advance the cause to which I have devoted my life, liberté. I believe Ecclesiastes was wrong: there is something new under the sun. It is the United States of America. Go forth and help preserve it by freeing it of its original sin. Adieu my *bel esprit*."

CHAPTER TWENTY-TWO

NASHOBA

AFTER ROBERT DALE HELPED FANNY and Camilla move their things from the flat bottomed, tall sided river raft to the home of Josiah Warren, Camilla remained to help Mrs. Warren settle them in and Robert Dale was instructed by Fanny to show her New Harmony.

New Harmony sat right on the banks of the Wabash and included two thousand acres of farm and orchards as well as a saw mill, a granary, a distillery, a church converted to a laboratory, several individual homes and two large dormitories.

Father George Rapp and his German-Lutheran flock had moved to Harmonie from Pennsylvania in 1817 to purify themselves for the Second Coming which Rapp believed was imminent. The men and women at first lived together, but when Rapp said Jesus was near at hand they built separate dormitories for men and women. When Jesus had not shown after a year of purification through celibacy, the frustrated flock grew restless. Rapp moved his congregation back to Pennsylvania in 1824 and sold the town to Robert Owen and William MacClure.

"Miss Wright, this area without tombstones is the Harmonist cemetery. Since they believed the Rapture was imminent, there was no need to mark the names. We are probably standing on someone's grave now."

"Robert Dale, your town is much more than I ever envisioned. I offered to come to the American frontier to join the struggle for equality and enlightenment and I find a beautiful modern community to live in. It is already my home. Your father is a wonderfully generous man whose vision is well underway. What uniquely talented and brilliant people you have drawn together. I know it must succeed. I am grateful to be allowed to be part of it."

"Miss Wright, it is I, I mean we, who are fortunate to have you with us. When you speak you put words to my thoughts. I never dreamed that I would meet a woman whose passions are my goals. Just how do you plan to eliminate slavery so easily and quickly? What do you know that the rest of us don't?"

"Everyone already intuitively knows what I believe to be the best hope to free all manner of slaves. Human beings are motivated by self-interest. We just need to harness this powerful engine in the right way. And the universal education you value so highly is a necessary component of my plan. It is not just the Negro that I believe needs to be freed. The oppression of the ignorant by religious leaders and the oppression of women by the institution of marriage are matters of the highest concern to me."

"Miss Wright, Fanny, if I may, I certainly agree with your abhorrence of that Peculiar Institution, but to accuse true believers of ignorance and clergymen of manipulation seems to me to paint with a wide and indiscriminate brush."

"Well, Robert Dale, and, yes, you may, I note there are no clergy-women and I direct your attention to the book many Christians swear by but few have read. 'When I was a child I thought as a child, but now that I am a man, or in this case a woman, I have put off childish things.' What could be more childish than myths, legends, false hopes and superstitions being used to control otherwise rational thought?

"And as to marriage, women lose their property, their autonomy and even their identities to the men who have the legal authority over women who cannot even vote on the laws used to oppress them. My body is not for sale. I have sympathy for women who have to make their living selling themselves, but I give little quarter to women who willingly bind themselves as lifelong chambermaids and heir producers. Women are not chattels, they are people with much more to give than they are allowed to."

"But Miss Wright, Fanny, what of the children of a couple? Are they all to be bastards? What of the laws on inheritance? How are families, the cornerstone of all societies, to be fostered?"

"All children are born legitimate by the laws of nature. It is only the artifice of positive law that requires a man-made pedigree. Why cannot the law provide for inheritance by descent or the free will of a testator; isn't that pretty much what prevails now anyway in probate? Marriage adds nothing to the biology of children or carnal passion. Do not most people truly believe that coitus outside of contract is much more satisfying?

"And that brings us to my ultimate solution to the problems between the races, cenogamy. With free interbreeding without concern for status or contract, eventually, probably within three generations, the races will be so pooled that no one will be able to arrogate themselves to assumed superiority. I came to America to found a society for Negroes where they can learn to support themselves and breed freely with whites without recriminations. With the resources and contacts of the Marquis, I have located a likely site in Tennessee along the Wolf River near its mouth into the Mississippi. My sister and I have already made a deposit on it. Camilla and I had hoped LaFayette would be involved with us. But even though he has encouraged our endeavors, his heart requires him to return to France. So, we have his blessing, but not him."

"Fanny, my community is strongly committed to the rights of all men, and women too, of course. Indiana is a free state, but Tennessee would be fertile ground for freeing and preparing Negroes for independence. And the area you speak of can be reached from New Harmony via the Wabash, Ohio and Mississippi rivers. Depending upon the time of year and the condition of each river, your Utopia is just about two days down river by flat boat and four days to one week back. If one were fortunate enough to catch on with one of the new steam packets, such as the Memphis Belle, we, I mean .... It would take one down and two back. What can our community do to help?"

"I envision a sanctuary where men can learn skills such as carpentry and women can study the arts as well as business. It is especially important that it be a haven for women to have babies without fear of retribution or ostracism. Sexual relations between the races among those of free will is what can free the slaves and, perhaps, prevent armed conflict among the states. People are less likely to feel they have a right to own or control people who look like themselves and may even be blood kin. It is not just equality of the races, but the right of any person of any race, male or female, to control their own body without recrimination that is essential. The best way to avoid this is cenogomy, the voluntary sharing of all mates, and the communal raising of all children.

"As to what you can do, Robert Dale, you can first come with me to this land I have not seen and use your experience in communal living to help us organize a successful society founded on freedom and free will. Should we plan to seek this Garden of Eden together? Maybe we can provide the Adam and Eve of a new world. Of course, we could take one of your famous New Harmony raintrees to plant as our symbolic Tree of Knowledge. And who knows, temptation for forbidden fruit might arise."

Robert Dale was amazed by this candid offer. He had little experience with women and was unable to enter the easy sexual repartee. He, also, felt disloyal to LaFayette and worried he would be taking advantage of a guest who had to rely upon him. He was in awe of this woman. He knew what he wanted, but he had no idea of what to say or do.

"Robert Dale, is it the Marquis that is on your mind? If so, please know that he brought me to America to say goodbye and god speed on my dream of equality for all. He still pines for Adrianne and, although he loves me too and I him, France is his life. That is where he must return."

"Fanny, we can do this. We shall fulfill your vision and incorporate mine with it. Isn't the Wolf River in the land of the Chickasaws?"

"It was until Andrew Jackson from Tennessee removed them from their home. I guess when he lost the 1824 presidential election to John Quincy Adams in his back door deal with Henry Clay, he was so angry he took it out on the Chickasaws. I bought the land at a fair price from an agent appointed by the federal government to represent the Indians. I hope they got the benefit. In their honor I have decided to use the Chickasaw name for the Wolf River as the name of our new Eden. It is called, Nashoba."

CHAPTER TWENTY-THREE

THE CONSTITUTION

ON SATURDAY MORNING, JANUARY 18, 1851, Alvin P. Hovey presented a Petition signed by one hundred and thirty citizens of Posey County.

Hovey and Robert Dale Owen were Posey County's delegates to Indiana's Constitutional Convention which was convened to draft a new Constitution to replace the original one of 1816.

Hovey and Owen arrived at this moment of shared destiny via different routes. Owen was the eldest son of a wealthy Scottish industrialist whose vision of an earthly paradise was founded on the pursuit of knowledge and equality of opportunity.

Hovey was an orphan who had raised himself since the age of fifteen. Hovey craved the respect and financial security Owen was born into.

Owen did not need a group to feel better than, but in 1851, Hovey still did. Where Owen could dream of building a brighter future for all of society, Hovey lived in constant fear of losing the present for himself. Hovey's façade of certitude masked his gnawing doubts about his homespun education and social status.

Owen and Hovey had a relationship founded initially on a belief by each man that the other had a sincere desire to serve the public. As their friendship became more personal, their differences added to their mutual respect. Hovey admired Owen's heritage, education and social status. Owen envied Hovey's ability as a stonemason and builder and respected his knowledge of literature and history, especially military history. Most of all, Owen was impressed that Hovey was a product of his own efforts, not those of his family. Hovey had been saved by fate from what caused Owen his worst self doubts. Hovey could do things with his hands; he did not have to hire other men to do things for him.

Owen did not know the depth of Hovey's deference to Owen's family background as Owen, himself, was habituated to it. And Hovey accepted Owen's professed interest in Hovey's technical abilities as genteel rather than genuine because of Hovey's sense of himself as part of a lower caste.

When the two men discussed the Negro problem, Owen, the born aristocrat with his sense of noblesse oblige and financial insulation, gravitated towards the greater good for all while Hovey, the born plebian who ached to be a patrician, argued that laws that reflect the will of the current electorate in Posey County was their representative duty at the Convention.

Hovey's petition was a preemptive strike against Owen's attempt to force a clear choice by the Convention between citizenship for Indiana's Negroes and their voluntary removal to Liberia.

Hovey knew Owen's plan was to appeal to the delegates' best hopes and worst fears, hopes that the Negro problem would resolve itself and fears of their constituents if the resolution required the imposition of extra taxes.

Owen's experience with Fanny Wright's failed experiment of Nashoba had convinced him that repatriation was a cruel hoax. Owen, also, knew that Hoosiers, especially those in Posey County, would rather suffer Negro migration to Indiana than pay any of their own money to prevent it.

In 1851, Hovey was not willing to risk his nascent career on the reed of Enlightenment appeals to fairness. His prudence was validated most clearly later by the lynchings of 1878 when some of the Posey County petitioners of 1851 eschewed representative democracy for direct involvement.

Although Hovey admired Owen, he knew that Owen's egalitarian beliefs were at odds with those of most Posey County voters.

So, when Owen set forth his, "Give them citizenship or pay them to leave dichotomy," Hovey was ready with his anti-tax petition that ostensibly had no connection to the Negro issue.

Owen spoke to the Convention:

CB

"Since, then, public opinion is as it is, what is the ultimate remedy? Separation-colonization. To those whom we are not willing to treat here as men ought to be treated, let us afford the chance of seeking a free home elsewhere.

There are about sixteen thousand Negroes now in the State, which, at thirty dollars a head (the estimated cost of transportation to Liberia), would make the total of four hundred and eight thousand dollars. A tax about thirty-five cents on the hundred dollars would raise the amount. This, spread over seven years, would be but five cents a year."

CB

Both Owen and Hovey well knew the penurious nature of their citizenry. Owen fully expected to buy civil rights for Indiana's Negroes with this unimposed tax. But Hovey, also, knew the Hoosier white man's unwillingness to bear even this modest financial burden, and he had anticipated Owen's scheme to exploit it.

This was the beginning of the marginalization of Owen's political influence in southern Indiana and the ascendancy of Hovey's. However, their personal relationship did not suffer.

Owen recognized Hovey's deep seated fear of failure and accepted his façade of bigotry because Owen understood the futility of sacrificing an otherwise good man on the altar of public ignorance.

Hovey respected Owen's passion for justice but saw nothing to be gained for Negroes by supporting a beau geste which would result in his own demise. And Hovey opined that whoever replaced him as Posey County's Moses would be less apt to cautiously intercede for individual coloreds.

However, when some of those good citizens for whom he undermined his good friend participated in the lynchings of 1878, Hovey saw a direct connection to his frailty in 1851. He feared his treachery so understandingly forgiven by Owen might, "Well the mighty Ohio River incarnadine make with the blood of the murdered Negroes."

Hovey doubted that his courageous war service outweighed his political cowardice.

He was glad that Owen had died in 1877 before the lynchings.

Hovey knew that his words from 1851 would someday be reviewed by history and that his weakness would be shown. Who could have foreseen the events of October 1878 from January 1851?

After the lynchings, the ghosts would not leave him alone. He remembered guaranteeing his constituents that if they would choose him he would help draft an Indiana Constitution that would prohibit Negroes from settling in Indiana and that would deny them rights of citizenship. The voters would not have elected him a delegate otherwise.

Of course, Robert Dale Owen was elected, but he was wealthy and insulated by his influential family. And his opponent had been the irascible Judge John Pitcher who was hard for voters to warm to. Besides, Hovey's and Pitcher's public promises on how they would vote on the Negro issues were the same. Privately Hovey was not averse to some of Robert Dale's positions, but Hovey's fear of popular opinion kept him from going against the majority of his constituents.

Hovey's words to the Convention came with facile ease in 1851. After October, 1878, their lack of humanity attacked Hovey with the reproach he might have justly received from Owen:

ଓ

"The article reported back by the committee would compel the people to pay an annual tax of twenty or thirty thousand dollars for the privilege of protecting themselves against that unfortunate though reckless and abandoned class of immigration.

I regard the whole article reported back by the committee thus coupled with colonization, as an insidious attempt against Negro exclusion ...."

ଓ

When the Civil War began, Hovey had been so eager to go to war for any reason that he asked no questions of himself. But as the deaths built up, he found that the etiology of the complex conflict caused uneasiness in him.

The War might truly have been about Union as Abraham said, but it was the Peculiar Institution that was the dividing issue.

What if political leaders before 1861 had shown Owen's courage and passion? Perhaps there were too few Robert Dales and too many Alvins. Of course, there also may have been too few Madisons and too many slave owners a hundred years earlier. It is easier to assuage one's collective guilt with the half a loaf theory if one shares in the half.

Hovey often mused about these personal foibles with his friend, Judge Parrett, after the War. He and Parrett were more akin than Robert Dale Owen to either. Parrett recognized the vanity in arrogating one race over another but he, also, saw the personal folly of publicly opposing it. Parrett and Hovey could convince themselves that it was not courage but hubris that caused some to call for the abolition of legal and cultural separation.

Besides, they agreed that they could effect more justice for Negroes from within the Bench and Bar than as discredited Jeremiahs. For example, it was Hovey's representation of Jim Good and Judge Parrett's finding in Good's favor on the false charge of raping Jennie Bell that had saved Good from prison. Justice was served and, yet, Hovey had not risked his position nor had Parrett lost his judgeship.

Parrett and Hovey trusted that just as the Holy Trinity of the Thirteenth, Fourteenth and Fifteenth Amendments to the United States Constitution had corrected the problems left unaddressed in 1789, time would cure the country's and, particularly, Indiana's, racial divisions. They saw nothing to be gained from throwing themselves on the bier of an idea whose time had not yet come.

Chapter Twenty-Four

LEGACY

JUDGE EAGLESON HAD READ THE sepia colored news articles that he found stuck between the pages of the 1878 Order Book. He had kept the old book on his desk in his private chambers since the day Tom Hanson asked him what to do with it.

In the weeks since Eagleson had realized the import of the Order Book, he had begun to research other newspaper archives kept on microfilm at the Alexandrian Public Library in Mt. Vernon. He, also, had read the Indiana Constitutional Debates of 1850 and 1851 maintained at the library.

The vitriolic feelings of the Hoosier white population against Negroes in the second half of the Nineteenth Century shocked Eagleson. He had grown up in a segregated state but had always thought that Indiana had no endemic racial problems. Of course, he knew of isolated instances such as the Marion, Indiana lynching of 1930 and the race riots in Evansville in 1970 and 1971, but he had thought these to be anomalies.

Eagleson's study of the Coroner's Inquest from October, 1878 in which the official conclusion was that the victims had been lynched by, "persons unknown to the members of the Coroner's Jury," reminded Eagleson of Supreme Court Justice Clarence Thomas' assessment that his confirmation hearing was simply, "a high class lynching".

Closer to home, Eagleson reflected that maybe Indiana had changed only in its method of eliminating young black men with prison terms rather than locust trees or constitutional amendments. Eagleson had just received his annual Indiana prison report showing that black males represented only four percent of Indiana's general population but thirty-nine percent of its prison inmates.

And *Western Star* editor, John Leffel, made it clear that right next door to Posey County in 1878, Evansville and Vanderburgh County could not claim any moral high ground on racial matters. On the front page of his December 5th edition Leffel wrote:

છ

"The *Evansville Journal* and *Tribune* never lose an opportunity to make the late lynching in our city a text for statements the only inference from which is that our people are a band of ruffians who set all law at defiance; usurp the function of the courts, and deal out to the subjects of their malice and wrath swift and sanguinary punishments. If the facts justified these statements we would have no right of complaint. But the reverse is true.

We would further intimate that chidings of us from that source are hardly becoming or consistent. If it be true that people who live in glass houses shouldn't throw stones, it illy becomes Evansville to toss bricks at us. The only difference between her and us in the negro hanging business is, that she hung hers on lamp posts and we ours on trees."

છ

Eagleson's thoughts kept returning to the news accounts of the 21st Century sentencing of the young black boxer in Evansville, Indiana. Did he plead guilty out of fear or lack of resources? Or had he relied on the false hope of mercy that so many other Negroes had clung to? And why did those thirty police officers in full uniform form a ring around the small courtroom and stare fixedly at the judge? Was the message clear that the judge might pay a political price for a lesser sentence?

But most of all, Eagleson wondered if only the level of sophistication had changed since 1878 in southern Indiana's system of controlling black people. As to the fear of political reprisals or public criticism, Eagleson concluded from his study of the Order Book and newspaper articles from 1878 and his knowledge of contemporary events that only the names and dates had changed.

CHAPTER TWENTY-FIVE

LYNCHBURG

GEORGE DANIELS WAS NOT A man cursed by introspection. Things happened. He did not engage in etiology. When he left Lynchburg, Virginia on March 15, 1840, the twenty-three year old blacksmith took with him his ability to work with iron and almost every penny of the meager wages he had earned from five years of working for his uncle, Simon Combs.

Simon's only child, William, and George, who was the only child of Simon's sister, had been raised together and were as close as brothers. George had always looked up to his cousin. William was only two years older than George but had a rebellious nature that the naïve George secretly envied, especially in matters involving women.

George's mother had died of cholera when George was eighteen and William was twenty. George's father had died in a steamboat accident when George was ten.

George's mother had been a devout Quaker who was strongly against violence and slavery. She had often taken pains to explain to young George that whereas early Virginia Justice of the Peace, Charles Lynch, was known for rough justice, Lynchburg, was named for the humanitarian businessman, John Lynch. George never saw any irony in lynching versus Lynchburg, not even after the events of October 1878.

When he lived with his mother, he would have said he was against slavery if anyone had asked. By the time he moved to Indiana in 1840, much of his mother's sympathies for Negroes had been tempered by his uncle's views that coloreds were lucky to be cared for by their white masters. Simon had often told George that the only thing that was worse for the negras than slavery would be freedom, as they would not be able to make it on their own. Although none of their relatives had ever owned slaves, for Simon, that was more a function of economics than principle.

William and George had been separated by events five years earlier when William had spent too much time for Simon's liking with a twelve year old slave girl named Inola whom Simon had rented from a tobacco planter named Caleb Crider. Simon used her to help around the house and yard. When Simon came upon William in a horse stall with the struggling girl's dress pulled down to her waist, Simon slapped the girl across the back with a buggy whip and sent her back to the planter.

The planter moved the girl out of her kitchen duties to the tobacco fields. Inola disappeared soon thereafter, but it was rumored she had sought sanctuary among freed slaves near Memphis, Tennessee. However, the bounty hunter the plantation owner commissioned to bring her back reported the community where she had last been sighted was little more than a series of shacks on the Wolf River, and Inola was either not there or was being protected by the crazy white woman who lived among the Negroes.

William had left Lynchburg for Mt. Vernon, Indiana to try and establish a blacksmithy. He had settled there because it was located on the banks of the Ohio River and it was near the teeming metropolis of Shawneetown, Illinois. Shawneetown was close to the spot the Lewis and Clark Expedition had first noted the confluence of the Wabash and Ohio rivers in 1803. William had been told about Mt. Vernon by the legendary boatman, Mike Fink, who had stabled his horse at Simon's shop in 1834. Fink's braggadocio about his well deserved reputation as a brawler was tempered by his self deprecation over an incident earlier that year at a tavern in the young, vibrant and ribald river town. The six foot three inch one hundred eighty-five pound Fink laughingly related to William and George how he had challenged everyone in the tavern to knock the red feather from his cap. Just as he was claiming that he had cowed the entire town of Mt. Vernon, a massive brace of antlers that had been hanging from the ceiling came loose and knocked him cold. When he awakened, he found himself floating down the Ohio River in his flatboat. As he told it to the impressionable cousins, this was the only fight he had ever lost and that to a dead stag. But he also told the boys that Mt. Vernon was a promising site for barge and steamboat traffic due to its flood free setting and the extremely fertile surrounding farmland.

Once William settled in Mt. Vernon, he sent word to George that the demand for metal working among the farming community was greater than the need for a farrier, and together they ought to be able to do much better than either of them had ever done with Simon. William suggested that the route from Lynchburg to Nashville to Memphis then up the Mississippi River to Cairo, Illinois and on up the Ohio River to Mt. Vernon was the easiest route.

In a private correspondence to George, William told him he believed that Inola was indeed at the commune known as Nashoba just fifteen miles from Memphis on the Wolf River. William suggested that if George could capture Inola, he could have her held in Memphis and earn the two hundred dollar reward for her return. George could have the reward money forwarded on to him at Mt. Vernon. Then George and William could use the money to start their business.

George had saved over one hundred dollars while working for Simon. George put the gold coins in a money belt he had fashioned out of horse hide. He carried a well turned knife he had forged in a scabbard attached to the money belt. He attached a cotton bag to a backboard. And he supported the backboard with a headband and a length of hemp rope going around the bag and the backboard then encircling his torso.

He wore his only pair of brogans and his only coat along with his second best shirt and pants. He carried his Sunday shirt and trousers in the bag with the letters from William and jerked beef. He had no socks or underwear. He, also, packed the reward flier on Inola that included her description at age twelve. Inola's back had been deeply cut across the shoulder blades by Simon's whip. The flier mentioned the possible scarring and Inola's unusually light complexion. At age twelve she was five feet two inches tall and one hundred and ten pounds. Her teeth were good.

He could have traveled most of the way to Nashville then on to Memphis by stagecoach at the rate of five miles per hour and a cost of three bits per day plus one and one half cents per pound for his belongings. He decided to walk over the Allegheny and Cumberland Mountains to Nashville then take the stage on to Memphis. He figured the stagecoach trails over the mountains would require that he and any other passengers walk a great deal of the mountain passage anyway. And since he estimated that he could walk about a third as fast as the stage, he could walk daylight to dark and arrive only a week later than if by coach. His money meant more to George than his time.

George followed the stagecoach route and slept in the brush along the road. He drank from the innumerable clear streams and managed to make it to Nashville from Lynchburg in less than two weeks and about ten dollars better off.

The stage from Nashville to Memphis took him three days and cost him a total of four dollars. He could have slept inside the stagecoach depot and been served a meal each night for an additional four bits per night, but George eschewed this extravagance and slept in the barn with the horses.

CHAPTER TWENTY-SIX

INOLA

MEMPHIS, TENNESSEE IN 1840 WAS not much. It had only been in existence since 1819 when Andrew Jackson helped establish it. In 1840 there were only about eighteen hundred white residents.

Memphis did have two distinguishing characteristics. It was a major steamboat landing for boats plying the Mississippi up from or down to New Orleans and to or from St. Louis and Cairo, Illinois. The Missouri River poured its rapidly moving waters into the Mississippi just north of St. Louis and the Ohio and Mississippi rivers met at Cairo. And there was a large volume of river traffic upon the Ohio originating in either Pittsburg, Pennsylvania then on to Cairo or from Cairo to Pittsburg.

Memphis of 1840 was, also, one of the largest slave markets in the United States. Since federal law forbid international slave trading in America after 1807, the domestic market in slaves became extremely lucrative as did the trading of slaves born in the United States or the capture for resale or reward of escaped slaves.

Memphis, Tennessee was ideally located below the Mason-Dixon Line with ready access to other slave states.

Shelby County, Tennessee in 1840 still held its court sessions in the community of Raleigh that was located in the center of the county but on the outskirts of Memphis and on a bluff above the Wolf River.

The two thousand citizens of Shelby County were proud of their new two-story, forty by fifty foot, brick courthouse with its fine wrought iron fence. It was an impressive edifice and it leant dignity to the important legal proceedings. Judge L.M. Bramblett was the circuit court judge in the small clapboard structure that was replaced in 1835. Judge Bramblett had often felt the lack of respect the frontier justice center had engendered. And now he took pride in his new courthouse. It was a proper place to instill the majesty of the law. Decisions made here, such as the slave auctions held on the front steps, were not just approved by a judge, they were the will of the people.

The courthouse stood high above the beautiful, clear and swift flowing Wolf River and it was only fifteen miles downstream from Frances Wright's community of Nashoba. The two thousand acre plantation was established there in 1825, but by 1840 the dreams of LaFayette and Frances Wright and Robert Dale Owen had floundered. The plan to have slaves learn trades and help the commune earn money to buy other slaves so that all could be freed had failed miserably.

But, at least, in 1835 when Inola had escaped from Lynchburg, Virginia she had a refuge to hide in. She had been encouraged and helped to run from her tobacco plantation owner by members of the Quaker church. The church's connections with the Underground Railroad were the twelve year old's life line to the atheistic Mad Fanny Wright.

Inola had not used the last name of her owner and father, Caleb Crider, since escaping to Nashoba. Fanny called her Iphigenia, Eppie for short, and if she was ever in need of a surname, Frances Wright had her use Harrison. Wright chose Harrison because of William Henry Harrison who had served as governor of the Indiana Territory from

1801 to 1812 before he was elected President of the United States in 1840. Wright liked letting people assume they had cleverly figured out that Inola was secretly related to him. Such precautions should have been a help to prevent Inola's true identity from becoming known by blackbirders. But the ignorance of Inola and the hubris of Frances Wright worked in favor of the seventeen year old Inola Crider being found by the erstwhile Quaker, George Daniels.

When Inola arrived at Nashoba, she was housed with two Negro women in a small log and mud cabin. Although Frances Wright knew that Inola had arrived via the Underground Railroad, she made no effort to locate Inola's owner and buy her. By 1835 the financial footing of Nashoba was already precarious and a comely twelve year old woman might bring five hundred dollars at the auction. Mad Fanny decided to believe that Inola's past was better left unexamined. And Inola was too frightened of white people to discuss with Wright her true circumstances.

So Inola remained a runaway slave and Frances Wright was committing the hanging offense of stealing her. In 1836 a Shelby County jury had found Nimrod Hooper guilty of slave stealing and Judge Bramblett had presided over the hanging. Frances Wright and Inola (Crider) Harrison lived in fear fifteen miles away. Their fears arrived in persona in 1840.

Neither Inola nor Frances understood that the tide could not be held back. Nor did they recognize that the catalyst for the coming irreversible upheaval in their lives was the hubris of Mad Fanny. Fanny had refused to follow the advice of Robert Dale Owen who knew the deep well of racial, religious, and gender bias that pervaded not only the South but, also, the supposedly more egalitarian southern Indiana.

Frances had refused to temper her public comments on her plans to free Negroes and women. She reveled in the opportunity to rub her intellectual superiority in the noses of such bigots as Judge John Pitcher and the other white men who controlled Posey County, Indiana. Indiana might be a free state by law, but when it came to equal rights for blacks and women, Mad Fanny could not distinguish it from Tennessee. And she loudly said so.

She would even occasionally bring her newly acquired slaves to New Harmony and Mt. Vernon to show their progress on the road to self-determination. Of course, she did this in hopes of shaming or encouraging more contributions for Nashoba.

Frances was particularly proud of the golden skinned, beautiful and bright Inola who by the age of sixteen had learned to read and write and speak as a white lady might. To counter Robert Dale's argument for caution, Frances boldly took Inola to meet the Posey County community in 1839. Wright's confidence that her transformation of the twelve year old Negro slave into a young woman who could pass for white was so strong that she even had her attend a public reading at the courthouse in Mt. Vernon. Unfortunately, the reading was attended by Judge John Pitcher. Pitcher told his newly made friend, William Combs, about the light skinned uppity negra whom Mad Fanny Wright from Nashoba was trying to pass off as white. Pitcher did not catch the woman's name, but he told Combs she was supposedly helping Wright run Nashoba. The next time Combs wrote his cousin, George Daniels, he told him of his suspicions that maybe the old rumors about Inola being hidden near Memphis were true.

CHAPTER TWENTY-SEVEN

MEMPHIS

GEORGE DANIELS ARRIVED BY STAGE coach at Irvine's Landing in Memphis, Tennessee in the spring of 1840. He asked the stagecoach driver for directions to the courthouse then walked up the high bluff to Raleigh. Daniels perused the captured and escaped slave fliers posted beside the double wooden doors at the front of the courthouse. When he found no mention of Inola being held for a reward, he entered the courthouse and inquired of Sheriff J.K. Balch and Circuit Clerk Joseph Graham about Nashoba.

The sheriff told Daniels they had recently hanged a man for slave stealing and that if there was any legal way to hang that nigger lov'n meddlesome Yankee he'd furnish the rope. He just needed someone to give him a reason.

The fact that George Daniels did not find any notices about Inola did not greatly concern him as five years had elapsed since she had disappeared from Lynchburg. His copy of the flier described her as a, "Nappy headed pickaninny girl with good teeth. Twelve years old, may have scar on back."

George remembered her as a skinny child who was so quiet that even when William Combs was trying to rape her she barely made a sound as she struggled. Had George not run to tell his uncle, the girl would have most likely just accepted her fate without complaining.

Daniels figured that if Inola was hiding out at Nashoba, he would not get any cooperation from the owner of the place. Of course, anyone harboring her would be subject to being hanged, but first George would have to discover the runaway slave and prove who she was.

Daniels did not want to alert anyone that there might be a reward to be claimed at Nashoba. He found out that Nashoba had only a few Negroes and that the commune was reputed to be engaged in educating and, perhaps, even allowing them to engage in miscegenation. Although, as yet, the authorities had not been able to discover any reliable evidence of these capital crimes as all statements from Nashoba were made by the crazy white woman, Frances Wright, who kept the Negroes on the plantation or with her at all times. It was reported by the *Memphis Appeal* recently that a woman at the commune who may have been at least a quadroon appeared at a gathering in Indiana and gave a public reading. However, as the news item had been given to the *Appeal* by Frances Wright herself, it seemed unlikely the woman was a slave.

CHAPTER TWENTY-EIGHT

THE SEARCHERS

INOLA SAW THE POWERFULLY BUILT young white man approaching Nashoba from one of her favorite resting places beside the Wolf River. He was poling a small dingy along the northern bank of the swiftly running waterway.

As the man came closer, she noted how the morning sun caused him to squint and the exertion of the poling brought out his hard muscled shoulders and arms. Inola was always alert around white people, especially grown men. She did not want the stranger to see her in her working clothes for two reasons. She looked more like a runaway slave and she wanted to show off at her best.

Inola was wearing a one-piece grey cotton sleeveless dress that she had tied up above her knees. Her hair was black, but had been heavily oiled by Frances Wright every night for the five years she had been at Nashoba. It was shiny and smooth and the natural curliness was controlled in large waves. Her skin was luminescent and her large brown irises were surrounded by pure white sclera with wide dark pupils that seemed to exude a warm invitation.

At seventeen her body was naturally firm and her perfectly aligned teeth had never been dulled as her only drink was water and the taste of sugar did not appeal to her.

Frances Wright was well aware of the effect the beautiful Inola had on almost all men and some women also. Even brilliant worldly men such as her husband, Count Phiquepal d'Arusmont, and her erstwhile lover and fellow dreamer, Robert Dale Owen, were dumbstruck by the nymph-like Inola.

As for Inola, since men had been trying to win or steal her favors since she entered puberty, she was well aware of her presence. What those who desired her did not realize was that the stirrings in Inola were every bit as powerful as those she caused.

Although she had been prevented from delving into these great mysteries by the watchful eyes of Frances Wright, Inola had spent many private moments exploring both her desires and her easily responding body. She did find it ironic that what Miss Fanny said was to be the salvation of both Negroes and women, i.e., cenogomy, was denied to her by Fanny's curiously inconsistent standards for Inola. She sometimes felt that when Fanny oiled her hair or helped her dress that Fanny's lingering touch signaled other messages than what were spoken. And sometimes after she was alone, Inola just had to put out the fire by caressing herself.

So when George Daniels stepped onto the shore just below where Inola had been observing him approach, Inola was both apprehensive and tingling with those feelings that bubbled ever closer to the surface. Here was an interesting new man who seemed to have appeared out of the morning mist in the middle of Inola's secret desires. Inola hurried to the main cabin to alert Fanny.

George had been concentrating on navigating the snags and sawyers along the river bank. His eyes did not immediately filter out the sunlight so he missed the striking young woman looking down upon him.

CHAPTER TWENTY-NINE

UTOPIA

GEORGE HAD BOUGHT A SKIFF for a dollar and poled it the fifteen miles from Memphis to Nashoba. When he saw the grand sign proclaiming, "This is Nashoba. All Who Seek Justice are Welcome", George was impressed. He tied his skiff up to the landing, strapped on his back pack and began to climb the high bank to a cabin at the end of a worn down dirt path. The cabin faced the river and to its sides were four smaller huts. George imagined that these were just the outlying elements of a larger community.

Suddenly a loud voice boomed out to him from the top of the bank, "Come on up here, sir!"

George heard the voice of command and knew that if Inola was at this compound he would almost certainly have to deal with this strident, tall, reddish-blonde haired woman who towered above him from the top of the river bank.

Frances Wright called for George to follow her up to the largest of the enclave of shacks that sat above the Wolf River surrounded by poorly tended fields. George thought, so this is what all the trouble is about, a large white woman trying to run a huge plantation with a few

Negroes? Where were the men? Where was the evidence of some dangerous conspiracy to free slaves and overthrow the government?

George looked first for other men then for available weapons. He could not see that these people could protect themselves much less threaten him. He did sense that this forceful woman thought a great deal of herself in spite of her surroundings. George, also, knew there had to be some Negroes around somewhere, but he had not seen any in the fields nor near the cabins.

"My name is Daniel Elkins. I was traveling through Memphis and I heard that you folks were running a large plantation and might need someone to repair and sharpen your farm implements. I thought I might could pay for the rest of my way to Indiana if you needed any work done. I am a blacksmith by trade. Do you have the need for some forge work? I would have to make do unless you have a bellows, anvil and some tools. But I can repair wheels and shoe horses without a real shop. If I could get some work here and put up in one of your slave quarters, I could help you out and be on my way in a few days. I figure I saw about fifteen dollars worth of smithy work just walking up here."

"We do not have slave quarters. We do not have Negroes except for the two men and two women who are on the other end of the plantation working to cultivate the cotton crop. They are no longer slaves but are working here because they have not, as yet, earned enough money to reimburse me for what I paid for them. They will be truly free soon enough."

"Ma'am, I apologize if I offended you in any way. I just was looking for work. If you have no need of a wheelright or a blacksmith, I can take my leave. Although I could do some repairs just for a day or two's room and board and fee of two dollars per day if you do not feel the need to do much at this time."

Frances did need to have numerous things fixed and neither her effete husband nor the poorly motivated and ignorant Negroes knew how to properly repair anything. Further, her money was slowly draining through the holes in her grand plan to revamp the morals of the whole nation.

She sensed that this stranger did not appear at Nashoba by chance nor was he forthcoming as to his true purpose. But she needed things done and he claimed he could do them and cheaply. She decided to take him up on his offer.

"Alright, I will pay you two dollars per day for a maximum of twenty days and provide board and a cot in the empty cabin next to the workers home. You will not be paid until the end of the term and I will be the judge of whether the work you do deserves compensation. Can you start today? If so, you can try to repair the broken axle on that corn wagon right outside this house. Then, you can clean and hone the tools and the plow. And I do not want you talking to anyone but me and my husband, agreed?"

"Perhaps, Ma'am, let me see the cot and the corn wagon. Do you have a nigger who can help me if I decide to stay?"

"We do not have niggers, Mr. Elkins. Please remember that. I will get Mordecai to help you, but do not mistreat him. He is a sensitive young man. Do not try to engage him in conversation except about work."

"Ma'am, if I might inquire of you? I was directed here by a man at Levine's Landing in Memphis. When I asked for information about getting to Indiana, he suggested that someone here might be able to help me. I am trying to get to a place called Mt. Vernon. Have you heard of it?"

"Perhaps, why are you wanting to go there?"

"Well, as I said, I am a farm implement maker by trade, and I have heard there is a great need for a craftsman there. Would you know if that's true?"

"It is an area of rich river bottom land with the Ohio on the south and the Wabash on the west. Farming is on the rise there. And, if you truly are able to fix wagons and plows, you might find some work there."

"My plan is to be in Indiana within the next month. Can you tell me how long it might take to get there?"

"My husband, my young ward, my daughter and I recently returned from New Harmony, Indiana, which is quite close to Mt. Vernon. We traveled by flat boat down the Wabash to Shawneetown, Illinois on the Ohio where we caught a steamboat packet to Cairo, Illinois then on to Memphis. It took three days. So, if you do know how to repair things, you should be able to stay with us a few days before traveling on."

George had no desire to waste his time dealing with this woman who appeared to be totally out of place in this rundown shanty. However, this would give him an opportunity to see if Inola was being secreted on the grounds. On the other hand, he had not seen any Negroes yet and he wondered what kind of man this forceful woman's husband might be. Where was he?

"My husband is giving lessons to my ward and my daughter. They are in the education building that you saw to your right as you came up to our main edifice. We provide education and music training for our freed Negroes and young ladies. Of course, we do not educate slaves as that would be illegal. Come with me and I will introduce you. You may leave your pack by the door for now. Are you staying?"

"Could you let me consider your generous offer for a little while? I need to think through my plans."

George could not believe that these few miserable cabins were the entire complex that caused such vitriolic hatred in Memphis. Where were all the freed slaves? And what about the salacious rumors of inter-breeding and promiscuity?

"My name is Mrs. d'Arusmont and my husband is Count Phique-pal d'Arusmont, the famous educator. You have surely heard of Dr. d'Arusmont and me, also, perhaps. I am quite well known as Frances Wright."

George had never heard of any of them except for Mad Fanny, the nigger lovin' white woman of Nashoba. However, he just bowed his head and followed her out the cabin door. She slightly ducked to avoid the lintel. George managed the doorway without difficulty even though he was five feet eight inches tall. He noted that Mrs. d'Arusmont was a large woman. He did not care for her.

Fanny and George approached the education building and entered through its only door. It was dark except for the sunlight entering the window opening that could be covered with a burlap flap. As they entered, a small reedy white man with a goatee rose from a rough desk and looked at them quizzically.

"Count d'Arusmont, this is Mr. Elkins. He may be staying with us a few days to repair some things. He represents himself as a farm imple-ment expert. Mr. Elkins is on his way to Mt. Vernon, Indiana to work on farming equipment."

D'Arusmont did not acknowledge George's outstretched hand which he soon dropped in embarrassment. George did not care for him either.

As George's eyes acclimated to the darkness of the crude hut he noticed a woman seated behind d'Arusmont at the desk. George could just make out the shape of the woman whose appearance was obstruct-ed by the bony shoulders of d'Arusmont. The woman did not get up from the desk until Mrs. d'Arusmont said, "This is my ward, Miss Iphigenia Harrison, whom we call Eppie. You may call her Miss Eppie. My daughter, Sylva, is seated beside Miss Eppie; she is eight years old (actually nine and conceived out of wedlock)." As Fanny motioned to Inola, the young woman came into the window light that framed her face and body from behind her.

George caught himself staring awestruck at the most beautiful woman he had ever seen. She was about five feet tall with shoulder length black hair that fell in waves around her face. Her skin gleamed as if it had been rubbed with olive oil and her rounded lips were full and almost pouting. When she smiled her teeth were a contrast of brilliant white. She gazed directly at George with wide dark eyes that caused him to react deep within his loins.

Inola noticed the handsome stranger's eyes steal a look at her breasts and felt herself getting warm as she blushed with pride. He had light brown hair and clear blue eyes. His beard was full and dark and it excited her. She noted that his forearms were rippled with interlaced muscles and pronounced veins. Inola wondered about the rest of his body.

Inola felt Miss Wright's disapproval of the smile she had involuntarily flashed when she was introduced to the young man. She immediately cast down her eyes and moved backwards towards the desk. But she felt an exciting stirring when Miss Wright said, "Mr. Elkins may be staying a while to work on our equipment. He will sleep in the empty cabin next to the women's quarters. Count, would you show Mr. Elkins his cabin and where we keep our tools?"

"I am finishing up with Sylva on her elocution exercises. Let Mordecai do it."

"Mordecai may be across the plantation working cotton and I must finish justifying the accounts."

"Would you want me to show Mr. Elkins around, Miss Fanny? I do not mind."

Inola moved swiftly out the door before Fanny could react. George hesitated only long enough to bow his head to Mrs. d'Arusmont and the Count. His heart was raging in his chest. All he managed to say was, "Let me get my things."

CHAPTER THIRTY

INTIMATIONS

GEORGE KNEW EVEN LESS ABOUT women than Inola did about men, but he knew he could not catch his breath when she said, "Would you like to follow me; I'll show you your place?" He watched as her trim rounded buttocks moved within her thin cotton dress. They had no quiver to them at all. They appeared to be one with her entire legs. Her small feet fascinated George as they moved one directly in front of the other as if there was nothing separating the strides. How could anyone be so perfectly formed he wondered? He sensed that this marvelous creature actually liked him. What was it that made him feel as if there could be something more to her?

Inola's body swayed gently in front of George as they moved towards the implement shed. He could not feel the ground beneath him.

The shed was open on three sides. A dusty anvil was sitting in a corner and a few dirt encrusted long handled tools were piled beside it. George saw no bellows or any fire pit. How did these people tend crops, he wondered?

"Will this do, Mr. Elkins? I might be able to find some more implements out in the fields. And the corn wagon with the broken axle you saw on your way up the bank. We, also, have a couple of wheels that are missing spokes."

"Miss Eppie, I am sure everything will work out fine. It may require some nigger-rigging, but I am used to that."

Inola was not caught off guard by George's colloquialism. Even the Negroes used the term at times. But its use reminded her of her years in Lynchburg and reminded her to be cautious. Besides, this powerfully built white man had something about him that felt like the past she had hidden from for so long. On the other hand, when their eyes met in that first moment, she had felt a wonderful sensation that dispelled other concerns. Was this the man who would finally answer those needs she had been wondering about? Should she try to discover if he had any hidden agendas or just rely on her intuition to carry her along? What was it about the stranger that caused consternation yet made her feel safe? Or was she just sensing his passion rising to meet hers?

"Would you like to see your quarters, Mr. Elkins? They are next to mine." Inola heard her words and flushed. Did he take anything from the tone she had not intended to let into her voice? "I mean next to the women's quarters."

"Yes, Ma'am, I would like to put down my pack. Will I be in the company of others?"

"No, sir, you are our only guest and this is our guest cabin."

Inola entered first and pulled back the oil cloth from the lone window. The cabin was spartan with a narrow cot and a table with a wash basin on it as the entire furnishings.

"The facilities are just out back, Mr. Elkins. Miss Wright will want you to dine with us in the evening. As to other meals, you may need to ask Mordecai when you begin working with him."

As Inola turned to exit the cabin she brushed up against George's shoulder. He jumped back as if she had slapped him. Neither of them understood the other's reactions. Inola asked for his pardon and George could not voice any response.

Inola could feel the power of George's body through his shirt. George had never touched a woman's breast until hers met his shoulder. He had not anticipated the contact and had no explanations for the fire it caused within him.

"I must get to work on the corn wagon."

"Will we see you for dinner about eight o'clock in the gathering house? That is where we first were."

"Yes. Thank you, Miss Eppie. I would be pleased to see you, see all of you then."

Chapter Thirty-One

MORDECAI

FIXING THE CORN WAGON WAS so simple George wondered how these people survived. Mordecai had been brought to him by Frances Wright who had found him down below the cabins fishing. George had started out with the notion that he would show Mordecai how to make the repairs so he could do it next time. All it entailed was propping up the wagon by using a sapling as a lever and a stump as a fulcrum, then what appeared to be a broken axle was revealed as a missing cotter pin from behind the wheel.

George could see that Mordecai understood the problem but did not care to learn how to fashion a new cotter pin on the anvil. His attitude appeared to be that he had no ownership interest in the problem. He did help George move the wagon to the stump.

But what of the so-called Count, what kind of man would live off of a woman? Was he too smart to come out and learn to do this mundane task? Or was he too good to work with his hands? George may not be a doctor or a Count, but he could read and write and fix a wagon.

On the other hand, George did not envy the man's relationship with the overbearing and manly woman. Even in his state of involuntary celibacy, George could not summon any sexual interest in such a prideful and domineering woman.

George adhered to Fanny's admonition to stick to business with Mordecai until they finished the wagon. But he wanted to know about Inola, and Mordecai came across as not particularly bright when George tried to show him how to use the hammer and anvil.

"Mordecai, how long have you been here?"

"Oh, Mister Elkins, I don't rightly know, awhile tho'."

"Who is here to help run this large plantation, Mordecai? Who does the cooking and washing?"

"Why, the folks who live here, sir. There ain't nothin from here to Memphis, so we duz for ourselves."

"I can see that, boy. What I was asking is, who all is here to do the work?"

"Oh, Master Elkins, we is all here to do the work. That's how we can be free."

"Now, boy, don't get uppity with me. Are there any negra women around here? Surely you got a woman to take care of you, don't ya?"

"No, sir, my wife and two children were sold off into Arkansas before Miss Wright paid to get me away from my master over by Nashville. When he sold off my fambly I guess I just couldn't rightly understand it and complained a little too loudly for my master's liking. He put a collar on me and kept me separate from the other niggers. Then Miss Wright came and paid four hundred dollars for me. I still got's a long way to go to repay her. But it don't seem as tho' it matters much. Miss Wright says she can't afford to buy any more niggers right now and I reckon I'll never see my wife and little ones again."

George wasn't sure if Mordecai was telling him the truth or was just changing the subject. But it had become clear to George that Mordecai was not as dull as he had thought. He was going to have to make his own inspection for Inola.

George told Mordecai he wanted to look around for other things that might need fixing. He started walking the sorriest looking fields he had ever seen. The land held promise but was spotty with trees and brush. A great deal of clearing needed to be done.

George finally came across an area where two Negro women and a Negro man were leaning on hoes or squatting down until they caught sight of him approaching. George was accustomed to coloreds trying to escape work, but usually when they knew they were being watched they at least pretended to do something. These three did come to erect positions when he neared but did not exert any effort in doing so. It was as if their only response was out of curiosity, not respect or fear.

"What ya'll doing? I'm here to fix equipment. Do you have anything that needs sharpening or repaired?"

"No, sir, we is about to get this field chopped and ready. We's been hitting it real good today."

The spokesman was a large black man about thirty years old. He locked onto George's eyes as he relaxed his position on his hoe.

"We was just getting ready to go back for supper. Is there anything we can do to hep you along?"

"Is there anyone else working around here? Who else helps you?"

The two women looked down and pretended to clean their hoes. The large man's voice had a slight edge to it when he answered.

"You come from de main house didn't ya, sir? You's seed it all. Ain't no one else to help do all this work. We's best be going in if you don' mind?"

George realized that Mordecai and these field hands were wary of white men asking questions. Of course, that could mean they were hiding something. But that something was probably not Inola because he believed that this run down operation needed every listless helping hand it could muster. She would be pretending to work like the rest.

"Well, who does the cooking for the white folks?"

"She and I does the housework when we get out of the fields. We's going now to start things. Is you staying to supper, mister?"

George looked at the graying older colored woman who had spoken up. Her companion was a skinny teenager who just gazed at her as she spoke to George.

"What do the white people do?"

"Oh, they's real busy readin' and ciphr'n an' play'n music. They ain'ts gots time ta work."

CHAPTER THIRTY-TWO

DINNER AT EIGHT

GEORGE USED THE HARSH LYE soap and the water from the wash basin to clean his important parts. He put on his Sunday shirt and pants and used a little axle grease on his brogans. In the small mirror of his cabin he appraised himself as rather handsome.

He had difficulty concentrating on the lies he had told. He needed to make sure he was consistent. But his mind was constantly being assaulted by thoughts of the beautiful woman he was soon to see again. Now that a few hours had passed he was beginning to doubt that she had evinced interest in him.

Had she truly been trying to see down inside him or was he just projecting his intense feelings onto her? Such thoughts were difficult for George. He had rarely had to struggle with his inner and outward thoughts. Usually he just went about his life as though it were a straight line. But this woman had caused him such excitement, and he was not used to practicing intrigue anyway. His cousin, William Combs, could have handled this quandary much better. George wished he were there to advise him.

George had long been ready when Mordecai knocked on his door and said, "Mister Elkins, dinner be ready now. We's set up in de big house."

George was not quite sure what Mordecai meant by the "we" part. Surely these people did not eat with Negroes. The thought made George slightly queasy. He immediately banished his uneasiness by remembering the Count would not even shake his hand. Surely they would not eat with Negroes. What would they do with the plates and utensils they used? Another thing that bothered George was the "women's quarters." When Miss Eppie had shown George the guest cabin, she had pointed to the one next to it and said, "This is where we sleep." Surely she did not sleep with the black field hands.

George followed Mordecai across the yard into the main cabin. When they entered, the light from four lanterns made George's pupils contract. When his sight adjusted, he saw that the furniture had been arranged in a square with two small tables at a ninety degree angle then four chairs completing the box.

Doctor d'Arusmont and Fanny were standing on either side of Inola. Inola had her arms around Sylva who was in front of Inola. The two colored women and two colored men were positioned behind the four chairs. There were three place settings on one of the tables and two on the other.

Fanny motioned for George to sit at the table between her and the Count. Inola and Sylva sat at the other table. George was disgusted when he saw the Negroes sit in the chairs. Although he was ravenously hungry, he was not sure he would be able to force down any food while subjected to supping with niggers.

As George waited for the blessing, Fanny said to the older Negro woman who had told George she did the cooking, "Playella, you and Rachel will please serve the table starting with Mr. Elkins. Then you and Rachel can help Samson and Mordecai. Are you waiting for the permission of some deity to eat, Mr. Elkins? We are not superstitious here. I have found that food tastes no different with or without conjuring over it."

"I just was appreciating the smells from your fine table. What are we eating?"

George was still hoping that somehow the tide would turn and the coloreds would leave before they began to eat. He was hungry but he feared the food would hang up in his throat.

"This is sure a fine table you set, Mrs. d'Arusmont. My mother used to use pewter things, but these candlesticks look like silver."

"We may be on the frontier, Mr. Elkins, but my family is of ancient Scottish descent. My late sister and I regularly dined with royalty and ate with such notables as President Jefferson and the great Marquis de LaFayette. Of course, Count d'Arusmont's title is hereditary, not honorary. These linens are the finest and irreplaceable."

George did not need the bright light of day to see the fraying edges on the white damask table cloth and the napkin he left beside his plate that had a scene of a large manor painted on it.

"That is La Grange, Mr. Elkins. I assume you are familiar with the Great LaFayette's home near Paris. LaFayette himself gave me this set and the crystal comes from Prussia. It once graced the table of Frederick the Great who sent it as a gift to George Washington as a token of his admiration for the American Revolution. General Washington presented it affectionately to the Marquis in appreciation for LaFayette's service to America."

George had never heard of Frederick or La Grange and did not wish to learn about either. He regretted using his insincere comments about the table to buy time for his stomach to settle. He was hungry, but eating with coloreds was a high price to pay for a meal.

These asinine braggarts were so proud of their fraying possessions yet they obviously were just putting on airs. And on top of that, they were consorting with Negroes.

George decided to concentrate on the beautiful Miss Eppie as he tried to swallow small bites of the stew made with leeks and lamb and what appeared to be mushrooms. George's mother had often warned him against eating mushrooms and George had never been able to stomach mutton. Yet here he was eating mutton and mushrooms with niggers and pompous inept white people.

When he mustered the courage to look towards Inola he found her staring directly into his eyes. He dropped his large spoon on the white table cloth leaving a greasy brown stain. In his attempt to apologize, he caught a glimpse of the large and scowling Samson glaring at him.

What did he care, George wondered? It wasn't his table cloth and George was a white man. And if Samson was upset about his interest in Inola, a white woman, unless Samson was charged with protecting her, that certainly was none of his affair.

As George tried to rub away the spot made by his spoon, Fanny haughtily said, "Use one of these *serviettes de collation*, Mr. Elkins." George stared blankly at her outstretched hand with the wet towel. "The towel, Mr. Elkins, the towel." George took it and wondered what sort of fool would feel the need to call a towel anything but a towel when they lived with Negroes in a shack surrounded by fallow fields?

After the stew and coarse homemade johnnycake, Fanny produced a bottle of wine that she proclaimed had been made from peaches grown at Nashoba. George was not a frequent drinker but figured anything that would get the slimy taste of mutton out of his mouth would be an improvement. He was wrong.

The wine contained particles of fermented fruit and the fumes invaded George's nose as the harsh taste stuck on his tongue. "This is very tasty, Mrs. d'Arusmont. Thank you for a fine supper. I don't think I should trouble you for another glass though as I plan to be about your repairs early in the morning."

Although George was ready to forego even being in the same room with Eppie to escape from Mrs. d'Arusmont, Fanny was not going to easily lose an opportunity to expose her erudition and intellectual superiority.

"Are you a follower of Jefferson or Hamilton, Mr. Elkins? Are you a Democrat, Whig or free thinker?"

"I am a blacksmith. What I know of politics is I don't care to know about politics or politicians. I prefer men who work for a living, no offense, Count."

In the midst of his anger at what he supposed was a put down, George caught Inola's eye and thought he saw a hint of a smile on her full lips. He suddenly lost his edge against Fanny as he felt movement against the inside of his fly. He feared the buttons might be too far apart for decency. Then he thought he saw Miss Eppie glance quickly in that direction. Surely he was mistaken. Beautiful young ladies did not think on such things.

Samson loudly said, "Will you need me to show you back to your cabin?"

"No, boy, I can find my way if I can have a candle."

Mordecai handed George a tin holder with a lighted candle he took from the silver candelabra on the table. "I can show ya around some more tomorrow if you needs me to, Mr. Elkins."

"Thanks. I will let you know in the morning. Goodnight, Count, and, Mrs. d'Arusmont, and, Sylva. Thank you for supper. Miss Eppie…"

"Mr. Elkins, the path to your cabin is hard to follow in the dark. I will show you the way if you wish?"

Samson snorted and started to interject when Count d'Arusmont said, "Fanny, we have business to discuss if you can take yourself away from memories of the "great" LaFayette. Let Eppie leave now and show Elkins out."

Before anything else could be said, Inola reached up to George's hand and took the burning candle and candleholder. As she did her small, thin fingers brushed the hairs that covered the back of his hand causing him to shudder involuntarily. George wondered, did she touch me on purpose? Can this marvelous woman actually be interested in me?

George did not want to look the fool so he tried to disabuse himself of the ridiculous notion that this refined and beautiful woman might not be repulsed by him. He would concentrate on his mission of finding Inola and not be distracted by his foolish fantasies.

CHAPTER THIRTY-THREE

MOTHS TO THE FLAME

COUNT D'ARUSMONT DID NOT ACKNOWLEDGE George's exit. Just as Inola's candlelight disappeared out the cabin door, d'Arusmont directed Samson, Mordecai, Playella, and Rachel to leave.

"Frances, you may believe as you wish, but others have the right to seek salvation as they choose. I resent you claiming to speak for the rest of us on such matters. I want Sylva to have the benefit of a Christian upbringing. Then, if she chooses, she may take up your anti-religion crusade when she is an adult. After all, she is only nine ..."

"She is eight!" interjected Fanny.

"There is no need to maintain that charade when we three are alone," said the Count. "Sylva is aware that her early arrival is all that causes us to maintain our relationship. I have long ago explained to her your unorthodox views on marriage and relations between men and women. She knows but for me she would have been born a bastard. She need not have our sins compounded by blasphemy. Sylva and I shall soon return to France and you may go or stay here as you see fit. Your performance tonight with that ignorant transient is just the type of incident Sylva does not need to see."

"And just how do you plan to pay for your passage and yours and Sylva's care? You will not work and you have already dissipated a great deal of my money."

"It is not your money. You are my wife and I am entitled to your estate. Should you be so foolish as to take the matter to the law, I will not even grant you an amount for dower. And because we have a child, under the doctrine of curtesy, she, not you, must receive any lands or tenements you possess during coverture."

"I have supported you completely. You had nothing but an empty title and a worthless education. You dare to threaten to take my child and my fortune? You are indeed a scoundrel!"

"I have heard the last of your past indiscretions and your desire to curse our daughter and our Negro wards to perdition with your prideful atheism. When Sylva and I return to France, I will initiate legal action concerning our marriage."

"Do what you will! Your superstitions can not make reality from fear. Believe what you choose, but why subject others to your ignorance, especially Sylva? As for our marriage, I never wanted that. Had my beloved sister, Camilla, not died during our transportation of freed slaves to Haiti, I would still be with Robert Dale Owen. You played on my grief while I was alone. Sylva is the only thing you have ever given me and now you wish to steal her. I will not countenance your filling her head with superstition. Religion's only role is to help men subjugate women. I want Sylva free from such bondage."

"Momma, I do wonder why so many brilliant and powerful men appear to side with Father in religious matters. Are they all wrong? And I am eager to go back home to France. Our life here is very hard. Why can't we just give this place to Mordecai and Playella and the others and go home?"

"Child, most of the world's brilliant and powerful men used to believe the earth was flat and the sun revolved around it thanks to their superstitious views on such things. Just because most people are convinced of something does not mean it is correct. And we cannot just turn Nashoba over to our black charges because Negroes are not allowed to own property in Tennessee. If we did leave here, they might be put back into bondage. They surely would end up having little opportunity for happy lives. We cannot just throw up our hands and leave them to the furies."

"Your pride and stubbornness are clouding your judgment on how best to help our Negro friends, especially Inola. And her name is Inola. She is not Iphigenia and you are not Artemis. Instead of saving her, your desire to flout your self-perceived superiority in Indiana then return her to Tennessee just puts her in danger. If we cannot afford to purchase her and let her earn her freedom through work, we should help her escape permanently.

"But you have an unnatural attachment to Inola. She is as an acolyte to you. You are grooming her to be your vestal virgin and priestess. Have you asked Inola what she wants? Not all women hate marriage and religion – nor do very many beautiful young women care to forego a normal life for someone else's cause no matter how worthy."

"Your words are very hurtful and full of ingratitude. Once you claimed to have the same passion to free slaves and women as I. Now that the realities of hard work and hardships have arisen, you want to steal both my money and my only child and abandon me and Nashoba.

"It was not out of hubris but out of pride in what Eppie has accomplished that I took her to Mt. Vernon. I have gained nothing and have lost nearly everything in my desire to free slaves and married women from bondage. Is it not ironic that after you came to me because of those dreams you now wish to make me the eponym of what we have so long struggled to save?"

"Ah, Fanny, you cannot see what is obvious to everyone else. Religion is not the enemy. Marriage is not the enemy. Slavery and stubborn pride are the true enemies. And we cannot eliminate the former without first eliminating the latter. Let us quarrel no more tonight. Tomorrow Samson and I must go to Memphis to replenish our stores. I will try to do so as frugally as possible. Then when we return we will try to assuage these words spoken in haste and anger. We are all, and you most of all, under a great deal of stress. The appearance of Mr. Elkins, if that's who he really is, has exacerbated an already difficult time. Do we not all wonder why he happened to appear? Is this Elkins to be believed? Is it not strange that he found his way to Nashoba when he says his destination is Indiana? Wouldn't you think he would have tried to work for his passage at Irvine's Landing or even on a steam packet itself?"

"I agree, Count. He has told us very little about himself. And he seems willing to delay his trip just for a little repair work. On the other hand, according to Mordecai, he did fix the axle on the corn wagon in an efficient manner. We are captives of our lack of knowledge in such things and of our waning resources. Perhaps we should not be too eager to examine this Trojan horse. Maybe he is in trouble and in need of a temporary sanctuary, although Samson, who often sees people for what they are, seems to be put off by him. That may be because Samson perceives that Eppie is a little too quick to be the Samaritan to this bearded stranger. Samson's interest is more in Eppie than Elkins. We have long been wary of strange white men who might be looking to do some "blackbirding" or looking for an easy encounter. Maybe I should alert Eppie and see if she can divine any nefarious motives in Mr. Elkins. He seems smitten with her so he may let his guard down if he, in fact, has one up."

CHAPTER THIRTY-FOUR

THE SPIDER AND THE SPY

"EPPIE, COME SIT WITH ME, girl. Did you enjoy last night's dinner? How did it go when you showed Mr. Elkins to his cabin?"

Inola sensed that Fanny was in her investigative mode. Often Fanny tried to garner information by what she thought were cleverly disguised questions. It was not long after Inola had come to Nashoba that she learned that the first part of the inquisition was just such an entreaty.

Her antennae were on high alert when she answered, "Oh, Miss Fanny, we barely talked. I just showed him to the door."

Inola felt herself warm just thinking about her confusion from the previous night. George had followed closely behind her and when she turned to show him through the door their faces were inches apart. Eppie had slightly raised her head and was filled with excitement when George said, "Excuse me, Miss Eppie. I didn't mean to startle you."

Inola had wondered, was I mistaken, didn't he like me, did I do something wrong? Then George had gone on past her and she had left.

"Eppie, you know how much I care about you and how proud I am of you?"

"I guess so, Miss Fanny. I know that I am very different from five years ago. It seems like that other life is just an awful dream. I am happy here and want to stay with you and the Count forever."

"You know that there are evil men who may still be searching for you. We must ever be vigilant to avoid slave traders and men with other bad intentions. You are young and do not understand what some men might seek from a pretty girl like you."

Inola blushed and put her head down. She hoped Fanny had not seen the recognition and amusement on her face. Inola knew better than most what men were seeking. It was what she had wanted to experience for some time, most recently with Samson. Samson's large and powerful body was fascinating to Inola. But he always kept his distance from her, especially when white people were near. She wished he would enfold her in those massive arms and let her take things from there.

But this white man seemed as stiff around her as Samson. Inola wondered if maybe she was not really that attractive to men.

"Why do you say that, Miss Fanny? Have I done something wrong? Were my manners bad last night? I tried to remember all that you have taught me."

"No, child, you did very well. I would be proud to show you off even to the great Marquis if he were still with us. Although since I wasn't much older than you when we met and you are much prettier than I ever was, the greatest hero in the world might well have chosen you over me."

Inola blushed again. She often dreamed of being loved by a great man as Fanny had often claimed to be.

"Miss Fanny, I could never be as you were, are. I could never be loved by any great man, or maybe even anyone."

"Your day will come, girl. And I promise you the fulfillment of all your dreams is possible. Of course, you must not allow yourself to be owned by any man whether slave master or husband. Take what you want when you care to but do not tie yourself to an emotional bondage."

"But, Miss Fanny, I have often thought you disapproved of any such contacts by me."

"I do not encourage you to consort with low brow men when you can find happiness in many fascinating men of intellectual superiority. I have always hoped you would see men as equals. But more importantly, I want men to see you as an equal. Do not barter away your freedom. Take what you want but give only what you must."

"Are you and the Count happy, Miss Fanny? Why did you decide to get married?"

"I did not decide to get married. I just got married. My child has a mother and a father. I am married."

"I am sorry, Miss Fanny. I didn't mean to be impertinent."

"That's okay, Eppie. Let's talk about Mr. Elkins. Do you feel comfortable around him?"

"He doesn't seem to like me much, although he is polite. I am not sure what you mean, Miss Fanny."

"Do you think he is truly just a traveling tinker? Could he have some other agenda in coming to Nashoba? Do you think he might show himself to you? He is probably going to keep his distance from the rest of us."

"Are you concerned he might be trying to find information for the authorities to use against your great plan to free Negroes and women?"

"Perhaps, or maybe he is exactly what he says. Either way, there is no harm in keeping a watch over him. If you believe you can do so without harm to yourself, would you try to observe him? You are naïve in such matters, but often men will divulge to women things they would prefer to keep to themselves. And I would not worry too much about Mr. Elkins not liking you. With men, such is not required where women are concerned."

CHAPTER THIRTY-FIVE

THE SPRING

INOLA FELT HER BODY TINGLING as she went to the guest cabin looking for George. She had a premonition that Fanny might be correct. She had almost immediately sensed danger when she met George. There was something about his physique and manner of speech that reminded her of someone. On the other hand, her thoughts about this mysterious memory were not negative. She let caution ease behind her excitement when she first noticed what she thought was his interest in her breasts.

"Mr. Elkins. Mr. Elkins!"

George had long been up and feigning attention to his work as he looked for signs of Inola. He had at first thought Rachel might be the runaway slave, but realized she was too young. Inola would be a grown woman now and might even have children of her own. This thought piqued George's interest even more as any children born to a slave belonged to the slave's owner. And Caleb Crider would happily pay George for the pickaninnies too, if they were healthy, of course.

George found poorly maintained farm equipment everywhere he looked. He was surprised to find a large cotton gin with a horse hair belt crudely attached to the hand crank. It was obvious that Eli Whitney's basic engine had been bastardized by someone who number one, was too lazy to crank it by hand and, two, was inartful in trying to harness a horse or mule to it.

The cotton gin's screen and hooks had been pulled off cant by the excessive force of the animal. George opined that from the looks of the fields the efficacy of the cotton gin was irrelevant. However, since all it took to repair the gin and earn two dollars was to remove the belt, pull the screen tight and re-bend the hooks, he spent about an hour at the task.

Just as he was completing his repairs in the heat of the Tennessee spring, Inola came around the lean-to where George was working. He had his shirt off and his hair tied back with a red cloth he had found hanging in the lean-to. His years of farrier work had built up his arms and shoulders and tapered his waist. The perspiration flew from his arms as his veins and muscles rippled in the sunlight.

Inola thought that he looked like one of the Greek gods in Fanny's book of paintings. She could barely withstand her excitement as she came up behind him and stammered, "Mr. Elkins." George was stopped with his hammer in mid strike. His heart almost burst from his chest. He was unable to respond until he put down his hammer and grabbed his old shirt up about him.

Inola misunderstood George's reaction. She thought he was perturbed to be interrupted. In fact, he was so immediately excited by her voice that he had to cover himself. What would this refined lady think of him? She surely had never seen an aroused man nor should she.

"Yes, Miss Eppie." He was almost immediately able to put his shirt on and face her. Inola was disappointed to see those glistening shoulders disappear beneath the thin grey cotton.

"Were you able to fix the gin? We haven't been able to use it since the Count tried to hook a mule to it. Samson tried to tell him there wasn't enough cotton to worry about anything but hand cranking. Miss Fanny was furious at the Count, but he just went back to the main house and started reading."

"You look different in your work dress, Miss Eppie. I like your hair up like that." George embarrassed himself by this statement and immediately sought to insulate himself from any possibility that she would be offended.

"I mean you probably need to put your hair up so you can help Mrs. d'Arusmont."

Inola felt herself getting flustered. What did this man really think, she wondered? Does he like me? Am I pretty? Or am I going to bother him if I stay?

"Miss Fanny asked me to check and see if you needed anything. If you want a drink, there is a spring just over that rise. Would you like for me to show you?"

"I guess I deserve a break; lead on."

George noticed that she was barefoot and that her one piece work dress hung loosely about her down to her knees. He was surprised to see a refined white lady dress like a colored servant. But in this place he expected to be surprised.

From behind Inola George could see the smooth rhythm of her rounded hips moving just to the inside of her dress, first to the right, then the left.

When she turned to hold a branch for George, he could see her breasts outlined against the beltless dress. He saw her nipples clearly defined. He purposefully brushed up against them.

Inola felt a rush of blood to her head. Had he done that on purpose? She had often wished for her breasts to be admired and caressed by a man such as George, but other than that ogre back in Lynchburg five years ago, no one had done so except Inola herself.

"Here it is. The water tastes sweet. Count d'Arusmont says that's because it is filtered through both flint and limestone and it bubbles up through sand."

When George walked past the branch held by Inola he saw a natural rock basin surrounded by cedar trees and large basalt rock. The pool of water was so clear George could see individual pebbles on the bottom. It looked as if it were no more than two feet deep.

"Be careful, Mr. Elkins. It's way over your head just as soon as you leave the edge. I come here a lot to watch the butterflies, especially in the spring when the giant monarchs have returned. It is so peaceful here you can almost hear their wings flutter. This and a spot above the landing are my favorite places."

George squatted down and cupped his hands to get a drink. Later George would blame Inola for pushing him, but Inola thought George used the excuse of slipping to grab for her. The reality was more prosaic.

When George stood up too quickly he suddenly lost his balance and began to flounder. Inola reached for him. As she caught his strong right hand, it reflexively closed upon hers, and when George fell in Inola was attached.

As they came up splashing and laughing Inola yelled, "I can't swim!"

"Well, why don't you just try putting your feet down, it is not as deep as you thought. And, by the way, neither can I."

Inola kept her grasp on George as she tested for the bottom. When she stood on her tip toes her head rose just above the surface. George did not encourage her to let go of him.

Although George was several inches taller than Inola, her lips were close to his when they finally stabilized their positions. Neither of them noticed the coldness of the spring fed lagoon. Just as George had mustered the courage to move the few inches between them the branches parted and Samson and Rachel appeared.

"Here, Mr. Elkins. Let me take Eppie from you first then I's git you out. We heard Eppie yell for help and come run'n."

George helped Inola up to Samson then he took the huge right hand of the black man. George and Samson were both used to being the strongest man they knew. Each felt the power and resentment of the other. Both had the thought that the other would someday have to be dealt with.

"Thank you, Samson. Miss Eppie was showing me the spring to get a drink. I must have lost my footing on the mossy rocks."

"Come, Eppie, Rachel kin hep you back to de house to git dry clothes. Does you needs to change clothes, Mr. Elkins?" George noted the familiarity in Samson's use of Miss Eppie's first name. Such uppitiness was uncalled for.

"Go along. I am okay and I have more work to do on the cotton gin so you can get back to your real work instead of checking up on white people."

Samson seethed with anger, but was still a slave by law and he was not sure how far even Miss Fanny would back him against another white person. He held his comments and followed Inola and Rachel away from the spring.

As for Inola and George, each felt as though the opportunity they had waited years for had slipped away. The cold water had begun to soak them through.

CHAPTER THIRTY-SIX

THE LORD HELPS THOSE WHO HELP THEMSELVES

INOLA LAY NEXT TO RACHEL in their small bed in the southwest corner of the cabin they shared with Playella. The burning that had begun earlier that day when she and George were body to body in the spring had grown more intense.

Fourteen year old Rachel's back and buttocks were inescapable. Inola tried to lie with her left side hanging over the side of the thin pine board that served as the frame. But there was no way to balance even her lithe body on the narrow slat. Their mattress was a ticking of straw that rode over a rope lattice and the east and south walls served as part of the frame. The lone bed post was at the northeast corner and had the thin slats on the north and east sides nailed to it.

The young women slept in their cotton work dresses without under garments. Playella's cot was similarly made and attached to the southeast wall about six feet away.

Rachel did not snore and Inola often lay awake trying to discern if Rachel was sleeping. This particular night Inola tried several ploys of heavy breathing and feigned coughing to test whether Rachel was awake. Finally, she could wait no longer. She had to seek relief from the fire the powerful stranger had ignited. She made a slight movement against Rachel and then tried to stay absolutely still and wait for any reaction. When there was no response from Rachel, Inola carefully caressed herself with her right hand as she did her best to keep her arm and the rest of her body immobile.

After only a few moments of imagining herself back in the spring with George, Inola felt the joyful release she sought. Now she could put her desires and her imagination to sleep.

Next to her, Rachel, who often daydreamed about Samson, vicariously enjoyed Inola's virtual experience with George. When Inola's warm body shuddered along with an involuntary moan, Rachel silently thanked her.

Chapter Thirty-Seven

ONAN REDEEMED

GEORGE'S MOTHER HAD NEVER TALKED to him about sexual matters other than when she had come upon him examining himself at age eleven. His mother had ceased bathing him years before, but on this warm summer afternoon she had not expected him to be cleaning himself after mucking his uncle's stable. George used the large tin washtub on the rear porch. In the winter he rarely bathed, but, if his mother insisted he do so, he would heat water in a kettle on top of the wood burning stove. During warm periods he would just use lye soap and cold water.

When she pushed aside the curtain they used for a back door when it was hot outside, she saw the young George in a turgid state and so engaged he did not notice her until she gently said: "Son, tonight we will study about Onan. Dry yourself and come to the kitchen table."

George was embarrassed to be seen naked by his mother and sensed he had disappointed her. He dressed and sat with her at the small table next to the cook stove.

"George, your father should be here to explain such matters to you. As the good Lord has taken him from us, you and I will need to talk about this. I should have recognized that you are growing up, but a boy is always a boy to his mother.

"I have opened the Bible to *Genesis* because I remembered that God's commandment as to this matter is set out there. Give me a moment and we will study it together."

Anytime George heard his mother use the words, "God's commandment", dread would arise in him. God never commanded anything good. It was always some sacrifice that, if not made, brought eternal damnation.

"Here it is, chapter thirty-eight, you read this slowly and try to understand your duty to God."

George read the passage but did not know what it meant:

"Go in to your brother's wife,
and perform the duty of a brother-in-law to her."

George's mother looked at him expectantly. "Now do you see what you were doing? Do you see what God did to Onan? It is a deadly sin, to cast your seed upon the ground. God damned Onan for wasting a chance to have offspring."

George still had no idea what God wanted him to do or not do, but he loved his mother and she clearly did not want him doing what she had seen him doing. It was interesting and felt good, but George did not want to go to hell. He did not know that semen was seed, but he was pretty sure offspring were children. He decided that what his mother wanted him to do was to leave himself alone so he would not have children.

"I'm sorry, Momma. I won't do that anymore. No one ever told me it was wrong. I don't want to die, Momma," George sobbed as his mother hugged him.

"Now child, don't you fret. God forgives and especially children. But now you know so do not backslide as our Baptist friends might say."

For all the years since, George had heeded his mother's and God's warning about the consequences of onanism. Sometimes in his dreams matters were out of his hands, but he would pray for forgiveness when he awoke. And when his cousin, William Combs, bragged to him about girls or told George what William did in the privy, George would just listen.

But George envied William's experience with women. He wanted to have girlfriends too. William would laugh about taking neighborhood slave girls whether they wanted to or not.

"Of course, George, you don't kiss no niggers. It's okay to do other things with them. You got to try it. You know, even the ones who act all uppity and squirm away really want it. You just have to put up with some pretend struggling so they feel better about it. Hell, they can't say or do anything about it. And if they get knocked up, their owners are happy to have another slave, especially one that's half white and a lot smarter than its momma."

George's mother would have been extremely disappointed with George if he had forced himself on some woman. And, since she believed God intended men and women to copulate only to have children and, then only during marriage, even a willing girl was off limits to his mother's way of thinking.

All of these thoughts raced in and out of George's head as he lay on his cot. He wondered if the beautiful ladylike Miss Harrison could actually bring herself to like him. She had appeared to be genuinely enjoying their contact in the spring. But George had never had even a close relationship with a woman much less any sexual contact. What was she really thinking?

And even though his loins were on fire, he dare not incur God's wrath. Perhaps a dream would bring surcease. For now he would try to concentrate on finding Inola.

CHAPTER THIRTY-EIGHT

MYSTERIES REVEALED

GEORGE WATCHED FROM THE TOP of the river bank as the Count and Samson shoved the skiff into the Wolf River. The golden morning mist was beginning to clear, and when Samson's and George's eyes locked, George felt Samson's unspoken menace.

Rachel, on the other hand, was elated that Inola and George were so obviously drawn to one another. She planned to encourage the situation. Maybe then Samson would finally pay her some attention. She was only fourteen, but the thirty-five year old Samson might be surprised at what she could offer. Besides, Miss Wright had long ago clearly put Eppie off limits to Negro men. She was being groomed to fulfill Nashoba's vision of racial and sexual equality. The irony of discriminating against Inola's fellow Negroes and not allowing her to control her own body was lost on Miss Fanny, but not on Rachel or Samson or Inola.

Rachel approached George and said, "Mr. Elkins, you recall where you saw us working yestiday? There be some tools down there that needs filing. Mordecai and I has to help at the big house, but, if you wants, I can ask Eppie to show you?" George was again put off by this nigger wench's casual use of Miss Eppie's name and even more by her statement that she would tell a white woman what to do. But the excitement he felt by having a chance to be alone with Miss Eppie dispelled his peevishness.

"Alright, girl, you can ask Miss Eppie if she is available and, if so, if she cares to accompany me. Be quick about it now."

Rachel was used to being dismissed by other people, especially white men. She normally did not mind and, this time, was not at all put off; she hurried to find Inola.

"Eppie, Mister Elkins needs you to show him back to the spring. There's some tools down there that needs tending to and Mordecai and I must help Miss Fanny start packing Sylva's and the Count's things to go back across the water. He's down by the landing."

As soon as Rachel left, Inola combed her hair and put a drop of eau de cologne on the underside of her wrists. Then she rubbed a small amount through her hair and combed it again. Inola knew that Miss Fanny would not like for the expensive perfume to be used so casually but Inola reminded herself that she had been instructed to find out about Mr. Elkins. A little distraction might help. At least that is what Inola used to justify her nervous preparation.

After putting on a fresh cotton dress over her one piece bodice, Inola slid her small feet into her open toed sandals. She was tingling with anticipation as she set out to find George.

George was heading back toward the cabins along the dirt path when he noticed Inola's head above the high weeds along the curved trail. He felt a rush of blood throughout his body. His excitement caused him to move more rapidly forward.

"Mr. Elkins, Rachel said you needed someone to guide you back to the spring. If you want me to, I'll show you?"

"Thank you, Miss Eppie. I need to stop by the guest cabin and get my bastard file to hone the tools. Then, I would surely like it if you would lead me there."

After they procured George's file, Inola headed across the field towards the spring. George could not make his tongue form any words except, "uh huh" when Inola would ask about his work.

"Mr. Elkins, where did you learn to be a blacksmith? Who taught you?" George could not think about her questions as he watched her gently rolling buttocks in front of him. What was she saying over her shoulder?

When they reached the high cane around the spring, Inola pushed it aside and stepped onto the sandy bank. She stepped out of her sandals then bent at a ninety degree angle from her waist to pick them up. George was so close to her their clothing touched. He did not know what to do.

Surely I am not to be permitted to touch her, he thought. But, as she bent over, she appeared to lose her balance and he instinctively grabbed her from behind. As she steadied herself in his hands, she turned towards him.

He is more afraid than I am, thought Inola; I will have to take the lead and hope that it works out.

Inola dropped her sandals and reached up to feel George's beard. It sent such excitement through her that she quit thinking and started feeling his hard shoulders and arms.

George did not yet believe this beautiful and sophisticated woman was attracted to him. And he was without any experience with such matters. Surely she will be offended if I hold her close, he thought. But Inola was already losing herself in this strong man's power and she could feel his response through her clothing.

As Inola stroked George's beard he began to caress her black hair. George was surprised at the feel of her hair. It was smooth to look at but more coarse to his touch. Its thickness felt wonderful in his hands.

Inola lifted her face up to George's. He still did not dare to kiss her until Inola placed both of her hands behind his head and pulled George to her. Fire swept through George's loins as they embraced. George felt the fullness of her lips and the need flashing from her tongue.

Now what, George wondered, what will she think of me if I take advantage of her all alone like this?

Inola took George's large right hand in both of hers and placed it on her breasts. She felt his excitement as her own coursed through her breasts to her thighs. This is what I have been waiting for, she thought. This time I will not let this magic get away.

George slipped his left hand down to Inola's right leg and moved her dress up to her waist. Then he found the buttons on the back of her bodice and was confused on how to proceed. He began to realize what most men eventually learn. In these matters the woman is always the more experienced. Nature has seen to that.

Inola easily managed to undo her bodice and then slip it down while all in the same motion she removed her dress over her head. George was in awe. He had never seen a naked woman. She was beautiful and she seemed to actually want him to touch her.

George was surprised at the dusky, smoky color of Inola's skin beneath her clothing and when his eyes were drawn to her pubic area the hair appeared more wiry and thick than the lightly oiled hair on her head. And her areolae were larger and darker than her facial complexion.

As Inola moved into him, George fumbled with his pants while Inola undid his shirt. She had his shirt completely undone before he could get his belt unbuckled so Inola took over for him.

Inola managed to get George out of his shirt while she worked on the top button of his trousers. But, because he was so aroused, she could not get the other two buttons loose. So together they wriggled George out of his pants.

When Inola saw the turgid state George was in, she reflexively held it with both hands. Inola lost control and let George take the lead. For his part, George was amazed that this lovely creature wanted to touch him there. He felt himself almost out of control before he carefully removed her hands.

George turned her around and placed his hands on her breasts as he rested her buttocks on him. Her posterior was firm and exciting but somewhat larger than it appeared under her dress. Once again he was near exploding.

Then George saw the scars on her back. He was so startled by this realization he lost contact with her. Inola felt the loss and turned around. As she looked deep into his soul with her large brown eyes they both knew who they were.

"Inola?"

"Are you the man who saved me in Lynchburg? Did you come looking to take me back?"

George was fighting with himself. "It's okay to have sex with nigger girls, but not to love 'em," his cousin, William Combs, would say. And while George's mother taught that Negroes were humans deserving of fair treatment, she, also, taught that sex was reserved for procreation within marriage.

Inola was frightened and frustrated. She was not cursed with the disgust George felt over interracial emotional attachment and she was finally on the verge of sexual discovery. But she was not going back into slavery no matter what. She would die first or maybe Samson would kill this man for her.

George said, "Yes, Inola, my mother taught me to respect people of both races and especially women. It is difficult for me to believe that you are a negress. I do not think it matters to me in spite of how it matters to others."

"So you still want me, Mr. Elkins?"

"My name is George Daniels and I did come searching for you to get the reward. That is something else my cousin, William Combs, is responsible for. But now I find that I want to protect you and make love to you if you will still have me."

"You know that it is a capital offense to harbor a slave? And we cannot legally marry in Tennessee, Virginia or even Indiana. Or would you even want to marry me?"

"Inola, I am older than you, but I know less about things than you seem to. That is probably due to your Mistress and the Count. Maybe I shouldn't admit it, but I have never known a woman Biblically. And my mother demanded that I marry before I ever did know one in that sense. Maybe you know how we can proceed when society says it is a crime?"

"Let me ask you again, do you still want me now that you know who and what I really am?"

Inola felt the answer to her question through the expression on George's face. To her surprise, the fact that he had never had another woman filled her with happiness. They could start their lives together as equals, she thought. The improbability of the rest of the world accommodating their love was pushed aside by their desire.

George wrapped his large arms with their veined muscles around Inola's lithe body. Somehow he seemed to know what to do now. He laid her down gently in the soft sand beside the gracefully flowing spring and they both were assured of the rightness of their faith in the other. Their loving was as exciting as they had each anticipated, but now it was to last beyond the moment.

CHAPTER THIRTY-NINE

WHAT NOW?

GEORGE WAS NOT SURE HE had done things the right way, but Eppie seemed happy to just lie in his arms beside the spring. He was surprised that when they kissed he had felt no repugnance. Her clear skin felt just like his mother's cheek when she would kiss him good night. And although Eppie's hair was thick in his hands, it smelled clean and fresh. His earlier confusion was dissipating into a sense of wonderment that this beautiful woman had put her body and her trust in him. He knew that he could not go on without her by his side no matter what others may think. But George was not able to think clearly about protecting her while her warm body nestled so perfectly into his.

"I guess it is 'Eppie' from now on? What can we do now? What will we say to Miss Fanny?"

"I am so happy that I do not want to miss this wonderful time by worrying about future troubles. Let's just think about now," Eppie said as she slowly and gently moved her long thin fingers across George's chest and reached up to kiss him.

George felt the miracle begin to once again stir within him as the sound of a meadowlark trilled from the tall cattails. He forgot his concerns until they fell apart again exhausted and fulfilled.

"Eppie, I cannot lose you now. What are we going to do? We must tell Miss Fanny and we must protect you."

Eppie knew that reality had irrevocably entered upon her reverie. After waiting and wondering for years about this great mystery of life, she planned to memorize and treasure every detail. But after escaping from Lynchburg and living Mad Fanny's fantasies for five years, she had no doubts that the white man's world would overwhelm her dreams.

"If you truly want me, and I am not quite sure as yet, we know that nothing will be easy. I am not even sure what to call you."

"Why, George, of course. And I want you with me forever. But how can we manage things when you are legally a slave and we cannot legally marry? It is certain that we must leave Tennessee and we cannot return to Virginia. The only place I know where we can live in freedom and where I can make us a living is Indiana with my cousin, William Combs. Of course, he may recognize you. But we are very close and he would not want me to be imprisoned for marrying you."

"But he is the man you saved me from! How can I ever feel safe around him?"

"Eppie, that was a long time ago and was before I fell in love with you. William would never betray me by betraying you. He will not bother you if you are living with me. William is the least of our worries. How will we fit into the town and maintain our secrets? And we still must face Miss Fanny."

"Miss Fanny will be upset and disappointed, but she loves me and will help us. After all, we will be living her vision of America. We cannot marry, and she is against marriage. We will not receive a blessing on our lives from the church, and she is an atheist. And we will be a Negro slave and a southern white man living as though we were husband and wife. How can she deny our love and remain intellectually honest to her own vision?"

"Well, we must tell them sometime. Let's return and tell them all together at dinner tonight. I do not think Samson will approve. He appears to me to have more of an interest in you than that of a friend."

"That may be true, but I guarantee you that Rachel will be thrilled. She has long set her young cap for Samson. Now she will have full rein as he will accept whatever makes me happy, and that would be you."

CHAPTER FORTY

REASONING TOGETHER

"Miss Fanny, there is a subject of much difficulty that our guest and I must discuss with you and the Count. Now that everyone is together, we can ask for your understanding and your help. This is extremely important and extremely hard."

George had been dreading this meeting ever since he and Eppie had returned from the spring. George expected that Eppie would look different after they had made love and he feared others would know. He was confused when he next saw Eppie and she looked and acted as if nothing had changed. George wondered if he looked different and if people could tell what they had done earlier that day.

George sat silently and closely watched Samson. George was most concerned about Fanny's reaction, but knew he would have to leave that situation up to Eppie. As far as Samson was concerned, George feared a more violent reaction. The Count was weak and Playella, Mordecai and Rachel were without real standing in the matter. It came down to Fanny and Samson.

"You know that we do not air personal matters at dinner or among guests. Although, as you have indicated Mr. Elkins is involved, perhaps the prohibition against guests may not apply. Let us finish dinner before we take up any family matters."

Eppie fought the desire to raise her voice to Fanny. Fanny had always encouraged her to speak up as an equal, but now she was being dismissed. It was apparent that Fanny was aware that something of importance had occurred. It was, also, apparent that she was not happy about it.

After Playella and Rachel cleared the table, everyone moved their chairs into a circle in the center of the cabin and Fanny said, "Alright, Eppie, tell us about your problem that involves this itinerant tinker."

The Count was averting his gaze by fiddling with his pipe and tobacco and Samson was staring right through George. His huge forearms and hands were within inches of George. The veins were popping out as he gripped and re-gripped his fists. Playella was watching Fanny and Rachel watched Samson. Mordecai sensed that his world was about to change.

"He is a man I used to know from Virginia. He befriended me when I was just a girl of twelve, just before I escaped to Nashoba."

The others, except George, reacted as if Eppie had slapped them. Fanny stood up to her full six feet and the Count dropped his pipe. Samson's eyes blazed at George.

"He knows who I was and he came here looking to take me back." Samson reached for George who was ready for the move.

"No, Samson! Leave him alone. He is not taking me back. I love him!"

Fanny gasped, "You love him? You don't even know him! He is a common laborer and a slave hunter! You were not educated and trained to waste your life on such as him. I forbid it!"

Samson stood menacingly by George and said, "I's not going to let ya' leave here with Miss Eppie. Ain't go'n to be no capture!"

George moved a step back from Samson. "It's true I came here searching for Inola Crider, but I did not find her. I found Eppie and I love her. When we leave here it will be to go north together. You need have no fear of me. Eppie and I need your help. We want your support."

"Support, you expect to just come to Nashoba and remove its heart? Eppie is all I have worked for and spent my fortune on. She represents my vision for women and Negroes. She is not just some lovely girl. She is an icon of what is Nashoba. The Count is going to take my only child, Sylva, to France. My beloved sister is gone, my fortune is depleted. I have lost the great LaFayette and my fellow idealist Robert Dale Owen. And now you want to destroy the one thing that I traded all them for. No! No! A thousand times, No!"

"Fanny, do you not hear yourself? Is Eppie nothing but a symbol? What of her desires? Is your pride and arrogance going to do to Eppie what you have done to us? Other than our brief moment of creating our daughter, we have wasted our lives wishing for other people and other things. Why can't we listen to Eppie and Mr. Elkins? Are you once again so absolutely sure of your views that no one else's opinions and desires matter?"

"Thank you, Count. I have flown under false colors and I am ashamed of my lies and of my reasons for coming here. My mother raised me as a Quaker. She taught me that God did not mean for people to be treated like property. Unfortunately, greed and prejudice led me to put love of money ahead of her teachings. But, now that I have fallen in love with Eppie, I want only to protect her and Nashoba too. My true name is George Daniels and I knew Eppie in Lynchburg, Virginia. I beg your forgiveness for my deception and I beg your understanding and help for us now. We must have your help. We would like your blessing."

Fanny slowly sat down and slumped in her chair. She appeared to shrink to normal size. She, also, somehow seemed to age right in front of them. It was as if the pride and certitude that had ruled her life oozed out of her with her realization of the consequences of this confluence of events.

CHAPTER FORTY-ONE

THE BRIAR PATCH

"FANNY, I KNOW MY WORDS hurt you. But you do not listen. Your philosophical approach to these issues is morally sound. Negroes and women should have the right to choose their own way. Religion is sometimes used to control the ignorant and superstitious. It is not the rightness of your cause, but your obtuseness in attempting to advance it that is the real issue. I have watched as your hubris blinded your splendid vision. You have enormous talent and courage. It is your tendency to ignore the views of the majority in spite of its power that has led us to this current pass. For once, consider the realities of this backwoods country. Americans talk freedom, but they live money. Until the profit goes out of slavery it will not die. And until women are worth more as equals than chattels, marriage and the church will keep them oppressed. Your writings, speeches and especially this debacle of Nashoba are of no consequence. If we are to help Eppie, you must set aside or rise above your pride."

"What would you have me do, Count? Are you finally going to do something besides live off of me? Do you have plans that will protect

Eppie and the others from a return to bondage? Is your effete study of philosophy going to save them from ruin?"

"Miss Wright, it seems to me we have but one course to follow. Eppie and I must get north to get her beyond the reach of any return to slavery. As we must make a living, entering the farm implement business with my cousin in Indiana may be our best option. No one on the frontier asks to see a white couple's wedding license or proof of their status as freemen."

"Well, Mr. Elkins or Daniels or whoever you claim to be, it may be news to you that Indiana was established as a free state when it was carved out of the Northwest Territory in 1816. Slavery was prohibited in the Northwest Territory by the Act of 1789. Indiana's Constitution forbids slavery. It is not the law of Indiana that I fear, but the men who control it. There are several well respected Indiana businessmen and farmers who purchased their financial success by forcibly taking Negroes across the Ohio and Wabash Rivers to Kentucky and Illinois where they languish without hope and without the law's protection.

"If we could rely on the law, there would be no lynchings even in slave states. Unfortunately, my experience as a resident of Posey County, Indiana has been that the men of the law subvert or ignore the law as it suits them. As the great LaFayette wrote, it is the love of justice, not money that is called for. As I see it, the love of money will usually win out."

"All that may be true, Miss Fanny, but we must deal with the here and now. And that means we must do our best to avoid disaster while striving to make a good life together. George and I know that trying to make a living in Indiana will be difficult and dangerous. What are the alternatives? Should we go our separate ways? That will not happen. Can we stay at Nashoba when even your generosity must cease soon. It is obvious that Nashoba cannot support us. We must live in a free state and, at least, I have been to Posey County and you and the Count have friends there who believe as you do. Also, George is a trained black-smith and toolmaker whose cousin has already done the preliminary work on a business.

"I know that the great ideal of Nashoba may have to wait. But won't George and I be living examples of your vision? If we enter white society and build a life together without the sanction of church or state, isn't that part of your plan for America? It has never been your way to let financial concerns control moral decisions, but if you close Nashoba for now you can save a great deal of money and, perhaps, regenerate it later on a stronger footing. You would be free to return with the Count and Sylva to France if George and I took Samson, Playella, Mordecai and Rachel with us. You would need to furnish them with manumission papers that could be recorded in Memphis, but they are already free in all but the details. George, could we not provide room and board for them in return for their work, at least for a short while? Maybe, if your business prospers you could continue providing for them or even pay them. Of course, you would all be free to stay or go as you wanted."

Eppie was not at all sure she should be discussing George's busi-ness. But she did not want to lose the only family she had known for five years, and it was clear that Miss Fanny, the Count and Sylva were soon going to be gone. Also, even though she loved George, she barely knew him. Having her friends, especially Samson, around would help ease her fears.

"I have some money, but do not think I could support more than the two of us until I can get a business going. We will need to pay for steamboat passage to Indiana and pay for food and shelter once we get there. And I am not sure that Samson and the others would care to trade Nashoba for the unknown of Indiana. There are no guarantees that even you and I can survive there. They might just be trading themselves into a situation they won't like. I cannot pay them any wages and I have never even been to Posey County."

"Fanny, you would save the cost of their food and other care if we just declared all debts for reimbursement liquidated. And if you close Nashoba, for now, there will be no cost to put out a crop this year nor will you need to pay to feed the mules. They can be sold. Could you not give Eppie a dowry of half of what you had already planned to spend here this year? If no changes are made, Nashoba will surely drain you of all your funds. If you choose a hiatus, if Mr. Daniels' business prospers, perhaps he can repay your generosity. Do as you like, but Sylva and I are going home."

"It is true that we cannot continue to carry this burden much longer. In order to save our dream from complete disaster, perhaps we can, in a sense, put it in the bank with Eppie and Mr. Daniels and the others too. Maybe they will all, someday, be able to make Nashoba the paragon of freedom and justice that we have all dreamed of. As for me, I am ready to return to Scotland for now."

"Scotland, what is left for you there? Father Milne who raised you is gone. And Sylva will be in France with me."

"But my heart is in Dundee. France with the great Marquis was exciting, but I was young then. Everything was exciting. Home is in Scotland. I must first return there then, perhaps, I can meet you and Sylva in France later?"

Fanny knew the strain that Nashoba had put on their financial status. The money that LaFayette gave towards it in 1825 was exhausted long ago. Robert Dale Owen had ceased his involvement when he learned about Fanny's relationship with the Count in 1832. Fanny feared that she would not be able to support even herself and her family if they continued to care for the freed Negroes. And the Negroes did not seem capable of helping to make Nashoba a viable operation. They were a product of the slave system and the slave system was the antithesis of individual incentive. Fanny had sensed some time ago what she refused to acknowledge. The awful truth was that real freedom from slavery would take generations. Fanny loved her black charges, but love could not change the facts. American slaves were first torn from their culture in Africa then prevented from establishing themselves as part of America's white culture.

Fanny knew how naïve she had been. It did surprise her that brilliant and experienced men such as LaFayette had not understood that Nashoba, or even a thousand Nashobas, could never bring about the changes they desired. Robert Dale had grown up in America and even he had not seen the folly of Nashoba.

It had taken both France and America violent revolution to change just their political systems. Why had it not been obvious that changing the culture of slavery was not just a matter of freeing people and expecting them to pull themselves up by their own bootstraps? Eppie was an exception, but she had received five years of intensive and very personal education, training and love. And Eppie was a person of exceptional intelligence and beauty who looked white. Of course, she was half white.

Fanny had always thought that the fast track to the end of the slave culture was through interbreeding. The more people looked alike the more they accepted one another. Of course, this had never prevented civil wars and discrimination on other grounds. But, at least, it allowed individuals to be a part of a country's culture. Eppie was the proof of that. Although as long as white men held exclusive sway over the political and legal systems, even she was not secure.

Without interbreeding there would always be two distinct races in America. How many years, if ever, would it take for whites to accept blacks as equals? America had made its bargain with the devil and there may be no way out without a total upheaval.

Be that as it may, the Count was no longer willing to go down with Fanny's ship. And Fanny herself was relieved to be forced to end the vain hope of Nashoba and to have a chance to be free of the freed Negroes.

"All right, I do not agree with your conclusions about Nashoba, but it may be time to step back and reorganize. First, we must ask Samson and Playella and Mordecai and Rachel what they want."

"Miss Fanny, Mordecai and I wants to stay with you no matter what. Can we's just go where you go? I's know I be afraid to go across the Ole Water, but you tell me dat's where we come from anyhow. We don have nobody but you. We won' be no trouble, Miss Fanny."

"But, Playella, you and Mordecai are free. Why would you want to remain servants?" Fanny was not unhappy that she might have servants to help her. She recognized that she would have to hire servants wherever she went and provide them with room and board too. If Playella and Mordecai stayed with her, she could save money. Besides, she had paid to free them and had known them for years. And they would have food and shelter they could not furnish for themselves. It did not occur to Fanny that such maternalism was the same justification slave owners used to assuage their consciences.

"Let me think about these things. We do not have to make all of these decisions tonight. For now, we will do nothing. Tomorrow we can discuss the options."

What Fanny wanted was time to think through the details, but her mind was made up and she was on the way to convincing herself that the ideas were hers. The next morning she set forth her plan.

"I can furnish Samson and Rachel with forty dollars each if they wish to go with you to Indiana or if they wish to travel north with you then go wherever they choose. What do you want to do, Samson? Rachel?"

"Well, Miss Fanny, if Rachel wans to we's can go with Eppie, I means, Miss Eppie, and Mr. George if theys wants us to. I don know about the money. Maybe Mr. George and Miss Eppie could look after it. White folks in Indiana might be like white folks in Tennessee. Theys may not like Negroes having all that money. Whats' you wans to do, Rachel?"

"I's wanna go with you, Samson, and Eppie and Mr. George too if they wans us to. All that money just scares me. Mebbe it would be best to let Mr. George handle it."

George could not believe that these people were going to put such trust in a stranger. He kept thinking of his mother. What would she want him to do? What would be best for Eppie and himself? What would William Combs think? What story would they tell the people in Indiana? And could he trust himself with Samson's and Rachel's money and their lives? Was it even legal for Negroes to own money even in free Indiana?

"As for our beloved Eppie, if you must leave us and go with Mr. Daniels, you may take your clothes and personal items including your trunk. And I will endow you with one hundred dollars. It is all I can afford now and that should provide well for you if you use it wisely."

"Oh, thank you, Miss Fanny, and you too, Count. You have done so much for me. I owe you everything. How can I ever repay you for all you have done? That is a great deal of money. It will help us make a new life together. I am sure that George will manage it wisely."

"Now, Eppie, I did not raise you to be a kept woman. That is your money to use for you. Do not turn your life or your money over to any man."

"Do not worry, Miss Fanny. I love Eppie. I know that I am still a stranger to you. And you have reason to withhold your trust. But not all white men are evil. I assure you that I will do my best to protect all of them for you. I know that your generous gifts belong to Eppie, Samson and Rachel. I will keep that ever in mind and use the money carefully for them."

George kept adding up his new fortune. He still had almost all of his own one hundred dollars. He decided it would not seem gentlemanly of him to ask for the money he had earned at Nashoba in light of Fanny's generous gift to Eppie. And it appeared that he would have not only the services of Samson and Rachel, but the use of their money too. This caused him to remember another thing his mother often said, "Where a man's treasure is, there will be his heart also." George remembered the advice, but may not have grasped its significance.

"I guess things are settled then. We will leave for Indiana tomorrow. Only Eppie has much to pack. Perhaps my things will fit in her trunk and Samson and Rachel will have one sack, I suppose. We will leave for Memphis at first light to catch the steam packet north."

"I will post a letter on ahead so that my cousin will know we are coming. Perhaps he will be able to have temporary lodging for us. Samson and Rachel, what will be your last name?"

"By God, we will have a wedding here and now and they will be Mr. and Mrs. Wright! I don't care what Fanny says about marriage Stand up here, Samson and Rachel. Counts can marry people I figure. For once, the rest of us will proceed as we see fit."

"All right, my husband. You perform the ceremony and Sylva will be the bridesmaid. But if you are going to 'marry' Samson and Rachel to be Mr. and Mrs. Wright, why not make it a double rite and have Eppie and George exchange vows? Sylva can serve for both couples and

I will be their matron of honor. Playella and Mordecai can hold the broom for both couples to jump over.

"At least as far as the people we care about know, all four will be married. I know that my acquiescence in this arcane rite may be out of character, but the last two days have all been out of character. Congratulations newlyweds!"

CHAPTER FORTY-TWO

FAUSTIAN BARGAINS

IRONICALLY, FRANCES WRIGHT WAS IN favor of George and Inola swearing out a marriage license in Memphis as George Daniels and Iphigenia Harrison. But, Count d'Arusmont's more cautious approach of just declaring themselves Mr. and Mrs. Daniels won out.

Why invite scrutiny from a local court system that had recently hanged a man just for stealing a slave. What sort of justice would be received for subverting the entire social order through miscegenation and education of slaves?

Perhaps they could live without incident in free Indiana. And with the push of such men as Robert Dale Owen, the Indiana Constitution of 1816 might be amended to allow for interracial marriage.

Of course, George and Eppie would have to be alert around the Posey County blackbirders and they would have to be particularly cautious around William Combs. But, as it was illegal for anyone, without a court order, to forcibly remove a person regardless of race out of the state of Indiana, Combs would himself be subject to arrest if he recognized Inola and tried to return her to Lynchburg. Unfortunately, the

Federal Fugitive Slave Act of 1850 was just ten years away and the 13th, 14th and 15th Amendments were a whole Civil War away.

But, even before the Fugitive Slave Act, it was a felony for whites and blacks to attempt to marry or live in a marital relationship in Indiana. And Indiana's prohibition against miscegenation was not repealed until long after the Civil War. It was okay for white men to have a little black understanding on the side. And it was even okay for some white trash women to take up with blacks in some northern states. What was a serious social and legal matter was any attempt to have the sanction of either church or state on such relationships in free Indiana.

And no matter how Mad Fanny might rail against the ignorant white men who passed and enforced what she condemned as arcane social bans, the possible consequences to George and Eppie of someone such as William Combs divulging their secret were severe.

So George and Eppie, with Fanny's help, created a written family history for Inola as Iphigenia Harrison with just a slight connection to William Henry Harrison. As fate would have it, the two escaped Negroes, Nicy and Fredunes, who had, also, recently borrowed the family name of Harrison, were settling in Mt. Vernon, Indiana about this same time.

Neither Fredunes nor Nicy Harrison was sure when they had been born, but they thought they were in their teens in the 1840's. Their name came from a story told by a freed Negro they had met through the Underground Railroad run by the Quakers. This freed man told them about how he had received his freedom upon his master's death in Macon, Georgia. That master's name was Harrison, and he went by that name. Nicy and Fredunes followed suit.

As for George and Inola, who now must forever be Iphigenia or Eppie, they both were able to see many dangers and obstacles, but were sure their love would see them through the difficulties.

Fanny did not want to lose Eppie, but she feared George would destroy Nashoba if she tried to deny him Eppie. She, once again, put her vision of America ahead of everything. Fanny foresaw nothing but tragedy for Eppie with George, but she felt powerless to save both Nashoba and Eppie. At times such as these, Fanny wished she could believe in some god or even poetic justice. But as Robert Dale used to tell her, the facts keep getting in the way. Fanny could not even wish Eppie, god speed, on her travels to her new life in Posey County, Indiana.

CHAPTER FORTY-THREE

THE FIRST CHARADE

WILLIAM COMBS' INITIAL SHOCK AT the beauty of his cousin's bride slowly dissolved into curiosity. As Eppie gracefully walked down the steamboat's gangplank to the Mt. Vernon landing, her long red velvet dress clung to her small waist and firm full bosom. The matching parasol was held for her by Rachel who was overshadowed from behind by the huge Samson. Even before he was introduced to Samson, Combs felt the ominous power in the hulking giant. George Daniels followed the tableau he and Eppie had carefully planned as a first impression to the large crowd that always greeted the arrival of a steamboat.

Eppie wore her long white gloves and lace trimmed velvet hat to cover as much of her olive colored skin as possible. And she had instructed Rachel and Samson dress in white so that their coal black skin would contrast with their clothing.

Eppie and George had alerted Rachel and Samson that they might expect a public display of master and servant type directives upon arrival in Indiana. The new Mr. and Mrs. Wright, with their eighty dollars of new wealth, were at ease with the charade. They were just happy to be in free territory with Eppie and George to help protect them.

"William, this is Eppie. As I wrote to you, we married in Memphis last month. Have you been able to find suitable quarters for us and our servants? Samson, Rachel, this is Mr. Combs, my cousin. Get the trunks and take them up to that bluff at the top of the riverbank." George pointed to the highest point on the bank. The original "Mc Fadin's Bluff" was where in 1795 old Tweedle Dee Dum Mc Faddin had built the first cabin in what was later to be called Mt. Vernon.

"My wagon is at the bluff, but the seat will only accommodate the three of us. Your niggers can load the trunks, but they will have to walk. The house is about four blocks from here."

Eppie had to look away when Combs used the hateful term for Rachel and Samson. When Negroes referred to themselves or other black people, they often used the term without rancor. But when prejudiced white people called black people niggers, it connoted all the evils of subjugation and inferiority. Her greatest fear was that Combs would recognize her. But she, also, had hoped his attitude towards Negroes had mellowed after spending five years away from Lynchburg.

After Samson and Rachel had loaded the wagon, George and William aided Eppie onto the single bench seat of the wagon. William took the reins and started the team from the Ohio River landing north along Main Street. They first passed Judge Pitcher's vacant lots, then the Pilot House Tavern, the comfort houses of Rosa Hughes and Jennie Davis, the Damron Hotel, and the county courthouse.

The courthouse had been built in 1825 and had been sketched by the Swiss artist Karl Bodmer on June 6, 1834 during his North American expedition with Germany's Prince Maximilian zu Wied-Neuweid.

The courthouse was centered on the village square. A log jail was on the southeast corner and a clerk's building was on the northwest corner. The courthouse was two stories with a steeple that contained a bell for giving signals and warnings.

Combs paid no attention to the courthouse or anything else as he was fixated on the beautiful young woman whose left thigh he kept purposefully rubbing up against with his right hand as he guided the horses.

But the rest of the party was impressed with the courthouse and its young locust trees bordering the south edge of the square and the flowering golden raintrees on the north.

"William, your courthouse appears to have bed clothes hanging out of the windows to air. Are there people living there?"

Combs laughed and replied, "You've heard about how the new presidential residence of Andrew Jackson was invaded by his supporters who claimed it belonged to all the people, haven't you? Well, several Mt. Vernon families and at least one school teacher have moved into the courthouse and refuse to leave. Judge Elisha Embree has been trying to get them out, but his orders are ignored by the squatters. We may have to tear it down and build a new one if Embree can't get the sheriff to evict them. Heck, we probably ought to move in there ourselves and save the rent money."

"That's okay, William. Where is our place?"

"Just up ahead another block then one block west to College Street. The college part is rather pretentious. Some of our townsfolk call our private school a college, but it ain't anymore than a two room shack where our better off families send their kids after they get out of the public school. Our house is within sight of the "college".

"Your coloreds can sleep behind the main house in the carriage shed. There are two bedrooms in the house and a summer kitchen attached to the back of it by a runway."

Eppie was hesitant to speak up, but when George did not respond to William, she said, "How long might it be before we have our own home, George? Surely it would be cheaper to buy a place than pay rent."

George did not care much for sharing quarters with William either. It was going to be difficult enough to keep Combs from prying into things if they lived separately. George feared that proximity would lead to carelessness and that carelessness might lead to catastrophe.

"My dear, we will begin at once to look for a home of our own. For now, we must thank Cousin William for his thoughtfulness."

That evening after supper George and William sat on the front porch to smoke pipes and talk. They found that their pooled resources would enable them to quickly expand the nascent farm implement business William had started and leave sufficient funds for them to buy two modest homes. George did not tell William that almost one third of his money actually belonged to Samson and Rachel.

At William's suggestion, the cousins decided to approach Judge John Pitcher about making him a partner if he would contribute his vacant property on the banks of the Ohio River. This was a prime location for receiving raw materials and shipping finished products. Besides, Pitcher could provide free legal services and he was well respected in the community.

Chapter Forty-Four

A THREE WAY SPLIT

Judge Pitcher recognized Eppie as the young woman Frances Wright had brought to Posey County from Nashoba, Tennessee just a year earlier. He had his suspicions then that the beautiful and refined lady might have just a hair of Ethiopian blood running through her. But now that she was married to a promising young white man, he was less sure of his conclusion. Also, she appeared to be totally at ease ordering her Negro servants around and her husband's cousin was clearly infatuated by her. Pitcher decided to bide his time and see if there was more to the matter than what appeared.

Pitcher had been invited to dinner at the rented home of the two enterprising young businessmen. They had made it clear beforehand that they wished to discuss a business proposition and had given Pitcher an outline of their plan. After Eppie and the servants cleared the table and left the room, the three men spent several hours reaching an agreement to manufacture tools and equipment to service the rapidly growing agricultural industry in Posey County. Pitcher observed that if their business prospered, the only area for expansion was into the Belleville section where the Negroes and prostitutes were.

Pitcher was not worried about forming a three way business arrangement with the cousins. He had already decided that Combs could be controlled by his greed and that Daniels was naïve.

Pitcher had noticed how Combs followed Eppie's movements and how he managed to frequently brush up against her. Pitcher relished the opportunity that was sure to come to divide the cousins by driving Eppie between them.

Judge Pitcher could relax and let his partners make him rich as he filed away the small incidents that would allow Pitcher to manipulate the cousins should he need to. He, also, resolved to keep observing Eppie to see if, in fact, she might be hiding something from her husband. Perhaps he could gain a bit of knowledge about Eppie's lineage that he could hold over her head or even over Daniels and Combs; that would be a real bonus.

George was elated that such an important local dignitary as Judge Pitcher would associate with them in business. Pitcher's assets, legal training and reputation would greatly enhance their business. And he appeared to have an interest in them personally. George was concerned that he, Eppie, Rachel or Samson might slip up around the quick witted Pitcher. But, so far, not even Combs seemed to have any suspicions. If they just remained cautious, things might be okay. And William appeared to have a genuine interest in Eppie as a member of the family. George convinced himself that life was going to go well in Posey County.

For his part, Combs had little concern whether Pitcher cared for them as individuals. Combs knew that Pitcher's name and influence were vital to their growth from a cottage smithy type farming business to an operation that might make them wealthy. Combs felt no warmth for or from the judge. Such feelings were irrelevant to Combs. What he wanted was to use Pitcher as he expected Pitcher wanted to use him. On the other hand, his cousin's wife aroused more basic emotions in Combs. What was it about her that unsettled him?

CHAPTER FORTY-FIVE

THE DEBATING SOCIETY

ABRAHAM LINCOLN HAD DECIDED TO accept Alvin Hovey's invitation to stop over in Mt. Vernon on his way to visit his mother's grave in Spencer County, Indiana. The detour to Posey County would add approximately one full day and night to the trip, but Lincoln had missed Hovey's company. They had not talked in person since 1849 in Warrenton, although they frequently exchanged frank views by letter.

Both men counted as extraordinary their close relationship. Each man had the ammunition to derail the other's political career and maybe their personal lives by publishing their friend's letters. But no topic was taboo and no punches were pulled. It was good, but rare to have such faith in another man.

Hovey had asked Lincoln's permission to have Judge John Pitcher and his Mexican War hero son, Thomas, and a few other friends join them for dinner that evening. It was expected that Robert Dale Owen, Frances nee Wright d'Arusmont, Mr. and Mrs. George Daniels, and Henry Jones would be arriving.

Alvin and Mary also invited their friends, William and Juliette Harrow. Alvin was aware that Lincoln and Harrow were close friends from the time they had ridden the law circuit together in Illinois. Harrow had moved to Mt. Vernon in 1850 to practice law and marry Juliette James. Juliette was the daughter of Enoch James who owned the only private bank in Posey County.

As Hovey was the sitting circuit court judge in the county in 1852, and as Harrow regularly practiced law in his court, they knew and respected one another. And they had realized early on they had a mutual friend whom they both admired in Abraham Lincoln. When Lincoln arrived at Hovey's door at five o'clock p.m. on that October evening in 1852, Mary ushered him in and was gently chastised for calling him Mr. Lincoln.

"Now, Mary, you and I are closer than that. Although this is our first chance to meet in person, I feel I know you well from Alvin's letters. I have heard of your lovely dark eyes that peer deeply into his soul. And now that we have met, I understand Alvin's anguish when he must be apart from you. Please, Alvin is like a brother to me which would make you my sister. A sister must call me Abraham."

Mary's initial shock at meeting this very tall, angular man dressed all in black quickly dissolved in his warm gaze and gentle manner. She was surprised at Abraham's thin voice. It did not fit such a large man. But after a few moments of catching the sparkle in the laconic rhythm of his speech patterns, Mary found herself captivated by this man so admired by her husband.

She soon found her manners and said, "Esther, this is father's friend, Mr. Lincoln. Say hello, then you must get ready to go to Grandmother James' home for tonight."

"Hello, Mr. Lincoln." Esther only saw Abraham Lincoln this one time, but never forgot how he looked right at her as if she were the most important person in the world.

Lincoln lifted her high in the air and said, "Will you come back with me to Springfield? Mrs. Lincoln would be greatly cheered by your smile."

"Oh, I cannot, Mr. Lincoln. I am not allowed to go anywhere but Church and school and Grandmother's."

Lincoln gently let her down as he grinned at Mary. "Goodnight, Esther. It was very nice to meet you."

Mary turned Esther over to Fredunes Harrison then said, "Alvin tells me your wife's name is Mary, also. I wish she could have accompanied you. We will have to all meet somewhere between here and Springfield."

"I wish she could have accompanied me too, but she prefers Springfield to the wilds of Indiana. She believes you folks still keep the flintlocks handy to ward off the Indians."

Mary laughed and took Abraham's hat. "Put down your valise. Alvin is at the court, as always. But you understand that. He will be home soon and then you and he can catch up while I see to dinner. Is ham alright? If you need to wash up, there is a ewer and basin in the guest room. The door is the one to your left. Please feel free to rest there or in the parlor."

"Thank you, Mary, although I am not as tired as I might have been just a few years ago on this trip. The roads are substantially better now than they were when Alvin and I met in Warrenton three years ago. Alvin's leadership in Indianapolis must have helped."

"Maybe so, but as for me, I am glad to have him serve as Posey County's judge. I did not like traveling to Indianapolis. Posey County has always appreciated his efforts. Let the rest of the state take care of itself. Well, listen to me. Alvin says I take these things too personally. He is right. I do not like to see him mistreated and some of his positions in the constitutional debates were misrepresented in the India-napolis newspapers. Alvin is more forgiving than I."

"I will keep that in mind, Mary. Alvin is fortunate to have you behind him."

"Who is that gangly creature in my house? Mary, call the constable! Oh, it is just Abraham. Welcome, dear friend. It is surely good to see you."

"Well, that's some greeting for someone it is good to see. Mary tells me you have been at court. Were you judging, prosecuting some poor widow for back rent or helping some miscreant escape justice?"

"Yes."

Alvin led Abraham into the parlor and bade him sit on the new horsehair loveseat. Alvin sat across from him in a hardwood maple chair he had turned on his own lathe. By sitting on the edge of the chair, Hovey could comfortably look Lincoln in the eye as Lincoln slumped into the cushioned loveseat.

"Excuse me, gentlemen. I must at least make an appearance in the kitchen as Nicy and Fredunes prepare dinner."

"Well, my friend, she is as lovely as advertised. After meeting your Mary, I predict you will grow old and fat without ever again leaving Mt. Vernon. And Esther is going to break the hearts of many Mt. Vernon boys."

"How is your Mary, Abraham, and your boy, Todd? I grieved for you greatly when Edward died. Has Mary recovered? At least young William is now here to cheer her up."

"Mary cannot be cheered. She is generally determined to be un-happy most of the time. But when she is happy, a better mate no man could have. And speaking of good companions, I am greatly looking forward to seeing William again and to meeting Juliette.

"But, please brief me on these other intellectual lions you have gathered to devour me. I know Mr. Owen and am well familiar with his erstwhile companion, Frances Wright. When did she marry? I thought she was a front line soldier in the gender wars. It will be good, if philosophically exasperating, to see our old friend, Judge Pitcher. And Thomas has lived the life that you and I have always dreamed of. How is his injured leg? But first, who are the Daniels, and what of Mr. Jones?"

"By my count, I have about twenty questions to respond to in that monologue. Let me first tell you that our new home is in a district developed by Mr. Jesse Welborn. Our home is on the northwest corner of Fourth and Walnut Streets. You saw the courthouse across Fourth Street and, if you look out the east parlor window, you will see Walnut Street. Going north up Walnut towards Black's Grove live some of the world's best neighbors, George Daniels and his intriguing wife, Iphigenia, known as Eppie. When you see her you will believe that her Greek name fits her. She has the dusky look of a modern day princess, but she is far too pretty to be a sacrifice to any god. She has been tutored by the brilliant but mad, Fanny Wright, who raised her as her ward after her parents were lost at sea in the Mediterranean. Her education was received much as yours and mine. However, she was blessed by the constant presence of Mad Fanny and the frequent influence of such brilliant thinkers as Robert Dale Owen and Count Phiquepal d'Arusmont, who is a marvelous educator in his own right. Fanny and the Count have an arrangement. He spends her fortune and rears their only child while she saves the world. Most people do not know that Mrs. d'Arusmont and the Count are now divorced, but Fanny pretends it never happened. Her façade of marriage seems strange for a woman who sees the institution of marriage as anathema to feminine rights.

"Fanny now lives full time in Cincinnati, Ohio where she had a bad fall on the ice last year. She has never fully recovered physically. She is in town now to visit old friends. I sense she may be making a farewell tour. You will note that she walks with a cane and is often in pain.

"Mr. Daniels and his cousin, Williams Combs, own and operate one of our most successful businesses. They manufacture and repair farming implements. I confess I find Mr. Combs rather boorish, but the Daniels are quite pleasant, although George says but little. He does not have much interest in anything but commerce. But Eppie is a woman who will give even you a fierce battle of wits. And on a more somber note, she is the woman I mentioned to you at Warrenton who was causing such a stir due to a supposed liaison with a Negro.

"As with most small town gossip, the facts fell far from the source of the rumor. It turns out the Daniels' manservant, a huge Negro named Samson, was trying to force himself on Mrs. Daniels when Mr. Combs happened to arrive and save her. The nigger and his wife fled to avoid his being hanged. Unfortunately for Mr. Combs, the gigantic assailant almost killed Mr. Combs with his bare hands before Mr. Daniels appeared and intervened. The Negro and his wife were aided to escape by members of the local colored community.

"Anyway, that is more than you needed or probably cared to know about my neighbors. That was years ago and needs no new airing. She was saved and the niggers are gone. It was unfortunate how the story first did not come out as an assault on Mrs. Daniels but as a liaison. Of course, the colored community here was afraid of reprisals. Some of the Negroes were even trying to claim that Mr. Combs was the culprit and the nigger was the savior. But that story was apparently started by one of our local madams. In fact, if it hadn't been for Combs' soiled dove lady friend, the whole thing would have blown over quickly. Combs spends a lot of his time and money at Rosa Hughes' house. Rosa may be a whore, but she holds out some vain hope that Combs will make an honest woman of her. She apparently assumed that Combs was going for Mrs. Daniels so she told a negress who cleans her establishment that Eppie had led him on. When the colored community began to repeat this outrage, Mr. Daniels and Mr. Combs paid a visit to the home of the negress who was carrying the tale for Rosa Hughes. That stopped that nonsense. I regret that I fell victim to the rumor myself.

"Oh, and Mr. Henry Jones is a young and energetic businessman who keeps books for and owns part of the rapidly growing Pittsburgh Coal Company. He, also, just purchased a home near here in anticipation of finding a wife. Rumor has it that he may have to wait until the one he has his sights on gets out of puberty. Mr. Jones is, also, the son of the first white man to settle in Posey County. And if I haven't quite yet titillated your taste for Mt. Vernon's racy social scene, the local gossip mongers say young Mr. Jones is hiding a history of Indian blood. Of course, that is most likely due to his efforts to help the Shawnees when he lived in Vincennes. As you know, most good Christian folk who love their neighbors still do not love Indians."

"Well, I see that Mt. Vernon continues to be a hot bed of wagging tongues. It must be a place inhabited by people. I am eager to meet our old friends and am looking forward to making new acquaintances."

CHAPTER FORTY-SIX

THE DEBATE

MARY HOVEY SET HER TABLE with the china and silver her mother had brought from Ireland. The handmade linen table cloth and napkins were usually brought out only for Christmas and special dinner parties. Mary had to always carefully watch Alvin's tendency to invite too many guests. Her table and her service could only accommodate twelve and she had insisted on serving dinner in honor of Mr. Lincoln.

She had sought Alvin's advice on the seating arrangements. Mary and Alvin would sit at the ends, of course, and no one would feel slighted to have Mr. Lincoln sit to Alvin's right. And decorum dictated that the unattended Mrs. d'Arusmont would sit next to Mary, However, the rest of the arrangements were problematic.

Mary decided to sit Judge Pitcher to Alvin's left so that he would be directly across from Mr. Lincoln. On her own left she would have Mr. Daniels and to his left she put Juliette then Henry Jones.

She seated William Harrow to Fanny's right and Eppie next to Harrow. Although Mary was concerned that Robert Dale Owen and Judge Pitcher might clash over some of the Negro issues that were bound to be discussed, she decided that such sparks would assure a lively discussion. So she placed Owen next to Judge Pitcher and Captain Thomas Pitcher on Abraham's right.

Robert Dale Owen had married in 1832 when Mad Fanny got pregnant and married Count d'Arusmont. But Mary suspected Owen and Fanny still carried on their relationship. Owen's wife, Mary nee Robinson Owen, and Owen lived separate lives, and other than keeping Sylva from being born a bastard, Fanny had always done as she pleased with whom she pleased. But Mary's sense of decorum would not allow for an illicit relationship at her table. On the other hand, Mary thought inviting Mrs. Owen was unnecessary and probably ill-advised.

As to her other guests, she could not help bragging just ten years later that once gathered in her home was a cadre of men who were on the cusp of the war effort. And when the Civil War broke out, the Union's Commander in Chief and his three generals from Mt. Vernon, Indiana would often reflect on this propitious dinner party and its confluence of destinies.

Lincoln and Hovey owed their earliest knowledge of the law to the same man, Judge John Pitcher, who only moved to Mt. Vernon because his first wife had died. John Pitcher's son, Thomas, spent the first seven years of his life in Rockport, Indiana hanging onto Lincoln's pants legs before Lincoln moved to Illinois. And while in Illinois, Lincoln became friends with fellow lawyer, William Harrow, who ended up practicing law in Mt. Vernon.

But in 1852 the Mexican War had just ended five years earlier and, due to the compromise of the Fugitive Slave Act of 1850, the twelve people who shared dinner in Mt. Vernon at the Hovey home saw another war as unlikely. Of course, they had no way of knowing that the Kansas-Nebraska Act of 1854 and the *Dred Scott* case of 1857 were just over the horizon.

"Abraham, what do you know about the new senator from Illinois, Stephen Douglas? I have read some of his public comments and I cannot tell where he comes down on the expansion of slavery into new states."

"Well, William, you have, as you always did when we were in court, gotten right to the nub of the issue. No one can pin him down. My contacts with him lead me to believe that he is exceptionally bright and well intentioned. He is one of those rare politicians who appears to actually believe in democracy. In fact, his approach to government reminds me of our friend Alvin's philosophy. I believe that Judge Hovey saw his job as a delegate to Indiana's Constitutional Convention as a true democrat would. Is it not true, Alvin, that you saw your duty as one of getting the consensus of a majority of Posey County's citizenry then voting as they directed?"

"Correct, Abraham. I believe a leader should advance his own views if he can convince his constituents of their correctness. However, once he has fought the good fight for his positions, if the majority disagrees, I believe, a representative is just that, a representative of the common will and weal. On the other hand, my dear friend, Mr. Owen, for whom I have the highest regard, takes a more republican approach. We often had the opportunity in Indianapolis to respectfully lock horns over our different views. But fairness dictates that I let Robert Dale speak for himself. I assure you all that he is much more able than I to defend his policies."

"Ah, damned with faint praise. Be that as it may, Alvin, I will attempt to rejoin your rapier with my clumsy broadsword. We did accomplish much with our new Constitution. Unfortunately, much of what was accomplished would have been better left undone. As Alvin will tell you, my political science has one constant element. I believe that government is best that governs least until the tyranny of the majority needs governing. When the majority uses its power to deny basic rights, I become an advocate for change. Often this has meant voting against what those who elected me want, particularly in the areas of Negro citizenship or the rights of women or religious freedom or Indian issues. I know that one person's views may be the product of ignorance or arrogance. But so may those of the majority."

Fredunes Harrison was carefully clearing the table as she pretended to be unaware of the conversation. Her husband, Nicy, had cooked the meal and remained in the kitchen. Fredunes knew that Judge Hovey had forbidden Mrs. Hovey from using Fredunes' sister, Mattie, who cleaned Rosa Hughes' place, due to the problem with Samson and Mrs. Daniels. Mattie had been helped out of Georgia and guided to Mt. Vernon by the Underground Railroad and she used her connections with the Underground Railroad to help Samson escape. But the judge was like many white people. He cared little about the family relationships of colored people. He had not made the connection with Fredunes and Mattie. Mrs. Hovey needed the help and she did not care to get involved in the gossip.

Fredunes could sense Mrs. Daniels' eyes following her, but Fredunes avoided looking her way. Fredunes knew that Samson and Rachel had fled due to Mr. Combs. She, also, knew the closely guarded secret that Mr. Morita Maier and Mr. Lowery had swiftly hidden Samson and Rachel in the false cistern at Mr. Lowery's Robin Hill home then moved them out of Indiana to Ohio through the Quaker's Underground Railroad. Fredunes was not sure how much of this Mrs. Daniels knew.

Fredunes planned to tell Mattie everything she could remember from the evening, although she had to make sure that Judge Pitcher did not catch her listening in. He was known as not liking slavery and not liking Negroes. And Fredunes sensed that even though the tall stranger and Judge Hovey spoke to Judge Pitcher respectfully, they seemed to differ from the Judge on the rights of colored people.

CHAPTER FORTY-SEVEN

PEACE IN THEIR TIME

"Mr. Owen, what has become of the plan you advanced to either give Negroes citizenship or ship them back to Africa? When Alvin wrote to me during the Convention he mentioned there was substantial support for the idea, at least among the northern counties. Of course, they are not inundated with freed or escaped coloreds. I was impressed by your ploy of tying the return to Liberia with a head tax. Your reliance on the average Hoosier's abhorrence for taxes was quite clever and almost worked. But I warned Alvin of your true purpose in proposing a tax. You expected your fellow representatives to be so afraid of paying for the return to Africa that they would opt for citizenship."

"Judge Pitcher, my plan was not for a 'return', as few of America's living Negroes were born there. I simply called for either citizenship here or citizenship there if any chose to go. As for the tax, my thought was if white men were so eager to avoid black people, a thirty-five cent tax per person was a reasonable expenditure. However, my friend Judge Hovey's eloquence kept the Convention from adopting either of my positions. I postulate that your advice to him was a strong factor. It would appear that even though you lost your bid to be elected as one of Posey County's representatives to the Convention, you still managed to help deny Negroes any chance for citizenship."

"Now, Robert Dale, do not suppose that I have no thoughts of my own. It is true that Judge Pitcher advised against both the Liberia tax scheme and citizenship for Negroes, but his opinions were in lockstep with virtually everyone's in Posey County. And, as Mr. Lincoln has pointed out, I see my role as a representative of the people who is for the people. Therefore, I had no choice."

"In Illinois, we had the same schisms, Abraham. Don't you remember how we would try to avoid any attempt to place us in one camp or the other when we rode the circuit? It was dangerous to come down on the wrong side in some of those little towns. In fact, one reason I left Illinois for Indiana, other than to win the heart of the lovely Juliette, of course, was because "Old Rough and Ready" died and the southern politicians were emboldened. President Taylor may have been a slave holder himself, but he would brook no movement towards secession. I fear Millard Fillmore is too pliable and Chief Justice Roger Taney interprets the Constitution as if he were holding court in his native Maryland. Come on, Abraham, favor this table with some of your sage legal analysis."

"Ah, William, you would have me unmask my pedestrian brain to this erudite assemblage. I thought you my friend. But, if the lovely Mary would not mind having my wine glass re-filled, I may foolishly take the bait. Thank you; Fredunes is it? Not too much now. I have found that my tongue is usually already too loose for my own good or for the forbearance of others.

"Anyway, so far as I understand the case before the Bar this evening, we have two issues: is government and the law that guides it to be one of true democracy where a majority always rules or is it better to let the majority have sway as long as it does not abuse those who are not a part of it?

"I must be ever mindful of my mentor, Judge Pitcher, and the sensibilities of others. However, with this long and vacillating opening statement, my argument to this august panel of eleven jurors would be that just as a benevolent dictator, or god, would be best, the conundrum is: how can we assure that the majority will be benevolent?

"In the noble experiment that is America, that safeguard is the separation of powers. Unfortunately, even our Founding Fathers could not find any gods to serve as executives or legislators or judges. And here I cite our present United States Supreme Court and Chief Justice Roger Taney.

"When Taney decided *Prigg v. Pennsylvania* in 1842, I sensed that the grand plan of separate but equal had failed; although there is a case involving a former resident of Illinois that is currently struggling its way through the federal court in St. Louis that may test Taney's mettle. A slave named Scott has sued for his freedom. I predict, based on the Missouri Compromise of 1820 and the Northwest Ordinance of 1789, that he will win.

"Now, William, see what you have done? The ladies are yawning and the gentlemen are shaking their heads at my ignorance."

Fredunes finally pulled her eyes off Mr. Lincoln and saw both Judge Pitcher and Mrs. Daniels staring at her. She hurried to put the wine decanter back on the sideboard then flew into the kitchen.

"Nicy, you must see dis man. Judge Hovey's fren, Mr. Lincoln, says somb slave is going ta be freed by somb judge. I's so excited I near dropped de wine. An he spoke ta me in front ob all dem big peoples. He membered my name. He spoke right at me an looked me right in de eye."

"Now, girl, you bes be keeping yourself on de groun. Ain't no white man going ta care who's you are. He's just showing out ta dem judges an sech."

"No, no, Nicy. He be somebody. He looked at me likes a real person. An dem others was jus as struck as me. De didn't say nuttin whiles he was talking. You's gots to sneak a peek ats him."

Nicy dried off his forehead and arms with a dishtowel. Then he grabbed the container of finger bowls and motioned for Fredunes to raise the dumbwaiter door that filled the opening between the kitchen and the dining room. As he pushed out the finger bowls filled with warm water and sprigs of peppermint from the herb garden, he ducked his head down to look at Mr. Lincoln who was peering right into Nicy's eyes. Lincoln nodded his head at Nicy who felt himself tremble.

Who was this man, he wondered. He appeared to actually see Nicy, not see through him as most white people did. Then Nicy felt the scornful gaze of Judge Pitcher and backed away from the opening.

"What's he mean a nigger going ta be freed by some judge? Judge Hovey?"

"Alls I heard was St. Louis and freedom. Mebbe Mattie wills know sumpin. Lordy, I wish she could see Mr. Lincoln. He be somebody."

"Abe," Judge Pitcher insisted on keeping Lincoln in his place, "you surely aren't suggesting that Negroes can be made citizens. The United States Constitution should have never sanctioned slavery, but it does not allow for Negro or Indian citizenship. Free the coloreds, but do not give them the right to bear arms or vote. I am against slavery because it is like trying to finance government through gambling. Citizens and businesses must not expect to get something for nothing. It is not the slave who concerns me but the slave owners. When we enslave others to do our own work, we lose our ability to innovate and succeed on our own. Slave owners are like those who try to live by games of chance. Something for nothing breeds nothing."

CHAPTER FORTY-EIGHT

THE HEAT OF BATTLE

PITCHER TURNED TOWARDS EPPIE AS he spoke to Robert Dale Owen. "Surely, Mr. Owen, you do not believe the Negro race could ever be equal to whites. What civilization in history was ever developed by Africans?"

Fanny had had enough. "And what of women, Judge? Can they not be educated? Are women to ever be citizens of America?"

"But women are citizens, Mrs. d'Arusmont. They live as full partners of their husbands. They are protected by the laws of curtesy and dower. They are protected by our male army from Indians and foreign invaders." And, while looking directly at Eppie, Pitcher said, "And they are protected from rogue niggers. Of course, some women flaunt the law and convention and have children out of wedlock and take up with niggers. But that is by choice not due to oppression by white men."

"I do not choose to be protected. I want to vote. I want to have the same rights as white men to live as I please with whom I please. And when it comes to white men being concerned with the dangers of truly freeing black men, I find they are often more concerned with possible liaisons with white women. That is the true reason Posey County refuses to allow Negro children to be educated with whites. And the true reason young Negroes are so often decried as shiftless or worse is they have no education and, therefore, few options to be anything else."

Judge Pitcher was surprised that a woman would speak up at a gathering of men, especially in a formal social setting. But he was aware of Mad Fanny's reputation and he had been present on July 4, 1828 in New Harmony when Frances Wright made America's first formal and public address by a woman to an audience composed of both men and women.

Pitcher was, also, surprised to be talked to so boldly in front of Lincoln and Hovey whom he still managed to control by understanding their deep seated need to succeed. On the other hand, this large woman seemed to relish the opportunity to be ostracized. But Fanny's health prevented her from continuing her exposition of Pitcher's misogyny. She wanted to attack, but she needed to rest.

Mary Hovey reveled in Fanny's put down of Judge Pitcher. During her six years of marriage to Alvin she had come to realize that Pitcher had his thumb up against Alvin's political jugular. Abraham had managed to escape because he lived far away, but Hovey remained subject to Pitcher's pernicious control. But Mad Fanny was fearless and brilliant; too bad she was not a man.

Fredunes, too, could not believe that a woman would speak up at dinner much less take on Judge Pitcher. Fredunes knew Judge Pitcher disdained women and coloreds. But his views on Negroes were colored by greed. Fredunes and Nicy knew that Pitcher wanted the colored people and the prostitutes out of Belleville. Pitcher owned land right on the Ohio Riverfront near property owned by Mt. Vernon's first Negro property owner, who was Nicy Harrison. Pitcher had tried to buy that property, which consisted of two lots. But it had been owned by Morita Maier, and he let Nicy buy the two lots on contract. Nicy and

Fredunes planned to pass the lots on to their first born son, Daniel, now that he was married and had baby Jane.

Pitcher owned the land from the corner of Sawmill and Water Streets down to McFadin's Creek and the river. Nicy owned lots 28 and 29 of the Kimball Enlargement to Mt. Vernon. Harrison's lots were separated by Elm Street and were at the southwest and southeast corners of Second and Elm. Over the years, the names of First, Water and sometimes, Second streets, had become garbled and confused. One had to refer to the descriptions in the deeds for the lots in Belleville to know for sure who owned what.

Pitcher had plans to develop the area for wealthy whites, but he refused to pay money to Negroes because he did not believe they should have the right to own property in Indiana. He was ever alert to some means of taking Negro property through the courts via tax sales or other liens. Pitcher despised Nicy and Fredunes for standing in his way.

CHAPTER FORTY-NINE

SABRE RATTLING

HOVEY COULD SENSE THE DINNER table camaraderie disintegrating. "Now, ladies and gentlemen, let none of us play the role of Old Hickory in ending the Era of Good Feeling. I suggest that we ask young Captain Pitcher about his experiences in the Mexican War. Abraham and Mr. Harrow and I admire your courage and envy your time in battle. Of course, just speaking for myself, I am glad to have escaped your wounds.

"How is your leg, Thomas? We know from your letters home to the Judge that you were in the thick of the fight at Buena Vista. Was that not when you won your early promotion to First Lieutenant?"

"Judge, you flatter me with your plaudits. I was but one of many in that war. And as for battlefield promotions, there was a fellow West Pointer who rose from major to lieutenant colonel to colonel in the space of three engagements. The civilian world will never hear of him, but Robert E. Lee of Virginia was the most honored officer of the war except, of course, for General Taylor.

"Lee graduated from the Academy in 1829, twelve years before I started there. But he was famous among the cadets even when I attended because he never received a demerit. Unfortunately, I cannot claim that distinction. Lee would be an excellent choice to lead the Army. However, my understanding is that he has resigned his commission and returned to his family plantation.

"As for me, it was my high honor to serve directly under the command of Zachary Taylor whose brilliance and bravery carried the day at Buena Vista. My immediate superior was another West Pointer from Kentucky, a man named Jefferson Davis who graduated in 1828. Davis was as brave as any officer, but he was of a kind and forgiving nature. He wanted to allow the Mexicans to share Texas. His position was not appreciated by President Polk.

"The West Pointer who appeared to be the most aggressive was a man from Ohio who attended the Academy when I did. He graduated in 1843. He was the son of a tanner from Ohio, but he was a true student of military strategy. He and I often talked of the Roman siege tactics under Julius Caesar. His name is Ulysses Grant. I do not know what became of him after the war."

"Thomas, did you know that Mr. Harrow was born in Kentucky as I was? And President Taylor was born in Virginia, but raised in Kentucky? Now you tell me your fellow West Pointer, Mr. Davis, was, also, born in Kentucky. I believe that when Mr. Davis was a captain during the Black Hawk War of 1832 he gave me my oath. I remember his military bearing and his gentle manner. The two did not seem to mesh. Of course, I never saw battle and that has been a deep regret. On the other hand, I might have run as soon as the Indians attacked. After all, my grandfather, Abraham Lincoln for whom I am named, was killed by Indians before I was born."

"Now, Abe, I do not remember you running from any fights in Spencer County. In fact, you were known as the best scrapper in the area. Other young men learned to give you a wide berth. I do not think you would have been found wanting in battle. And I remember how you studied Weems' *Life of George Washington* and Washington's military strategy. You have a ready grasp of military matters. Fortunately for all of us, the saber rattling over secession has been put to rest. But if the South were to secede, what do you gentlemen think would be the outcome, a good war or a bad peace? What say you, Abe?"

"I campaigned for Old Rough and Ready because of his position on secession. He believed as I do, that the Union must be held together by any means, including force. The United States must remain united. And, if that means we will have to permanently have some slavery, then we must accept that. Eventually, slavery will most likely die of natural economic causes. That is preferable to our country dying in an attempt to end it earlier.

"But, Judge, that does not address your question. From a military standpoint I believe the Mississippi River is the key. When I took flatboats to New Orleans to sell goods, I noted the high bluffs at Vicksburg, Mississippi. That point reminded me of what George Washington did at West Point, New York on the Hudson River. General Washington had his headquarters near West Point at Newburgh, New York. To control access to the interior of the country he had a huge chain installed across the Hudson. The South may have the same opportunity at Vicksburg. Although a chain would be impractical, military installations might work to keep out Northern armies and keep Southern supply lanes open. In that event the North would have to pray for a Southern Benedict Arnold to sell the plans."

"Speaking of George Washington, Mr. Jones' father who was Posey County's first white settler, personally knew both William Henry Harrison and Thomas Posey who served under Washington. Mr. Jones' father, Tom Jones, ran a trading post near the confluence of the Ohio and Wabash rivers during the time that Harrison served as the Territorial Governor of the Northwest Territory and later when Posey served as Governor of the Illinois Territory between 1816 and 1818. Perhaps Mr. Jones can enlighten us on the salacious rumors about Thomas Posey being the child of George Washington. When you enter my courtroom you will see portraits of both Washington and Posey. They do bear a striking resemblance. May we have the benefit of your knowledge, Mr. Jones?"

"Judge Hovey, all my father ever told me about General Posey was that his family lived next to Washington's home of Mt. Vernon for which our Mt. Vernon was renamed in 1825. Washington did keep an unusually close watch on young Posey's military and political career. However, President Washington never acknowledged any children, including Posey. And as we know, portrait painters are not above trying to make a profit from the image of the Father of Our Country. Many figures of that time were flattered to be made to resemble Washington.

"But, I have a question. Now that the talk of civil war is past, what will be done about the Indians? Will we follow Old Hickory's method of taking Indian leaders such as Oceola prisoner under a flag of truce? Can we keep pushing the Indians west until we drive them into the sea?"

"Now, Henry, surely you would not want those savages to keep us from God's plan. It is a sin to let land lie fallow. The Indians nether plant nor sow, they do not deserve the land. Perhaps your impressions were formed in Vincennes where you and the Shawnee, Christian Willis, tried to bring the savages to Jesus. I see even he gave up and is now outside of Mt. Vernon in Brewery Hills trying to redeem Negroes. I am curious about what happened to that young squaw I saw you with in Vincennes a few years ago. Just what was your interest in her?"

"Oh, Judge Pitcher, I had no interest in her. And I am not concerned for the Indians. I am a white man. My concern is what plans our government has for western expansion. Not much has happened in this area since Lewis and Clark stopped here almost fifty years ago."

Henry Jones could tell that Judge Pitcher was trying to drag him into a conversation about Soaring Bird. Henry had long ago accepted his loss due to his fear of being labeled either an Indian or an Indian lover. He did not plan to also lose his reputation and business interest. He regretted bringing up the Indian issue.

"But one thing that has happened in Mt. Vernon is the rapid development of industry. My company, the Pittsburgh Coal Company, has grown at a phenomenal pace due to such businesses as Mr. Daniels' farm implement company. Can you tell us, Mr. Daniels, now that the war tocsin is no longer sounding, how do the prospects for Posey County's development look?"

George did not care to share his business information and predictions at such an open social event. He and his cousin, William Combs, were doing far better than most people would have guessed. They had experienced a near collapse when George came upon Samson beating William. William had at first accused Samson of attacking Eppie. But when Eppie said Samson was just trying to save Eppie from William, William told George that he had just been trying to spare George's feelings. He said the ugly truth was he had caught Eppie and Samson in a compromising position. As George tried to sort out the truth, William took George's loaded shotgun down from its place over the mantle and pointed it towards Samson. George did not want to believe William, but the seed of doubt had been planted. George remembered that at Nashoba Samson and Eppie had shown feelings for one another.

George, also, feared that William would either expose Eppie for the escaped Inola or that he might have George ridiculed because his wife had taken up with a Negro. George could see his entire life unraveling if he acted on Eppie's accusations against William. Surely William would never again dare to accost Eppie. It would be simpler to just let Samson and Rachel flee. George told them to immediately get their things and head for Robin Hill. William was threatening to shoot Samson or hold him for the Sheriff. But George just wanted the problem to disappear. A shooting or a lynching or, at the worst, a court trial, would just bring contumely upon George and Eppie. And the entire fraud upon which their lives were based would likely be exposed. George chose expediency over an exposé. It would be better to avoid embarrassment.

Of course, it seemed extremely unlikely that Samson would have assaulted Eppie in Rachel's presence. And when George arrived, Rachel was there trying to stop Samson from killing William. She and Samson must have, as Eppie told George, arrived together and just in time to save Eppie.

The problem for George with these facts was that he would have to go against William in a public forum. So George just took the shotgun from William and threatened to kill him if he told anyone about Eppie and Samson or interfered with their escape.

But on their way to Robin Hill, Samson and Rachel ran into Fredunes' sister, Mattie, who was told the whole story as they hurried to Robin Hill.

William had successfully played Iago to George's Othello. Although George loved Eppie and trusted her, she was his entire frame of reference in sexual matters. And from the beginning Eppie had been needier than George. Perhaps he had not been enough for her or had ignored her desires. George did not trust William, but he could not accept that his cousin and business partner would attack his wife then tell a lie that could get an innocent person lynched.

It was easier to let Samson and Rachel escape than confront the possibilities posed by believing Eppie. Besides, George had the eighty dollars Samson and Rachel had entrusted to him. Fairness dictated that George keep the money for the loss of their services.

"Henry, you are correct about the promising future Posey County has. My business has prospered thanks to low taxes and a state and local government that encourage business. But I am sure the ladies have had enough of this talk of war, politics and business. About the only subject we have neglected is religion and I, for one, am grateful for that omission. For now, Mrs. Daniels and I must regretfully take our leave. Thank you all. It has been a unique evening and, Mrs. Hovey, your dinner was superb."

After all their guests but Lincoln had made their exits, Mary, Alvin and Abraham moved to the parlor as Fredunes and Nicy cleared the table.

"Well, Mary, you set a fine table of food, wine and interesting guests. Maybe Alvin and I should stroll down the hill to the river. Do you mind if we leave the real work to you?"

"Abraham, you and Alvin are men; I would be surprised at any other course of action."

CHAPTER FIFTY

AN EVENING WALK

THE CRISP OCTOBER AIR WAS invigorating as Abraham and Alvin walked south along Walnut Street towards the Ohio River. The smaller golden raintrees on the north side of the courthouse glowed in the moonlight that filtered through their bushy limbs. On the southeast corner of the campus long ghostly shadows appeared as the full moon shone upon the locust trees.

"The great LaFayette planted one of those raintrees a quarter of a century ago. Robert Owen helped set these locust trees at the same time. I was only four years old then, but it would have been grand to see the Hero of the Revolution and Robert Dale's father. He was a man who believed in and lived the principles of the Enlightenment. Have we turned backwards from the Age of Reason to religion and superstition?"

"Why, Alvin, I did not hear such sentiments in front of Judge Pitcher. Of course, you will quickly point out that my lips oozed platitudes as well. We both continue to hedge our bets. Perhaps Americans will some day treat the Bible as a helpful compilation of the myths and legends of various Semites and the ancient Greeks. But, for now, why should we try to swim against the current? Would it help America to be the secular nation Thomas Jefferson envisioned? Does it hurt anyone for you and me to mouth the words that our constituents are comfortable with?"

"I see no harm in hypocrisy as long as we are not fooling ourselves. As community leaders, we can garner more support for secular goals if those who look to us for guidance think we believe as they do on religious matters. I suppose it is a little like drinking from the poisoned well. On the other hand, until the general population becomes educated in matters of science, superstition can be used by religious and political figures to flimflam and confuse. Our role is to work from the inside. We will do no one, especially ourselves, any good to point out the mote in the public's eye.

"Take my role as judge. What kind of general acceptance would my decisions receive in this small county if people did not think of me as a moral man? And for most Americans, morality and their particular religious beliefs coincide."

"Alvin, your courthouse looks a little worn even by moonlight. How old is it? And these locust trees are still young, but they are already hiding your courthouse from view."

"This courthouse was built in 1825, but, as with most things done at the local level, it was done as cheaply as possible. It will not be long until it will be an impediment to the administration of justice. I have already floated the idea of replacing it. If I ever convince our shortsighted County Commissioners and Council to act, I will probably have to issue a court order to both preserve the trees and provide for adequate space for all the county offices. I will most likely let some future brave-hearted judge fight that battle, for as you well know, the right judicial decision is often an unpopular judicial decision. And I do owe it to Mary and Esther to remain employed.

"You will note that the courthouse looks large, but only the court can fit in it. All the other county offices are in these surrounding shacks. Of course, the original 1825 log jail has had a stone and iron addition put on in 1845. It seems the public will always support money to lock up people. That is our jail right between the courthouse and the locust trees. It is eerie to see the shadows cast over the jail by the moonlight."

"Alvin, you are certainly right about the fickle nature of the public. I plan to never get involved in politics again. But if I somehow forget my own sage counsel in this regard, I will take no more stands on any controversial issues, including public building projects and religion.

"Dear friend, I treasure this time with you more than you know. Who else thinks on these matters as you and I? Maybe there are many fellow travelers, but I have found none in whom I can confide. I do wonder how such men as Jefferson and Adams and Madison could have devised their system of checks and balances if they truly believed the religious dogma they often expressed. If they truly believed that some omnipotent deity was in charge, why would they even worry about a Constitution? But they, as we, were captives of a superstitious majority. They had to make a nod to God or get nothing accomplished. Of course, the same is true of the slavery issue. They took what they could get and still end up with a country. We must do the same."

Sketches courtesy of Anne Doane

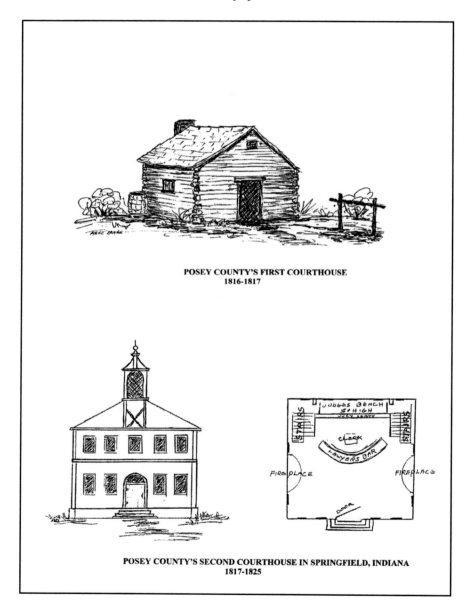

POSEY COUNTY'S FIRST COURTHOUSE
1816-1817

POSEY COUNTY'S SECOND COURTHOUSE IN SPRINGFIELD, INDIANA
1817-1825

First Courthouse at Mt. Vernon, Indiana, 1825-1876. Sketch courtesy of Anne Doane. Copied from a painting by Karl Bodmer (1834) by permission of The Joslyn Art Museum, Omaha, Nebraska.

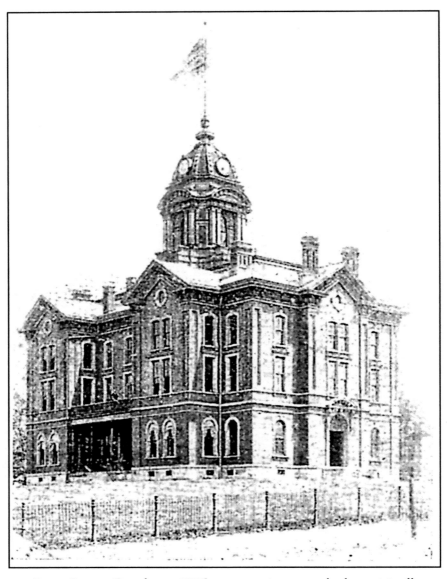

Posey County Courthouse 1876-present as it appeared when originally built and after the locust trees had died.

Photographs courtesy of Becky Boggs

Contemporary view of the Posey Circuit Courtroom facing the Judge's Bench

View from the Judge's Bench

Robin Hill, Mt. Vernon, IN

Brewery Hills School/Church
Sketch courtesy of Anne Doane

Photographs by Peg Redwine

Hovey House (Col. Gustavus & Esther Menzies' Home)

Former Hovey Home

Photographs by Rodney A. Fetcher & RAF Productions

Location of Daniel Harrison, Sr.'s Home (Second & Elm, Mt. Vernon, IN)

Old Black Church, Third Street, Mt. Vernon, IN

Nooses from the 1878 lynchings; currently on display at the Posey County Jail

Order Books

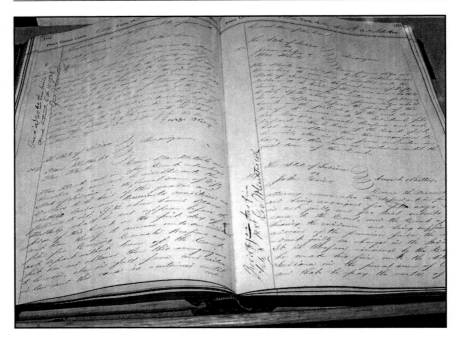

Sample entries in Order Book

Black Odd Fellows Cemetery, Mt. Vernon, IN

Alvin P. Hovey

William F. Parrett, Jr.

William Harrow

West Point Museum Art Collection,
United States Military Academy, West Point, NY

Thomas Gamble Pitcher

Frances Wright

From the collections of the Indiana State Museum And Historic Sites

Robert Dale Owen

Marie-Joseph Paul Yves Roch Gilbert du Motier, Marquis de LaFayette

Thomas Posey

Photograph by Peg Redwine

Giggy Family Sugar & Creamer Set resting on a doily crocheted by Agnes Giggy

John Giggy, Co. H, 44th Ind. Vol. Infantry

CHAPTER FIFTY-ONE

STRANGE FRUIT

HOVEY HAD HURRIEDLY CAUGHT THE train back to Mt. Vernon from Indianapolis as soon as he heard of the lynchings. He knew that his future and Posey County's reputation could well depend on how the matter was handled. When Hovey first heard the bits and pieces of the story, his understanding was that one or two Negroes had been lynched by some friends of a white prostitute who had complained of a sexual assault.

Hovey's initial reaction was outrage that the law had been by-passed by this group of hooligans. He certainly did not condone sexual assaults even on prostitutes, but the law was in place to punish such actions. He planned to make sure that swift action was taken against what he had assumed was a small handful of ne'er-do-wells who had taken matters into their own hands.

When he got back to Mt. Vernon and was told by Gustavus Menzies that two or three hundred white men may have been involved in the killing of as many as seven Negroes, he was overwhelmed. Menzies and Hovey's daughter, Esther, had been in Evansville that Friday and Saturday visiting Menzies' family. But when they returned Sunday night, October the 13th, Menzies had learned that the mob contained many of the prominent men of the county. The mob had broken into the jail and lynched at least four Negro men. Menzies told Hovey that according to Morita Maier there may have been three more black men murdered.

Hovey had managed to arrive after dark on Sunday, October 13, 1878, but that night sleep eluded him. He found himself compelled to carefully slip out of his daughter's home and cross Walnut Street to the courthouse campus where the boys had so recently been hanging.

After Mary had died in 1863, Hovey could not bear living in the home on the northwest corner of Fourth and Walnut Streets that Mary and he had loved so much. So in 1871 he bought the one year old home on the southeast corner of Fourth and Walnut and gave it to Esther and her husband, Gustavus Menzies. He sold his old home to his Masonic brethren to be their new lodge and lived with the Menzies.

Menzies had served under Hovey in the War and they now practiced law together. The home served as their law office as it was just across the street from the courthouse with its large locust trees. The golden raintrees had died in the winter ice storm of 1863. Hovey was not superstitious, but he did think it apropos that the raintrees Mary had loved so much went out when she did. The fifty-seven year old Hovey often reflected on how much of his life had been connected to this small geographic area.

He had read for the law under Judge John Pitcher whose home and office was only a block west of the courthouse. Hovey had practiced law and been judge in the 1825 courthouse. He had been instrumental in getting the new courthouse built. He had spent much of his adult life living at the intersection of these two streets, Fourth and Walnut, and working at the two courthouses.

Years later when Judge John Eagleson, who was an Elk and whose father had been a Mason, began to study Posey County's history, he found it interesting that Posey County's favorite son's two homes had been so closely affiliated with the Elks, the Masons and Posey County's government. Hovey's home with Mary had housed the first Masonic Lodge in Posey County before the Masons sold it to the Elks Lodge. After Hovey died, Esther and Gus Menzies sold their home to the Masons who moved across the intersection. And in 1995, the "Hovey House", as it was called, was sold by the Masons to Posey County. The county uses it to house the Prosecuting Attorney's office and the meeting rooms for both the County Commissioners and County Council.

As Hovey crossed onto the courthouse campus that October evening in 1878, he thought back to his last walk with Lincoln. What was it Lincoln had said as they watched the moonlight make long shadows from the locust trees? So much had changed between that October of 1852 and this October. His Mary was dead. Lincoln was dead. Frances Wright was dead. Hovey was thankful that Robert Dale Owen had died in 1877 before he could remind Hovey of the different positions they had taken on Negro rights at the Constitutional Convention. Had Robert Dale's predictions been right? Had Indiana's failure to protect the rights of Negroes in the 1852 Constitution led to this catastrophe? Of more concern to Hovey was his realization that his political expediency a quarter of a century earlier may well lead to the demise of his political future. How was he going to survive the inevitable fallout from this tragedy of seven Negroes murdered in one October week? He was thankful that he had been out of the county on business when the vigilantes decided to act, but it was almost certain that he would be drawn into the vortex of the aftermath.

Hovey suspected that he knew most of the white men who were involved. Judge William F. Parrett, Jr., the current Posey Circuit Court

Judge, had to suspect who the ringleaders were. And Hovey had been told that John Leffel, who published the *Western Star* newspaper and Tom Collins the editor of the *Mt. Vernon Democrat*, had been eyewitnesses and even interviewed the men just before they were murdered. Leffel's photographer, Mr. Jones, had photographed the hanging bodies just a few hours after the lynchings. It was likely the Coroner's Jury that Judge Parrett had ordered Coroner William Hendricks to immediately impanel to investigate the deaths contained members of the mob. Hovey appreciated Parrett's quick thinking. It was better to start appearing to be vigorously responding locally than delaying things until the state or federal government got involved.

Hovey had been told by Menzies that Prosecuting Attorney William Gudgel, and Sheriff John Wheeler, were already urging Judge Parrett to keep the rape charges pending against William Chambers, Jim Good, Ed Hill and Jeff Hopkins and the murder charges pending against Daniel Harrison, Sr., even though they had all been lynched or cut into pieces. This would allow the focus to be returned to the misdeeds of the Negroes whenever questions were raised about the lynchings. Although their public argument to Judge Parrett was that by keeping the charges active it would allow for a more thorough and comprehensive investigation. Parrett had already announced that a regular Grand Jury would soon be impaneled to, "thoroughly investigate the lynchings."

Hovey wished that the group of white men who had hired Ed Hayes to lead a vigilante committee had kept their mouths shut. William Combs had been so proud of this move to handle the Negro problem that he encouraged Leffel to publish it in the newspaper along with his running editorial comments about how Sheriff John Wheeler should rid the town of the colored scourge by whatever means it took. Hovey was aware that there had been several recent reports of colored men committing serious crimes. He noted that most of these reports had not resulted in convictions in court. Hovey did not think it coincidental that Rosa Hughes and her girls were the source of most complaints.

Hovey knew that Combs and Hughes still had close business connections even though Combs had turned his personal attention to Rosa's young prostitute, Emma Davis. Apparently, Hughes had given up on her long held dream of a legitimate relationship with Combs when he had married a few years back. Or maybe she just put up with the new arrangement for financial reasons but still secretly clung to her vain hopes.

Hovey had wondered about Combs and Hughes since the incident involving Combs, Eppie Daniels and the Negro, Samson Wright. He remembered that Rosa Hughes had been a prime instigator in riling up public sentiment against the colored community then.

Hovey could not escape his memory of his own failings. He had realized that he was choosing the easy path during the Constitutional Convention. There were men such as Robert Dale Owen who had warned then that denying Negroes their full rights of citizenship might lead to war. Owen, also, had foreseen that if whites continued to treat blacks as less than human, their resentment of their status would inevitably lead to violence. But Hovey's fear of Judge Pitcher's veiled threats to bring down Hovey's career coupled with his own deep sense of inferiority kept Hovey in his place.

But what was Hovey to do now? Perhaps he should have taken the path of the harder right then, but he did not see how trying to change history would help anyone. How could you imprison or hang two to three hundred men? The entire county would be devastated by such an approach. Besides, where would the blame stop? How could justice be served by selecting some for punishment and ignoring the involvement of the rest? With two or three hundred men taking part, it was likely that practically every family of Posey County's twenty thousand residents had some friend or relative involved.

What would Abraham say? What would he do? Hovey thought back to their mutual understanding about their political cowardice. But Abraham had set aside his fears and acted in spite of his sure knowledge of the cost to him. Could Hovey find such courage? What was it Abraham had said as they had walked this same walk that October so many lifetimes ago? "What good would it do?" Wasn't that what Abraham said? Wasn't he right back then? Wouldn't he counsel Hovey the same way today? What good would it do the dead men for Hovey to sacrifice his career? What good did it do Lincoln to ignore his own cautionary advice?

It seemed clear to Hovey that the "right thing" was impossible. There was no practical way to determine the identity and degree of involvement of everyone who contributed to the week's mayhem. And if the legal system selected just a few to be the scapegoats, would that not be just another form of lynching?

Of course, if the murdered men had been white, the county would find some way to punish several of the ringleaders and compensate the victim's families. But there was no need to be concerned about the Negro community. They were impotent to demand either punishment or compensation. Besides, there had been numerous complaints that the dead men had committed serious crimes against white people in general and white women in particular.

Hovey concluded that, although he hated the violations of the law by the mob, the best approach would be to ignore the mob's actions and apply the method that usually worked for those in power, blame the victims.

Hovey decided the first thing that needed to be done was to talk to the people who had the most to lose from an independent investigation. Hovey knew the most important thing was public opinion. If momentum towards an unbiased accounting got started, there might be no stopping it. Then Hovey would be forced to choose between the law and his political supporters. The best thing would be to avoid that disaster. For that to occur, the control of public sentiment was paramount. The key to controlling public sentiment was the newspapers. Since John Leffel had publicly called for the hanging of Jim Good just a few days before Good was lynched, Hovey had little doubt Leffel would be amenable to suggestions as would the bombastic editor of the *Democrat*, Tom Collins.

And while Hovey thought that Judge Parrett had a good legal mind, he, also, knew that Parrett was not likely to delve too deeply into matters that could derail his judgeship or cause him to lose popular support. After all, during the War, Parrett had no trouble ignoring the law and imprisoning Confederate soldiers because of public pressure. The Confederates had performed a raid into Posey County in 1862 and should have been treated as prisoners of war and turned over to the authority of the federal government. But Parrett succumbed to popular opinion in Posey County and tried them in his own court. It took the intervention of Governor Morton in his role as Provost Marshall of Indiana to have the soldiers released from the Posey County jail.

On the other hand, Parrett had managed to get done what Hovey could not when he was judge. He had convinced the other county officials and the public that the fifty year old courthouse had needed to be replaced. In fact, the beautiful new courthouse that Hovey had been honored to lay the first brick for had just opened for business ten months before the lynchings.

As for Parrett, he appeared willing to do whatever it took to maintain his position and accomplish his goals. Hovey was confident that

Parrett would not stand in the way of a practical approach to the current problem.

CHAPTER FIFTY-TWO

SEPARATE OR EQUAL

JUDGE JOHN EAGLESON WAS NOT a superstitious man. He did not believe that his life had been planned for him. He did not believe that good and evil were competing entities. He did think that much of what was detrimental to the world was brought about by the superstitions of others.

Therefore, he found it disquieting when his thoughts turned to the possibility that his old courthouse was drawing him into the events of 1878. He had occasionally wondered about how he came to be the judge in this place. But until he had begun to read Judge Parrett's entries in the long missing Order Book, he had concluded his life was just a series of colliding coincidences.

Eagleson had always silently disdained those people who arrogated themselves to be children of destiny. It took a lot of egocentrism for someone to believe supernatural forces had taken a personal interest in them. So Eagleson had tried to dispel his own uneasiness by denying it existed.

That had worked to overcome his initial reaction when he first opened the old Order Book. However, as he continued to read Parrett's entries and the newspaper accounts of the murders and the cover-up, he could not shake the notion that somehow he was being called upon by someone or something. These feelings intensified when he worked alone at night at the same massive oak desk in the same third story chamber that Judge Parrett had sat at in 1878.

Eagleson had always enjoyed exploring the old courthouse by himself. He would rummage through the dungeon-like basement or take the rickety old stairs up into the attic of the dome. Over the years he had been startled from time to time by eerie sounds, but he had always been able to laugh at his reactions. It was a lot like when he had been a child alone in church.

Occasionally when he was young his mother or father, who were elders in the church, would send Eagleson in to get a hymnal or some other item. Eagleson remembered how the hair on his neck would rise when he saw the stained glass windows and heard the wooden floors creak. He always walked in to the church, but often ran out once he had accomplished his mission. He sometimes thought back to his silliness when he returned to his hometown and attended church services.

Even before Eagleson started to study the old Order Book he had often been struck by the similarity between the old brick church building of his childhood with its basement rooms, large sanctuary and balcony and his brick courthouse with its catacombs, large courtroom and balcony.

Eagleson remembered how proud his mother had been that the first, and only, time black people had been allowed in his church was for his father's funeral. American society in general may have pushed aside the memory of those "separate but equal" days, but Eagleson's family made it a point to remember.

Separate schools, separate restrooms, separate restaurants, separate seating, separate rights, were a vivid memory for Eagleson from his childhood in the southwest. He still remembered how he and the rest of his high school football team had gone hungry after Friday night games because their coaches refused to leave their three black players on the bus while everyone else went in to a restaurant to eat.

Eagleson's father had grown up poor and he easily related to colored people. He had stood up for them and they wanted to show their respect by attending his funeral. Eagleson's mother had to get permission from the church board for them to come in the back door and sit in the balcony. Eagleson remembered thinking it was just like the local picture show where black people could pay the same price for a ticket but could only sit in the balcony.

Eagleson had not given much thought to segregation when he was living with it. He had noted that his parents helped colored people with paperwork or gifts of food or money, but no colored people ever came to their home nor to any other white person's home except to care for white children, clean or do yard work. Now as Eagleson read about the events of 1878 that occurred in the northern state of Indiana he was struck by the de facto segregation that had been as strictly enforced as the dejure segregation he had grown up with.

Eagleson's father's family had served in the Confederacy under the South's only Indian general, Stand Watie, who was a Cherokee. Eagleson's father's family had settled in Indian Territory long before the Civil War. When the War broke out, they joined with many whites and Indians to oppose the federal forces. The ideology in Indian Territory had more to do with being left alone than either slavery or states rights.

On the other hand, Eagleson's mother's family had come from Indiana and was staunchly pro-Union. Eagleson remembered much good natured bantering between his loving parents over the righteousness of the Blue or the Gray.

Eagleson's only connection with Indiana before moving there had been through his great grandmother, Agnes, whose father had fought for the North. She would try to tell young Eagleson about the old war hero, but he was not interested. Of course, now he wished he had paid attention.

Eagleson did remember that his great-great grandfather was from LaGrange, Indiana. Eagleson's mother, Clarice, had told him many stories about Indiana and her family with its long tradition of military service. Eagleson's first American relative on his mother's side was Benedict Giggy from Berne, Switzerland. Benedict had served as a professional soldier for twenty-one years before bringing his family to America.

Benedict's son, John, settled in LaGrange, Indiana and worked as a stonemason and farmer before and after the War. John Giggy was the man in whose memory his mother had named him. And, when John Eagleson settled close to Evansville, Indiana his mother excitedly reminded him that John Giggy had been hospitalized there after he was wounded at Shiloh on April 6, 1862.

Eagleson's mother was convinced that everything that happened was somehow God's will. She claimed to be spiritual, not superstitious. Although John loved his mother, he did not see a distinction in those beliefs. Regardless of what John thought about the reasons for his ending up in Posey County, Indiana his mother saw this as a circle of life. John was returning to his family's roots.

And when John was elected Posey County's judge, his mother knew there was a special reason for this unlikely occurrence. To commemorate this auspicious event, at the first Christmas after his election, his mother passed on to John the only objects she had that were directly connected to the Civil War hero, John Giggy.

That Christmas morning she had waited until just the two of them were in the den by the Christmas tree. "Johnny, I want to pass on to you my most treasured possessions from my family. Your great-great-great grandfather, Benedict Giggy, brought these, and almost nothing else, from Switzerland to America. He bought them in Germany for his bride. Your great-great-great grandmother gave them to her son John Giggy when he got married. Then, your great-great grandfather, John Giggy, who was from LaGrange, Indiana, gave these to your great grandmother on her wedding day. She gave them to my mother on her wedding day and my mother gave them to me when your Dad and I got married. I have never been able to give them up before. But I know now why I have held on to them. You are here for a reason and these were meant for you. When you moved here your great-great grandfather came to me in a dream and asked me to make sure you received them. This photograph of him as an old man in his Civil War uniform looks just like you will look someday. I want you to have it too. It is the only picture we have of him"

John had done his best to keep the cynicism out of his voice. The women in his mother's family had often claimed they had special abilities to connect with the past and foresee the future when it involved their family. John figured this illogical behavior was both innocuous and entertaining so he had never disrespected these women he loved by voicing his opinions. Now that all three of them were gone he was glad he had, for once, kept his superior wisdom to himself.

"Mom, you seem pretty serious about this. What items are you talking about? Grandpa Giggy didn't leave some gold double eagles by any chance, did he?"

"Now, quit it, Johnny. This is important to me and should be important to you. It will now be your duty to safeguard these precious connections to our family's history so they can be passed on. I feel strongly that Great Grandfather Giggy wants you to have them."

Eagleson's mother had carefully opened the small cedar chest and slowly removed the cream and sugar holder set. Eagleson would have preferred the double eagles or even a Civil War sword, but it appeared that his only current connections to his great-great grandfather were to be his mother and these old dishes. He tried to act enthusiastic and appreciative, but his mother was not placated.

"Johnny, I know you do not share my beliefs about these matters. But keep these things close to you and someday they may mean as much to you as they do to me. I do know in my heart that there is a reason your Great-Great Grandfather Giggy wants you to have them. Look closely at his photograph; you can connect with him if you give yourself a chance.

"There used to be an old newspaper clipping with the dishes but it's gone now. When we would visit her, your great grandmother used to have me read it to her over and over the last year or so before she died. She had asked your grandmother and me to place the clipping in her casket when she died. Of course, we honored her wishes and she was buried with it between her crossed hands. I should have made a copy of it, but I didn't think of it until it was too late."

CHAPTER FIFTY-THREE

CREAM AND SUGAR

EAGLESON CAREFULLY LIFTED THE SMALL cedar chest from the shelf in the dusty attic. After his mother had died he had not wanted to be reminded of his loss each time he saw it on the fireplace mantel. So, he had wrapped it in one of the doilies his great grandmother had crocheted and stored it away. But on this anniversary of the hangings he felt a need to connect with his family.

Earlier that day he had been the invited speaker at a joint meeting of the Posey County Kiwanis and Chamber of Commerce Clubs. He was frequently asked to speak to clubs and schools simply because he was the Posey Circuit Court judge. No one expected him to be particularly witty or entertaining. He was usually invited to fill an obligatory speaking slot, often as a last resort, when a real speaker had canceled. Eagleson knew if he just told an opening joke and ended by thanking the group, he could give the same speech he had given for twenty years.

But this time Eagleson had been excited to be asked to speak. Tom Hanson had given him the 1878 Order Book just a week before and Eagleson was filled with the enthusiasm of new discovery. He was sure the business leaders would be amazed to hear of the incredible events of October 1878.

As Eagleson had never heard of the lynchings, he assumed this was information that had been lost to history. Posey County would want to expiate this dark chapter. On the other hand, this would not be the first time a community had used a shameful event from its past to become a tourist attraction. Salem, Massachusetts had made an entire industry out of its treatment of witches. And in southern Illinois just across the Wabash River to the west, the Old Slave House with its slave quarters and "Big Buck Bob's breeding room" was proudly on display for "donations".

The community leaders were constantly decrying the need for economic development. Here was an opportunity for Posey County to both do the right thing and turn a profit. Eagleson thought that he had discovered what every small town was looking for, fame and fortune through its unique history.

One of the first things Eagleson had done after reading the 1878 Order Book was to go out to the new Posey County jail and talk to the sheriff. Years before he had seen four hangman's nooses displayed in the artifact cases in the outer office of the jail. But then no one knew where they had come from. Most people assumed that many years ago some bored inmate had just tied them as a hobby and left them with a past sheriff. Now Eagleson believed they were the only remaining direct connection to the lynchings. Eagleson decided to go all out and use the nooses as props for his speech.

There had been a large crowd there for the noontime joint meeting. There were many of Eagleson's friends and political supporters as well as a few of his implacable enemies in the group. Over the years not everyone had found his decisions to be Justinian.

But, for once, Eagleson was so excited about the prospects for doing well and making good that he had pushed all other cares away. This could lead to real changes in the declining economic and cultural environment of Posey County and maybe make him a folk hero to boot.

Judge Eagleson had been introduced to polite applause and low expectations. Several of the audience had taken note of the four nooses he had hung over the chalkboard in the front of the room. Eagleson planned to point out to the assembly that they were meeting in the basement of the Elks Lodge that had once been Alvin P. Hovey's home. And they were just across the street from Hovey's daughter's old home and, most significantly, less than one hundred yards from where Old Dan Harrison was butchered and four men were lynched.

It was a serendipitous confluence of the anniversary of the lynchings, the Order Book, nooses, locations and an audience of shakers and movers. Eagleson just knew his personal and political stock was about to rise.

After Eagleson told his joke, he pointed to the nooses and asked if anyone in the audience had ever heard about the lynchings that occurred on the courthouse campus in 1878. He was met with total silence. He continued recounting the events from the old Order Book in spite of the growing hostility he felt from the crowd.

When one of the most influential community leaders who, also, was one of Eagleson's good friends, thrust back his chair and stormed out, Eagleson mumbled his thank you and sat down. An officer of the Kiwanis Club turned to him and almost spat in his face as he asked, "When are you up for election?"

Not one person came up to Eagleson afterwards and said anything to him. He was left to collect the nooses and his notes and go back across the street to his courthouse.

Judge Eagleson slumped into his chair behind Judge Parrett's old desk and tried to reconstruct the events of the last half hour. So, some people did know of those awful happenings. And, it appeared, some people still did not want anything done or even said about them. Eagleson wondered how he could have so badly misjudged the reaction to the murders. Of course, he had known that it was almost a certainty that some of the audience had ancestors who knew of or were even involved in the lynchings. But how was that different from having ancestors involved in blackbirding or slavery or criminal activity. Many people relished their spotty family history. Why would this be any different?

Eagleson feared that he knew why this was different. It was the same thing that still permeated the white majority in southern Indiana and much of the United States. It was what kept the media and legal system from demanding investigations into cases such as when those thirty policemen packed the courtroom at a young black man's sentencing. It was what contributed to the constant reappearance of a huge percentage of Posey County's small Negro community in his courtroom. It was what Robert Dale Owen in 1850 and Abraham Lincoln in 1863 had demanded change. It was the pervasive vestige of two legal cultures, one white and one black. It was deep seated prejudice and the shame caused by its realization. It still was better to blame, or ignore, the victims than to boldly address the problem.

And Eagleson was not sure he wanted to face this reality either. Why should he lose friends, incur the ire of powerful people, maybe lose his judgeship and most assuredly be uncomfortable every day all over some people who had been dead over one hundred years?

But as he looked at Giggy's photograph and held the iridescent creamer and sugar holder, he felt a stirring deep in his being he could no longer deny. How old must they be? Benedict Giggy brought his family to America in 1841, so they were, at least, one hundred and sixty-seven years old. But they were pristine, no nicks, no scratches, no loss of color. How had they survived the ship voyage, several wars and numerous hard times such as the Great Depression?

John Eagleson carefully removed the lid of the sugar holder. He noted how it must have been hand crafted as it did not nestle perfectly on the bowl. The painting had been done meticulously but one could still follow the slight irregularities of the glass. If it had not been for the watermarks on the old dishes, John would have guessed a local Swiss glazier had made the items in his barn.

John's mother had always loved flowers and she was particularly fond of poppies. As he studied the dishes he was struck by the small burnished orange poppy that was flanked on both sides by smaller flowers that appeared to have come from the imagination of the artist. John was glad that for some reason he had chosen to send his mother poppies several times over the years.

John decided to try to let his mother's belief in transcendentalism at least have a chance. He turned off all the lights and held a dish in each of his hands. He closed his eyes and told himself to open his mind. But after twenty minutes of meditation all he felt was the pull between further exploration of the Order Book and the thought that he would be better off just sending it to the Clerk's Office to be put in its proper place, after he had destroyed the newspaper clippings. He heard no voices and had no visions. He did put the cedar chest back on the mantel beside Giggy's photograph.

CHAPTER FIFTY-FOUR

GLORY

GENERAL HOVEY WAS COMING HOME a hero. He could not believe that his number one dream was coming true. He had led men into battle at Shiloh and had been promoted to general on the spot for gallantry and leadership. He had to find a reason to come home and bask in the glory. What would Judge Pitcher think of him now? And Mary who had been so afraid for him would be so proud when they walked into church with Hovey in his uniform.

Hovey decided that the best approach would be to plan a trip to the makeshift military hospital in Evansville to visit the soldiers who had been wounded at Shiloh. This would not only deflect any criticism for his furlough home, but it would show his compassion and concern for his soldiers.

When General Hovey entered the large tent where John Giggy was lying with both of his legs covered in bandages, Giggy raised himself up on his left elbow and saluted with his right hand. Hovey looked the young private in the eye to avoid looking at his legs.

"What outfit were you with, soldier?"

"Company H, Forty-Fourth Indiana Volunteer Infantry, General. Most of us are from northern Indiana; my home is LaGrange."

Hovey noted the clipped manner of Giggy's speech. Somehow it reminded him of his friend, Morita Maier. "What's your name, son?"

"John Giggy, I am a stone mason by trade." Giggy was not sure why he told Hovey this, but he was nervous around all officers and this was a general.

"Now, soldier, so was I at one time. I greatly enjoyed the work and still can handle a hod and trowel. What type of masonry work have you done?" Hovey's plan had been to just move quickly through the tents and then catch the train back to Mt. Vernon. But he saw something in the clear blue eyes of the blond haired young soldier that reminded Hovey of himself at that age.

"I built my own house and several others while I was farming. I guess the biggest thing I done was work on the county courthouse just before I mustered in at Indianapolis on August 28, 1861."

"We all remember our muster date, don't we, Johnny? I just pray our muster out date won't be far off.

"You know, Johnny, I hope to get a new courthouse built in Posey County when this war is over. Maybe you can come down and give us a hand. For now your war is over. I'm sending you home."

"Oh, General, you can't do that. I got to get back to my boys. I ain't sitting home while's there's a war on. My wife, Samantha, has several brothers serving right beside me. If I was to quit, I'd never hear the last of it from those Hart boys. And my daddy was an officer in the Swiss army for twenty-one years. He would die of shame if I stayed home."

"But, John, both of your legs are shot up. How would you do your infantry maneuvers? You would just hold 'em up. You don't have any choice. You have done your duty. You're going home to your Samantha."

"By God, no I'm not! I'm getting out of here and getting back to the 44th!" Giggy's outburst shocked Hovey who had assumed John's initial protests about returning home were not sincere. What did this young man have to prove now that he had done his duty and been shot for doing so?

"Listen here, Giggy, you will do as I order. Why should you go back? You have already done enough."

"General, the day I got wounded a buddy of mine that I had met during the fight at Fort Donaldson had the left side of his head blown off by a Rebel minie ball right next to me. His name was Bill Newby and he was from Mill Shoals, Illinois, you know, right across the Wabash. I don't know if he survived but even if he did he ain't going to be the same. And he had a wife and six kids. Hell, General, I ain't that bad. I'll heal up and be good as new. I got to get back for Newby and the rest."

Hovey was drawn to the young soldier and envied his wounds. It would be just perfect to be shot but not lose any parts or get disfigured. The problem was, of course, war was not a cafeteria.

"Alright, Johnny, I will talk with the sawbones. If they say you can go back, I'll let you. But you might want to rethink your decision. Here's my address in Mt. Vernon. If we both survive this great dustup, I want you to contact me about that stone work. You take care, John."

CHAPTER FIFTY-FIVE

THE FOUNDATION

JOHN GIGGY WAS GLAD THAT General Hovey had not visited the military hospital in Nashville, Tennessee after Chickamauga. He had been wounded in the hip that time but was again determined to return to his comrades. The General might have turned him down flat that time.

After fighting all four years with the Iron Forty-Fourth as they came to be called, Giggy was happy to muster out in October of 1865. He had followed Hovey's career and was grateful to have such a great hero take an interest in him. But he was not sure he should contact Hovey when he read about Posey County's decision to build a new courthouse in 1876. He needed the income to supplement his farming and it looked like he might be able to do some inside structural work during the winter months. But he doubted if Hovey would remember him.

When Hovey got the letter from Giggy dated February 10, 1876, all it said was:

ය

"GENERAL, IF YOU STILL WANT ME TO WORK ON YOUR COURTHOUSE, I CAN COME AFTER THE SPRING CROP IS PLANTED

IN MAY TILL HARVEST THEN BACK IN OCTOBER. THANKS, JOHN GIGGY, COMPANY H, 44TH IND. VOLS., LAGRANGE, INDIANA."

ଔ

Hovey was elated and relieved. He knew how many fierce battles the 44th had been in and its heavy losses. He had often reproached himself for not demanding that the special young soldier go home to stay. He had not heard any more of Giggy since the hospital visit, but he did know the odds were not good for a brave young soldier with vengeance on his mind.

Hovey immediately checked with his daughter and son-in-law and invited Giggy and his family to visit in July for the laying of the cornerstone. Hovey suggested that Giggy's family could return to LaGrange after the ceremony and Giggy could stay on to work on the courthouse. Hovey knew that he had sufficient connections to get Giggy a job. Esther and Gus Menzies would be gracious hosts in their large new brick home. The details of the visit were worked out through an exchange of letters between Hovey and Giggy after Hovey's short initial response and invitation.

ଔ

"GENERAL, SAMANTHA IS IN THE FAMILY WAY AND WILL BE LYING IN THIS SUMMER. BUT MY LITTLE GIRL, AGNES, AND I WOULD BE HONORED TO SEE YOU AND MEET YOUR DAUGHTER AND FAMOUS SON-IN-LAW, COLONEL MENZIES. IF IT IS NOT TOO MUCH TROUBLE, I WOULD LIKE FOR AGNES TO STAY WITH ME IN MT. VERNON. SAMANTHA'S SISTER WILL BE HELPING HER WITH HER LYING IN AND IT WOULD LESSEN THE BURDEN ON SAMANTHA AND HER SISTER TO NOT HAVE AGNES UNDER FOOT AND TOO CURIOUS ABOUT THE BABY. AFTER THE BABY

IS BORN, AGNES CAN PROBABLY BE A HELP. SHE IS SIX YEARS OLD, IS NO TROUBLE AND CAN BED WITH ME. WE CAN ARRIVE BY TRAIN ON JULY 2 AND DEPART ON JULY 5 IF THAT IS NOT TOO MUCH BOTHER.

JOHN"

CB

"Johnny, I will meet you and Agnes at the train at about noon on July 2. You will connect with the Mt. Vernon train when you get off of the train in Evansville. Bring your tools and prepare to stay until the fall. There is plenty of stone work to be done on the courthouse and I have already talked to the architect, Mr. Hafer, about you. My daughter, Esther, and her husband, Colonel Menzies, are looking forward to having you stay in our home. Young Agnes will add joy to the summer.

Alvin Hovey"

CB

John Giggy was surprised that a great man such as General Hovey would even remember who he was. He was amazed to be invited into his home and to be included in the impressive ceremony purposefully scheduled for America's one hundredth birthday. General Hovey, Colonel Menzies, Judge William Parrett, Jr., and all the county officials were present along with the architect, Edmund L. Hafer, Jr.

Giggy was humbled and embarrassed to be called General Hovey's friend and comrade in arms when the great man introduced him and Agnes to the large crowd. And when *The Western Star* editor, John Leffel, put out his paper for that week, he mentioned John and Agnes by name. When he returned to La Grange in October, 1876, John put a copy of the clipping in the bottom of the small cedar chest where they stored the creamer and sugar holder from Germany.

General Hovey had arranged for Giggy to work directly with Hafer on the courthouse's granite foundation and brick arch supports in the basement. On July 5, 1876 at 6:00 o'clock in the morning Hafer and Giggy met to outline the important first phase of the project. Hovey had "laid" the first brick, but, in fact, he had simply been presented with one of the locally fired building blocks that included the date and an outline of Hafer's conception of the completed courthouse.

Giggy was concerned that he would somehow let Hovey down. He had Hafer slowly explain how the massive central column and each of the outlying basement supports were going to withstand the weight of the three story building. Then Giggy worked from six a.m. until eight p.m. implementing the complicated design. Most of the brick work required Giggy to constantly hold his arms above his head. He was exhausted at the end of the work day.

Giggy took a lunch break each day at noon and met with Esther and Agnes. Sometimes they would walk the three blocks down to the river but usually they would sit under the huge locust trees and eat the lunch Esther prepared. Colonel Menzies and even General Hovey would occasionally join them. And a time or two General Hovey took John's trowel from him and laid bricks while wearing his three piece suit. Giggy would listen as the general talked about the war and how he had known President Lincoln. From time to time Hovey would inquire about Giggy's wounds from Shiloh and Chickamauga. Giggy was surprised that Hovey appeared to wish he had been wounded. Giggy's aching legs and hip made him wish he had not.

The summer of 1876 flew by. John and Agnes were eager to get home but were sad to leave General Hovey, Esther and Colonel Menzies. Also, John had earned enough money to harvest his crops and provide some necessities for his growing family.

John made an agreement with architect Edmund Hafer to return the next summer as the courthouse was scheduled to be finished in the winter of 1877. Giggy declined General Hovey's generous offer of the Hovey House guest room and made arrangements to stay at the Damron Hotel just south of the courthouse.

When Giggy returned to work on the courthouse, Hovey made it a point to spend time with him socially and on the job. Samantha would not allow Agnes to go back with John as she was needed to help around the house after the baby arrived. But Agnes always treasured her time watching her father work on the courthouse. She, also, never forgot the time she had spent under the shade of the locust trees.

When John finished helping erect the massive rafters for the dome, he and Hovey said their goodbyes just before Thanksgiving in 1877. "General, Mr. Hafer says all that's left is the roof and I am not a roofer, especially when the roof is one hundred and nineteen feet off the ground. I know I don't usually show much feeling, but I hope you know how grateful I am to you. It has been just like being back in the war, but this time having you there to keep me from getting shot, although I have left some considerable sweat and not a little blood from the basement to the dome."

"Johnny, from that time in Evansville when you put me back on my heels for trying to send you home, you have meant something special to me. I hope you will come back and see us from time to time. Our latchstring is always out for you."

"General, I know you had a lot to do with getting this courthouse built. Can I ask you how you feel about it now that it's done? For me, it's like some of the best of me is deep in the brick and mortar."

"John, I will tell you what it represents to me. It says the citizens of Posey County care about what you and I and so many others struggled for. This magnificent structure says to the whole world that in Posey County you can get justice. I hope it stands forever. Goodbye, Johnny. Say, 'hey', to little Agnes for me; I truly enjoyed her being here."

CHAPTER FIFTY-SIX

REGULATORS

ED HAYES HAD SERVED AS a First Lieutenant in Company H of the First Indiana Cavalry in 1862 and '63. He had been stationed in Memphis, Tennessee as part of the quartermaster corps. While there he visited the fabled Nashoba. He found it had been converted into a sanctuary for unwed Negro mothers who had been impregnated by Union Soldiers after they had gained control of the former slave market.

It was not much more than a collection of dilapidated shacks with cots for delivery beds. Hayes had heard so many rumors of Nashoba as he was growing up in Posey County that he was shocked to see the reality. Where was the evidence of Mad Fanny's plan to bring down the Peculiar Institution of slavery and the institution of marriage?

Hayes had been told by William Combs that Eppie Daniels had lived at Nashoba before she married George. Combs and Judge Pitcher were concerned that Eppie Daniels and Robert Dale Owen were trying to rejuvenate Nashoba as a model of Negro self-government. They feared the long term agenda was to hold up Nashoba as proof that Negroes should receive citizenship after the war. And rumor had it that

Mad Fanny's daughter, Sylva, had returned to Nashoba to bring Christianity to her atheistic mother's venture.

Combs and Pitcher had asked Hayes to investigate Nashoba and report on its status as a viable operation. What Hayes told Combs and Pitcher was that there was little to fear from Nashoba. It was occupied and operated by freed Negroes who had neither education nor resources. If anything, it could be cited as an example of why freed Negroes would not benefit from being made citizens of Indiana. And Sylva d'Arusmont appeared to denounce everything her deceased mother had advocated.

When Hayes mustered out he returned to Mt. Vernon and began to lay the groundwork to run for sheriff. But Hayes and his family were affiliated with the Democratic Party that was out of favor immediately after the war. Practically all of the community leaders were Republicans until Judge Pitcher and many of his supporters switched when the Party of Lincoln pushed through federal rights for Negroes.

By the spring of 1878 the incumbent Republican sheriff, John Wheeler, looked vulnerable so Ed Hayes and O.C. Thomas, who served as part-time deputies under Wheeler, both sought the nomination for sheriff from the Democratic Party. It was not politically wise for Wheeler to fire the deputies, so Wheeler had decided to just bide his time and hope that Hayes and Thomas would do enough damage to one another during the primary campaign for Wheeler to beat whoever won the nomination. If Wheeler were reelected, he could fire both of them in 1879. Wheeler was disappointed that Thomas did not seem to grasp the unwritten rules of local politics. He surely knew about Hayes' rumored relationship with his young Negro housekeeper, Jane Harrison, but Thomas never mentioned it or anything else about Hayes. Fortunately, Hayes was less charitable about Thomas.

Hayes engaged in a campaign of innuendo and rumor against the popular young war hero while publicly maintaining a façade of respect for Thomas' battlefield service. Hayes had never seen a shot fired in anger while performing his quartermaster duties. Hayes' secret jealousy of Thomas seethed within him every time he heard someone speak well of Thomas.

And when Thomas won the nomination by the razor thin margin of twenty votes, it was all Hayes could do to keep from publicly endorsing Wheeler for the fall election. Hayes did go to Wheeler privately and offer to support him if Wheeler would keep him as a deputy after the election. Wheeler agreed, but as Thomas' popularity kept growing after May, it appeared that soon neither Wheeler nor Hayes would have a job.

So when Judge John Pitcher, William Combs, Henry Jones, George Daniels and John Leffel asked Hayes to meet with them in secret at Black's Grove just north of downtown Mt. Vernon, Hayes was open to their proposition. The meeting took place amid ominous thunderclaps and swirling clouds on the evening of June 8, 1878.

After swearing one another to secrecy, the men aired their individual grievances against Posey County's colored community and the state legislature that was poised to grant Negroes full rights of citizenship in Indiana. There had been several recent instances of young black men acting uppity to white men. The blacks, also, were rumored to be assaulting white women who were too embarrassed to make public complaints.

Of course, each of the men had their private reasons for wanting to rid Posey County of the Negro scourge so they found common ground in calling for the end to lawlessness by the Negroes. As for Hayes, he needed the money they offered him to replace what he had spent in his losing campaign. Plus, he saw the chance to lead a committee of regulators as an opportunity for the "combat" command he had not had. Further, Hayes hoped this cadre of wealthy and influential men would be the foundation for his next run for sheriff in two years. He did not plan to let that son-of-a-bitch Thomas enjoy the office for another term if Thomas did beat Wheeler this time.

Pitcher suggested that before any real action could be taken against the coloreds, the public needed to be firmly on board. Also, there were many white men who might oppose a Ku Klux Klan type of endeavor. So, John Leffel was to just mention in his newspaper that Ed Hayes had been privately engaged to protect law abiding citizens from the lawless black element. Leffel's editorial comments could plant the seeds of vigilante activity. Then, perhaps, a larger portion of the community might approach Hayes and offer their support.

CHAPTER FIFTY-SEVEN

A TANGLED WEB

SARAH JONES DID NOT KNOW how she could face Henry after what she and Da had just done in Henry and Sarah's bed. She felt so wonderfully fulfilled, but terribly frightened for herself and Da. She was surprised that she felt no shame. She knew that adultery was a stoning offense under God's law. And, when a Negro man and a married white woman were involved, it was a hanging offense for the Negro and banishment for the woman under white man's law.

Yet, she had not felt so satisfied and justified since she and Henry were trying to have a child many years ago. However, she still knew that she had to hide her joy from the world. She, also, knew that she and Da could never be by themselves again. Sarah did not trust herself to be close to Da's pulsating, muscular body with its promise of creation.

Sarah hurriedly tore the sheets and pillow cases from the bed and replaced them with the starched white muslin ones Elizabeth had recently washed and ironed. She thought about burning the ones she and Da had just been lying on, but she could not part with them. She put them in the basement clothes hamper instead. Sarah did not know how she could face Elizabeth again either.

Sarah dreaded the sound of Henry's footsteps on the wooden porch. When she finally heard him coming she almost threw herself at him and begged for mercy. What had she done? How could she atone for this mortal sin? How could she have betrayed her husband, her religion, her race and Elizabeth? She was perspiring profusely and her whole body was flushing when Henry opened the door. She thought she might faint.

Henry walked past her to his study without speaking. He spoke through the open study door, "What's for supper?"

Sarah sat down on the chaise lounge and tried to stop trembling. Her voice cracked as she responded, "Your favorite, meatloaf, but it will be awhile. You can get some more work done if you want."

Henry walked past her again carrying some account books under his left arm. "Should I come back in a couple of hours?"

"That should be fine."

And that was it. Henry suspected nothing. In fact, after a few weeks, Sarah began to doubt her memories of the time with Da. Then she noticed that she was late. At first she was not panicked as she had begun to be somewhat irregular once she turned thirty-five. But after forty-five days she was on the verge of hysteria. She had forced herself to approach Henry when her normal time had run. She loved Henry, but they had not made love for months before her time with Da. He had to be coaxed to come to her, but appeared to enjoy the surprising interlude Sarah had arranged. Sarah realized that any child she might have from Da would almost certainly be recognized as non-white, but she did not know what else to do. And then she began to dread the mornings.

Chapter Fifty-Eight

FRIENDS

SARAH'S ONLY EXPERIENCE WITH PREGNANCIES was when she and Eppie Daniels had attended to Elizabeth and Eliza Harrison when they were giving birth. By the spring of 1877, Eliza had already delivered ten year old Georgia, eight year old Eva, seven year old Albert, six year old Augustus and three year old Mattie who had been named for Eliza's aunt.

Sarah and Eppie had attended all of Eliza's deliveries as well as the youngest three of Elizabeth's children.

All of Elizabeth's children were lighter complexioned than Eliza's, but when Jane was born in 1852, it was remarkable how white she looked. It was a common occurrence for a newcomer to the area to assume Jane was white.

There were no black doctors and the white doctors would have been shunned had they delivered black babies. Usually a Negro midwife such as "Doctress Maggie Caldwell" would help, but both Sarah and Eppie wanted children so badly they had learned enough to help Elizabeth and Eliza just to be somehow involved.

A bonus for Sarah and Eppie, who were of different generations, was they became best friends. Once they had shared in the wonder of birth and the good feelings of doing good works for those in need, Eppie and Sarah had become inseparable. In addition to their common interest and lack of children or grandchildren, their husbands preferred being at work to being home, so both women had a great deal of time to fill. Over the fifteen years they had been friends they had come to share almost every part of their lives.

Each woman knew of the other's sense of emptiness from being childless. They readily shared their resentment of their husbands' inattention and preference for material things over personal closeness.

So, after years of watching young Sarah show no squeamishness or superiority in going into the Harrison homes, Eppie had confided her darkest secret to Sarah. Now Sarah had only Eppie to turn to.

"Eppie, I have done something that I dare not talk about but I must, somehow, address. I have tried to talk to the new priest, Father J.J. Schoentrup, at St. Matthews Parrish, but I fear eternal damnation even if Father would tell me God understands. I have actually thought my only way out is through ending my life. I do not know what to do, but time is quickly running against me."

"Why, child, nothing could be that bad. When I was denied by my own father and ran away from slavery I thought I would be better off dead. But had I gone down that irreversible road, I would never have met Frances Wright or Sylva or you, dearest friend. Do not despair. If we have survived slavery and barrenness, we can face whatever crisis looms now. Come let me hold you while you cast out whatever demons have their clutches on you."

Sarah sank gratefully into Eppie's bosom and sobbed for almost half an hour before she could regain her thoughts.

"Eppie, I believe I am with child."

Eppie was stunned, but almost immediately recovered, "Oh, how marvelous, how long you have waited and me too. It will be as though I have a child of my own. I am so happy for you, Sarah. But, girl, why are you crying? You are like Sarah in the Bible. A miracle has taken place. Are you sure? What does Henry say? He must be absolutely beside himself with joy."

"I believe I am about one month or so. I have not had my womanly time this month and I am quite ill each morning. Henry does not know."

"Does not know, why, Sarah, you must share with him immediately. This may well be what will bring you and Henry back together. You know he has always wanted a child as much as you. And you told me you have always felt that he blamed you somehow for being childless. Surely he will 'rejoice and be exceedingly glad,' as the Good Book says."

"Oh, Eppie, Henry must not know. How can I tell you what I have done? I have sinned and there is no way to atone for this."

"Now, Sarah, you get a hold of yourself. I do not know what you have done, but you certainly would not be the first wife to stray and never let on. Henry wants a child. If he never suspects that he is not the natural father, he will bless you for giving him offspring. And I am confident you did not lie in the manger with some cur, so your child will be much as Henry's own would be. Pull yourself together, now. Do not feel the need to confess further. Whoever the father is most likely is married so he has as much to lose as you do. He will keep quiet even if you were to tell him. And men are so ignorant of these things, if you do not tell him he will never suspect the child is not Henry's. Where women usually pray for seed to take root, men are often happy with a crop failure. No, the thing for you to do is make an end of this tryst and celebrate yours and Henry's baby."

"Ah dearest Eppie, if I only had such an option. That is what I desire most in this whole world. I do love Henry and my indiscretion was only once. If we could be a family, I would give my life for that."

"What do you mean, that is not an option? I guarantee you that no one need ever know. In fact, after a few years even you may lose track of the origin of the matter, especially if it was simply a fleeting loss of control."

"You do not understand and I do not know how to make you understand. I have betrayed not only Henry, but one of our friends. It is not just a matter of hiding the source of the fruit."

Eppie hesitated to delve deeper. It appeared that the husband of one of their mutual friends was involved. Eppie loved Sarah, but she did not feel right about helping to betray another friend. She would not take it upon herself to divulge Sarah's indiscretion, but she could not be actively involved in a course of action that might destroy someone else who trusted her.

"Sarah, perhaps I have overstepped my bounds. If you are unable to let this other man go, maybe my advice will not be helpful."

"That is not it, Eppie. I have already given him up and he has no choice but to leave me alone. The problem is not susceptible to what we women might often do in these cases, that is, pretend it never happened. This did happen and it is neither reversible nor ignorable. And time is rapidly taking any solution, if any there can be, out of my hands. Maybe I should do the right thing and tell Henry, but in this case the consequences of that would be horrible."

"Okay, Sarah, you have persuaded me that my initial joy and my secondary easy solution are both inapposite. But unless you fully explain the problem, I doubt that I can be of any help. Take your time and decide if you wish to confide in me?"

"I do not have time. Something must be done within the next three or four months. I might be able to keep from showing with long full dresses until about six months, but I fear in this small town of wagging tongues, my secret will not make it beyond this summer. I did not want to come to you now but I had nowhere else but the river to turn. I cannot bring myself to kill my baby, so I need you desperately. Forgive me for involving you, but what was I to do?"

"Do not reproach yourself. I sought comfort from you for my deepest pain. You have preserved my confidences and my sanity with your love and understanding. I will stand by you as you have by me. But it is time for you to tell me what you feared to tell even your priest."

CHAPTER FIFTY-NINE

THE SURROGATE

"Oh, Eppie, I am so ashamed. I do not mean about the baby, I feel only gratitude for this wonder of life growing inside me. No, I am ashamed because I have betrayed the trust that Elizabeth and Daniel Harrison placed in me. Eppie, do not hate me; I have taken advantage of young Daniel Harrison and God has seen fit to both bless and punish me for my sin."

Eppie could not speak. The first image that arose in her mind was being attacked by William Combs when she was twelve. But then her mind began to recover and differentiate between a seventeen year old virile young man who almost assuredly enjoyed his time with Sarah and the forceful assault she had only barely avoided so long ago.

"How could this have happened, Sarah? Did you not know you both and maybe Da's whole family might be destroyed? My God, Sarah, what ever possessed you to do such a thing? What has Da done since then? You know he is not a sophisticated man. He may have already let slip what may bring down the whole thing. What a selfish, stupid thing to do!"

Suddenly Eppie heard her own words and compared them to her lifelong charade after Lynchburg. Who was she to be casting stones? And her best friend and Da's family too needed help, not recriminations. She had better quit being such a hypocrite and try to keep this situation from raging out of control.

"I am sorry, Sarah, I certainly am in no position to judge you or Da. You know who has more experience than we do in assuaging such black/white catastrophes, the colored community. I know you are ashamed to face Elizabeth and Daniel, but nobody has more to lose than they do if this thing leaks out."

"Oh, Eppie, how can I face them? They trusted me and I have placed them and their son in mortal danger with my weakness. Do you think it might be better if you approached them? Maybe I could find the courage to go with you, but I know I cannot go alone. And, of course, there is not time to waste."

"Alright, let us go now while we have mustered the strength. I fear if we wait I will be found wanting. It is only about a fifteen minute walk to the Harrison home if we go first to the river then walk through the trees on the bank until we reach Elm Street. We will leave a note for George and Henry that we are at church and try to go after the sun has gone down."

When Eppie and Sarah knocked on Elizabeth's flimsy backdoor, Elizabeth wondered why they would come to the rear entrance as coloreds might. But Elizabeth was always glad to see Miss Sarah and Miss Eppie who had done so much for her family.

"Why land, Miss Eppie and Miss Sarah, does ya all wants ta come in? Lordy, my little house ain't ready for company, but do come in, now. Ain't nobody here but me and Jane. Daniel's gots de res of em outs working on de farm."

"Elizabeth, we are here seeking answers. Mrs. Jones and I are very much in need of your help. The matter is most grave and very delicate."

Elizabeth and Jane were totally perplexed. High class white women did not come to black people's homes except to give help or hire help. They certainly never looked at coloreds as able to solve white people's problems. What on earth were these ladies talking about?

Jane was watching Sarah while Eppie was talking to Elizabeth. Jane had seen how Mrs. Hayes coped with her husband's controlling nature. Ed Hayes was a deputy sheriff and relished the power the position provided, and he never willingly relinquished it even at home. Hayes would frequently become upset with his wife, Darly, and reduce her to tears in front of Jane. Hayes made a point of commenting on Jane's body in front of Darly and comparing Jane's lithe build to the frumpy Darly. Hayes made no attempt to hide his lust for Jane, but Jane was extremely careful to never be alone with him. She knew better than to confront the situation; her family needed the small pay she received. Besides, Hayes had the authority to cause Jane great harm and he would not hesitate to do so.

Jane had noted over the five years she had cleaned for the Hayes family that Darly's manner of coping with the situation was to remain silent in the face of Ed's tirades then cry when he left. Sarah Jones had that same redness in her eyes and the same wilted and frightened look about her. Jane figured that whatever the problem these white ladies were seeking help on was probably Mrs. Jones'.

"Mrs. Jones, would you's like to sit out of the sun? I can get you some water. Is you going ta be all right? Let me get a damp cloth to cool you off."

"Thank you, Jane. Mrs. Jones is having some difficulty. We thought we might talk to your mother about it. It might be better if you left us for now."

Sarah had felt the sympathy in Jane's gaze. Jane had frequently struck her as a sensitive person who understood how to help others. Sarah had noted how Jane had been a calming influence when her three younger sisters were born. Sarah and Jane had formed a special bond over the past few years due, in part, to their similar appearance. Sarah's eyes and hair were dark and she had an olive complexion, and they both were thin but had well formed breasts. But mainly Sarah felt that Jane was of a good and generous nature.

"Mrs. Daniels, please let Jane stay. Elizabeth may feel more comfortable with her here. This matter is of import to both of them."

Jane felt her stomach turn. She looked at her mother who did not appear to catch the significance of Sarah's statement. But Jane now knew whatever these white ladies were bringing to the Harrison household was indeed a grave matter and not just for Mrs. Daniels and Mrs. Jones. When white people said that black people had a problem, it always turned out they were right.

"You are correct, Mrs. Jones, this is a matter of concern to Elizabeth's entire family as well as to you and me. It might be better if Jane were here to support Elizabeth and to advise us. Well, I do not know how to begin, but the situation will not improve with age. Elizabeth and Jane, let me first say that no one regrets bringing this problem to your door more than Mrs. Jones. She has been devastated by this and comes to you with a heavy heart and a great deal of shame. This is the most delicate and embarrassing situation you can imagine.

"Please try to remain calm and help us address this grave dilemma. And please accept Mrs. Jones' sincere apology for bringing this to your home. What she did was out of a momentary and solitary time of weakness. She acted out of her deep need to have a child and her love for Da as a member of your family."

Elizabeth still did not grasp what Eppie could not bring herself to say directly. But Jane shot to her feet and had to muffle a scream. Sarah began to sob and shake from side to side.

"Momma, does you understand? Oh, God! Oh, God! How? Does Da know? He must get away. Does Mr. Henry know?"

Elizabeth continued to deny what her mind now told her Jane was saying. It was too horrible to contemplate. This could destroy her whole family and cost Da his life.

Then Jane and Elizabeth almost in unison began to let their human and female sides dominate the vestiges of slavery that caused their initial reaction. Jane spoke first.

"How much time does we have? Who else knows?"

Sarah managed to stop crying but she could not look at Elizabeth or Jane. "I think we have about two months before people might notice. No one knows but us. I am so very sorry. I would never hurt your family, especially Da. He is a good boy and I am totally to blame."

"Not totally I suspect, Miss Sarah. My little brother gots some devilment in him too as we's alls know. But what's you ladies wanting to do. Da must get away or the white men will hang him even if Mr. Henry were against it. And how wills you get along? What's you going ta do?"

"Not long ago I received a letter from my childhood friend, Sylva Wright d'Arusmont, who has returned to Nashoba, Tennessee to run a Christian mission for pregnant Negro girls. I have been thinking that Mrs. Jones and I could go there for awhile to help run the mission. After the baby is born we could find a good home for it and return here. If we could have been sure no word about the baby would leak out in Posey County, we could have just gone down ourselves and kept our secret. But I just found out myself a few hours ago and I fear for Da if word should get out. We knew that in spite of Mrs. Jones' anguish and shame we had to warn your family as soon as possible. Also, I am not sure Mrs. Jones can give the baby up, so going to Nashoba might be to no avail. For her sake we must find another way."

Jane had only lived twenty-five years but life had already convinced her that God was fickle. His ways may be higher than man's ways, but they often seemed cruel to Jane. She expected that no matter what they did, all of them would regret it later. On the other hand, if they did nothing but wait for events to play out, Da and Sarah and the baby and maybe a whole lot more people might suffer greatly or even die. As always, life would be a struggle but the struggle is all we have.

"Miss Sarah, I knows yous did not do this with a bad heart. I's mindful of alls you and Miss Eppie has done for us. I knows yous loves us and we loves you all. Now, Momma, I knows you's scared for Da and the rest of us. But we's ain't the first fambly that's been up dis creek. Miss Sarah, what's you wants ta do?"

"Oh, Jane, and Elizabeth, too, I feel such shame for the fear and pain I have brought to you. But I have waited a lifetime for a child and no matter what it costs me I cannot lose it now. I will die before I give up my baby. I am sorry for Da and will do whatever I can to protect him and to atone for my great sin, but my baby and I will be together. I plan to go somewhere and not return. Henry will be better off without me. It would hurt him terribly to find out, so I will just disappear."

Jane respected Miss Eppie and Miss Sarah. These women had helped her family in many ways for many years. She knew that Miss Sarah was a good and caring person who would never intentionally harm anyone. And Jane herself had on more than one occasion come close to giving into the very same desires Sarah and Da had. She had always managed to pull back but she had to suppress her excitement and her burning need to have a child. Jane truly believed that Jesus wanted her to get married before she engaged in the great wonder of love. But she was not judgmental about others. She understood how this could have happened. There was no time to wring hands and place blame. It had happened and Da and maybe others would be killed if word leaked out. And that brought Jane back to these two loving and naïve white ladies.

Jane respected Miss Eppie and Miss Sarah, but she had no confidence that they understood the world as Jane knew it. After years of surviving as an attractive black woman in a white man's world, Jane felt better equipped than these wealthy white women to navigate this dangerous situation. And she wanted Da's baby to be part of her life.

Jane did not recognize that this last issue was the controlling one. She believed she was acting out of a sense of sacrifice and love for Da, but the driving force in her improbable solution was her desire to have a child.

"Miss Sarah, what if I's was to go with you and Miss Eppie to Nashoba? If we tells people that it is me who must go away to have some white man's child, the colored community will not doubt that I's been taken against my will and the white folks wills just write me off as another shiftless nigger. Then we's could come back an I's could raise my niece or nephew as my child. You all could still see and be around him from time to time. Mebbe that's would work, huh?"

Jane thought she was acting altruistically. What a wonderful selfless thing she was doing for her family and Sarah. But as with many good deeds, the motivations were more complex.

All four women immediately grasped Jane's idea close to their hearts. Elizabeth would get to protect Da and still see her first born grandchild. Eppie could return to Nashoba and see Sylva and enjoy vicarious motherhood through Sarah and Jane. Sarah could begin to atone for her sin by working with Jane and protecting Da. Most importantly, Sarah would finally have the baby she had always dreamed of. And Jane could be everyone's heroine, and have her own child. It was a marvelous plan of feminine wisdom and sharing and was filled with good deeds all around. So why did all four women somehow already sense that their desires for a child were clouding their judgment? Was this child to be a savior or a harbinger of God's retribution for the sins of adultery and bearing false witness?

The irony of how this potentially disastrous situation was an embodiment of Mad Fanny's grand scheme of bringing equal rights to Negroes and women was not lost upon Eppie. Interracial breeding in violation of marriage and a plan to escape its consequences devised by black and white women would have elated Fanny. Of course, just as Fanny's own plans often arose out of her pride, this effort had its genesis in these women's unreasoning desire to be a part of the unborn child's life. Eppie feared that this current female effort to avoid the wrath of white men who would think themselves wronged by women, black and white, was as likely to fail as Fanny's Nashoba had. But Eppie wanted this child to be born. Suspending rational thought came easily when Eppie and Sarah had waited so long for this moment that they thought had passed them by.

CHAPTER SIXTY

TRAVEL PLANS

EPPIE WROTE TO SYLVA AT Nashoba and asked if she and her friend, Sarah Jones, could bring an unmarried pregnant Negro woman to stay at Nashoba until the child was born. Eppie named Jane Harrison as the pregnant woman and, also, commented on the coincidence of Jane's surname being the same as Eppie's maiden name.

Sylva responded to Eppie and warned of the primitive conditions at Nashoba but expressed her excitement at seeing Eppie again. Sylva, who had been only four years old when Eppie arrived at Nashoba, had never known her as Inola Crider. Therefore, Sylva had no thought of what Eppie's reaction might be when Sylva included in her letter that she was sure Eppie would be pleased to see Samson and Rachel who now went by the last name of Crider.

Sylva informed Eppie that when Samson and Rachel had fled Posey County in 1847, they were taken in by Frances Wright in Cincinnati, Ohio. Sylva's mother had thought it would help them hide from any blackbirder or Posey County law enforcement officials if they changed their last name. Fanny had suggested they take the name of Crider. Sylva assumed that her mother had chosen this name because Cincinnati had a number of former slaves who went by that name. Sylva, also, wrote that Samson and Rachel had a twenty-seven year old son, Ajax, and that he was with them at Nashoba.

After Frances Wright had died in 1852, Samson, Rachel and Ajax had continued to live in Fanny's house with Sylva's permission until 1867 when Sylva asked them to come help rejuvenate Nashoba. Samson and Ajax would be the only men there and there was a great deal of heavy physical work to be done. Sylva informed Eppie that Playella and Mordecai had both passed away in France during a cholera epidemic in 1874.

When Eppie read the name Crider she felt emotions she had suppressed for over forty years. Her father may not have acknowledged her, but she realized that she had needed his love then and still felt a connection to Lynchburg. Eppie thought that maybe Fanny had somehow understood Eppie's unspoken need because Fanny and Camilla had themselves lost their father when they were young. Regardless of whether Simon Crider saw his daughter as offspring or property, Eppie now realized that she had spent a lifetime yearning for him as a father.

Eppie was not sure why Fanny had chosen Crider, but when she read her old name she felt an initial icy shock followed by a flood of tears. Perhaps Fanny had foreseen the possibility that some day Eppie would see Samson and Rachel again and that, if so, the name Crider might help close the open wound in Eppie's heart.

Eppie cried as she yelled in anger, "Father, why? Why couldn't you love me or at least protect me? Wasn't I a good girl? Didn't I do everything you asked of me? I always loved you. You did not have to tell other people you loved me or were proud of me, but you could have told me, or, at least, shown me some kindness. Now it's too late for us. But I must forgive you for my sake. I thought I had done so years ago, but, now I know I have always had this inner battle of love and hate."

As she calmed herself, Eppie silently thanked Fanny for her unexpected understanding and her foresight in planning for this unlikely reunion of people and emotions. The world may have maligned her as Mad Fanny, but Eppie thought of her as the mother she had never known and the father figure she had always needed. Fanny's impractical idealism was exceeded only by her generosity of spirit and her self-destructive pride.

Eppie smiled when she read the name, Ajax. She knew that just as Fanny had named her Iphigenia, she must have asked Samson and Rachel to name their son for the Greek warrior and boxer. Mad Fanny was a dreamer unto the last. She must have hoped that Ajax would grow up to avenge his parents, his race and Fanny too.

Eppie knew that Rachel and Samson harbored no ill will towards her for the events of 1847. They knew that the facts in an alleged assault by a black man on a white woman were often irrelevant. They did not blame Eppie or even George for William's actions. Unfortunately for Eppie, her conscience was not as charitable with her.

Eppie had known, even before Combs had made it clear, that he had long ago figured out she was Inola Crider. Combs reminded her and George that he could expose her or even take her back to Lynchburg. Eppie decided to handle this assault by Combs just as she had the first. And George decided to believe his cousin's version, although he indicated that it would not be good for William to be alone with Eppie again. But now Eppie would see Samson and Rachel again and maybe somehow atone for the frailty of her youth.

Eppie and the conspirators decided that they would have to inform Da, Daniel, Sr., Charles and Eliza. They knew that every additional person who knew of this plan was a potential source of an inadvertent leak. But they, also, knew if they did not tell these members of Jane's family what they were doing and why, when they were called on to explain Jane's absence, they might raise suspicions with inconsistent stories. And when Da was informed of the pregnancy and the desperate solution to it, he confided in his best friend and older brother, John Harrison.

Eppie felt inadequate to coordinate and execute the group's plan. On the other hand, she had managed as a twelve year old ignorant slave girl, with the help of the Quakers, to find her way to Nashoba and successfully pass for white for over thirty years. She wished someone else could take the lead, but she knew that Sarah was near breaking already and it was unlikely that any of the Harrison family could negotiate the perilous contacts with the white world.

Eppie's first move was to have Jane act ill around Darly Hayes until Darly concluded on her own that Jane was pregnant and the father might be a white man that Jane refused to name.

Darly was happy to get Jane away from Ed, so when Jane mentioned that Miss Eppie and Miss Jones had made arrangements for her to go to Nashoba, Darly spread Jane's story throughout Mt. Vernon under the guise of soliciting financial help for Jane. As so often happens when a guileless person such as Darly attempts to manipulate others, the result Darly worked so hard to avoid, i.e., any connection between her husband and Jane, led to just such a connection in the minds of Posey County's mongers of salacious gossip.

Those familiar with Ed Hayes' designs on Jane took this opportunity to add two and two and get five. The rumor spread rapidly that Ed Hayes was the father of Jane's baby, although Ed had tried to ignore the gossip until Judge John Pitcher skillfully used the rumors to enrage Hayes.

CHAPTER SIXTY-ONE

A GOOD DEED

"HENRY, YOU KNOW JANE HARRISON, Elizabeth's girl? She has found herself in a bad situation and I feel as though I should help her."

Sarah had waited until after Sunday dinner to raise the topic of Nashoba to Henry. She hoped the morning church service and Father Schoentrup's message coupled with a stomach full of meatloaf would make Henry more prone to supporting her travel to Nashoba with Jane and Eppie.

"Eppie Daniels and I believe we should accompany Jane so that we can help her. You know that no local doctor will attend to her and Elizabeth says Jane is anemic and already having problems. I know she is to blame for giving into the flesh, but the rumor is the father is a prominent married white man and she may have been put upon. And, if that is true, she might even be in danger if she stays here. The white man might try to force Jane and even her family to leave so that he is not exposed. Darly Hayes has already collected some money and things to help Jane. But Eppie and I fear for Jane's health and safety if she has to go off alone. She is Da's sister after all."

This last had slipped out before Sarah could catch herself. She was afraid to look at Henry. He might see right through her lies.

"How long would you be gone? Can Elizabeth go with her instead or Eliza?"

"Elizabeth and Eliza can barely read and write and who would watch their children? Daniel and Charles must work and the boys don't know how to care for things. But, if you cannot spare me here, I will not go. It would be a long time to be gone."

Sarah fought hard to keep the panic in her throat from flying out of her mouth. What could she do if Henry insisted she not go?

"Eppie can only travel with Jane to Nashoba. She cannot abandon her duties at the Methodist Church. You know that she is deeply involved in the effort to help Reverend Jacob Bockstahler get another church started at Caborn Station. The fledgling congregation might fail if she were to be gone for long. I can have Elizabeth look after the house and fix whatever meals you might need."

Henry was not at all reluctant to have some time alone. He had recently spoken with Christian Willis who had mentioned to him that Soaring Bird had joined the community at Brewery Hills. Willis told Henry that Bird's French trapper had abandoned her and gone to Nevada to look for silver. Bird's only child had taken his wife and son and followed his French trapper father to Nevada. Bird decided to make a fresh start in Posey County. She told Willis and the Negro preacher Ben Wilson that she had heard much from the trapper about the white man's deal with the Great Spirit Jesus. As she now had no man, no child and no place of her own, she wanted to see if she could still get this deal for herself. She remembered that Willis and Henry Jones had tried to give her this bargain years before. She thought it might be okay now. Bird told Willis and Wilson that she could help provide pelts for the community if she could stay.

Willis had told Henry that Soaring Bird had changed in some ways and that she had asked about Henry when she first showed up at Brewery Hills. Willis had filled Bird in about Henry and Sarah. He had invited her to remain at Brewery Hills as long as she attended the church. As for her material contribution, Willis had told her that her services as a trapper would be helpful and she could, also, help care for the Negro children while their mothers performed their outside chores such as farming.

A flash of excitement had rushed through Henry's body when Willis mentioned Bird's name. Henry had not expected to ever feel such intense emotions again, although Sarah's unanticipated passionate advance of a few weeks ago had, for a moment, awakened his old hopes of creating a child.

But his emotions upon hearing Bird's name were far more intense and basic. Henry had assumed that he was past those fires of his youth. He and Sarah had filled their early years with wonder and excitement, but, as they drifted apart due to his business and her social work, their emotions waned long before they stopped embracing physically. And when it appeared that their great desire to have a child was not to be realized, they engaged in sexual relations so infrequently and unsatisfactorily that neither missed it.

CHAPTER SIXTY-TWO

SECOND CHANCES

HENRY JONES WAS EASILY PERSUADED that the Christian thing was for Sarah to attend to Jane. He provided Sarah with money and a farewell kiss on the cheek as she, Eppie and Jane boarded the steamboat for Memphis. Henry convinced himself that his motives in visiting Christian Willis at Brewery Hills were, also, altruistic.

As Henry pulled his carriage up to the ramshackle log building that served as both church and schoolhouse, he was filled with dread and anticipation. He feared that Soaring Bird would be disappointed at the changes in him since they parted. For years their time together had seemed as if it had happened to someone else a long time ago. But now Henry had the same image of Bird that he remembered as he had left her. While he knew that time had taken its toll on him, he assumed the beautiful sixteen year old girl would appear in life as she remained in his dreams. Would this teenage beauty be repulsed by the old man he had become?

When Henry got down from the carriage a heavyset Indian woman came out of the building and held his horse. She tied the horse to the hitching rack. The woman kept her eyes downcast until Henry asked her where Christian Willis was. When her eyes met Henry's he felt the shock of recognition. Could this be the lithe, golden skinned beauty who had been his first love? Her skin remained smooth and clear and her long hair was full and dark, but her teeth were no longer white and her body had lost its angularity. Her eyes held a sadness that cut deeply into Henry's memory of his abandonment of her.

"Soaring Bird?"

Bird had seen Henry's carriage approaching as she was sweeping the floor of the meeting house. Even at a distance she could tell who the driver was. She felt every one of the years her body had endured since they were last together. If he had left her when she was young, he surely would have no interest in her now. As for Bird, she had never forgotten the wonder of Henry's touch and the joy she had felt the first time they had lain together. It was not Henry's golden hair and beard she thought of when she recalled those days when her life was filled with happiness, it was his passion for helping Bird's people that kept Henry in her heart.

Henry had tried to help the Shawnee without trying to steal their land. Henry had warned the Shawnee that the onslaught of white men would soon destroy them if they did not learn the white ways. Soaring Bird understood why her people had preferred to maintain their own culture. In fact, if she had the power, she would have prevented the destruction of her tribal way of life. But Henry had explained the coming of such things as steamboats and preachers and he had been right. Bird had felt Henry's love for her and his sincere desire to help her people. Although he had left her to return to the white world, Bird had always blamed the Indians for not heeding Henry's warnings. She, also, blamed herself. She had loved Henry unconditionally, but somehow she had failed him. She had never stopped loving him.

"I think you no remember me. Many seasons now passed. I no longer think of next summers. Winters fill my spirit."

Henry's sense of loss was profound. He had recognized long ago that his fear of being identified as an Indian and his shame at loving Soaring Bird had cost him his best chance at true happiness. At first, he had suppressed his knowledge of his mistake in his relationship with Sarah. But as they had failed to achieve their goals together, Henry's thoughts had often returned to Bird. He had admitted the awful truth long ago. He had thrown away what most people never find. His pride had cost him his soul.

"How have you been, Bird? Christian told me that you were here. What do you hear from your son and his father?"

"He well. He not return."

Henry was pleased to hear this, but he was not sure who Bird was talking about. "Is your man coming back or your son?"

"Man gone, son no come back. Maybe son come back sometime. Where your woman?"

Henry picked up the reproach in Bird's voice at Henry's third person treatment of Bird's life. He had spoken to her as white men often spoke to Indians. He regretted his insensitivity.

"Sarah has gone to Tennessee to help a young Negro woman who is with child. She will be gone for some time. You may know that we never had children ourselves. I am happy for you that you have a son. What is his name?"

"Michelle. His father would not allow me to give him an Indian name. But, I always call him Storm Child because he was born during a storm. He is thirty-five years old. He took his woman and their child with him when he left."

Henry was familiar with what sounded to most white people as a lack of emotion in Indian speech. Henry could sense the loneliness and pain in Bird's voice. She missed her son and grandchild.

"I am sorry they are gone, Bird. I am sure you miss them very much."

Soaring Bird heard echoes of the young man she had loved so much. Henry still saw Indians as individuals. But what was left of their youth? Surely this man who had gone on to prominence and wealth would feel nothing for her. After all, she had been found wanting when she was young, why would he want her now? And what sort of connections could she hope for when he was married and had other obligations? Bird decided Henry had just come to Brewery Hills to see Christian and Reverend Wilson.

Christian Willis was glad to see Henry. Henry had not wanted anyone else to know of his involvement in Christian's missionary efforts to help area Negroes, but he never failed to give money when Christian asked for it. Christian was surprised that Henry would take the chance of being seen at Brewery Hills, although when he had told Henry of Soaring Bird's presence, he had seen the flash in Henry's eyes.

"Well, my friend, it is good of you to come. Let me show you where your contributions have been put to work. We could not help my people to come to Jesus, but we have been able to give refuge to many Negroes, especially women and children. We have taught many to read and write. We use the *New Testament* as our *McGuffey's Reader*. It serves to educate and save souls at the same time. We, also, teach women how to cook and clean as white people expect and men how to farm and handle money. Some of our people have even gone on to own their own homes and farms. You know the Harrison family. Daniel and Elizabeth both used to come to Brewery Hills before they got their property in Mt. Vernon, and their forty acres. Bird, we will be back in a little while."

"You have carried out our hopes quite well, Christian. I wish we could have done more for the Shawnee, but, at least, Soaring Bird is here. Maybe she can carry on in the future. It was good of you to tell me she was here. Is she happy? Has she asked about me?"

Henry could not hide his excitement from his old friend. Christian had no more questions about what, or who, had brought Henry to Brewery Hills. He, also, knew why Soaring Bird had come to Posey County. Christian was not sure of the morally correct way to address the situation involving his old friends. He did not want to encourage any illicit relationship and he certainly did not want to see Soaring Bird hurt again. Christian knew that Henry could retreat into his monied white society, but Bird might be, once again, used and discarded when her presence became inconvenient. Christian resolved to be direct with Henry on this point.

Chapter Sixty-Three

HOME AGAIN

Eppie looked up the bank of the Wolf River at the worn dirt path. Her heart began to race in her chest. She felt herself sway backwards against Jane who thought Eppie had just lost her balance. But Sarah immediately sensed what was happening.

"Steady, Eppie, give it some time."

Eppie tried to calm herself by slowing her breathing. She had clenched Jane's left arm with her right hand to keep from falling. She asked the porter they had hired in Memphis to stop. She sat down on the trunk he had removed from the wagon. No longer did one have to take the river to Nashoba. There was now a dirt road along the north bank that connected Nashoba to Memphis.

Eighteen thirty-five reappeared in Eppie's mind as though that twelve year old escaped slave had captured Eppie's soul. She remembered how frightened and confused she had been when the Quaker man had taken her hand when she turned to run away. He had been firm with her because he had to be. Inola Crider was, with good reason, suspicious of strangers and strange places.

The Quaker had turned her over to Frances Wright whom Eppie remembered cowering from. Even forty-two years later Eppie had not lost her initial image of the large, forceful white woman who had none of the motherly characteristics the little black girl so needed. But when Playella appeared behind Fanny with a small Negro girl, Rachel, in tow, Eppie's fears began to subside. She had no realistic option but to stay where she was told, but she had almost bolted away when she had seen the cabins that looked like her old slave quarters.

So many memories were competing with the present. Yet all of them were combined in one emotion. This was her true home. This was where Inola Crider was loved and cared for just for her sake. This was where her first sexual awakening took place when she noticed Samson's huge muscles. Here her love with George was uninhibited and without the slow and relentless battering that life had brought over the following thirty-seven years.

"Are you okay, Miss Eppie?" Jane's question brought Eppie back from Inola Crider to the present.

"Yes, thank you, Jane. I just needed to catch my breath. We had best proceed."

Samson and Rachel had caught sight of the party just as Eppie recovered. They raced down the path as fast as Samson's seventy year old knees would allow. When they reached Eppie they hesitated, but Eppie grabbed Rachel in her arms and began crying. Then they were both laughing and crying. Eppie let go of Rachel and tried to put her arms around the still massive Samson. At first Samson let his arms hang at his sides, but then he enveloped Eppie who sank up against him.

"Oh, my, I have forgotten my manners. Samson and Rachel, this is Mrs. Jones and this is Jane."

Rachel bowed her head to Sarah and nodded to Jane. Samson took off his broad brimmed hat and nodded towards both of them. Then

Samson unloaded both of the remaining trunks as Rachel yelled, "Ajax! Git down here an help yore daddy!"

Ajax had been watching the events from the doorway of the largest cabin. He had been told by Sylva that a young black woman was coming with Miss Eppie to have a baby at Nashoba. But all he saw were three white women. He assumed that the oldest woman who hugged his parents must be Miss Eppie. One of the other women looked younger than Eppie, but older than the beautiful young white woman who was not dressed as fine as the older women. But where was the pregnant black girl?

Ajax ran down the path to help Samson and the porter bring up the three trunks. When Jane saw Ajax she could not take her eyes off of him. She felt herself staring but she could not help it. He was black as ebony and the largest man she had ever seen. Samson was certainly huge, but time had stooped him and his white hair made him seem smaller. But this man looked as if he were the one who could bring down the pillars of the palace. And when he lifted Jane's heavy trunk that Sarah had given her as though it were a shoe box, a thrill went through Jane.

"Miss Eppie, Mrs. Jones, Miss Jane, this be my boy, Ajax. Miss Fanny named him that 'cause when he was just a baby he was always clinching his fists. Miss Fanny said he must be a boxer from de Greeks gods come to fight for his fambly. He ain't much, but he's alls God has giv me."

"Now, Momma, you know I's your favorite."

"Shore nuff that's be true. You's alls I got."

Jane was reminded of the love her mother, Elizabeth, and her brother, Da, often showed by their teasing. She could tell that this large young man was gentle with his mother.

"Ajax, yous takes that trunk up to de empty cabin. Miss Sylva says ta puts de ladies dere."

Jane noted how when Samson spoke, Ajax paid respectful attention. She, also, noted that both men had voices that carried the rumble of thunder. Jane figured it would not do to rile up either of these easy going giants.

"Momma, is there anybody else?"

"Mind your manners, boy. Don be nosin in ta sompin dat ain't none of your bizness."

"That's alright, Rachel. Ajax is just trying to help get all of our things and us unloaded. No, Ajax, we three are alone and I can only stay a few days. But Mrs. Jones and Jane will be with you until next spring."

Ajax, Rachel and Samson did not miss that Eppie referred to one white lady formally and to one by her first name. Jane must be a servant. But where was the pregnant Negro girl? The Crider family decided individually to ask no more questions. Miss Sylva would let them know anything they needed to know.

Then Ajax was ordered by Samson to help the porter unload the food stuffs and other provisions that the women had brought.

CHAPTER SIXTY-FOUR

FAR FROM THE TREE

WHEN EPPIE SAW SYLVA SHE was surprised that she could find none of Fanny in her. She was small and thin, a female version of the Count. And she was wearing a cross.

"It was so good of you to take us in, Sylva. I have thought of you and your parents almost every day since George and I left for Indiana. I owe them my life. Now I will owe you for my friend's life. Mrs. Jones and I have brought you a contribution for your mission, but no amount of money is adequate to repay you for your kindness. How many girls do you have here now?"

"Eppie, we were girls together. My mother thought of you as a daughter too. Often I think she felt you were more a daughter than I. I have no interest in her insane causes of mixing the races, eliminating marriage or outlawing religion. My mission work is to glorify Jesus. But just as Jesus said to suffer the little children, I am working to help wayward Negro girls to repent of their sins of the flesh. We require strict adherence to God's will here. We teach the girls to read and write and skills such as cooking and cleaning. Our goal is to prevent them from sinning again."

Eppie was glad to see Sylva who was the only link Eppie had to Fanny. But Eppie could sense the disapproval and condemnation in Sylva's voice. Eppie was concerned that if Sylva was judgmental with ignorant Negro girls, she might turn Sarah away for her sin. Eppie knew that she would have to tell Sylva the truth in a very delicate manner.

"Perhaps we can have a nice dinner this evening. We have brought stores that should last for some time. As I wrote, I must return to my church work in Mt. Vernon, but Mrs. Jones, Sarah, and Jane plan to stay until the baby is born." Eppie thought it might help if she let Sylva know about her church involvement. Eppie had long ago decided that whether she believed, or pretended to believe, made no difference in the world, but it made her life a lot easier to have others think she believed. It seemed to Eppie that the Fanny Wrights of the world were quite rare. Most people needed confidence that some great power took an interest in their lives.

Religion was often used to justify injustice, but it was, also, often the motivation for people to do justice. Unlike Fanny, Eppie had concluded that religion was here to stay regardless of anyone's efforts to eliminate it. Eppie thought that Fanny's sad life was a testament to the triumph of faith over fact. Eppie saw no advantage to herself or anyone else to ignore the inevitable.

"Sylva, it is marvelous that Nashoba is accessible by a short road from Memphis. What is it, about fifteen miles?"

"Fourteen now actually; yes, it is a real improvement from our childhood when we had to pole up and down the river."

Eppie had asked if she might speak to Sylva in private. "Is the spring still across the field? Could we walk there together?"

"I have found that the spring is the only thing that hasn't changed. It would be good to return to it with you, Eppie. We spent many wonderful hours there as girls."

Eppie kept trying to work up the courage to tell Sylva the truth. As they walked together across the still desolate cotton fields where yellow top grew so thick the occasional cotton bole looked like a weed, Eppie was awash with fear. She and everyone who knew the facts fully expected disaster to befall Sarah and the entire Harrison family at the next turn. Eppie felt the full weight of responsibility. She was the runaway slave. She was educated in the ways of the white world. She was a pillar in the Posey County social community. She had cared for the Daniel and Charles Harrison families. She was the one who suggested that Sarah tell the Harrisons when a better course might have been for Sarah to try to abort her baby or to go away and have the child then give it up and return to Mt. Vernon or for Sarah to simply go away and never return.

But the real guilt that Eppie struggled with was her knowledge that this whole house of cards was built on her desire to have a child by any means possible. She realized that Sarah and Jane were, also, victims of this fierce maternal aching. However, Jane was without power in this white society and Sarah was in no condition to even think clearly, much less plan a viable solution.

No, the fault for the pregnancy may lie with Sarah, and to some extent Da, but the responsibility for this labyrinthine scheme held together with gossamer lay with her. And Eppie was beginning to feel more like Inola Crider than Iphigenia Harrison. How could she save all these people?

CHAPTER SIXTY-FIVE

SISTERS

WHEN THEY ARRIVED AT THE spring where George and Eppie had first made love, Eppie felt a fresh flood of memories overtake her. She savored those feelings as they sat down on the limestone ledge around the spring where she and George had sat so long ago.

"Let's dangle our feet in the spring as we did when we were girls, Sylva." Sylva hesitated but then shrugged her shoulders and kicked off her sandals. As the two women transformed back into the nine year old Sylva and the seventeen year old Inola, memories of their shared mother overcame them and they hugged and cried as two sisters should.

"I have never been able to apply my father's Christian forgiveness to my mother. I have always resented how she put everyone and everything in the world ahead of me. I know that if I can forgive others I should forgive her, but I just can't. I confess that until you wrote asking for help, I had always resented your relationship with my mother. I grew up seeing you as the daughter mother wished she had instead of me. For some reason when I received your letter it awakened our time as sisters. I have ever thought of you that way. After all, you are the only family I have left."

Eppie smiled and said, "And if one cannot impose on their family, why have them?"

"Oh, Eppie, it is no imposition. I have missed you greatly as have Samson and Rachel. They told me about George's cousin and how they had to flee. They have longed for you ever since."

"I felt so guilty that I could not protect them. That was before the War and I was still my father's property. I did not know what to do."

"They hold you to no blame. They told me how you helped them connect with your old saviors, the Quakers, so they could escape. It worked out well for them and my mother. She got to enjoy them for only about five years, but they brought her great solace during that time. And after Mother fell on the ice, they cared for her as you and I would have. Most importantly, she got to be around little Ajax who was the grandchild we never gave her; although, he is certainly not so little now."

"Sylva, your mother loved you more than her life. Think, girl, she married your father to legitimize you even though she thought marriage an abomination for women. She allowed your father to raise you as a Christian when she saw religion as the root of much of the world's troubles. She gave you her remaining fortune while she struggled to maintain her life. And she abandoned her great dream of Nashoba because it broke her spirit and her heart when your father took you away to France. You were all she lived for. She was just too proud to tell you so and too proud to give up on her great dreams of justice and equality for Negroes and women.

"Pride is a great sin, my little sister, but one many of us often commit. Unfortunately, a more original sin is what brought us back together. Sylva, I must now put the lives and futures of several families in your hands. I hope you can forgive me for bringing you this quandary that you had no part in creating.

"Sylva, I could not chance putting in my letter all that is involved in this matter. You and Nashoba were the only way we could turn. Please, for the sake of our childhood friendship and out of your Christian duty, do not judge too harshly what I must tell you. The lives of several people may be in your hands."

Sylva's need to seek the approval of Jesus was awakened by Eppie's statement. She was being called upon to help others in dire circumstances. Heavenly rewards were possible. "Why, Eppie, it is no problem for us here. This is what we do. We help wayward Negro girls. I am glad you came."

"Oh, Sylva, if only a wayward Negro girl was the problem."

"What do you mean, Eppie? I realize Jane looks white, but that should help her and her child be accepted. Why would anyone else be in jeopardy? Jane looks healthy enough and she has you and Mrs. Jones to help when she returns home. It is not unusual, unfortunately, for these Negro girls to be rather careless with their morals. I am sure Mt. Vernon will not ostracize her. Oh, I am sorry, Eppie. I did not mean anything by that. I know you have lived a good life as a loyal Christian wife."

"Do not fret about it, Sylva. I am not offended. We live in our times and you are correct. There are many Negro girls who seek acceptance from the white community the only way they know how, with their bodies. But, my friend, that is what I am trying to tell you. Jane is not one of those girls. This situation is far more grave and delicate than you imagine. It is not Jane who is with child, it is Mrs. Jones."

"Well, why doesn't she have the child in Mt. Vernon? If she is married, she and her husband will be blessed in their middle years with a child who can look after them in their old age. I surmise Mr. Jones may not want the child now but fathers often do not see the miracle of creation as a miracle until the child is born. He will surely come around when he sees and holds his son or daughter."

"Little sister, the irony is that Mr. Jones has always wanted a child as much as Sarah has. They hoped for years to have one. He is twenty years older than she, but they never gave up on their desire for a child. The problem is far more complicated and grave than you can imagine. The child she carries is not her husband's."

Sylva pulled her feet from the spring and stood up. "Adultery, you brought an adulteress to my home! You know that according to God's law that is a stoning offense!"

"Actually, Sylva, if your god is Jesus, according to His law, it is a forgivable natural act. The stoning law is man's, not God's. I beg you to look into your heart and find forgiveness and kindness. Isn't that what Christians are taught?"

Sylva did see the anomaly in her running a place to help pregnant Negro girls while she condemned Sarah's transgression. Why was Sarah any worse than the young black girls who needed Sylva's help. And as an upper class white woman, she certainly had much farther to fall. Perhaps God would reward assistance to Sarah even more.

"Maybe I was too hasty in my judgment. What does Mrs. Jones plan to do with the child? We do not condone abortion here, that I will not be a party to."

"Sylva, if abortion were the plan, why would Mrs. Jones need to come here. There are midwives and even medical doctors in Evansville or Louisville, Kentucky who can provide such services anonymously for a fee. I fear the time has come to truly test our sisterhood and your Christian mercy. Sarah's baby belongs to Jane's brother."

"What? For the love of God, what manner of animal is he? He must be punished for this rape of a genteel white woman. Why are you and she, and even his sister, protecting this beast? You should have told me this first. I would have never held a forcible assault against her. I know some would, but not I. Of course, she is welcome here, but what about this animal being on the loose in Posey County? She will have to spend the rest of her days in fear."

"Settle yourself, dear sister. You have jumped to a normal but incorrect conclusion. There was no force involved. This was a one time weakness of the flesh brought on by an inordinate longing for a child, not carnal desire. Reach into your deepest roots and ask what our beloved mother would do. Can we not, also, put aside our conventional pride and prejudice and offer help to ones who most need it?"

"I do not know if I can deal with all of this at once. Perhaps we will need to proceed slowly and deliberately. You are right. Mother's grand plan of cenogomy has appeared incarnate. Give me time to withstand my staid conventions. With your support, dear sister, I may yet make our mother proud."

Chapter Sixty-Six

LIGHTING THE FUSE

"Say, Ed, what happened to your pretty little colored maid; she leave town with the family silver?"

Judge John Pitcher enjoyed watching Hayes' color rise into his cheeks. Pitcher figured that Hayes had probably heard some of the rumors flying around about Hayes and Jane Harrison.

Hayes knew he was being baited, but he was so eager to absolve himself he jumped at Pitcher's leering tone. The irony was that Hayes had tried for years to get Jane to agree to an arrangement, but she had consistently rebuffed him. Now some other white man had gotten the fruit and Hayes was being ridiculed for it.

"Judge, she let out for that nigger place in Tennessee. You know, Nashoba, that place Mad Fanny Wright set up years ago. When I saw it during the War, it was being used to let colored girls lay in while they were pregnant. Mrs. Daniels and Mrs. Jones saw to it that Jane got there. She's pregnant, you know. Some son-of-a-bitch got to her then probably tried to get her to kill the little bastard. She must have tried to blackmail him. She likely got a bundle of hush money to keep his name quiet. You have any idea who it might be? And who's trying to hang me with this thing?"

"Now that you ask, Ed, my first thought was it might be a political enemy. I can't think of a better way to bring a man down. After all, you are the choice of the Democratic Party. Sheriff Wheeler wouldn't have a chance against you. Do you think Wheeler might be floating this canard?"

Pitcher knew that Wheeler and Hayes had already agreed that whichever of them won in the November, 1878 general election would hire the other as his chief deputy. Pitcher, also, knew that the popular young war hero, O.C. Thomas, was going to run against Hayes for the Democratic nomination in the spring of 1878. Pitcher relished the opportunity to stir up controversy. He figured that his own political and economic prospects were brightest when other ambitious men were off balance. Besides, Pitcher just enjoyed watching others squirm.

"Judge, do you think O.C. Thomas might have a hand in this? Wheeler wants to beat me, but he, also, wants to stay on if I win. He'd be a fool to think he could slander me then work for me. Thomas seems okay, but I am not convinced he's on the up and up. Sometimes he comes on a little strong with his supposed charitable attitude. I hear he wants to be sheriff. Have you heard anything, Judge?"

Pitcher was elated to have an opportunity to stir up bad blood. He had always resented people who claimed to be happy just as they were. He believed that deep down everybody was as eager as he was to get the better of people. Pitcher always questioned ostensibly selfless acts. He believed everybody was motivated solely by self-interest and his greatest pleasure came from finding evidence to support his belief. O.C. Thomas was one of those people Pitcher detested. Thomas appeared open and without envy. He came across as a modest war hero who liked everybody. And it seemed that everybody liked Thomas, except for Pitcher. Pitcher saw an opportunity with Hayes to bring Thomas down a notch or two.

CHAPTER SIXTY-SEVEN

THE CRIDERS

EPPIE AND SARAH DECIDED TO name Sarah's new born baby Hattie Crider. Their thinking was that both Hattie and Crider were common names in the black community. Also, they knew that someday the child should be told the truth about her biological parents and the reasons for the subterfuge surrounding her birth. They were glad Hattie was born female. A woman was more likely than a man to be understanding in a matter such as this. But the most important reason was that Jane and Ajax had fallen in love. When Jane returned with Hattie to Mt. Vernon, Ajax planned to go with her, the baby and Sarah. Having Ajax Crider appear with Jane would help convince people that Hattie was Jane's and Ajax's child.

Sarah and Eppie had regularly corresponded while Sarah was lying in. They were careful in their letters, but Eppie was able to keep the Harrisons informed. The Harrisons were happy that Jane had found Ajax who appeared to accept Hattie as his own.

Jane and Ajax had decided that Jane and Hattie would live with the Harrisons until Ajax had established himself as a laborer. Once Ajax had regular work, he and Jane would get married and set up their own house.

Eppie frequently checked with Henry who, also, received frequent letters from Sarah. Eppie and Sarah sought help for Ajax from Henry. Henry was happy to work through Christian Willis to find temporary lodging for Ajax at Brewery Hills. This gave Henry another reason to make contact with Soaring Bird.

Christian needed Henry's financial assistance for the missionary work at Brewery Hills. Christian and Reverend Wilson did not condone an illicit relationship between Henry and Bird, but they decided it was not their role to police it. Sight unseen was sin unknown. And the important work of bringing the Gospel to poor Negroes was surely of more value to God than searching for a mote in Henry's eye.

And so when Henry suggested that a strong young black man would be willing to work for his room and board at Brewery Hills, Willis and Wilson saw this as God's unspoken approval of their approach to the matter between Henry and Bird.

Christian Willis accepted Henry's invitation to meet Sarah and the future Crider family when they arrived at the Mt. Vernon landing on April 10, 1878.

Chapter Sixty-Eight

HELLO AGAIN

THE SIX WEEK OLD HATTIE was in Jane's arms. Ajax towered over both of them from behind while Sarah hung back until the "Criders" had disembarked together. Both the Daniel and Charles Harrison families had gathered to welcome Jane, Hattie and Ajax. As they crowded around them, Sarah walked over to Henry who was flanked by Christian Willis and Eppie.

Sarah felt her legs trembling under her hoop skirted dress. She was afraid they would give out and she would collapse. Eppie moved quickly to her and put an arm around her waist.

"Henry, perhaps you'd like to introduce Christian to Ajax while I help Sarah see to the luggage? She and I will join you momentarily."

Henry was glad to have some time to adjust his feelings before having to speak to Sarah. He feared his guilt was written across his face. The fear that drained the color from Sarah's face and her wobbliness escaped Henry's notice.

Sarah whispered to Eppie, "Isn't she beautiful? I do not know how I will stand to see her go."

"Quiet, child, you must stay strong. Plus, Da is there with his family. You do not need to see him at this time. Let them leave while we deal with the trunks. And here comes Henry. Be glad to see him."

Henry took over dealing with the removal of Sarah's things. As he saw to the loading of the carriage, Sarah squeezed Eppie's arm and begged her to go with them to Sarah's home.

"Can you not stay with me at least until we get into the house? I do not trust myself to be alone with Henry. He seems okay, but he may have questions I cannot answer without raising suspicion."

"Now, Sarah, you know the answers to any questions he may ask. Jane and Ajax have a baby girl, Hattie, and they will marry as soon as Ajax finds work. Other than that, all you need to do is tell Henry you are glad to be home. The less you say, the better things will go. However, you must find it in your heart to show Henry some affection. After all, you have been away for months. It will appear strange if you do not return to him as a loving wife would. Here he comes. Get hold of yourself."

Sarah found she was glad to see Henry and, to Henry's surprise, he was glad to see Sarah. Soaring Bird almost immediately began to fade into history again as Sarah touched Henry's brow with her delicate and perfumed hand. Henry realized he had sorely missed her. And Sarah felt herself gravitate towards Henry as he gently kissed her cheek and said, "Sarah, you look good."

By the time Sarah, Henry and Eppie arrived at the Jones' home, Sarah was able to say, "Thank you, Eppie, Henry and I can handle things from here. Henry, please take Eppie on to her home while I unpack. I will be here when you return."

CHAPTER SIXTY-NINE

ALL'S WELL

EVEN SOARING BIRD WAS GLAD for things to return to a quiescent state. She would no longer be disappointed by Henry's promises they both knew he would not keep. And out of his sense of guilt and fear that Sarah would discover his activities with Bird, he now regularly gave her money. Since Bird found his old man's touch held none of the magic she remembered from their youth, she was glad to have the money without having to pretend she wanted Henry.

Henry and Sarah discovered that the absence had brought them a new appreciation for one another. Their mature love had a sweetness that surprised them. Henry no longer dreamed of the beautiful young Soaring Bird and Sarah reacted to Henry's gentle touch with a deep love of her own.

Sarah and Eppie found great joy in being around Hattie when Elizabeth or Jane would bring her to their homes. Neither Henry nor George was ever present when Hattie was with Sarah or Eppie. The women irrationally feared that the bond that existed between them and Hattie might, also, arise with Henry and George. But men are less often captured by someone else's offspring than are women, especially when children are in swaddling clothes. Once a child develops a unique personality and displays talents that a particular man takes an interest in, it is not unusual for an avuncular relationship to arise. However, at Hattie's tender age most men, including Henry and George, are content to eschew any more than a passing comment that the child may be cute.

Jane and Ajax were steadily working towards saving up enough money from Jane's housework at Darly Hayes' home and Ajax's odd laboring jobs to start their own housekeeping.

Elizabeth got to see her grandchild on a regular basis and Da had but little interest in Hattie, so he was comfortable having his sister and mother raise her.

Ed Hayes had convinced himself that Wheeler was likely to beat O.C. Thomas in the sheriff's election in November so the wounds from his twenty vote loss to Thomas in the May Democratic primary were starting to scab over. Hayes had started treating Jane with some respect ever since she had introduced him to her huge future husband.

All in all, Eppie, Sarah and Jane were pleased and amazed that their convoluted plan appeared to be working out better than they had dared to hope.

Of course, the gods were not about to allow such a boring state of affairs to continue. The first hint of trouble was the outcome of the Widow Watson's claim that the Negro Jim Good had assaulted her.

CHAPTER SEVENTY

THE ERSTWHILE VIRGIN

EMMA DAVIS WAS SO EXCITED she could not make her fingers work the hooks and eyes on her high top shoes. The shoes were hand-me-downs from a by-gone working girl who had abruptly left the business to marry a riverboat deck hand. The entire courtship had started the previous Saturday night and culminated in undying love Sunday morning. The new bride had also bequeathed her bustier and a red boa to Emma.

Although Emma had just turned fifteen, she had spent her years since the onset of her menses working around her mother, Ida, and the other prostitutes at Rosa Hughes' house. Her mother knew how valuable the beautiful and fresh Emma could be but she was reluctant to get her started into the life Ida hated but could not escape.

The progression was rarely deviated from. First a young whore could sell her false virginity. Then she could earn her best money as an experienced but still physically attractive woman. Next she could start her own house if she had been wise enough to save any money. Or, as was usually the case, the tired out older woman ended her days as a charwoman for younger whores.

Rarely, some lonely and invariably ne'er-do-well customer would deign to make an honest woman out of a prostitute. In Ida's experience, these satanic bargains led to more heartache than did growing old alone.

Ida had planned to keep Emma out of the family business. Emma's older half-sister, Susan, was already past phase one and Ida rued each time some drunken, smelly river boater would trade his two dollars for her daughter's soul. She did not want that for Emma, but without Rosa Hughes, neither Ida nor her two daughters would have a home.

So when Rosa came to Ida asking that Emma fill the slot left by the newlywed, Ida asked Emma how she felt about it.

"Honey, you don't have to do this. It ain't much of a life as your sister and I can tell you. I should have sent you to school but children of women like me are not welcomed. Maybe you could have stood the name calling but the other mothers would probably never have let you be with their little darlings. Now you need to make some hard choices. What do you want to do? Rosa says she needs you and we need Rosa."

Ida was aware that the first trick she was asking her daughter to pull was to sell her body so that her mother, her sister and she would not lose their home. Ida had long ago forgotten who the first, second or hundredth man was for her. She did remember how she hated the smells of the men who used her as if she had no more significance to them than a privy. She did not want that for Emma. On the other hand, Ida and Susan had provided for Emma by the only means they knew. Why was Emma any better than they were?

"Emma, will you do this for me just this once, Honey, and for your sister? Maybe Rosa can find some new girl soon and you won't have to do it anymore."

"Momma, I'm scared. What if the men don't want me? How do I do it, you know, how does it work? Won't it hurt? What do I say to the men?"

Ida was ashamed to start Emma down a road that had no u-turns and few y's. She, also, was embarrassed to try to teach the sordid details of sexual encounters to her own daughter. Ida considered having Emma's sister begin her training, but she decided that would double her sins upon her daughters. And as the boatmen would be arriving within a few hours, there was not time to waste. If Ida was going to force this life on Emma, she would, at least, try to soften the blows herself.

"Now, Honey, you will find that very few men know anything about the intimate details of a woman. So you start out, even at fifteen, far more knowledgeable in these matters than men. On top of that, whether you realize it or not, you are a beautiful girl. Men will fight to pay high prices to have you. Men like young girls. It makes them believe they know more than the girl. They don't, of course, but with men, their perception of themselves is what makes women money. One of your jobs will be to convince the man you are with that you think he is a wonderful lover. At first, that will be easy for you because you will know no better. But, as you become more experienced, you will find that a woman's best lover comes from her brain not a man's body. And then your true job will begin, that is, to convince yourself you are enjoying things. Unfortunately, you will not be able to trick yourself after your first few men."

"But, Momma, does it hurt? What if I get pregnant? No one will want me then will they?"

"Child, it may hurt some the first time or two, but just remember that girls have been doing this since the beginning of time. I did it, your sister did it, all the other working girls and wives have done it. These things come naturally. I suggest that at first you close your eyes and think of something else, something pleasant, like the waves on the Ohio River or the smell of fresh baked bread. It is likely that the smells will be harder for you than the man will."

"How will I know when it's over and I can come back downstairs? Do I say anything at the beginning or when he's through?"

"Don't fret about it, girl. He won't take long and then he will be the one who wants to get away from you. You don't need to say anything except maybe to sigh a little if you can. Rosa takes care of the money up front so that's none of your concern. You are going to have to wash the men off first. Just use the washcloth and soap. You will learn as you go along to help shorten your time with them by extending the cleaning. But, as you have not ever seen a man, for now you can just wash them and get onto the bed. Afterwards you must thoroughly wash yourself and use the aloe and cotton root douche in the syringe. That will help prevent any pregnancy."

"Momma, can I ask you something?" Ida knew what was coming. She just nodded. "Do you like the men? I mean, will I enjoy them?"

"Emma, I hope you do like it. Over the years I have enjoyed it with a few men. For example, I thought the two men who gave me you and your sister really loved me, and maybe they did for awhile. But honestly, girl, the circumstances of how we survive do not often lead to love. I suggest you will get through this easier if you do not expect too much."

CHAPTER SEVENTY-ONE

INGÉNUE

ROSA HUGHES HAD BEEN KEEPING her eye on William Combs and Emma Davis for some time. After having her fantasies of a normal life with Combs dashed by his marriage, Rosa had accepted the half loaf of an arrangement. But she did not intend to lose her arrangement to some new rival.

At first Comb's interest in Emma appeared to be paternalistic. He had bounced her on his lap when she was a toddler and he began giving her advice and small gifts about the time she entered puberty. But Rosa had noticed that recently he found opportunities to touch Emma in ways that Rosa's professional experience catalogued as unsavory.

Emma did not appear to understand the import of Combs' attention to her. She had a light hearted, open spirit in general and seemed to gravitate to his frequent contacts as if he were a father figure. But Rosa knew Combs well. She, also, knew professional women. Even if Emma was truly obtuse in the matter, when money entered the picture, Rosa suspected that Emma's bloodlines would take over. And Rosa was going to do her best to protect what was hers. Time was of the essence as the beautiful young Emma was blossoming right before Rosa's eyes.

Rosa saw the unexpected marriage of one of her best working girls as the opportune time for a preemptive strike.

Unfortunately for Rosa, her scheme to remove the bloom from Emma played out much the same as her earlier dreams of marriage. And this time Rosa would bring Emma down with her.

Rosa feared that Combs would try to intervene if he knew that Emma was about to be sacrificed. But earlier that day, Combs had told Rosa he could not come by that night for their regular time together. Mrs. Combs had decided to delay her normal shopping trip to Evansville until the following weekend. And the Memphis Belle with its Captain and a crew of five deckhands was due to dock at the Mt. Vernon landing when night fell. Rosa planned to sell Emma's virginity to the highest bidder.

Emma had spent the past two hours primping and asking her sister every question she could think of. When the knock on the side door finally came, Emma was surprised to find herself not only frightened but, also, excited. Susan had assuaged much of her fear of inadequacy by giving Emma a step by step procedure to follow. Susan had told her that she had been extremely nervous the first time their mother had brought her out. But a wealthy merchant had outbid everyone for her and presented her to his handsome Civil War hero son for a pre-wedding gift. Susan confided to Emma that when the young man had to ask Susan what to do, she had no trouble taking the lead and enjoying it immensely. Maybe Emma would get purchased by some strong young man herself. Emma was excited by the prospect.

Rosa had ordered all three of the working girls to remain upstairs while Rosa and Ida whetted the boatmen's fantasies. Rosa opened the side door and showed the boat captain and his crew into the parlor with its red flocked wallpaper. The oil lamps were dimmed and cheap whisky was available for premium prices. Rosa and Ida grabbed each man as he entered and put a tumbler filled with watered down liquor into his hand. When all six men had been seated on the worn horsehair sofas, Rosa collected a dollar from each of them for the drinks.

"Gentlemen, you are in for a special evening. Some of you have stopped by before with Captain Granger. You already know Jennie Summers. You know you can't get that at home. Would you like to see what's in store for some lucky man tonight? Well, let me see two silver dollars in each of your hands. That's just to start the bidding for the beautiful Jennie. Jennie, come down and meet six of the handsomest men you'll ever see!"

Jennie Summers had worked for Rosa from the time she was twenty-five. At age thirty-five she had begun to show the ravages of untreated venereal diseases and the occasional beating some drunken john had administered. But in the dim light, her pocked marked and painted face was scarcely noticed by the aroused men. And Jennie knew how to keep the light to her back as she worked the room.

When Rosa got a five dollar bid from a burly deckhand with filthy fingernails, she deftly took the coins in one hand and placed Jennie's arm around his neck. As the other men moaned in disappointment Rosa sent Jennie and the man up the stairs.

"Well, I guess that's all boys. The rest of you should have bid more."

The men suspected that Rosa was just playing with them so they did not react violently. As Jennie disappeared with their crewmate, Rosa winked at Captain Granger. "Alright, Captain, do you think your men deserve more?"

"To hell with my men, what about me, I ain't that old you know. Where's mine?"

"Now, Captain Granger, I am surprised at you. What about poor little Mrs. Granger back home? Or didn't you tell her about your last trip by here?"

As Granger's men laughed and pointed at him, Ida signaled up the stairs for Susan to come down. When the men caught a glimpse of a well turned ankle they suddenly got silent in anticipation.

Granger spoke first as Susan's face came into view, "Ten dollars! By God, she's mine!" The rest of the crew muttered to themselves, but could not outbid their captain. Rosa was disappointed that she was going to lose Granger's deep pockets in the bidding for Emma. She decided to hold up on Emma until Granger and the other crewman came back down. Her greed resulted in her undoing.

"Boys, don't worry. Women are just like candles. All of you will be able to get a light if you are patient. I make no promises, but there may be an even more beautiful and special flower waiting for the man who wants her bad enough. For now, have another drink or two as Ida and I make sure your mate and your Captain get more than their money's worth."

Emma had watched from behind a curtain as Jennie and then Susan had brought their customers up the stairs. Emma felt her fear dissipating and her excitement rising. She had seen the six men as they arrived. One looked to be about her age. He had wavy brown hair and fair skin and Emma could see his muscular build outlined by his thin cotton shirt. Emma had commented to Susan about him. Susan looked at Emma as she passed the curtain. Susan winked at Emma and pointed towards the fresh faced young boatman looking up the stairs.

Rosa knew that anticipation was the best way to raise prices. She decided to wait until well after the men were done with Jennie and Susan to bring out Emma. Rosa knew men needed some recovery time and she wanted all six digging into their pockets for Emma and then seconds with Jennie and Susan.

Granger came down first followed a few minutes later by the crewman. Ida and Rosa were now prepared for the *piece de resistance*.

"Gentlemen, I have preserved a very special treat for you. Ida's youngest daughter, Emma, who has never been with any man, is willing to share her treasure with one of you. She is fifteen years old and a beauty to behold. Think about what a rare find like this is worth. Sight unseen, what am I bid for this virginal flower?"

The six men did not believe for a minute this old pimp's and madam's ruse of selling virginity. On the other hand, four of the men were eager for any relief. Even Granger and the crewman felt their interest rise.

"Come on, boys; give me a bid in the dark. Where's your sporting blood?"

Captain Granger started the bidding at two dollars. The other five took the price to eight dollars before Rosa told Ida to bring her lovely daughter down the stairs. When the men saw Emma, all but the handsome young man she had hoped for gathered around her. The bidding rose rapidly until the shy young man asked Granger what was the most advance he could get on his three month wages. When Granger told him if he wanted to work for free until they got back to Pittsburgh he could have thirty dollars, the young man bid it all. Emma was so excited she would have contributed to her own price for the young man.

Amid the laughter and commotion no one had heard the back door open. William Combs had a key to the house because he secretly owned it. He had slipped in to be with Rosa after his wife had changed her plans once again and left for Evansville.

"Thirty-five dollars," Combs quietly said as he emerged from the shadows.

Rosa could not speak. She sat down on the arm of a divan as the six riverboat men bristled.

"Now see here, mister. This boy has never had a woman and, if Rosa's telling the truth, this pretty little girl is a virgin. It just makes sense for them to be together their first time. Why don't you back off? I'll even give you ten dollars if you do." Captain Granger was trying to keep his men from doing something rash in this place where they had no power. Besides, if something happened, the story might work its way back up the Ohio River to Pittsburgh and Mrs. Granger.

"Keep your ten dollars, sir. And I suggest that you control your crew. Yours would not be the first gang of river rats to meet their fate in Hoop Pole Town." Granger knew that this middle aged, well dressed man was referring to the famous incident where a crew of boatmen had been beaten senseless by a group of Mt. Vernon coopers who used hoop poles from their barrel making. Mt. Vernon was infamous for its reputation of vigilante justice to disorderly boatmen.

"Don't threaten us, sir. We ain't as easy to scare off as some. You may take note that there are six of us and one of you."

"I advise you to take note that I own this house. These women answer to me. Further, my business partner is Judge Pitcher who will make sure you rot in a Posey County jail if you do not leave peaceably and right now."

Rosa could not believe the turn of events. Her plan to prevent Combs from transferring his attention to Emma had assured just that outcome. Now, if she did not act quickly, Combs might abandon her completely and evict her besides.

"Captain Granger, you and your men had best leave quietly. Take two bottles of whiskey for your trouble. Perhaps the next time you pass this way, things may have settled down."

The handsome young man had to be held back by Granger. He stared first fiercely at Combs then sadly at Emma. Emma could not help crying although Rosa, Ida and Susan knew that for everyone's sake, Emma had to go through with this Hobson's choice.

Emma often returned to this night where she found herself in bed with the man she had thought of as a father while the handsome young man she had fantasized about drifted away on the river. Later, when Emma found that she was repulsed by the touch of men, especially Combs, yet had to pretend to enjoy it, she always returned to this first night.

Even after the induced, late term abortion that Combs had forced upon her, she had no thought of other women. Yet, when Jennie Bell had gently washed her hair and softly kissed her lips, Emma had finally found the passion she had dreamed of with the young boatman.

CHAPTER SEVENTY-TWO

A GRUESOME PASS

UNTIL TOM HANSON HAD DROPPED the old Order Book on his bench, Judge John Eagleson had paid scant attention to the sepia colored tintypes of Posey County's judges from the nineteenth century. He was entertained by their beards and quaint clothes, but they were history and he had pressing cases to decide. Eagleson had noted that several of the old judges were photographed, not in judicial robes, but in their Civil War uniforms. Their war experience must have been more important to them than their judicial service.

Since reading the legal entries from 1878 to 1881, and the yellowed newspaper clippings stuffed among the pages, Judge Eagleson had found himself drawn to the eyes of judges Alvin P. Hovey and William F. Parrett, Jr. Now when Eagleson worked after hours he would spread his files and legal research out on the ten foot long massive oak table in the room named in honor of Hovey who was the only person from Posey County to serve as Indiana's governor. The photographs of Hovey and Parrett faced one another as if in an eternal unspoken conversation. Eagleson was unable to concentrate on his work unless he was positioned where he could look up and immediately see his two colleagues from yesteryear. He found it eerily disquieting to have his back to the old judges.

In addition to the articles about how John and young Daniel Harrison had met their fates, Eagleson had found an account of old Dan's slaughter. This article had been neatly and carefully folded as if to assure time would not obscure its content. It was beside the order book entry describing the action of the emergency Coroner's Jury that Parrett had ordered Coroner William Hendricks to convene to investigate the shooting death of Deputy Sheriff O.C. Thomas.

Eagleson knew from his reading of other articles that Ed Hayes had claimed old Dan Harrison shot Thomas then Hayes had shot Harrison twice before the Negro escaped. When Harrison later that morning turned himself in through Morita Meier, he was weak from loss of blood. Harrison was placed on a pallet on the jail floor in the log portion of the jail near the four younger Negroes who were being held behind the locked iron door of the newer cell.

Eagleson read newspaper editor John Leffel's eye witness account of Daniel Harrison, Sr.'s last moments on earth:

 C3

"Old Harrison presented a pitiable appearance, looking weak and sick, but cool and unmoved. He lay on a pallet without uttering a sound, while the other four, who were locked in the first cell from the door, were kneeling on the floor, with their heads bowed to the wall, praying in the loud monotonous, thrilling tone of the camp meeting negro.

A single candle shed a sickly light upon the scene, and the last hours in the cell were terrible in their gloom. The old man, Harrison, was suddenly surrounded by men from whose hearts all humanity seemed to have fled, and their place filled with a demon. Without a word he was seized, a hand clutched about his throat to stifle any scream, and a knife plunged into his heart. In five minutes his body was cut into pieces like a hog, head, arms, legs, all separated, and the sickening mass of human flesh was flung into the privy."

☙

John Eagleson looked up from the grizzly account to see both Hovey and Parrett staring at him. He was not, at first, sure what their eyes were trying to convey. Then he understood; their shame had been there for all to see for over one hundred and thirty years. They might not have killed the seven African American men, but they had felt responsible for not stopping or punishing those who did. And they were beseeching Judge John Eagleson to help them and Posey County atone. First Eagleson had to try to understand what would bring the people whom Leffel described as, "two to three hundred of Posey County's best men," to butcher old Daniel Harrison and lynch the other four Negroes. Eagleson carefully removed the numerous newspaper clippings from the Order Book and spread them out on the antique oak table. He read alone except for the visages of Hovey and Parrett. When Eagleson finished it was after midnight. The old accounts contained much detail, but they, also, left huge gaps for Eagleson to fill in using his own experience with human nature as it had paraded in front of him on the bench.

CHAPTER SEVENTY-THREE

STORM CLOUDS

JIM GOOD HAD NEVER CARED much for work. His only regular income came from doing odd jobs for the Widow Watson whose husband had passed away in 1875. She was only thirty-two when he died and left her with little more than a small house with a large yard that she planted in vegetables. The widow had promised Good three dollars if he would plow the yard.

Instead of admitting to Good that she could not come up with all three dollars to pay him, Mrs. Watson claimed he had not got the land ready in time for her to plant it so she would dock his pay by half. When Good angrily demanded the rest of his pay, she became frightened and fell back on the white woman's fail safe plan of eliminating angry black men from their lives.

Her complaints to Deputy Ed Hayes that Good had tried to assault her resulted first in a beating of Good for "resisting arrest", then in charges against him. But after a jury had rendered a verdict of guilty and recommended two years in prison, Alvin Hovey had convinced Judge Parrett to set the verdict aside and set Good free.

Much of the white community was furious with the reversal and calls for *ultra vires* action were raised throughout Posey County. John Leffel even published an editorial playing upon Good's name. As Leffel put it, "A little hanging might do Jim some Good."

The atmosphere was roiled up further when Rosa Hughes' working girl, Annie Mc Cool, was found dead on the bank of the Ohio River. Annie was known by Rosa and William Combs to be involved with William Chambers. Chambers was a twenty-eight year old black man who slept most of the day and gambled away the money Mc Cool earned on her back. Chambers' hold over Mc Cool was difficult for Rosa to understand. He would not work. He spent Annie's hard earned money. And he beat her when he drank.

When Annie's body was found, she had numerous bruises on her body and one of her long black stockings around her neck. Chambers was saved from a lynching then by Annie's profession, the alibi he established through his fellow layabouts, Edward Warner and Jeff Hopkins, and Ed Hayes' knowledge of the unusual sexual tastes of Annie's most regular white customer. Hayes and Rosa had often remarked on this upstanding white man's weakness for sadomasochistic services. As Annie had an appointment with this friend of Hayes the night she was found by the river, Hayes did not wish to delve too deeply into who killed her.

But when Duffy the Dyer who ran a local gambling hall was robbed and murdered, his colored clientele were the prime suspects in the death of the well liked Duffy. However, in spite of the efforts of the law enforcement community, no individuals could be connected to the crime. This resulted in many of the county's white people casting suspicion on all young black men in general.

All of these events occurred between April and June of 1878. With newspaper editor John Leffel fanning the flames, the regular legal system was seen as inadequate to protect the community. Judge Pitcher and others had no trouble molding the atmosphere of bigotry and fear into calls for vigilante action.

The meeting held under the gathering storm clouds at Black's Grove on June 8, 1878 was the beginning of the end of the momentary tranquility Eppie and Sarah had enjoyed to the point that they had lost contact with the reality they had so rightly feared.

CHAPTER SEVENTY-FOUR

STEAMY POSEY COUNTY

THE SUMMER OF 1878 WAS the normal miserably hot and humid one for Posey County. Being only three hundred feet above sea level and having the Ohio and Wabash rivers as its southern and western borders, the county regularly endured humidity levels in excess of ninety percent. The humidity was often accompanied by summer time temperatures between ninety and one hundred degrees.

Sweaty irritability was a concomitant of all Posey County summers in those days before air conditioning. Young men, white and black, spent as much time as possible out of doors, often with beer to help ease the heat.

After a spring filled with several incidents that exacerbated tensions between the races, the hot, sticky, alcohol influenced summer of 1878 filled the newspapers and taverns with accounts of numerous fist and knife fights between testosterone teeming young black and white men and calls from both whites and blacks for vengeance. As predictable as young men spoiling to test themselves in impromptu boxing rings, often the catalysts for the brawls were women, particularly women who made their favors available for hire. However, the most volatile issue did not involve drunken young men but innocent, would-be students.

Eppie Daniels, who had been regularly appearing before the county school board for years demanding that colored children be allowed to attend the county's only high school, had decided that before this autumn she would force the issue. She and Sarah Jones were trying to organize support for school integration through each of their churches. They brought Daniel, Sr., and Elizabeth Harrison to the school board meetings that were held in the large courtroom of the new courthouse.

The Harrison children had shown promise over the years that Elizabeth had worked for Eppie and Sarah, but efforts to have Jane then John then Da and now their fourteen year old twin siblings, Nicy and Samuel, allowed into high school had met with vitriolic refusals.

If school integration and sex were not enough, the local political races helped salt the festering wounds. Ed Hayes had managed to put forth an image of the gracious loser to O.C. Thomas until it began to appear that Thomas might beat Wheeler in November. Hayes and Wheeler decided that something must be done to pull the popular young war hero down a peg or two. Hayes decided to use his law enforcement credentials and his symbiotic relationship with Rosa Hughes' house to smear the naïve young Thomas.

Posey County's whorehouses were a time honored tradition. The location of Mt. Vernon on one of the few accessible and flood free elevations between Louisville, Kentucky and Cairo, Illinois assured that Ohio River boatmen would regularly stop for supplies and other needs.

The community of McFadin's Bluff was founded in 1795 and the first case of prostitution to be prosecuted in what later became Posey County occurred in the Justice of the Peace Court in the Posey County settlement of West Franklin in 1816. Professional women had plied their trade while local law enforcement took payoffs in money and services for more than half a century before Ed Hayes made his accommodation with the only two "sanctioned" establishments, Rosa's and Jennie Bell's. Although, due to the recent brouhaha caused by Jennie Bell's falling out with her white patrons when she was caught in *flagrante delicto* with Jim Good, the kickbacks from Jennie's place were down substantially.

Jennie had cried rape, but most people had assumed Good was just a paying customer long before Alvin Hovey, once again, got the charges thrown out by Judge Parrett. Hayes had been in the Posey Circuit Court on both the Widow Watson case and the later Jennie Bell accusation. Even Hayes had to admit that nigger son-of-a-bitch was not guilty after Hovey had cross examined Watson and Bell. But Hayes thought he should have, at least, been horsewhipped for messing with a white woman, even a white whore.

Hayes was well aware that William Combs had a long association with Rosa Hughes. Hayes was, also, aware that the ridiculous old fool had turned his attentions to Emma Davis. Hayes was one of the few people who knew that Combs owned Rosa's house. Hayes thought that, perhaps, he could use this information about Combs to his advantage in the political arena.

He decided that the first thing he would do was approach Rosa Hughes about Combs. Hayes felt sure that Rosa must harbor some resentment over Combs acting the fool over Emma. Rosa was street wise in ways Hayes was not. She might suggest the best way to enlist Combs in the effort to bring down Thomas.

CHAPTER SEVENTY-FIVE

POLITICS AS USUAL

JUDGE JOHN PITCHER MAY HAVE had the influence to get the June 8, 1878 vigilante committee formed, but the idea originated with Rosa Hughes. When Hayes had approached her with the possibility of somehow weakening O.C. Thomas and driving a wedge between William Combs and Emma Davis, Rosa's intimate knowledge of much of Posey County's white male population was invaluable. For years, Rosa had carefully and secretly kept detailed records of the white male establishment's patronage of her house. This information coupled with Rosa's native intelligence and experience was more than Hayes could have hoped for.

Rosa was also motivated to see Thomas desecrated because she feared he might actually keep his campaign promise and shut down prostitution in Posey County. With all the black/white uproar and the church ladies beginning to organize against sin and corruption, O.C. Thomas' pledge to clean up Belleville might be more than the usual rhetoric. If so, Rosa, who could not even vote against Thomas, knew that she must prevent his election some other way.

Of course, Rosa's other strong motivation to work with Hayes was her raging inner anger at losing Combs to Emma. The knowledge that she had been directly responsible for her own demise only made her angrier.

"Before O.C. got married he spent one night with Susan Davis. He never came back. He has never come around asking for favors for himself or anyone else. In fact, Jennie Bell and I have been talking about Thomas ever since the May primary. He says he will close us down and he might actually try to do it.

"Jennie and I don't see eye to eye on much, but we agree Thomas must be stopped. One problem I see with Thomas is he has been trying to get the ladies in town to approach my girls and Jennie's too. He claims that instead of continuing to arrest the girls whenever public pressure requires it, he wants the church ladies to help the girls find other work. He says it's unlikely that men will stop their demand for our services so he wants to eliminate the supply. I know he has personally tried to get Susan Davis to leave my house and move to Brewery Hills.

"I do not see any mud sticking to Sir Galahad if we were to try to smear him. What might work is to show that his approach to fighting crime is dangerous. You have heard his stump speeches about alleviating street crime by helping young black and white men to find jobs such as at William Combs' factory. I know William hates black people, but Thomas appears unaware of this.

"My point is that O.C. is one of those Civil War veterans who believe the war was fought to give Negroes equal rights. You and I know that the majority of adult, white property owners in Posey County sent Hovey to the state constitutional convention for the express purpose of voting against such an outcome. I think that's where Thomas is most vulnerable."

"But, Rosa, how do we use Thomas' wacky ideas against him? He was saying the same things when he beat me in the primary."

"That is true, but he only beat you by twenty votes. And back then you were not attacking him for being soft on crime. Remember, Ed, since May we have had numerous incidents of Negro crime. The white community is angry and afraid. Even John Leffel has called for vigilante justice on the front page of *The Western Star*. The atmosphere is ripe for you to show the differences between Sheriff Wheeler and O.C."

Rosa did not tell Hayes that she was sure William Combs would eagerly jump on the anti-Negro vigilante bandwagon. Rosa knew that Combs still harbored deep resentment over the 1847 incident involving Eppie Daniels and Samson Wright. Rosa's hope was that Combs might somehow get crosswise with Susan Davis if Thomas was attacked. Then, maybe, Emma's closeness to her half sister might cause her to go against Combs. It was a long shot, but what other shot did she have to stop Thomas and get Combs back? Further, Rosa knew that Hayes hated the hulking young Ajax for getting from Jane Harrison what she kept from Hayes.

In fact, the whole Harrison clan had been in Hayes' personal and law enforcement sights for some time. Many white people in the county blamed young Daniel Harrison and his brother John for much of the recent turmoil. It seemed that old Dan Harrison was unable to keep his two boys in tow. They were uppity niggers who refused to back away from a fight. Such an attitude was just what a vigilante committee was for.

CHAPTER SEVENTY-SIX

BLACK MEN UNITE

ONCE JOHN LEFFEL ANNOUNCED IN his newspaper that a citizen's law enforcement assistance committee headed by Ed Hayes was seeking members, Hayes was inundated with white male recruits.

What the vigilante group had not anticipated was the open defiance from some of Posey County's young black men. Hayes, Combs, Daniels, Jones, Leffel and Pitcher could not believe their good fortune when crudely lettered leaflets exclaiming "Black men unite! White men beware!" began to appear throughout the county.

Pitcher told the burgeoning Citizens Committee that the leaflets had to come from a small segment of the three hundred Negroes who lived in Posey County. Probably no more than ten to twenty young black men would be idiotic enough to openly challenge the twenty thousand strong white community. The Citizens Committee should be able to guess with a reasonable degree of certainty who the trouble makers were. The young black hot heads were writing Wheeler's law and order campaign speeches for him.

So, when O.C. Thomas began to make public appeals for calm and dialogue between the races, Hayes was sure the tide would turn against

Thomas. For his part, O.C. did not appear to appreciate the depth of the vitriolic feelings against Negroes that recent events had engendered. He continued to call upon the church congregations, white and black, to seek a peaceful resolution of the ill will in the county.

The more he called for reason and good faith to prevail, the more Hayes and Wheeler tried to tie Thomas to a soft on crime stance. This caused some of the older members in the black community to become afraid. They remembered the days of blackbirding and slavery. The young black men did not appear to comprehend how impotent they really were and how precariously Negro welfare teetered upon a fulcrum of white largesse.

Daniel Harrison, Sr., suspected that Da and John were involved in some of the fights with whites and in the black group calling for action. Old Dan had never really believed he would live to see Negroes treated fairly. But he and his younger brother, Charles, did subscribe to the hope that their children might someday have the opportunity to live in peace with whites.

Daniel and Elizabeth had done everything they could think of to protect their children from becoming victims of hate crimes. They kept in their place. They never looked white people in the eye. If white people did not honor their agreements to pay them for work, Daniel and Elizabeth just smiled and said, "Yes sir, Boss." They had built their home on Daniel's lots in Mt. Vernon and bought their forty acres of farm land in Point Township by working six days a week and saving every cent they could without starving their family. They attended their colored A.M.E. Christian church every Sunday and prayed to Jesus with complete trust in His protection. They always stepped aside when they met white people on the streets or boardwalks. And, except for Da and John, their children and Charles and Eliza's children did the same. Da and John were too young to remember the way things were before the War. They acted as though they believed Mr. Lincoln's words. They saw no need to tuck at their metaphorical dreadlocks or turn down the opportunity to consort with white women. In fact, John and Daniel had been involved in the recent black/white brawl down on the Ohio River front that had started over complaints from young white men about Jim Good's visit to Jennie Bell's place. Instead of keeping his thoughts to himself, John bragged that not only Jim Good but he and other black men sometimes slipped into Rosa's and Jennie's houses. It took deputies Ed Hayes and O.C. Thomas as well as Constables Charles Baker and William Russell to quell the riot. Hayes made sure to relate to William Combs that John Harrison claimed to have spent the previous night with Emma Davis.

Old Daniel could sense that his family might well be in danger when he heard about the riot and word the Citizens Committee was organizing a response. Daniel decided to ask Morita Meier for advice.

CHAPTER SEVENTY-SEVEN

DA'S DEFIANCE

MORITA AND HAGAR MEIER HEARD the light rap on their rear door just after dark on September 25, 1878. When Morita opened the door he saw Daniel Harrison, Sr., and Ajax Crider standing on the ground below the stoop. Morita noted that even with white people they felt comfortable around, the Negroes were not sure they should be near the door.

Morita stepped out and called for Hagar to bring water and glasses. They sat out in the yard to catch what little breeze was available.

"Mr. Meier, Ajax an me was wondrin' if we's might ask you sompun? I's worried my boys Daniel an John is spilin for trouble. I believes they's mixed up in dis black men bizness."

"Vell, Daniel, youz and Elizabeth are not inwoled. Everybody knows youz are good people. Has anything happened?"

"No, sir, Mr. Meier, nots yet. But I have some bad feelins. My boys ain't like me. Des hot headed. Does ya thinks you could mebbe talk with Officer Hayes an tells him deys good boys jus a little filled wit ol Nick. I's heared some rumors about my youngins, particularly Daniel. He been say'n crazy things an I's feared sompun bad could happen."

"Tell me, Daniel, vat's Da doing? Vas he involved in that fight at the Pilot House last night?"

"He sho nuff was, Mr. Meier, an John too. They was both drinking and when Mister Hayes showed up with Mr. Baker and Mr. Thomas and Mr. Russell my boys was talking outs of school about white women. I's don kno if they was talking jus ta make de white men mad, but I hears the Committee is planning to use hickory clubs to beat em up. But what's I's feared of, Mr. Combs, Mr. Daniels and Mr. Jones is tole my boys deys goin ta shoot em if dey see em back in town. An I's knos my boys. Dey ain't goin ta stay out on de farm for long. Can you hep us, Mr. Meier?"

"Ajax, vas you inwolved?"

"No sir, Mr. Meier. Mister Harrison jus wanted me to come wit him in case you might need me. You's know that Jane and I plans to marry soon. Da and John is pretty dear to Jane. But I don' ever come to town 'cept to see Jane and her baby, Hattie."

Morita noted that Ajax had not said "our baby, Hattie", but his own English was so bad he gave it no more thought at that time.

"Daniel, I vill talk to Mr. Howey and see vat he says. Youz know youz can trust Mr. Howey. But try to keep your boys away from town. And tell them they are playing mit fire to talk about vite vemon."

"Thanks you, Mister Meier. I's know my boys ain't no angels but I's don wants to see em dead. Duz yous wants us to come back or jus waits ta hear?"

"Come right back if there's more trouble. But if you can vait it out I vill see vat Mr. Howey adwises. Go home now. Do not vorry. Mr. Howey vas a general. He vill know vat to do."

Unfortunately, Alvin Hovey was in Indianapolis working on an appeal of one of Posey County's most famous civil cases, the Estate of Robert Dale Owen. Hovey's good friend and long time political adversary had died in 1877 and Hovey had been named by Judge Parrett to administer Owen's estate. As Owen's assets were almost as large as his charitable nature, Hovey's duties in sorting out all the claims and bequests were quite time consuming.

So when Meier went to Hovey's daughter's house, he was told Hovey would not be back until October the fifteenth. Meier decided not to write to him. Surely, he thought, a week or two would make no difference.

CHAPTER SEVENTY-EIGHT

A NEW PLAN

SHERIFF WHEELER AND HIS DEPUTY, Ed Hayes, were beginning to panic. It was only about one month until the voters of Posey County would be choosing between Wheeler and O.C. Thomas. Thomas had refused to take the law and order, white on black, bait. He kept calling for calm and understanding from both races. What was worse, the church leaders were buying into Thomas' message. Thomas had spoken against vigilantism in at least one church every Sunday since Leffel had announced the formation of the Citizens Committee in June, 1878.

Church going women, white and black, rallied behind Thomas in his calls for justice, not vengeance. And even though none of the women could vote, they were a formidable influence. Many of the white male voters who wanted to join the Committee were too afraid of their wives, mothers and sisters to do so. Those who were already attending the weekly meetings in Black's Grove tried to keep a low profile. As for the blacks, most of the young Negroes would never dare to incur their mother's or grandmother's disapproval by being found to be part of the Negro male counter group.

Hayes decided to go back to Rosa Hughes to see if she had any better idea than waiting for O.C. Thomas to hang himself. Hayes' timing was good as William Combs seemed to be getting more infatuated with Emma Davis with each passing weekend. Rosa had been racking her brain for some way to solve her own problem. So, when Ed Hayes asked her to meet him after dark on Monday, September 30, 1878 down by McFadin's Bluff, Rosa hoped Hayes had good news. Instead, she found Hayes to be as hapless as ever.

"You've got to do something, Rosa. That son-of-a-bitch Thomas has every preacher in the county touting him for sheriff. I guess we're just supposed to turn the other cheek to those black bastards. And you know the next thing on the do-gooders' list will be you and your girls. You said that we could make Thomas look soft on crime. Hell, apparently that's what these idiots want!"

"Calm down, Ed. It's a whole month until the election. As you know, that's a lifetime in Posey County politics. Look at some of the fools and crooks that keep getting reelected to the county council and board of commissioners. That should give you and Wheeler confidence."

Hayes was not sure if he'd been insulted or not, but either way he decided he needed Rosa too much to take issue with her acid tongue.

"Well, what about you, Rosa? It looks like that old fool, Combs, is about to move Emma into his house with his wife and kids. What I do hear is that he's trying to get her to start her own house with his backing. If that happens, it will be Ida, Susan and Emma and you will be out. It is his building after all. From what I keep hearing on the street, Combs wants Emma to just service him while she and he make money off her momma and sister. I, also, hear that he wants Emma to approach Jennie Bell about combining their businesses. You know she seems awful tight with your competitor, don't you? I did make sure and tell Combs that brash nigger, John Harrison, claimed to get Emma Davis recently. Combs got so furious I thought he was going to kill Harrison that night."

Rosa had been aware for some time that Emma was sneaking off to Jennie Bell's establishment. Rosa mistakenly thought Emma was turning extra tricks for Jennie. Rosa saw this as a positive sign in that such an association might cause a rift between Emma and Combs. But Hayes' take on the situation put things in a different light. Maybe Rosa would have to protect herself on this flank too.

Rosa had thought when Combs forced Emma to abort her baby that he would drop her and she would hate him. Rosa was half right. Combs refused to give Emma up and Emma continued their arrangement for Ida and Susan's sake even though she despised Combs and sorely missed the comfort a child might have brought her. Emma, also, despised Rosa for selling her virginity to Combs and forcing her to follow a life she detested. Emma was on the look out for a way for her mother, her sister and her to escape from Rosa. However, Rosa was wrong to fear any plan that might involve Emma being owned by Combs. Unfortunately for the seven black men who were about to lose their lives, Rosa did not understand that the person Emma loved was Jennie Bell, not William Combs. Emma wanted away from Combs as much as Rosa wanted her away. Had Rosa had just a little more information and been slightly more streetwise she could have sent Emma to Jennie with her blessing. Then Jennie and Emma would have been forced to take their lesbian love far from Indiana where such acts carried grave criminal penalties. Ida and Susan would have had no place to go but with Rosa while William Combs would have had no option but to default back to Rosa. This time, however, the gods decided to amuse themselves by punishing discretion; Emma and Jennie had been too successful in keeping their illicit relationship secret.

Rosa misanalyzed the information she had and the convoluted and incomplete rumors Hayes brought to her just added to her miscalculations. Her wrong conclusion and her hastily devised plan based on this faulty premise were about to help bring disaster and dishonor raining down upon Posey County.

CHAPTER SEVENTY-NINE

TOO CLEVER BY HALF

ROSA'S FOLLOW UP PLAN HAD a few clear objectives. She wanted William Combs back. She wanted O.C. Thomas to lose the November election. She wanted to avoid helping Jennie Bell's business at the expense of her own. Most of all she wanted to repair the damage that had been done to the good name of prostitution in Posey County by having it known that white whores did not willingly consort with Negroes.

Rosa wished that she could test her thinking against someone in whom she had confidence. Alas, she had only Ed Hayes for a sounding board and there was a reason the Democratic Party had rejected Hayes. He just was not all that smart. Rosa was not sure why she even ran the whole scheme by Hayes. She knew that whatever she came up with would pass muster with the increasingly desperate Hayes.

Rosa did need to talk with William Combs about her plan. Her scheme played on the faulty judgment that pride and lust bring forth in all men. William Chambers was one of the ring leaders of the young Negro toughs and he did odd jobs for Combs. Rosa needed Combs to set things in motion.

"Let me check with Combs. If he okays my approach, you will need to bring Wheeler to my place next Monday evening. You must find some reason for Wheeler to send Thomas north of Big Creek so that he cannot be involved."

Big Creek bisected Posey County into two geographical north/south sectors. In many ways the county seat of Mt. Vernon was seen by those north of Big Creek as a foreign country and many of the southerners felt the same about any portion of the county north of Big Creek. Wheeler should have no trouble coming up with some reason for his political rival to have to go to, say New Harmony, Wadesville, Griffin, Poseyville, Cynthiana or even all the way to the county line to the old rundown Indian fort at Stewartsville. After all, the northern part of Posey County had plenty of taverns too.

Mondays were normally days of rest for the two whore houses. They were, also, when white men were back at work so Rosa and Jennie Bell, on the first Monday of each month, would slip in an occasional Negro customer. One working agreement Rosa and Jennie had always kept their word about was black men.

They knew that not only would both of their businesses suffer if white men knew that they serviced blacks, but the prostitutes might be tarred and feathered and the black men jailed. Until the recent drunken bragging on September 24th, the black men had always played their part.

At first, Rosa had relished Jennie's predicament over Jim Good. But when it began to affect her business, her self interest overcame her sense of *schadenfreude* at Jennie's misfortune.

Now Rosa saw an opportunity to use law enforcement to purge the disgust and anger John Harrison's statements and Jennie Bell's liaison with Jim Good had caused among white customers. She knew that William Chambers and Jim Good and several of their friends would jump at the chance to get some white women's favors while rubbing the angry white men's noses in it. Rosa would make sure that Combs furnished Chambers and his crowd with alcohol before he gave them the note Rosa planned to compose.

Rosa considered bringing Jennie Bell in on her plan but feared that she might warn Emma Davis. Plus, Rosa felt that her plan might result in positive publicity for her house and she saw no reason to help the competition. Rosa savored the dilemma Jennie Bell would be put in. No doubt Jennie would figure out right away what really happened. She would be livid when Rosa got the credit among their pool of white customers for putting the uppity blacks in their place, but Jennie would just have to take it because of her earlier carelessness with Jim Good.

The plan seemed simple enough: invite the young black trouble makers in for sex then cry rape. It was a time honored device. It should work particularly well with Hayes being in on the ground floor. Rosa assumed that the blacks would be arrested, jailed and then released after a few months when the prostitutes magnanimously agreed to drop charges if the Negroes admitted their wrongdoing and promised never to bother the working girls again. Combs did okay the scheme and let Hayes know that he should carry things through Monday evening about ten o'clock p.m.

However, as Rosa was about to find out, when one uses a purgative as powerful as racial hatred coupled with political dirty tricks, the end results may spew out of scatological control.

What Rosa had failed to include in her calculations was the venomous reaction of many of Posey County's white males. The prejudice and fear that existed merely from the clash of races and cultures had been gradually channeled into a rumbling volcano by the recent incidents of crime and crossing of the great social taboo of miscegenation. The terrible eruption began Monday, October 7, 1878. Its aftermath continues in southern Indiana yet today.

CHAPTER EIGHTY

SHARE THE SPOILS

ROSA HAD ALWAYS ASSUMED THAT Annie Mc Cool's sick white customer accidentally killed Annie during a sexual fantasy turned fatality. Still, she did not hesitate to encourage rumors that William Chambers had murdered Mc Cool in a jealous rage. Chambers had beaten Annie often enough that he deserved a lynching whether he killed her or not. Plus, the rich white businessman remained a regular and ever more generous customer.

Chambers continued to occasionally drop by Rosa's side door to claim he missed Annie, but Rosa never allowed any of her girls to have contact with Chambers. Now his sentimentality and anger over Mc Cool might come in handy. Rosa had sent word by Jennie Summers that black men would be welcome at the house that Monday evening. She instructed Jennie to make sure and tell William Chambers, Jim Good and John Harrison. These three took it upon themselves to invite Jeff Hopkins, Ed Hill, Daniel Harrison, Jr., and Ed Warner.

On the afternoon of Monday, October 7, 1878, Rosa wrote a note for William Combs to copy then she set out for the riverfront to secretly meet Combs. Rosa told Combs to re-write the note then seal it before he gave it to Chambers. Combs was to tell Chambers to hand the note directly to Rosa. Chambers and Good could read and print at a rudimentary level. Rosa told Combs to print the note with a blunt pencil on lined paper. It read:

ॐ

"You ain't treated us right. Take kere of us or we kil."

ॐ

Combs was fully on board as soon as Rosa told him that John Harrison would be one of the men arrested. When William Chambers finished repairing the fence at Combs' home on Monday afternoon, Combs stepped outside to talk with him.

"Boy, come over here. I need you to take this note to Rosa Hughes this evening about nine o'clock. Here's a couple of bottles of whiskey for doing it. Don't open the note. Give it right to Rosa and don't say nothing to nobody about it."

"Yas, sir, Mr. Combs, I's do what yous say. Thanks for de whiskey. I's git de note dere once it real dark."

Combs and Rosa had agreed that if Combs could not get the note to Chambers or if it looked like Chambers was suspicious, that Combs would get word to Rosa to call off the scheme. They knew that Chambers was aware of Combs' connection to Rosa and Emma so he would be likely to assume the note involved setting up something for Combs. They were right about Chambers' assumption. Further, his thoughts were clouded because he was already dreaming about replacing what he had been missing since Annie Mc Cool was murdered. Much as a male black widow spider's passion often leads to its death, Chambers had only one thing on his mind. He and his young black friends were easy prey.

But as Rosa and Combs would soon discover, when one sets out to trap fools, often the web also ensnares the hunter.

Chapter Eighty-One

LET'S PARTY

William Chambers shared Combs' whiskey with his six friends as they sat on the Ohio River landing at the foot of Main Street in Mt. Vernon and dangled their feet in the muddy water. That evening the temperature rose into the nineties.

The seven young black men laughed and teased one another about their sexual shortcomings and their odd sexual practices. John Harrison told the others that Emma Davis was his and he had seven dollars in his pocket to prove it. John's brother, Daniel, said he wanted some of that too and would take sloppy seconds for his two dollars.

Ed Warner said he'd had Jennie Summers before and planned to again if Susan Davis wanted too much money. Jeff Hopkins said he guessed Jim Good was going to have to settle for Rosa Hughes as he seemed to like old whores anyway. Ed Hill said he'd been to Jennie Bell's house before but never to Rosa's. He claimed he should get the first chance at young Emma as he was the best looking and she'd probably not charge him.

This alcohol fueled repartee got louder and more personal as the sun set over the Ohio. Orange and black hues filtered through the grey clouds as the blood red moon loomed on the horizon. The young men could wait no longer. They started towards Rosa's at a walk and ended up racing the last block.

William Chambers banged on the side door. When Rosa opened the top of the Dutch door that she used to make a preliminary culling of clientele, Chambers handed her the note. The seven inebriated friends laughed and tumbled into Rosa's parlor as she unlocked the bottom section of the door.

Rosa took the note, unsealed it and placed it on the mantle of the fireplace. Had Chambers been sober and not had other things on his mind he might have thought it curious that Rosa did not read the note. He certainly recalled this unusual fact later as he sat in the Posey County jail listening to the mob of white men beating on the jail door and calling for him to be lynched.

Rosa was concerned that the black men had arrived about an hour before she had told them to. She was, also, upset that instead of just the three men whom she wanted to see set up, four more came with them. She had no reason to want these four punished. Plus, there were only three prostitutes available as Susan Davis had fallen ill and Ida had taken her to see Dr. Spencer. Edwin V. Spencer was the only doctor who would chance incurring the good white folks' wrath and probable boycott of his services for treating the prostitutes. But he was prudent enough to require they come knock on the back door of his home office well after dark.

Ed Hill, who was sometimes called Ed Johnson, spoke up and loudly called for Emma Davis. John Harrison objected, saying he had seven dollars to bid. To the surprise of everyone, Hill pulled out seven dollars and fifty cents. Rosa decided to play the honest broker and pair up Emma and Hill. Rosa was only too glad to have Emma service a different Negro than one she had already been bedded by. She hoped that Ed Hayes and Sheriff Wheeler held off long enough for the soiled doves to make a little money and for Combs' new young plaything to get bedded by at least one of the black men. With there being seven riled up Negroes to take care of, Emma might have to take on up to three of them. That prospect brought a warm glow to Rosa.

Ed Warner said that he only had two dollars so Rosa figured she could mess around with him until he lost control without Rosa having to deliver. As Warner was almost passing out, he may not even realize he had paid for nothing but his own fantasizing. John Harrison and his brother, Daniel, wanted Emma Davis, but settled for sharing Rosa. John was already getting ill from the cheap whiskey. He threw up as he was trying to mount Rosa from the rear. Daniel did not hesitate to take his place.

Jennie Summers liked her work and sometimes gave seconds for free if a man made her happy and showed his appreciation by quickly rising for a second helping. She had often taken groups of friends together when they were willing to pay an extra dollar or two to watch one another, although she had never taken on more than one black man at a time. When William Chambers, Jim Good and Jeff Hopkins each angrily claimed her, she suggested that for five dollars a piece plus one dollar each as a premium, they could all three partake at once. It sounded interesting to the drunken friends.

Rosa collected from all seven of the boisterous young men as she gave instructions on who would be going with whom and where. She sent Emma Davis and Ed Hill upstairs first in hopes Hill would get started and finished before Hayes and Wheeler arrived. Next she laid the ground rules for the three men who were going to share Jennie Summers. Finally, she delayed John and Daniel Harrison as long as she could. It worked fine with John who started vomiting as soon as the pungent smells exuding from Rosa hit his nostrils. But young Daniel had not had as much to drink as his brother plus he was so eager for relief he would have mounted a heifer.

Daniel was finished so quickly Rosa was actually disappointed. She sent the Harrison brothers downstairs then cleaned herself before joining them.

Suddenly the front door burst open and Ed Hayes and John Wheeler came in with guns drawn. The Harrison brothers were near the side door and broke through it as they fled. Rosa started screaming that she was being raped. Jennie Summers sized up the situation quickly and called out for help upstairs. Good, Chambers and Hopkins had no where to run. They tried to conceal themselves in the closet and behind the curtains of Summers' room, but she pointed out their locations as Wheeler entered.

Emma Davis had used every device her profession had taught her to avoid having to have sexual intercourse with Ed Hill. She had slowly disrobed as she carefully cleaned and caressed him in hopes he would get overly excited and ejaculate in her hands. Just as she was resigned to performing on her contract, they heard the commotion from downstairs. Hill jumped off of Emma, grabbed his pants and tried to hide on the floor behind the bed. Emma started crying rape when she heard someone running up the stairs.

But when Hayes came in the room she could not bring herself to tell him where Hill was. Emma just pointed at the open upstairs window. Hill lay quietly until after Hayes and Wheeler had left with Chambers, Good, Hopkins, Warner and the note. Then he gratefully eased out of Rosa's house and was not seen again in Posey County, although Combs searched all of Belleville, including the Harrison home, trying to find him.

CHAPTER EIGHTY-TWO

ONE EYED JUSTICE

ARMED WITH THE NOTE AND the allegations from Hughes, Summers and Davis, Wheeler and Hayes went to Prosecuting Attorney William Gudgel to get rape charges filed against all seven of the young Negroes.

Gudgel asked the law officers what physical evidence they had. Hayes produced the note. Gudgel almost laughed when he read it.

"Who wrote this thing, Ed? Why on earth would those coloreds bring a note? And where is the pistol and knife the boys are supposed to have used to threaten the whores? This thing doesn't pass the smell test. You know we're going to have a riot on our hands if I file these charges. Maybe we'd better just let these boys go and tell them to stay the hell out of Posey County."

Wheeler and Hayes were not prepared for this outcome. If Gudgel wouldn't file charges, Rosa's scheme would fall apart. O.C. Thomas would not have a chance to alienate the white male voters by calling for calm and a thorough investigation.

"Now damn it, Bill, those women swear they were raped at gun and knife point. I don't know who wrote the note, but one of those niggers must have. It says they planned to kill if they didn't get their way. Maybe the niggers who escaped had the weapons." Hayes was near panic. He needed those charges filed.

Then Wheeler interjected, "Bill, you know I'm not the only one up for election next month. You and Judge Parrett could lose your jobs if this thing goes wrong. What are you going to say to Mr. Combs when he starts raising hell because both of his whores got done in by niggers? He and his cousin carry a lot of weight in this county. And you know that Judge Pitcher will have your hide if you don't do something. We got four in jail waiting charges. I think you'd better quit acting like O.C. Thomas and charge all seven of them."

Gudgel knew Wheeler and Hayes were right. On top of that, if no charges were filed, it would give Hayes and his Citizens Committee an opportunity to call for vigilante action. The whole county might blow up.

"Alright, boys, I'll take the warrant applications for all seven to Judge Parrett. But they'll never stand up to scrutinizing from Alvin Hovey and Gus Menzies. They'll have those boys out on the street before the prostitutes have time to spend the money we all know they got from those poor fools."

Gudgel may have been correct about how the law would have handled the situation. Unfortunately, the law was a non-factor.

CHAPTER EIGHTY-THREE

BILE BOILS OVER

WHEN WILLIAM COMBS FOUND OUT that Ed Hill had been with Emma, he became apoplectic. It had only been a week since John Harrison bragged about bedding her.

Emma may have courageously helped Hill escape even as she cried rape, but she did not have the strength to withstand Combs' wrath. She cried and embellished and lied and succumbed to that basest of all needs, survival. She and Jennie Bell had easily determined that the entire fiasco was a trap laid by Rosa and Hayes, but neither of them dared expose it. Emma did take the opportunity to wreck as much vengeance as she could for Combs' action in forcing her to abort her child and for the disgusting fluids and smells she had to pretend to enjoy when he came for her services.

Emma managed to work up a few tears and a trembling voice as she took Combs through every inch of her contact with first John Harrison then Ed Hill. She described their genitalia and compared them to Combs. She told Combs how she could barely stand the force and size of those awful dark young things. She immensely enjoyed watching Combs' neck and face boil beet red as she feigned terror.

Combs had been assured by Rosa that Hayes and Wheeler would arrive before any sexual activity could take place, so he was furious when Emma described her contact with Ed Hill. Combs planned to make Hill and the others pay with their lives for having the temerity to touch his property, even if he had helped entice them to do so.

Combs sought out Ed Hayes to get the details about the pending legal proceedings and to get more information about the Harrison brothers and Hill.

"Alright, Ed, when will those nigger bastards go to trial? And how did you let the others escape? Where are they?"

"Now, calm down, William. You need to get things in perspective. If William Gudgel is right, we're all going to be a lot madder when Judge Parrett throws out the rape charges."

"Throws them out, what the hell are you talking about! What about the note and the girls and the death threats?"

"Gudgel doesn't buy it and he says neither will Parrett after Hovey gets through. He says the Negroes will be back on the street before the election. How do you think I feel? That son-of-a-bitch, Thomas, will have a field day if word of what really happened leaks out."

"By God, those animals will not get out unless the Committee takes them out and hangs them. We need some help here. What's Wheeler doing? He's going to lose for sure if those niggers go free. What about Rosa and her girls? You know that if O.C. figures this thing out he'll drive them all out of the county.

"Where's your cousin stand in all of this? From what young Dan Harrison said about Eppie to Rosa last night, George might have more cause than any of us to see those boys hanged. Maybe you and George need to go see Rosa. Dan was drunk and talking about all sorts of craziness when Rosa was putting him and John off while she waited for Hayes and Wheeler to arrive. I don't believe anything that shiftless bastard says, but we still might be able to use it to rile up George and the rest of the Committee. One lie he ran on about even involved Sarah Jones. Henry will cut that nigger's balls off and feed them to him when he hears that bullshit."

CHAPTER EIGHTY-FOUR

NO TURNING BACK

WILLIAM COMBS SENT WORD FOR Rosa Hughes to meet him at the backroom office of Combs' and Daniels' company the evening of Tuesday, October 8. Rosa had met Combs there many times before. She knew to come alone and after dark. When she knocked on the rear door she expected to see Combs. She was taken aback to see George Daniels and Henry Jones too. She felt her stomach sink and her legs quiver. She knew that her simple plan was spinning out of control.

"Rosa, Ed Hayes told me that one of the Harrison boys said some things out of school. Do not dawdle. What scurrilous lies has he been spreading about Mrs. Daniels and Mrs. Jones?"

Rosa could not believe she had been so stupid. She knew that what Daniel Harrison said was as ridiculous as it was dangerous. Why had she rattled this nonsense off to Hayes? How could she put this genie back into the bottle? She saw no way out. If she denied that she had said anything to Hayes, Combs would tell Hayes who would finish her off with harassment. If she told these powerful businessmen what Harrison had said about the wives of Daniels and Jones, a torrent of hatred would be unleashed. The young black man had been drunk and acting the fool in front of his brother. If Rosa repeated what he told her, jail would be the least of the Negroes' worries. On the other hand, the damned fool had said those things, not Rosa. Why should she take a chance on hurting herself to protect him? She opted to take the easier path.

"It was the younger one, Daniel. He's just a boy and he was plastered besides. He was trying to impress me and his brother with his tall tales about white women. He surely did not mean to pull his own sister down with his babbling."

"Quit mouthing and tell us what he said, girl, or so help me I'll see you out of my house and out of this county. What did he say?"

When Rosa next spoke the fate of the young black men and Posey County's legacy of hate was sealed.

"He was hard to understand what with his nigger slang and mumbling, and being drunk didn't help, I can't be sure I got it all. He was talking about Mrs. Daniels and Mrs. Jones taking his sister to Tennessee. It came up because I was trying to hold them off until Hayes and Wheeler got there. I just asked about Jane's baby and that huge nigger she brought back with her from Nashoba. I said I knew Jane was awful light, but that with the child's father as black as Ajax I would have expected a darker baby. Of course, you know Daniel himself is pretty light skinned too.

"Anyway, Daniel started giggling and kind of whispered to John something about how he wasn't surprised at the baby's color since her mother was white. John was sick from the booze but he tried to put his finger up towards his lips. Daniel kept talking about how he had heard for years that Mrs. Daniels was part colored. I thought he was saying the baby belonged to Mr. and Mrs. Daniels but then he thumped his chest and said the baby was his. John tried to get him to shut up, but then I clearly heard Daniel say, 'I bet old Mr. Jones wouldn't treat me so high and mighty if he knew the real reason his wife had to go away.'"

Henry Jones put it all together: the unusual sexual advance from Sarah from a year ago; her story about having to help Jane; and Eppie's connection with Nashoba. He felt two strong emotions, embarrassment and loss. He knew he should hate Sarah for betraying him with Daniel, but what he actually resented was Sarah having the child they had always wanted and leaving Henry out. There was no choice for him as he saw it. If he and Sarah took the child, they would be ridiculed and ruined financially and Sarah might even be prosecuted for adultery. No, his only option was to somehow shut up Daniel and John before they could spread their stories further. He had no idea what to do about Sarah.

George Daniels realized that if something was not done immediately to staunch the flow of these rumors about Eppie they too would be destroyed socially and financially. More significantly, since the rumors were true, he and Eppie could be jailed for interracial marrying under Indiana law.

Combs, Jones and Daniels agreed to strike quickly. Combs and Daniels knew that Henry was going to have to decide for himself how he would confront Sarah. Daniels had already determined to say nothing to Eppie about her role in the deception until after the Harrisons were dealt with.

The three men put together a straight forward plan. They would arm themselves and go to the Harrison home after dark on Wednesday, October 9th. Their meeting place would be Black's Grove. They knew they had to act quickly before the salacious rumors infected the entire county. As to exactly how they would either drive the Harrison boys away or seal their lips, the men were not sure. They decided that some vigorous action must be taken immediately. The details would have to be filled in as changing circumstances required.

Chapter Eighty-Five

TO BE OR NOT

WHEN HENRY GOT TO HIS home Sarah met him at the door. He brushed past her and went to his study where he kept his pistol. Sarah was not sure what was wrong, but she knew Henry. Something must be terribly wrong. Sarah went to her kitchen and tried to busy herself with dinner.

Henry spent the night at his desk with his pistol being drawn to his right temple on numerous occasions. He knew that Sarah had done nothing worse with Daniel than he had done with Soaring Bird. He was amazed that he could not maintain his anger towards her or Da. His true fear was that he would be laughed at by his peers. If he could somehow prevent anyone from finding out, he would gladly just go on with their lives as they were. But he knew Posey County. Nothing would ever again be as it was. Da's pride, anger and drunkenness had made it impossible for whites and blacks to coexist in Posey County. The awful truth would hang as if it were a Sword of Damocles. The Harrison boys must be silenced. Henry could see no other way for the symbiotic relationship of the two cultures to continue.

The black citizens of southern Indiana dealt with race relations in two ways. The "good coloreds" accommodated every whim of their white neighbors. The "uppity niggers" aggressively evinced the "slave morality" of young men with no hope. The white citizens were paternalistic towards the good coloreds and wrathful towards any black who refused to "keep his place". There were many whites and blacks who believed that the only true solution to "the Negro problem" was to afford equal civil rights to both races. However, as the Indiana Constitutional Convention before the War and the de jure segregation after it proved, the ruling white majority had no wish to be equal.

Henry had no illusions in this regard. He saw his options clearly. He could do nothing and wait until he was humiliated and ruined. He could leave Posey County with or without Sarah. Or he could eliminate the sources of his problems.

He recognized that one way for him and Sarah to take their leave was for Henry to kill Sarah and himself. He could not see how they could start over somewhere else when he was in his sixties and the rumors might follow them wherever they went. To do nothing was to guarantee disaster.

Henry got up from his desk and went to the kitchen where Sarah had fallen asleep beside the dry sink. He wanted to hate her. But when he put the pistol near her head, the love of their youth overpowered him. As his hand trembled Sarah raised her head to look at him. She could not speak, but she silently prayed that Henry would pull the trigger. When he dropped his arm Sarah started to stand up. Henry involuntarily leaned towards her as she barely raised her arms to try to touch him. He tried to avoid her swollen red eyes and tears, but he desperately needed to hold her. Maybe they could go away. Then he remembered how George and William had looked at him when Rosa disclosed what Da had said. By God, Da had ruined his life and was laughing at him besides. Henry would wipe that smirk off his uppity black face.

CHAPTER EIGHTY-SIX

THE STEAM ENGINE

HENRY JONES, WILLIAM COMBS AND George Daniels met at Black's Grove at eight o'clock the evening of Wednesday, October 9, 1878. They each had a pistol hidden under the dark top coats they wore in spite of the warm temperature.

The three men walked their horses south on Walnut Street until they reached Second Street then they turned east on Second until they reached Elm Street. Daniel Harrison's two lots were located between Second and First (Water) Street. Daniel and Elizabeth lived in the house at Second and Elm and Charles and Eliza's home was directly south at First and Elm.

When the men reached Daniel's home they tethered their horses and knocked on the door. Daniel, Sr., lifted the latch string and barely opened the door. The three white men shoved Daniel out of the way as they loudly demanded to see young Daniel and John. As Daniel, Sr., tried to convince them that he did not know where his boys were, the rear door slammed. The three pulled their pistols and ran after Da and John who had been hiding among their siblings in the bedroom they all shared.

John ran towards the Ohio River and Da headed for Robin Hill. Jones, Combs and Daniels caught sight of Da going northwest. They mounted their horses and chased after Da as he fled west on Second Street past the courthouse then north on Main Street to Tenth Street. Da continued running west on Tenth until he reached Robin Hill where he pounded on Joseph P. Welborn's front door and screamed for help.

Mr. Welborn quickly awakened and rushed to the door. Welborn had only recently purchased the famous Underground Railroad house, but he had often participated in helping escaping slaves who found their way there before the War. He hurriedly pulled Da inside and led him towards the false cistern as Da fearfully pleaded for help. Just as Welborn closed the cistern cover over Da's head, the front door burst open.

"Joe, you'd better get that goddamned nigger out here or we'll tear this place apart!"

"Now, William, you boys had better settle down. This is my house and I'll not hesitate to call the law."

"Call the law you nigger lover. Do you think the law's going to help some nigger rapist? Produce him right now or you'll not fare any better than he does. You know he's been indicted for rape. Are you going to harbor a fugitive?"

Henry Jones interrupted Combs, "Joseph, it's no secret where coloreds are hidden in this place. You'd best get that boy; all we want to do is talk to him and turn him over to the sheriff."

The four men heard a window shatter at the rear of the house. Welborn tried to stop the vigilantes, but they threw him out of the way and ran for their horses. They caught a glimpse of Da running north towards the Evansville & Crawfordsville Railroad station where a train was waiting to depart.

When the men reached the train, they pointed their pistols at the frightened engineer and demanded to know where Harrison had hidden. The engineer pointed at the coal car attached to the engine. The three climbed into the coal and dragged Daniel out by his hair.

As Daniel struggled to escape, William Combs pistol whipped him across his face. Harrison fell to his knees and began begging for his life.

"Mr. Henry, don lets them kill me. Please, Mr. Henry, I do anything yous wants. I'lls go away. Please, Mr. Henry, I's don wants to die."

Da held on to Henry's legs as he cried and begged for mercy. Henry and George weakened in their desire for vengeance. "Let's turn him over to Ed Hayes," Henry said. George agreed.

But Combs hit Da in the head with his pistol and knocked him away from Henry. "You two make me sick. Maybe we should just wait until this nigger goes to trial and tells the world what he told Rosa. Is that what you want? Henry, do you want this whole county laughing at you?"

Henry grabbed Da's legs and asked Combs, "What are we going to do with him?"

Combs looked at the open fire box door. "Grab his arms, George." Combs guided Da's body to the firebox as Da screamed and pleaded for his life.

"Oh God, please don, Mr. Henry. Don throw me in there. Shoot me first; sweet Jesus, save yore pore lamb!"

As Henry and George hesitated, Combs struck Da across the face again and said, "That nigger son-of-a-bitch is already as black as coal and is surely going to hell for what he did with Sarah. Now throw his black ass in there!"

Henry threw up as Da screamed in agony. What had they done? George slumped down on the floor of the engine.

Henry and George knew that they had ended their lives when they took Da's. Combs did not care. They still had to find John Harrison. As Henry and George felt their souls leave their bodies, Combs instructed them to meet him the next night at Black's Grove.

Chapter Eighty-Seven

THE GUN

Daniel Harrison knocked on Morita Meier's back door as the sun came up on Thursday morning October 10, 1878.

"Mr. Meier, las night Mr. Jones, Mr. Daniels and Mr. Combs come ta my home ta git my boys, John and Daniel. Mr. Welborn tole me dat Daniel come ta Robin Hill but de white mens chased him away. I's feared dey killed him. I's fraid deys comin back tonight. Dey had guns. I's ain't gots no gun. Can ya loan me a gun, Mr. Meier?"

Morita knew very little about guns, but he did have an old muzzle loader. "Daniel, I don't have any shot, but vous can have dis ol gun. Maybe Mr. Shrieber vill sell you some shot. Vy don't vous go to O.C. Thomas an ask for his help? Vere is Ajax?"

Meier did not see how any good could come from Harrison using the gun. But if what Daniel said was true, the white men probably would come back.

Meier showed Harrison how to use the ramrod to load the old gun then told him, "Daniel, vous know all vites peoples ain't bad. Please think about talking with General Howey or Colonel Menzies."

411

Daniel thanked Meier as he took the ancient firearm. Daniel did not believe that there was anything he could do to save Da or John. However, a lifetime of bowing before white men had been of no help when they barged into his home and terrified his family. Harrison decided that he would not just meekly step aside if they invaded his home again.

And that night they did come back. This time Daniel had the loaded single shot shotgun by his door when Combs, Jones and Daniels knocked on the door demanding John. Daniel did not reach for the gun as the three white men charged into his house. He knew he could only shoot one of them and the other two might murder his whole family. What he did do was try to block the door to his children's bedroom. He managed to hold Jones and Combs back, but Daniels was surprisingly strong.

Harrison decided that he would at least try to use the shotgun to keep the men out of the bedroom. He grabbed the gun from the corner by the front door, but Daniels knocked it out of his hands as Henry Jones pulled his pistol and put it up to Harrison's head.

"I am going to kill you tonight!" Jones had decided after immolating Da that they had to, also, find and kill John Harrison. John knew what Da knew.

"John ain't here. He be outside of town at my farm." Daniel Harrison, Sr., was a good father, but a bad liar. The men knew that one place they did not need to check was Harrison's forty acres in Point Township.

"Daniel, your boys raped those white women. Now, we don't have nothing against you or Elizabeth, but if you don't tell us where John is, we'll burn this shack to the ground!" Harrison noted that unlike the night before, the men did not ask about Da. Harrison knew he must be dead.

"John be with Daniel. Y'all know dey left together last night. If ya finds Da, ya finds John."

"Now, boy, don't sass us. You don't want those pickaninnies to be without a daddy, do you?"

Combs did almost all the talking except when Jones forced himself to take a hand. George Daniels had his pistol drawn but did not look at Harrison.

"This is your last chance, Daniel. Either tell us where John is hiding or we are going to burn your whole damned family up in this house. Maybe you ought to ask Elizabeth. Get out here, Elizabeth, or we'll come in and get you."

Daniel yelled, "Don come outs here!"

Combs slapped Harrison with his left hand and jerked the thin bedroom door open. Elizabeth had the younger children behind her with the bed pushed up to the door.

"Where's Jane and the baby?" Jones asked.

Henry could not control himself. He wanted to see Sarah's child.

"Jane and Hattie be at de farm," Elizabeth told him. Once again it was a weak lie; the men correctly guessed that Jane and Hattie were with Ajax at Brewery Hills.

"Elizabeth, where's John? We don't want to hurt you or the kids, but if you don't tell us where John is, we'll be forced to."

Elizabeth was crying and trying to keep her five young ones away from Combs. She feared the white men would harm the children to get to John and she knew Daniel would not tell them anything.

"I's don kno for shore, but John sometime stays with dat colored man who looks after Mr. Duckworth's place in Caborn Station. You gentsmen know, where de court used to be."

The men knew Elizabeth meant Absolam Duckworth's old home-stead that had served as Posey County's first courthouse in 1816.

"You'd better be telling us the truth or we'll come back here and burn this place down. Boys, that rings true to me," Combs said.

It took the three men less than half an hour on horseback to get to Caborn Station. Travis Finley heard the galloping horses pounding on the packed dirt road. Running horses at night time were a bad omen if one was a Negro in southern Indiana. Travis snuffed out the coal oil lamp and looked between the calico curtains into the moonlit night.

William Combs had seen the light inside before Travis closed the curtains. The men got down from their horses and pulled their pistols.

"Finley, you open now, ya hear! We know you're in there. We want John Harrison right now!"

Travis lifted the bar and opened the door. Combs, Daniels and Jones pushed their way in.

"Where is he, nigger? If you do not want the same treatment, you better quit hiding him."

John Harrison did not want to be the cause of Travis getting hurt. He stepped out of the kitchen.

"Here's I is, Mr. Combs. I didn't do nutten to dem white womens. I gots sick from de alcohol and den run off when Mr. Hayes come. Please, suh, I's jus wants ta go away from here. If y'all lets me go, I's promise never ta comes back."

"It's too late for that now, boy. You should have thought about that before you started messing with white women and running us all over. Turn around so's Mr. Daniels can tie your hands."

Henry held John's wrists while George tied them together with the pull string for the curtains.

"Finley, you can either forget any of this happened or you can join this nigger where he's going."

John was about to faint from fear and Henry had to hold him up. John did have enough presence of mind to realize that Finley's death would be of no help to John.

"Don do nuttin, Travis. I's goin to be alright, ain't I, Mr. Jones?"

Henry could not believe how events had spun out of control in just two days. He had not slept since Da's terror stricken eyes had begged Henry for mercy as they had inched him up to the fire box. Now they had cornered John as if he were a varmint in a chicken coop. Henry knew that if there was a hell he and Combs and Daniels would surely meet there some day. And Sarah must have known about Da as she had spent the past twenty-four hours in a catatonic state clutching some ivory button.

There appeared to be no stopping Combs. He had tasted blood and he liked it. Henry and George were simply supporting players in Combs' tragedy. And unfortunately for John, he was the *tragós* who was about to be sacrificed.

John was dragged out of the building that had served as Posey County's first courthouse and taken out into the copse of trees about an eighth of a mile from the house. The men wanted to lynch him, but in the excitement of the hunt they had forgotten to bring a rope.

Combs ordered Harrison to kneel beside a huge oak tree with a rotten hollow trunk. The men could see the whites of John's eyes darting about for help. The bright moonlight flashed off of his mouth as his lips pulled away from his teeth. The fear in his face was palpable.

Combs told Jones and then Daniels to shoot him, but they both just stood there with their guns pointed at the ground.

"You yellow bastards. You are the ones these niggers have made fools of. I'll show you how to deal with these apes."

Combs put the barrel of his pistol up to the back of John's head and pulled the trigger. John jerked back then forward, but he was not dead. He cried out in pain as Henry and Daniels turned to run from the scene.

"Stop, you cowards, put him out of his misery. At least you ought to be able to do that."

But, neither Henry nor George could do it. Combs took Henry's pistol and shot John through his right eye. Harrison finally quit quivering.

The three white men tried to hide his body by stuffing it into the hollow tree, but Travis found it about a week later when the smell led him to where John Harrison's body had swollen so much it had burst out of the tree.

When the white men got back to Mt. Vernon, they went to Combs' office to talk about what they had accomplished and what was left to be done. While they expected no legal consequences for killing Da and John, they were still concerned about what Daniel Harrison, Sr., might say and do. Jane Harrison and Elizabeth too must know everything that Da and John had talked about to Rosa. Combs said the men could not stop until the threat of the information being leaked was entirely eliminated.

They decided to go to Ed Hayes and have him use the law to finally solve the dilemma of the Harrison family. If they could remove Daniel Harrison, Sr., Elizabeth and Jane could be scared into permanent silence or driven out of the county. It seemed like a good plan.

But what these three white men would soon find out was that they had not accounted for O.C. Thomas or Ajax Crider. Hayes made the same errors.

A more significant flaw was their inability to understand that when you start murdering people to quell the truth, there is always someone left to kill.

CHAPTER EIGHTY-EIGHT

PLAN C

ED HAYES WAS GLAD TO hear that the Harrison boys were out of the picture. But his main goal was to bring down O.C. Thomas and, as yet, nothing had happened to further this purpose. So when Combs, Daniels and Jones approached him on the evening of Thursday, October 10, 1878 with their plan to have Hayes arrest old Daniel Harrison for harboring a fugitive, Hayes decided to incorporate the demise of O.C. Thomas.

Combs told Hayes that John Harrison had confessed that Ed Hill was hiding out at the Harrison home and that old Dan was protecting him. Combs said that old Dan had threatened them with a shot gun and that he had vowed to kill any white son-of-a-bitch who came to his house. At a minimum, Harrison was guilty of harboring an indicted rapist. He deserved to be in jail with the four who were already in custody as did Ed Hill.

Hayes told Combs, Daniels and Jones that he would have to talk with Sheriff John Wheeler before he took any action. Hayes sent the three to their homes and he went to the Sheriff's Office located in the old jail on the courthouse campus. The old jail had originally been a two room log building built in 1825, the same year the county seat had been moved from Springfield in rural Posey County to Mt. Vernon. The 1825 courthouse had been torn down and replaced with the current one in 1876 with the first session of court being held there in January, 1878. A stone and iron addition to the old jail had been added in 1845. A new jail had been built two blocks west of the courthouse on Mill Street. It was scheduled to open January of 1879.

When Hayes got to the Sheriff's Office, volunteer deputies Charles C. Baker and William B. Russell were shooting the breeze with Wheeler and taunting Jim Good, Ed Warner, Jeff Hopkins and William Chambers who were all locked in the stone and iron cell of the old jail.

Hayes told Wheeler he needed to see him outside. He instructed Baker and Russell to watch the prisoners.

"John, William Combs told me that old Daniel Harrison is hiding Ed Hill at Harrison's house. He said Harrison got a shot gun from somewhere and threatened to kill anyone who tries to take Hill. I ain't sure what we need to do, but the election is less than a month away and it don't look good. We have got to do something about Thomas. Rosa's plan might have worked if he'd taken the bait, but, so far, he's playing it close to his vest."

Wheeler knew Hayes was right. When he had sent O.C. north on Monday he'd expected him to come back and raise hell about the Negroes being charged on the word of prostitutes. Instead, Thomas had kept calm as he gathered information. Both Thomas and Prosecuting Attorney William Gudgel had openly questioned the authenticity of the note and the veracity of the whores. Thomas had not hesitated to point out the role William Combs was rumored to have played. Wheeler could even envision O.C. and Gudgel figuring the whole thing out and bringing charges against Hayes and Wheeler. There was not enough time left to hope for a political miracle. Direct action was needed.

"Where's Thomas now?"

Hayes told Wheeler that O.C. was not scheduled until two o'clock the morning of Friday, October 11th. "He's supposed to take over prisoner watch then. We have about four hours before he shows up."

Wheeler said, "I think what you need to do is take Russell and Baker to arrest Hill before Thomas gets here. If Harrison should happen to shoot at you, you'll just have to make an appropriate response. Then we will have either arrested Hill and Harrison or eliminated them while Thomas was of no help. That ought to boost the value of our stock while he will look like a slacker. What do you think?"

Hayes knew that Baker and Russell were firmly behind Wheeler in the sheriff's race. He figured he could manipulate their accounts of whatever happened. If they got Ed Hill, that would be quite a coup just before the election. Also, Old Daniel Harrison might try to cause trouble over the deaths of John and young Dan. This could be an opportunity to shut Harrison up and look like a hero while doing it.

"Sounds good to me, John, let's go in and tell Baker and Russell kind of what we plan. We'll tell them only what we think they need to know. They both are part of the Citizens Committee anyway. I bet they will jump whatever way we say."

It did not take long for Wheeler and Hayes to lay out the plan for the arrest of Ed Hill. Wheeler told them to wait until after midnight so that they would be likely to catch Hill and Harrison asleep.

But sleep had been eluding O.C. Thomas who decided to make a surprise check on the prisoners and their treatment at 12:00 midnight. As with many good deeds, this one by O.C. Thomas did not go unpunished.

CHAPTER EIGHTY-NINE

A FLY IN THE OINTMENT

WHEN O.C. THOMAS WALKED INTO the old jail the four black prisoners began calling out to him.

"Mr. Thomas, hep us, Mr. Thomas, please, sweet Jesus, please hep us." The chorus of young Negro voices sounded like a spiritual to Thomas. He could hear the anger, bitterness and, most of all, fear. It reminded him of the a cappella choir at the local African Methodist Episcopal Church that he had recently attended to call for calm. The A.M.E. church was located in a clapboard structure with an almost comical steeple just eight blocks from the courthouse. The Negro congregation had never been able to afford a bell for the steeple, but generations of black ministers had used the "bells fund" to squeeze contributions from their parishioners. Thomas thought the resonating soulful voices were more poignant than any sound a carillon might provide.

"You boys doing okay?"

"Yas suh, we is for now. But Mister Wheeler been saying we's goin ta be tarred an feathered." Jim Good was the spokesman. Thomas figured that Good took the lead because he and Chambers were the only ones who had spent time in the jail.

"Now, Jim, you boys just need to settle down and go to sleep. Sheriff Wheeler's just funning you. Judge Parrett will make sure you get a fair trial. You did before, didn't you?"

"Yas suh, me and Chambers both, but we's been hearing lots of rumblins outside de jail. Mebbe de white folks ain't goin ta wait for no trial."

"Hush now! Quit that talk. The War put an end to old Judge Lynch. Calm down until Mr. Hovey gets back in town. You know he will take care of you."

Wheeler caught Hayes' eye and said, "I'm going to step outside for a smoke."

"Me too, John. O.C., why don't you see if the boys need any water?"

"That son-of-a-bitch is on to something, Ed. He didn't just happen to show up. Maybe you ought to let him try to arrest Hill and Harrison. Maybe they'll shoot the bastard. We can send him while we stay and watch the niggers. Russell and Baker can go home."

"How would that look, John? No, I think we better have Thomas go with me, Baker and Russell while you watch the jail. That way whatever happens he'll not be able to shout abuse or charge we let them escape. I'll team up with Baker at the rear and have Russell and Thomas go to the front. Hell, maybe the great war hero will get himself shot. You know he won't even carry a gun. Let's see if he can talk those niggers into jail. I will have my pistol and Russell always carries that double barreled gun of his that he's so proud of. He keeps hoping he'll get to kill somebody. Tonight might be his chance. Baker ain't of much use, but he can keep me company if the niggers try to run out the back."

Wheeler and Hayes went back into the jail and told Thomas, Baker and Russell part of their plan.

"Now, none of you needs to go if you don't want to. Ed and I can handle this ourselves if you want to go home. Alexander Crunk, Mt. Vernon Constable James L. Caborn and Town Marshall Joseph Musselman told me they'd help provide security during the day until these Negroes get tried. I plan to stay here at the jail until either you all come back or Caborn and Musselman arrive."

O.C. Thomas was too naïve to think he was being set up. He decided he'd better go and make sure that Ed Hill and Daniel Harrison made it to the jail alive. Besides, something about the operation smelled bad to Thomas. He found it difficult to believe that Ed Hill would stay around when his friends were locked up. Most of all, Thomas did not believe that Daniel and Elizabeth Harrison would endanger their children by hiding Hill at their home. And why were Wheeler and Hayes so eager to do this thing in the dead of night?

As for Russell and Baker, they could not wait to abuse what little power they could muster. They were in. Just such an opportunity was why they hung around the jail and carried guns.

CHAPTER NINETY

THE HARRISON HOME

ED HAYES HAD BEEN GLAD to hear that the Harrison brothers were beyond testifying about the events of Monday, October 7, but he had never contemplated the possibility that Rosa's plan would spin so out of control that deaths would result. When Combs had gleefully related the ghoulish details of Daniel and John's deaths, Hayes had to fight to hide his nausea. And in spite of his desire to see Thomas lose the sheriff's race and his own role in the false rape charges, his position as a law officer had given him the only status he had ever enjoyed. It was important to him. The cavalier manner in which Combs, in the presence of Daniels and Jones, had related their homicidal actions to Hayes, a sworn deputy sheriff, showed they had no respect for Hayes or the law. The growing undercurrent of lynch mob sentiment to deal with the situation Hayes had helped manufacture was eating away at Hayes. Unfortunately, he was neither brave nor smart enough to cure this social cancer. In fact, he was about to assure the deaths of six more men, one of whom was O.C. Thomas.

After the four men left the courthouse campus, they crossed Walnut Street, then Mulberry, Locust, Canal, Wood, Owen, Sawmill and

Elm before arriving at the Harrison home situated on two lots on Elm Street between First (Water) and Second. There was a small hog wire fence around the house with a wood slat gate in front and back. The two clapboard houses that Daniel and Charles Harrison had built abutted one another with Daniel's facing north and Charles' facing south towards the Ohio River one block away.

It took the four white men less than ten minutes to traverse the distance from the jail to Harrison's. Baker and Russell were excited to be in on the hunt for Ed Hill and were oblivious to any other agenda Hayes or Thomas might have.

Hayes was at a loss to figure out how he could work things around to embarrass Thomas or to make himself a hero. He was just following where the events were headed.

O.C. Thomas suspected that it would be up to him to prevent Elizabeth and her children from being harmed by the overzealous actions of the other three. If, in truth, Daniel Harrison was harboring Ed Hill, Thomas was confident that he could talk Hill into giving up without bloodshed. Thomas had not only agreed with Hayes' plan, he had demanded that Hayes allow Thomas to go to the front door and inquire about Hill before anyone tried to force entry.

Although Thomas had no knowledge of the deaths of young Daniel and John, he assumed that none of those indicted for the rapes would still be in Posey County unless they were already in jail.

Therefore, Thomas made it a point to cough loudly as they approached Elm Street and to stumble and collide with Russell as he entered through the front gate. The men could see light streaming out of the windows on the north end and west side of Daniel Harrison's home. As they entered the yard they could see old Dan seated at a table in the front room. Two Negro children were hugging Harrison and crying. Hayes would later be told by Harrison at the jail that he was trying to comfort his children because Travis Finley had told them about John being taken away. Finley also related that he had heard shots fired.

Elizabeth had taken their other children with her when she had left about two hours earlier to tell Jane and Ajax at Brewery Hills what Finley had said.

"Damn it, Bill, point that shotgun away from me! You know I'm unarmed and do not want to get shot by my own men. Ed, Bill and I will wait here in front until you and Charley get around back. Then I will knock on the door."

It was Thomas' hope that Harrison would hear and recognize his voice. But because Combs, Daniels and Jones had already invaded the Harrison home twice and had threatened to come back, old Daniel Harrison thought they were the ones returning. He grabbed his loaded shotgun and went to the window beside the front door. When Russell saw movement at the window he jerked his double barreled shotgun around and fired while O.C. Thomas, who had stood ready to knock on the door, turned towards Russell at an angle and put up his left hand to stop him from firing. The full blast was taken by Thomas who stumbled backwards.

Daniel Harrison thrust his shotgun through the lower window light and fired towards Russell who ran around the west side of the house and called for Hayes and Baker.

Harrison ran out the rear door as Hayes shot at him with his pistol. Thomas had stumbled away from the front door towards the west side of the house. When Hayes, Baker and Russell got to him Thomas was lying in front of the west side window. He said, "They shot me. Don't let the Negro get away."

Hayes could not at first see the extent of Thomas' wounds in the dim light from the coal oil lamp as it filtered through the window pane.

He responded to Thomas' complaint about being shot, "I guess not much. The Negro won't get far. I hit him at least once."

Hayes was not sure what had happened and Russell was too frightened to tell him. Hayes did not want to make a hero out of Thomas, but it looked like, once again, Thomas' luck was going to hold up. Here he was shot in the line of duty while Hayes was playing the part of back up. And to make things worse, it did not appear that Thomas' injuries were life threatening. Then O.C. Thomas died.

Now it would look like Hayes had not sought to help Thomas or catch his killer; Hayes wrongly assumed Harrison had fired the first shot at Thomas after which Russell fired at Harrison.

"That nigger murdered O.C.; he'll hang for this. Bill, what happened? Why'd the nigger shoot him?"

Russell turned away and threw up. He could see no use in telling Hayes and Baker what really happened. After all, the nigger had fired at him and then fled from justice. He was guilty of, at least, attempted murder. Where was the harm in letting Hayes' assumption become fact?

"When O.C. knocked on the door Harrison fired at him through the window. I fired back twice. I do not know if I hit the nigger. I saw O.C. go backwards when Harrison fired, but I didn't know he'd been shot."

Hayes was confused. Why would old Dan fire at a law officer who just knocked on his door? Surely he would be concerned about starting a gunfight at his home with his family there. And why didn't O.C. say the Negro had shot him? What he had said with his last breath was, "Do not let the Negro get away." If someone had just shot a person, wouldn't the more likely emotion be revenge? And now that Hayes had a closer look at Thomas' wounds from the shotgun pellets, he could see that some of them were in O.C.'s left rear shoulder. How did that make sense if Harrison had shot him face on?

On top of that, Harrison had his children in the front room with him and he hadn't even blown out the lamp. Why would he start shooting when he would know that he and his kids would be easy targets illuminated by the light?

Hayes instructed Baker to go to the back of the house to watch for anyone else trying to escape. Then he grabbed the shaking Russell by his shoulders and pulled him close.

"Russell, what really happened up here? Something ain't washing. Now tell me again. Where were you and where was O.C. and the nigger?"

Russell continued to shake and began to cry. "It wasn't my fault. I seen someone at the window with a gun so's I fired before he could shoot at me. O.C. was turned kind of half toward me as he was fixing to knock on the door. Hell, Ed, the nigger was going to kill us. I had to shoot. The black son-of-a-bitch was hiding a rapist and he did shoot at me. Don't tell nobody, please, it ain't my fault. What good would it do?"

Hayes agreed that Harrison was probably going to hang for harboring a fugitive and shooting at a law officer anyway even if reasonable people might normally see it as self-defense or a regrettable case of mistaken identity. With a dead white law officer and a Negro shooter, neither self-defense, nor mistake of fact would be viable defenses. It would little matter if the charge was murder or attempted murder. He was doomed.

"Well, let's search the house for Hill. Let me think on things a little."

Their search turned up two of Harrison's older children who were hiding beneath their bed, but no adult Negro males were found. Hayes was beginning to think Combs had set this thing up as a hedge against any charges for killing the Harrison boys. By God, Hayes would not let that treacherous bastard cause him any more grief. Hayes decided to start calling the shots. He would begin by making a hero out of himself and a lifelong sycophant out of Russell. Hayes pulled Russell aside.

"Alright, Bill, I see nothing to be gained from the truth here. Harrison is going to hang regardless. There's no harm in asking Mr. Gudgel to indict Harrison for O.C.'s murder. Just keep your mouth shut until the Coroner's Inquest. I'll be there with you. Just listen to what I say."

Hayes saw no harm in this version of Thomas' death. In fact, it even made the popular young Thomas look more heroic. How romantic would it be for him to lose his life in a stupid accident? No, Hayes was doing a favor for Russell, a favor to Thomas' memory and no harm to anyone.

Well, not quite, the entire Negro community of Posey County was about to feel the wrath of the white men who decided they had suffered enough at the hands of the lawless blacks.

The murder of O.C. Thomas in the line of duty was just too much to bear.

CHAPTER NINETY-ONE

A MOB WITH A MIND

ED HAYES AND WILLIAM RUSSELL testified together before the Coroner's Jury at eight o'clock the morning of Friday, October 11, 1878. Judge Parrett had convened the Coroner's Jury, ostensibly at William Hendrick's request, after Hayes and Russell told him how Daniel Harrison, Sr., had shot O.C. Thomas. Hayes decided to eliminate any thought that Russell might have shot Thomas by having Baker and Russell tell the story that Russell was unarmed. Hayes had not accounted for Russell's own sloppiness in interviews with John Leffel of the *Western Star* and Tom Collins of the *Mt. Vernon Democrat*. Russell let slip that he had fired his shotgun at Harrison. Fortunately for Hayes' scheme, no one seemed to pick up on this inconsistency.

Hendricks conducted the six laymen in their investigation, and at Hayes' suggestion, Hendricks allowed Hayes and Russell to be questioned together to save time so they could get back to guarding the five prisoners. Hayes managed to field almost every question. Based on Hayes' testimony, Daniel Harrison, Sr., was charged with the First Degree Murder of the popular young war hero who left three children and a pregnant widow.

The "secret" Coroner's Jury testimony spread throughout Posey County within a few hours. The Citizens Committee began to form up at the jail before Hayes and Russell could get out of the courthouse and walk the thirty yards to where John Wheeler was watching the prisoners.

Hayes was not too alarmed at this small group of angry white men who demanded that Harrison be brought out and hanged. Hayes, Russell and Wheeler took positions at the jail entrance with their pistols and shotguns and persuaded the men to disperse. Hayes told them the law would hang old Dan soon enough.

Things calmed down and Wheeler, Hayes and Russell went home to eat and sleep. Town Marshal Alexander Crunk, and volunteers, Matthew Nelson, William Kenna and Frank Wright, took over for the three who had been up all night.

Hayes and Russell returned to the jail as night fell. When they entered the south gate of the wrought iron fence surrounding the courthouse campus, they encountered a large group of white men who were drinking alcohol and brandishing firearms. It was only then that Hayes began to wonder if the events he had started on Monday night might get out of control. The morning mob had been small, sober and disorganized. But Hayes and Russell were now confronted with more than one hundred of Posey County's leading citizens, many of whom had military training. And they were armed and angry.

As Judge Eagleson read from Leffel's account in the October 17, 1878, *Western Star*:

ᙘ

"Your reporter and one or two others privileged to enter the jail ran out into the beautiful Court House yard, shaded with heavy locusts. The night was clear, and a bright moon pouring its light down, made the scene ghostlike and impressive.

(At Ed Hayes' command)

The crowd, consisting of two or three hundred, fell back across the street. For ten minutes it appeared to be a false alarm. But then was heard the steady tramp of two hundred feet, and a few minutes later fifty men entered the east gate and fifty men entered the north gate. The miserable guilty wretches on the inside began to pray and call on God to save them. But the one hundred men, the best of the county physically and probably in reputation, marched into the yard in files of two. Every man had on a long black mask, falling from forehead to chin, like the inquisition of old. All had changed their coats, some were turned inside out. Not a word was spoken until the leader demanded the keys to the jail."

&

Hayes would later wonder if he should have just given the men old Dan Harrison when they demanded him. Sure, Harrison would have been lynched, but he was the one the mob really wanted. Maybe that would have satisfied their blood lust. The problem was that Hayes knew Harrison had not killed Thomas and he knew the four young Negroes had committed no crimes at all. Most importantly, Hayes knew that he was responsible for this whole debacle.

The leader of the mob said to Hayes, "Ed, you damned fool. Give us the keys. Can't you see you are outnumbered?"

But Hayes had hidden the keys to the iron door of the inner cell. He refused to give them to the mob. Alexander Crunk pulled his pistol and fired up into the air just as a member of the mob discharged a shotgun. One of the shotgun pellets put out Crunk's eye. He dropped his pistol and was swept aside by the mob.

Several of the mob began to pound on the cell door with clubs as old Dan laid on the pallet in front of the cell. As the four Negroes inside yelled for help and pleaded for mercy, Daniel Harrison said, "Mister Combs, you know dem boys is innocent. Jesus be watchin you."

Harrison was grabbed by his throat and stabbed in the chest. Two vigilantes clasped Harrison's arms and legs as the leader began to hack at his body with his Civil War saber. Harrison struggled and screamed until his head was sawed from his body. Then the three men finished the slaughter and put Daniel Harrison's parts in the jailhouse privy where most of them became a permanent part of the courthouse lawn after the old jail was torn down.

By now the rest of the mob was in a total frenzy. Hayes fired his pistol into the air, but he was knocked to the ground. The mob disarmed Hayes, Russell, Nelson, Kenna and Wright as the cell door hinges gave way. The four young men were dragged out to the locust trees.

Jim Good, then Jeff Hopkins, next Ed Warner and finally William Chambers were each led to the large locust trees. Ropes and nooses that had been carefully knotted long before the cell was broken open were put around each man's neck and the ends thrown over limbs of two of the locust trees. Their hands were tied behind them with cords that had been brought just for that purpose.

A member of the mob said, "We got to give them a chance to confess." So before each man was pulled up, the leader said, "Say your piece before God. Confess before you meet the Devil face to face."

Of course, since none of the men had raped anyone, not one of them confessed. As John Leffel reported, once the four realized that death was unavoidable, "The doomed men uttered not a word of pleading nor faltered an instant."

This steadfast bravery and their denials of any wrong doing led some in the crowd to have second thoughts. One man said, "We ought not to hang an innocent man." For the briefest of instants the mob hesitated until the leader said, "No, but, by God, we must hang the guilty ones!"

Each young man was drawn up by his neck with his legs kicking as his eyes and tongue bulged out. It took several minutes for the men to suffocate to death.

Hayes knew that he would spend eternity seeing this ghastly scene while he burned in Hell. His only hope for salvation was to atone for his great sins by helping to bring the leaders of the mob to justice. He would start by telling Prosecuting Attorney William Gudgel the truth. First he had to go to his home and try to get some sleep.

As he wandered away from the strange fruit hanging from the locust trees that had been planted as symbols of justice and equality, Hayes was trying to comprehend how his envy and ambition had gone so terribly wrong.

Ed Hayes opened the gate and stumbled exhaustedly towards the long flight of steps leading up to his front porch. The Hayes home on the west end of Water Street was built to be above any possible Ohio River flood waters.

With his head down and the moonlight disappearing behind large dark clouds, Hayes failed to see the huge black man who was watching him from behind the large oak tree that loomed over the Hayes home.

Chapter Ninety-Two

A STEP DOWN

"Mr. Hayes, Elizabeth asked me to check on Daniel. I's been waiting ta talk wit you 'bout dat. I was skeered ta come ta de jail cause dere was peoples ever where. Daniel be okay, Mr. Hayes?"

Hayes eased his hand down to his pistol that he kept thrust in his waistband. He hated Ajax over Jane, plus he could not be sure what Ajax already knew about old Dan and the other four.

"Boy, you'd best git out of my way. If you want to know anything, you can check with Sheriff Wheeler on Monday. I'm on my way into the house, now move!"

"I's jus wants ta know 'bout Daniel, Mr. Hayes. Elizabeth and Jane be awful worried 'bout him. I's ain't no trouble maker, Mr. Hayes. Could's ya lets me see Daniel?"

"Nigger, I said move out of my way. And I mean now!" Hayes pulled his pistol and slapped Ajax across the face with it. Ajax started to lunge for Hayes.

"Come on, you big black bastard. I'd surely enjoy blowing your brains out. Then I'd make sure Jane and her half-breed were driven out of this county."

Ajax had always been slow to anger. It not only was his nature, but twenty-eight years of living in the white man's world had conditioned him to suffer insults and even blows because to do otherwise might be worse.

Ajax wiped the blood off his mouth and backed up. He now knew something bad had happened to Daniel.

"Okay, Mr. Hayes, I's going ta leave. But Daniel be in your care. You's supposed ta watch out for him. Monday, Mr. Hovey will lets me see him."

Hayes forgot that he had decided to expiate his sins by telling the truth. He could not believe this uppity nigger was lecturing him about his duties.

Hayes raised the pistol up to Ajax's face. Ajax brought his powerful right fist down upon the left side of Hayes' neck. The sickening sound of breaking bones was the last thing Ajax heard before he jumped the picket fence and ran the three miles back to Brewery Hills. Darly Hayes had been awakened by Ed's yelling. She looked out the window in the front door just as a large dark shape floated out of her sight. She thought it must be the shadow of the large leafy limb that extended above the fence. She told Sheriff Wheeler about the hulking phantom the next morning. Wheeler later made it a point to tell William Combs about the apparition Darly had seen.

Jane and Elizabeth heard the panting Ajax coming in the front door of the church. Christian Willis had allowed them to sleep in the pews as they waited on Ajax to give them word about Daniel. Eppie Daniels had already told them about Da and John. George had been unable to keep the horrible deeds from Eppie. George had, also, told her that Combs had lied to Ed Hayes about Hill being at the Harrison home. Daniels spared none of the details of what he, Henry Jones and Williams Combs had done. Eppie knew that without Combs' instigation neither George nor Henry would have done those horrible things.

But Eppie had come to Brewery Hills between the time Morita Meier had turned Daniel over to Hayes and when the mob killed him. To Eppie's knowledge, Daniel was badly injured, but alive and in jail. For all she knew, Daniel had shot O.C. Thomas and Ed Hayes was simply doing his duty guarding him.

Ajax fell exhausted into a pew as Jane and Elizabeth told the other Harrison children to wait outside until they were called.

Ajax told the women what had occurred between him and Hayes. "I's thinks Mr. Hayes be dead. Oh, God, I's jus trying ta keep him from shooting me. I's gots ta go tell Sheriff Wheeler."

Christian Willis and Soaring Bird entered the small church. Willis was carrying a lighted candle. "What did you find out about Daniel? Did Officer Hayes say anything about Da and John?"

"Oh, Christian, I thinks I killed Mr. Hayes when he was goin ta shoot me. I didn't mean ta. He wouldn't say nuttin 'bout Daniel. I's don know how's he is. I was 'fraid ta go ta de jail 'cause dere was lots of white men wit guns and swords downtown. I's goin ta tell Sheriff Wheeler. It was self defense, huh, Christian?"

CHAPTER NINETY-THREE

THE LAW FIRST

WILLIAM GUDGEL, ALVIN HOVEY, GUS Menzies and Judge William Parrett met in Judge Parrett's chambers on Monday, October 14, 1878.

Gudgel said, "Can you believe it, the only time we actually needed to hear from that idiot Hayes, he fell down his own stairs and broke his neck? Now how will we sort this mess out? He must have been fooling with his pistol as he was going up the steps. Darly found it beside him when she ran outside to check on him. It was dark, he was tired and he had just left the mob scene. I am sure there was a lot on his mind. Maybe I am being a little harsh on him. It's not good to speak ill of the dead. Well, I guess he isn't dead yet."

Colonel Menzies usually deferred to Hovey, but he spoke up first. "How much is there to sort out? We have five dead men and we all know who did it. And, from what I hear, the two missing Harrison boys were, also, murdered by the same crew. Our duty is clear. We didn't fight a war just so we could ignore this kind of vigilantism. How's this any different than the Ku Klux Klan and the night riders? I say we take the ringleaders before a jury then hang them."

441

Hovey admired his son-in-law. Menzies had been a brave soldier and he was just as courageous as an attorney. It was not that Hovey disagreed with Menzies' passionate call for justice; it was just that Hovey was not sure what justice would be in these circumstances. Hovey remembered how the fire had raged within him when as a young man the blackbirders would capture escaped slaves and return them to a life of bondage. But the years had taught him that the best outcomes to complicated problems were usually not arrived at easily or passionately.

"Gus, you are, of course, absolutely correct. These *ultra vires* actions are an affront to the rule of law and to what tore our beloved country apart for four years. We have paid a dear price for Negro liberty as have they for many years. We must not allow the Citizens Committee to be a law unto itself. After all, if we do not assure these horrific crimes against the colored community are brought to justice, who's to say that the next time such mob violence will not be directed at us?

"No, we must address this problem with courage and diligence. But do we not first need to gather all the facts and determine all who deserve punishment and to what degree? My information is that there may have been up to three hundred of our most influential citizens who were, at least, present when the jail was breached and the Negroes killed. Do we charge them all, and, if so, with what, murder? Then do we hang them all? And, if we only select the ones we wish to be the sacrificial lambs for the whole mob, are we any better than the mob?"

"But General, this whole mess was started when Ed Hayes brought me that phony note and insisted that the Grand Jury indict those boys on the word of three whores. And now we know that William Combs has been stirring this cauldron from the beginning with the help of Henry Jones, George Daniels and Ed Hayes. I don't know what happened at old Dan's house, maybe he did kill O.C., but he deserved a fair trial and a fair hanging, if he did. Hell, he was slaughtered like a hog and we all know who did it. Surely, we can pick them out of the mob and try them. Hayes should have been tried with them, but the gods may have saved us the trouble. By God, I'm going to do my duty and prosecute those madmen."

Judge Parrett knew he should not be a party to these conversations. How could he be fair if anyone was charged? On the other hand, he and almost everyone in Posey County already knew what had happened to all three Harrisons and the four other Negroes and, also, knew for certain several of the white men involved. It would be disingenuous for him to pretend otherwise. And while he often had to perform the mental gymnastic of setting aside something he may have inadvertently learned out of court, to set these events aside would be impossible. Parrett decided that his duty as the judge was to do his best to help the legal community deal with what was not just a legal problem, but an elemental social and cultural one. Nice conventions of law would not suffice.

"Gentlemen, let's impanel a grand jury so that Mr. Gudgel can investigate all of these matters. Bill, you can reopen the rape cases and thoroughly test the soiled doves. Members of the Citizens Committee must be put under oath. We all know that Judge Pitcher sympathizes with those who would deny Negroes civil rights. However, we, also, know that he would never condone murder. I direct you to seek his assistance in your investigation. And, at a minimum, you must hear from Combs, Jones and Daniels. It probably would be good to put Sheriff Wheeler and his deputies under oath and find out about the incident at Harrison's house as well as why the mob was allowed to disarm the law officers. I can have you a panel by tomorrow. We are not naïve here. We know that there is an excellent chance that the grand jurors themselves will have been members of the mob. It will be up to you to insist on a thorough report from the grand jury. We must have faith that other men will do their duty if we do ours."

CHAPTER NINETY-FOUR

SUICIDE WATCH

EPPIE DANIELS WAS SO REVULSED by George's account of the deaths of Da and John Harrison that she found it impossible to be near him. She could not reconcile her memories of their love with his involvement in those horrible deeds. When she read John Leffel's eyewitness account of the slaughter of that good man, Daniel Harrison, Sr., and the heartless lynchings of the four young men, Eppie knew George had to be involved. She, also, knew that Sarah Jones must be dangerously close to suicide. Sarah was convinced that she was responsible for all the evil that had occurred since her original sin with Da. Sarah had convinced herself that her life was the sacrifice that God required for her sin and the sins of Henry, George, William and the lynch mob.

On Sunday, October 13, 1878 Eppie decided to stay with Sarah. She wanted to keep Sarah from self-destruction and she could not stand to be in the house with George. Henry blamed Eppie for taking Sarah to Nashoba and he resented their closeness, especially at this lowest point in his life. Henry moved some of his personal things into his office and started sleeping there. It was just as well, Sarah's skin crawled just from thinking about Henry touching her.

445

Neither Eppie nor Sarah could bring themselves to attend their own churches where they knew the men who had murdered the Harrisons and the others would be gathered. Eppie suggested that they go to Brewery Hills. Sarah was so despondent that Eppie had to help her dress then almost drag her to the carriage. It was only when she told her that Hattie was at Brewery Hills that life returned to Sarah's face. When they got to Brewery Hills and Christian Willis came running out to greet them, Eppie knew she had done the right thing.

"Oh, Eppie and Sarah, I am so glad you are here. We need you badly."

Sarah looked up at Christian and said, "You need us?"

"We surely do, Sarah. As soon as the church service is over I must have you talk with Ajax before he goes into Mt. Vernon. He won't listen to me. I have never seen such anger. It was only Friday night that he was talking about turning himself in over Ed Hayes. Now he's spoiling for vengeance over Daniel, Da and John. He didn't know the four boys who were lynched, but he's calling for retribution for them too."

"What are you talking about with Ed Hayes? He fell down his steps and broke his neck. Darly found him outside right after she heard him yell as he fell down the steps. She almost saw it happen."

"Yeah, we did hear that ourselves. That's fine with me, but God may see it differently. Anyway, come in to church. We'll talk later."

Eppie knew that a church service with their true friends and especially Hattie would be a good thing for Sarah. Eppie had no personal delusions about religion, but she often felt better after church. Sarah was a true believer who badly needed her faith and Hattie, especially now. It felt good to sit with Sarah, Elizabeth, Jane, the other Harrison children, Soaring Bird and Ajax while an old friend who truly cared about them all spoke about redemption and heaven.

But when church was over life on earth returned, and it did not feel nearly as good as the one promised by Christian Willis. Eppie wished she could suspend reason and experience and buy into the Christian beliefs. Sarah certainly did and she was the one Eppie was most concerned about. Christian Willis had prepared a message directed at Ajax and the Harrison family that fit Sarah and Eppie as well. Eppie knew that she and Sarah must spend a lot more time at Brewery Hills. For now, Christian's involvement was paramount. Eppie decided to seek his help immediately.

"From what you said before church, I guess you know as much about the murders as we do. I understand why Ajax wants revenge. So do I, but why would he be concerned with Ed Hayes? Surely Ajax knew that Hayes was crooked and hated him over Jane. I think we'd better get all of us together and pool our information. Why don't you get Ajax, Jane, Elizabeth, and Bird too to join us here in the church? The kids had better stay away, although I do not think it possible to separate Sarah from baby Hattie."

CHAPTER NINETY-FIVE

SCHOOL'S OUT

TOM COLLINS WAS SO FURIOUS when he read the *Evansville Evening Tribune's* account of the lynchings and its aftermath that he published a special edition of the *Mt. Vernon Dollar Democrat* on Monday, October 17, 1878. Collins quoted the *Tribune* on its coverage of the Posey County School Board meeting held the last week in September and the *Tribune's* analysis of how the issue of integration of the high school had contributed to the lynchings:

❧

"It now appears that the question of the admission of colored pupils to the high school has been a factor in producing the excitement against colored people. The promotion of a couple of colored pupils to the high school grade brought up the question, which was discussed with some asperity, and decided against their admission, but the asking for admissions and an evident disposition to urge it, begot a great deal of passion, and those who participated in it were made the especial objects of abuse."

❧

Collins then responded:

Ꮖ

"The above is from the Evansville Evening Tribune, a paper,
that from some cause or other, has outrageously misrepresented
Mt. Vernon during her recent troubles."

Ꮖ

Next, Collins took umbrage at the *Evansville Evening Tribune's* re-
porting of the actions against Negroes after the lynchings. The *Tribune*
led with:

Ꮖ

"More of the Disturbance

The disturbance in Mt. Vernon has now degenerated into a
Confederate Cross Roads crusade against colored people.

The crusade is ostensibly directed against all who are not
old citizens, but even some of them are being driven out, leaving them no time to take care of their property or settle up
their business."

Ꮖ

The Evansville newspaper reported that practically all young Negro
males were being ordered out of Posey County on pain of death. Tom
Collins retorted that this was an exaggeration as no more than half of
the Negro men and their families were banished.

One young Negro man who planned to leave on his own schedule
was Ajax. As the white reign of terror spread throughout Posey County,
Ajax and what was left of the Harrison family along with Hattie stayed
at Brewery Hills and waited for justice from the Grand Jury. The Grand
Jury published its findings to Judge Parrett in the presence of a packed
courtroom on Wednesday, November 6, 1878. Judge Parrett read the
report then announced to the all white audience:

Ꮖ

"The Grand Jury is now adjourned after being in session twelve days. We understand they worked hard to find a bill against the parties implicated in the hangings of the negroes, but were unable to do so."

❦

When Eppie and Sarah took the November 7, 1878 edition of John Leffel's *Western Star* newspaper containing the Grand Jury's report to Brewery Hills, Ajax could no longer be cajoled into turning the other cheek. Just as Eppie and Sarah had lost all love and respect for George and Henry, Ajax was filled with a hatred for the three white men who had taken white resentment and turned it into murder. Even in his state of unquenchable passion for revenge Ajax knew it was neither possible nor proper to identify and kill every man who was involved in the mob or who condoned or covered up its actions. And while the white prostitutes may have been more than complicit in the rape charges, Ajax saw them more as he saw members of the colored community. They were simply pawns of powerful white men.

No, he could not extract a full measure of justice for the dead men and the displaced families, but he now knew from Eppie and Sarah the instrumental roles that Hayes, Combs, Jones and Daniels had played. Fate had helped him dispatch Hayes. He would take the destiny of Daniels, Jones and Combs into his own hands. But first he needed to make provision for evacuating Jane and her family.

CHAPTER NINETY-SIX

MIGHT IS RIGHT

EPPIE RECOGNIZED THE ROLE THAT she had played in this tragedy. She had been blind to her own pride for years in pushing the white community in a direction it was not prepared to go. And her childlessness had clouded her judgment on how Sarah handled her pregnancy.

Eppie now knew that her long time efforts to have Negro children admitted to high school could have and should have been approached differently. But she was truly a child of Frances Wright. Her deep commitment to equality was a product of nature and nurture. Inola Crider/Iphigenia Harrison/Mrs. George Daniels was the embodiment of Mad Fanny's dream.

Unfortunately, America was little closer to accepting a melding of the races and genders in 1878 than it had been when Nashoba floundered on reality more than a quarter of a century earlier. The Civil War bought the end of de jure slavery, but not even that dear price could buy equality.

Eppie now saw clearly what she had denied entirely until October, 1878. Just as slavery was only eliminated from the top down and by force, equal rights for Negroes and women would require either a great amount of force from government or a great length of time. Eppie knew that even the greatest amount of governmental force in American history had only ended slavery as a consequence, not a cause. She knew that the country would not and could not continue such coercion. She, also, knew that she did not have enough time to see discrimination fall of its own weight. Eppie would continue to hope for equal rights for all, but she would no longer demand them. There was not much of the present left for her and the people she loved. She was going to quit pushing for a future whose time may never come. Hattie the individual, not Hattie the symbol, would be Eppie's focus. She would often wonder if the horror of October, 1878 would have occurred had Frances Wright, also, just loved Inola Crider the individual.

On the other hand, was the life allotted to the Harrison family worth living if there was no hope for a better one? When Eppie had urged Daniel and Elizabeth to push for Jane, John, Da and the twins to go to high school, they were eager for the change education might bring in their children's lives.

Were the Harrisons better off in a permanent state of de facto slavery than they were losing the struggle for a brighter future? When Eppie had read John Leffel's account of Daniel, Sr.'s last moments on earth she was struck with his pride, defiance, and, Eppie believed, his victorious attitude in at first telling the world he was simply defending himself and his family from an unprovoked attack then his refusal to further beg the white man for largesse:

☙

"I am married, have eight children, and am 51 years old. Take me out and hang me, I have got no more to say."

☙

To Eppie with her own history and understanding of a black person living in a white world, Daniel's calm statement was a proclamation of victory. That even the white men who murdered him heard it that way was evidenced by their need to immediately silence him. Such unreasoned fury could have only come from their realization that they had not achieved what was more important to them than Daniel's death, i.e., his acceptance of their god given superiority.

Eppie had carefully folded this article as she had other articles from Posey County and Evansville newspapers that covered the events of October and November 1878. She feared that John Leffel's call for a county-wide conspiracy of silence would be heeded. The front page editorial from *The Western Star* edition of October 17, 1878 directed:

ᘓ

"Now let the appropriately dark pall of oblivion cover the whole transaction."

ᘓ

While she was not sure what use could be made of news articles when it was obvious that Posey County's legal, law enforcement and media communities had already decided that the murders were the product of good men doing good deeds, Eppie preserved the articles in the false bottom of her large jewelry box.

She, also, took the reserve fund of cash and gold coins that George kept in his small office safe. Eppie knew that some of this money came from Samson and Rachel when they had fled from Mt. Vernon.

Had Eppie known Ajax's plans for George she could have just waited a short while. All of George's property was soon to be Eppie's.

CHAPTER NINETY-SEVEN

DARK SHADOWS

DARLY HAYES WAS PREGNANT WITH her tenth child when she rushed to the front steps to find her husband face down on the walk. Her attention was on Ed, but she still caught sight of a large black apparition hurtling over the picket fence.

It was difficult for her to bend down, but she managed to get to her knees beside Ed's bleeding face. She pushed him onto his back and put her ear to his mouth. He was gurgling air through the blood pouring from his mouth and nose.

Darly screamed for her eldest daughter, Darlene, who ran out in her nightgown to help her mother set Hayes up so the blood would not suffocate him. Darlene then ran next door to get Mr. Jenkins who was already awake due to Darly's screams.

Jenkins and Darlene managed to get Hayes to his bedroom then Jenkins ran to get Dr. Spencer.

When Spencer examined Hayes he told Darly it appeared that Ed's neck might have been broken in the fall down the steps. Ed was in a coma and it would be up to God if he survived. Spencer knew of no treatment but rest and prayer.

The next day Darly went to the jail to talk to Sheriff John Wheeler. Wheeler had found it hard to believe Hayes could have sustained such damage from falling down six steps even before Darly told him about the black specter. His first thought was that the fugitive Ed Hill had been somehow caught by Hayes then escaped by clubbing Hayes.

After Wheeler assured Darly that he would ask the Posey County Council to continue Ed's salary until he recovered, Wheeler went looking for William Combs.

"It don't look good for Hayes. He may not make it and even if he does, he's probably going to be worthless. Combs, I think that nigger, Ed Hill, must have been waiting for Hayes and waylaid him with a club. You know that Hill's the only one left and he always was one to fight. Hell, I've had to have Hayes and another man hold him more than once so's I could beat some sense into him. Even then the black bastard would cuss me."

"John, ain't you jumping to some pretty big conclusions based on one shadow seen by a terrified pregnant woman? Dr. Spencer didn't seem to have any problem saying the fall did it. Don't go panicking on me now just 'cause them niggers were strung up. Everybody knows they had it coming. We just need to stay calm 'til things die down some. You know that with all the men involved in this thing no one's going to have any trouble unless we panic. Just go about your business and let Judge Parrett and the Grand Jury handle things. Ed Hill isn't crazy. Do you think after seven niggers got themselves killed that he would hang around by himself? He's probably all the way into Ohio by now. So quit acting like a trembling old woman. John Leffel is making sure the public stays in line and the niggers are being driven out so fast they are leaving food cooking on the stove."

When Wheeler left, Combs went to his cousin's house to get Daniels then Combs and Daniels went to Henry Jones' office.

"Wheeler thinks that Ed Hill may be hanging about and that he may have been the dark shadow that Darly saw fleeing from Ed Hayes. Wheeler says there's no way Ed's injuries came from such a short fall. He says it would take a strong man with a club to do such damage. We all know that Ed Hill was at Rosa's and he was always an uppity son-of-a-bitch. He'd have to be a damned fool to stay around, but I, for one, wouldn't put it past him."

"What are we going to do, Bill? Wheeler's worthless and Hayes can't help. After the hangings the whole county is sick of killing. We ain't going to get any help in hunting Hill down. Now that we got rid of their problems they are all getting religion. Even O.C. Thomas' family is calling for people to leave the niggers alone. I say we better make sure that black bastard ain't hanging around. If he did club Hayes, he may be lying in the bushes waiting to get us next."

"Damn it, George, you sound just like that coward, Wheeler. There's not a family in Posey County that's not somehow connected to this thing. All we have to do is not run around like chickens with our heads cut off. If we are not careful, we'll force the federal authorities to investigate this thing. Then we'll all be in a fix. Right now Judge Parrett and Alvin Hovey have made the right moves to keep outsiders out of this. But if we ain't careful, this whole thing may blow up in our faces."

Henry Jones had sat silently in his desk chair staring out the window towards the Ohio River. He knew Combs and Daniels were talking, but their words had no meaning for him. He kept seeing Da's eyes and hearing his terrified pleas for mercy. John's murder had made Henry nauseous, but Da's desperate turning to Henry was inescapable. Somehow Henry knew that neither Da nor even Sarah had betrayed him. He knew that whatever Da and Sarah may have done it was not done to hurt him. The only betrayal was Henry's of Da, and Henry could not find a way to forgive himself.

"Jones, are you hearing any of this? You're the one whose wife was bedded by that nigger. Now you act like we're the ones in the wrong. You are an ungrateful bastard. All we did was hasten them niggers to hell."

Henry could barely find the voice to respond to Combs. He slowly shifted his vacant gaze from the window to the floor.

"Combs, you know those boys didn't harm those whores. And we've all heard the rumors about what really happened with O.C. Thomas. I don't know what's true, but I do know what we did was wrong. I'm all hollow inside and I ain't going hunting for Ed Hill. Do your damnedest, but do it without me."

After Combs and Daniels left, Henry took a clean sheet of Pittsburgh Coal Company stationary and dated it November 20, 1878.

❧

"With only God and my conscience as witnesses I declare this to be my last will and testament. I do not ask for forgiveness or mercy; I deserve neither.

All that is or may be mine I bequeath to my beloved wife, Sarah Jones, to do with as she sees fit. However, if Sarah chooses, it would please me if she wishes to contribute some funds to Christian Willis and Soaring Bird.

If there is a child whom Sarah may select, I fully understand and support her choice of such child as our residuary heir.

Signed and sealed: Henry Jones
At Mt. Vernon, Indiana"

❧

Henry's attorney, Alvin P. Hovey, found the will in Henry's desk upon being appointed by Judge Parrett to handle Henry's estate when Sarah Jones could not be readily located after Henry's death.

CHAPTER NINETY-EIGHT

THE POGROM

"That sniveling coward, he's the one whose nigger loving wife caused all this. Now he's gone all weak-kneed. Well, it will just be up to us to let these niggers know they better get out of Posey County while they still can. George, get in this carriage. We are going to once again be God's avenging angels and let some more of these black bastards see the coming of the Lord."

Daniels had always deferred to his older cousin even when he knew that Combs had lied about Eppie and Samson. Now that Combs was the only person George had left to cling to, he was too weak to contest Combs' lead. On the other hand, he knew he'd done all the killing he could stomach. It would be up to Combs to find Hill.

"All right, Bill, I'll ride along with you again for now, but I'm not feeling well. You'll have to drop me by home before long."

Combs drove them all over Belleville as he stopped Negroes and ordered them to immediately leave Posey County or face the same fate as the lynched men. Daniels could not force himself to speak out, but he silently assented to the reign of terror promulgated by Combs.

The edict for Negroes to evacuate Posey County was successful. In the 1880 Census, fully half of the county's Negro population, as reflected in the 1870 Census, had been permanently driven out of Posey County and their property had been confiscated by whites.

Sheriff John Wheeler was quoted in the October 19, 1878 edition of the *Evansville Journal*:

ଔ

"He denies the story told by some of the refugees now in Evansville to the effect that the entire male colored portion of the population were forced to leave the city. He says that not more than half of them fled, probably one hundred in all, and that most of these were of the worthless class."

ଔ

But the Evansville reporter managed to talk with some of Posey County's Negroes who voiced doubts as to Wheeler's commitment to their safety.

ଔ

"In his perambulations about town yesterday afternoon and last evening a *Journal* commissioner met several of the refugees from Mt. Vernon. They are one and all undecided as to what it would be best to do. They are nearly all out of money and but few have friends here. When told that Sheriff Wheeler had stated that there would be no more trouble and that they could return to their homes in safety, they seemed to be skeptical.

....

In a communication received at the *Journal* office from Mt. Vernon last evening, it is stated that good, orderly negroes are not disturbed or molested. It is only the mean and worthless scamps who infested the place that have been driven away, and the citizens, so says the writer, have approved of the action taken."

☙

In *The Western Star* of October 17, 1878, John Leffel took umbrage at the following account taken from the *Evansville Evening Tribune* published on October 16, 1878:

☙

"A colored man, steady and industrious, a good mechanic and a man of some property, was met on the street yesterday evening after the 4 o'clock train had passed, and ordered to leave within five minutes. This order was given by two men who were going around town in a buggy, making a business of notifying colored people to leave.

An old doctress named Caldwell was ordered to leave and with her whole family obeyed;

. . . .

The colored people, instead of making preparations to burn the town are packing up and secreting their effects in the expectation of their houses being burned."

☙

But, as George Daniels and William Combs were soon to discover, there was one free young Negro male who was not quite ready to leave Posey County.

Chapter Ninety-Nine

MEASURE FOR MEASURE

AJAX LEARNED OF HENRY JONES' suicide and Ed Hayes' coma from Morita Meier. That left George Daniels and William Combs. Ajax would gladly leave Posey County when those two answered for their crimes. He would have to leave the rest of Posey County's citizens to answer to history.

With Eppie at Brewery Hills, Ajax decided to confront George Daniels inside the Daniels home. Well after dark on November 21, 1878 Ajax walked the three miles from Brewery Hills to Black's Grove then down Walnut Street to the rear of the Daniels house. He saw a lamp shining through a second story window.

George Daniels was lying on the bed he had shared for so many years with Eppie. He was fully clothed except for his shoes that he had dropped beside the bed. He heard the kitchen window break.

George grabbed his pistol from his nightstand and silently eased out of his bedroom in his stocking feet. He kept his back against the hallway wall as he slowly approached the stairs. He listened intently, but could not hear any more sounds from the kitchen.

As he entered upon the staircase he kept one hand against the wall and stepped on the end of the risers as near as possible to the wall.

George silently cursed himself for failing to nail down the loose step near the bottom of the stairs. He was amused that his thoughts turned to Eppie's repeated requests that he take ten minutes and fix the step. But then a powerful grip closed over his hand and the gun it held.

It may have been years since his blacksmith days, but George Daniels remained a powerful man. He jerked his hand free and fired wildly into the darkness.

Ajax was startled by the gunshot and the blaze from the end of the pistol. He fell back long enough for George to swing the pistol towards where he thought his assailant should be. But his wild swing missed Ajax who grabbed George and pinned his arms to his side. George lost his hold on the pistol which dropped from his hand and slid across the hardwood floor. Ajax then fell on top of him and placed his right knee in the middle of George's back. He gripped George's face in his two hands and began to pull George's head backwards.

The sound of George's neck breaking and the limpness of his body signaled Ajax to fall exhausted to the floor. Although the entire episode lasted only about two minutes from gunshot to George's death, Ajax feared that the shot would bring people to the scene. He forced himself to get up and stumble out the kitchen door into the cool blackness of the autumn night.

When he got back to Jane at Brewery Hills he felt no need to explain what he had done. In fact, he felt almost nothing at all. Somehow he knew that George Daniels had himself been a victim of both his times and William Combs. Maybe when Combs was dispatched to hell Ajax would achieve the vengeance he hoped would provide some relief.

CHAPTER ONE HUNDRED

A MAN

WILLIAM COMBS FOUND HIS COUSIN at the bottom of the stairs. This time there was no need for speculation. The pistol and the disheveled house left no doubt. Combs knew that someone or something was wrecking havoc on the ringleaders of the lynchings. He went directly to Sheriff Wheeler.

John Wheeler wanted to resign his office before he met the same fate as Hayes, Jones or Daniels, but Combs shamed him into staying on.

"You damned coward. How many niggers can there be out there? We have driven practically all of them out of the county. We know whoever's doing this is probably hiding out at Brewery Hills. There's no place else to hide. Now get some men and let's go raid that snake pit."

"I ain't going to do that, Bill. Enough is enough. No more killing. No more nothing. I'm through with this whole thing."

"You damned fool. You may be next. They are going to pick us all off one at a time. Is that what you want, to spend the rest of your life jumping every time you hear a noise?"

"I don't care. How will we face our children and grandchildren when they learn about these murders? No, I am done. If they come after me, so be it. You started this whole damned mess; you can try to finish it if you want. But I'm warning you, Combs, if you kill any more people it better be in self defense. Now go away and leave me alone."

Combs was so surprised by Wheeler's sudden shift in attitude that he just turned and left the old jail. He caught himself looking towards the rundown old jailhouse privy then up at the locust trees beside the majestic new courthouse. Just one month, is that all the time that had passed? He thought maybe that was what the Bible meant by six days; the whole world had changed in Posey County since October 7, 1878.

Combs mumbled under his breath, "Well, by God, I won't run scared from some spook nigger. I'll get that son-of-a-bitch Hill before he can get me."

Combs went to his house to get his pistol and his shotgun. Then he headed for Brewery Hills just as a bloody autumn moon rose over Black's Grove. But now that he was completely alone Combs felt doubt begin to work its way into his mind.

When Combs drove his buggy up to Christian Willis' church at eight o'clock p.m. on November 22, 1878, Christian opened the church door and stepped out.

"Mr. Combs, how can I help you?"

"Where's that nigger, Ed Hill? I know you're hiding him out here."

"Ed Hill ain't here, Mr. Combs. He never has been here. If anyone told you he was here, they were mistaken."

"Well, step aside, Indian. I'm going to look for myself."

Combs brushed past Willis into the small frame church where he saw Jane, Soaring Bird, Elizabeth Harrison and Ajax. Ajax's massive body barely fit in the pew.

"Why are you still here, nigger? Haven't you got the word to leave yet? If not, I'm telling you now. Get out of Posey County tonight or you won't see tomorrow."

Ajax looked at the shotgun Combs carried in his left hand and the pistol that was stuck in his waistband. Although he was filled with hate and anger, Ajax did not want to endanger anyone else.

"I's be leavin' soon, Mr. Combs. I's jus' gitting things tagether. I's jus' has one more thing ta do, then I'll gladly leave Posey County."

"Well, boy, if I see you again you will wish you'd left sooner. Now where's Ed Hill."

"I dons know Ed Hill and he ain't nebber been here. Why's you thinks he's here?"

"He killed George Daniels last night. There ain't no other place for him to hide."

"How does you knows he killed Mr. Daniels?"

"Why you uppity nigger, I don't have to prove anything to you."

Combs would have shot Ajax right then if he had not remembered what Sheriff Wheeler had said and if there had been no witnesses.

"Well, I'll be leaving for now, but I'll be back and you'd better be gone."

Combs had difficulty controlling his trembling legs as he exited the church. There was something familiar about the huge Negro who had stared calmly right into Combs' eyes. Combs had felt the hair on his neck rise even though he was the one with the loaded guns.

Combs backed out the church door and climbed up into his buggy. He was forced to walk his horse along the dark and narrow road with its ruts and chuckholes. The orange quarter moon gave only enough light to eerily filter through the overhanging tree branches. About a quarter of a mile from the church Combs heard the first sound that his horse and carriage had not caused.

Combs shifted the reins to his right hand and gripped the shotgun with his left. Every time the buggy was jarred by a rut in the road Combs felt his body stiffen. With each strange sound from the side of the road his sphincter muscle contracted as fear began to grip him. When Combs' horse flushed a covey of quail he lost control of his bowels.

Combs saw a silhouette gliding through the trees; he fired his shotgun towards the shadow and the loud blast frightened his horse. The horse bolted along the dark road until it tripped on a tree root and dumped Combs out into the shallow stream that ran beside the road. Combs lost the shotgun, but his pistol remained in his waistband. When he recovered from the fall he grabbed the pistol and hunkered down in the tall wet grass.

Then he saw the shadow again. He screamed, "Come on you black son-of-a-bitch! Come out in the open!"

"I's over here, Mr. Combs."

Combs turned completely around and fired at a moving branch. Now he had urinated on himself also.

"Over here, Mr. Combs."

Combs began to run down the bumpy road as he tried to reload his pistol. He was too nervous to get the cartridge into the chamber. Then he tripped into what he thought was a tree and fell to his knees as his pistol flew from his hand into the stream beside the road.

"Does you remember Rachel and Samson Wright, Mr. Combs?"

Combs was covered with feces, urine, sweat and fear. As he curled into a fetal position, Ajax asked him again, "Does you remember Rachel and Samson, Mr. Combs?"

Combs clasped Ajax's lower legs and whimpered, "Please, who are you? Don't hurt me."

"I axed you, does you remember Rachel and Samson Wright? Now, does you?"

"It was so long ago, yes, I remember them. Why?"

"They's my parents and you tried ta rape Miss Eppie and kill my daddy. Now does you 'member dat?"

"Oh, please, that ain't true. I tried to help your family. I don't know what they told you, but I didn't do nothing to them."

"An what about de Harrisons and dem boys you lynched? You didn't do dat neither I's suppose."

Ajax ripped open the back of Combs' shirt then jerked it off of him. Ajax tied one shirt sleeve around Combs' neck as Combs cried and pleaded for his life. As Ajax tightened the knot up against Combs' neck Combs began to struggle and swing wildly at Ajax with both arms.

Ajax grabbed Combs' gonads in his left hand as he held onto the makeshift noose with his right. The more Combs struggled the tighter Ajax squeezed as Combs screamed in pain until he fainted.

Ajax revived Combs by spitting in his face and slapping him. When Combs came to the pain was so intense he could not straighten out.

"Mr. Combs, is you ready ta meet the Devil? Just think 'bout burning in hell forever."

Ajax pulled Combs up by the knotted shirt and then he threw the other sleeve over a tree limb hanging low across the side of the road. Ajax slowly pulled Combs up until his toes were just off the ground.

Combs began to choke and gasp for air as his legs kicked spasmodically. Ajax kept tightening and then easing the tension on the knot for the twenty minutes he took to asphyxiate Combs.

Then Ajax dragged Combs' body away from the road to a brushy ravine haunted by foxes.

Ajax slowly worked his way back through the brush with the aid of the light from the now silver moon. When he reached the stream by the road he squatted down to carefully wash his hands and arms with water and sand.

He now had time to consider how he felt. He felt good. He felt like a man. He was ready to take his family and leave Posey County.

CHAPTER ONE HUNDRED ONE

WHY NOW?

ALVIN HOVEY AND WILLIAM PARRETT stood beside one another in Parrett's private chambers that occupied the northwest corner of the courthouse's third floor. Each chose to gaze out of the large windows into the setting sun glistening on the Ohio River three blocks away. Both men had known for ten years that such a day might come. But why did it have to arrive in 1888 when Hovey was involved in a close gubernatorial race and Parrett was running for congress?

Hovey had received a letter signed by Sarah Jones and Eppie Daniels informing him that Eppie personally and as Sarah's attorney-in-fact, wished to meet with Hovey. Sarah and Eppie had asked Hovey to wind up Henry's and George's affairs in 1878. He had liquidated all of their assets and arranged for both men's funerals and burials. Hovey had all funds transferred to the Cincinnati, Ohio bank accounts designated by a letter he had received from Eppie and Sarah in December, 1878. The final closing of both estates had been approved by Judge Parrett in October of 1879. Neither Hovey nor Parrett had heard any more from either woman until the letter had arrived on June 1, 1888. It was formal in tone with a return address of a post office box in Cincinnati:

&

"General Hovey:

Please be informed that Mrs. George Daniels is hereby appointed by me as my attorney-in-fact to act on my behalf.

Thank you for your past kindness. I respectfully request that you meet with her on June 8 if that is convenient. She will arrive on board the Memphis Belle that p.m. With all due regard I remain,

Sarah Jones
May 27, 1888"

&

Hovey had shown the letter to Parrett on June first. Now they were watching the river for the steamboat's arrival at the Mt. Vernon landing. Hovey had planned to meet Eppie at his law office across the street from the courthouse. But he wanted Parrett's advice on what he should do if Eppie was returning to reopen the events of October and November of 1878.

"Alvin, do you recall how proud and hopeful we were on July 4, 1876 when you laid the first brick for this courthouse?"

"I do, Judge, all things seemed possible then. Now it sometimes seems as if all we are doing is waiting for the sand to run out. What happened to us? How did we let things get to such a pass?"

"I don't know that we bear much blame for the actions of the mob. But we both know that if we are ever considered for admittance to heaven, our most grievous sin was the role we played in the aftermath. The thing is, Alvin, when I try to look back and honestly evaluate my actions, and those of others whom I respect, I still do not know what we could have done differently."

"Judge, I want to believe that, but I just can't. Men like Morita Meier and Christian Willis found the courage to speak out and try to help the colored community. If you and I and just a few others had stood up and called for justice, we might have been able to shame the county into trying to atone after the murders. Just as I now want to win the governor's race and you want to win a congressional seat, back then we feared losing all we had struggled to obtain."

"But what are we to do now, throw away all we have worked for? What would be achieved? Would our sacrifice bring even one Negro back to life or restore ownership of one parcel of real estate? It's been ten years since those boys were hanged outside this courthouse. We do not even know the location of the Negroes who fled.

"And what about the two to three hundred men involved in the tragedy? Do you think they and their families will take kindly to seeing this thing investigated? Your chance to be governor and my race for congress would end immediately."

"But how will history judge us? More importantly, how will God judge us? Are we to just go on pretending those boys ravaged those whores and that O.C. Thomas was murdered by Harrison? We know better."

"I do not know how history or God will judge us, but I know how our friends, neighbors and voters will judge us if we pull the scab off of this thing. John Leffel is still here publishing his papers. Do you think he will support an investigation? And for what, they are dead. I say we did all that we could under the circumstances. Surely Posey County can best prosper by letting this sad episode stay completely forgotten."

"Well, you may be right, but I fear for the legacy we are leaving to Posey County. History has a way of oozing out of unhealed wounds left open by those who hoped posterity would never find out about their sins."

"Well, there's the steamboat. Let's go see if Eppie can even recognize who we have become after ten years of fearing this day. Are you coming?"

CHAPTER ONE HUNDRED TWO

THE DAMRON HOTEL

Ten years had changed only the color of Eppie's hair. She remained the strikingly beautiful and graceful woman that Hovey had last seen as she signed the documents he had prepared at the end of November, 1878. While she moved slowly and with caution from the gangplank to the shore, her step was firm. The gangly girl who walked beside her had no need to help Eppie negotiate the landing.

Hovey and Parrett doffed their hats as they approached Eppie. "Mrs. Daniels, it is good to see you again," Hovey said. "You remember Judge Parrett, I presume?"

"Welcome back, Mrs. Daniels. If I may say so, the years have been more than kind to you."

"Thank you, gentlemen, it was good of you to meet me. This is an unexpected courtesy. Hattie, this is the famous General Hovey and Posey County's Circuit Judge, Judge Parrett. Please say hello. Gentlemen, you may recall the child who left with us in 1878; this is Hattie Crider."

Hattie shyly curtsied but did not speak.

"Why, hello little lady, I have not seen you since you were in swaddling clothes. You are almost as tall as Mrs. Daniels now. You must take after your father. I remember what an impressive specimen he was." Hovey reached out his hand and patted Hattie on the top of her head. She flinched, but did not move away.

"Eppie, if I may return to those days when we were more familiar, do you need help with your luggage? Where are you staying?"

"It would please me to hear the familiar sounds of Christian names, Alvin. As for you, Judge, I never knew you had a first name."

Parrett laughed and answered, "It is Bill, Eppie, and it would please me to hear it from you. People usually have the advantage of me as I am always 'Judge', and I may have no memory of what to call them. But I could never forget you or your esteemed departed husband, George, God rest his soul."

"I am staying only until the Memphis Belle leaves tomorrow afternoon. I have a room for Hattie and me at the Damron Hotel. The porter has already made arrangements to transport our things there."

Hovey and Parrett made eye contact at the last statement. Hovey said, "Uh, Eppie, Mr. Damron may need to make some arrangements. Perhaps Hattie would be more comfortable with her Uncle Charles. She might enjoy getting acquainted with her cousins and her Aunt Eliza. They still live at their place on Elm Street."

"The Damron will be fine. Hattie has been found good enough for the best hotels in Cincinnati and for passage on the Memphis Belle. We will try to keep her color from rubbing off on the sheets. I believe that is the least she is owed by this community."

"Now, Eppie, please do not take offense. Hattie will surely have no trouble if no mention is made of her lineage. After all, she somewhat favors my memory of Mrs. Jones. I just now remembered whom she reminded me of. But you know, Eppie, this is still southern Indiana."

"Let's move on to other matters. Can we proceed to your office or the courthouse to transact business?"

"Certainly, let me carry your valise, Eppie. Judge, would you like to show Hattie your beautiful courthouse while Eppie and I use your outer chambers?"

"I would be delighted to try to entertain Hattie. Perhaps she and I will inspect the seat of Posey County justice from the catacombs to the attic."

CHAPTER ONE HUNDRED THREE

A PRICE MET

"ALVIN, MRS. JONES AND I want to establish two trust funds at the Posey County Bank. A trustee will be needed to oversee them and we would like for you to accept those duties, for a reasonable yearly fee, of course."

"Why do you want the trusts to be established in Posey County?"

"For reasons she prefers to keep to herself, Sarah wants funds available locally in the form of a burial trust for Hattie and for herself. Sarah wants to be brought back here for burial and she wants a plot for Hattie too."

"But, Eppie, I cannot get a Negro admitted to Bellefontaine Cemetery. Even if I become the Governor of Indiana I will not have that power."

"Sarah knows that. But you can purchase plots for both Hattie and Sarah at the Colored Odd Fellows Cemetery on Upton Road. That is what she wants. And she needs someone of your stature to assure that her wishes are carried out. She does not plan to return to Posey County until it's time for her to be buried. She needs all the legal details to be in place for her and Hattie now. She has given me one thousand dollars. Is that enough for your fee, the plots and the burials? She wants no funerals for her or Hattie, but she does want Hattie and me to pick the plots out now."

"By coincidence, Hattie's uncle, Charles Harrison, is the sexton for the Colored Odd Fellows. I will see if he can guide you out there tomorrow. A thousand dollars is far more than necessary, but, of course, it will be good to have too much rather than not enough. Do you think Sarah would want any remainder after both burials to go to the upkeep of the graves?"

"No, that is where the other trust fund comes in. She and I wish to use any of her excess funds from the burial trust and the additional five hundred dollars that I will be entrusting with you to create a memorial for the lost souls of 1878. You are the only one who can get such a thing accomplished. We would prefer it be placed on the courthouse campus where most of the men were killed, but something permanent on the waterfront would, also, be acceptable. We must leave all details to you. We have no plans to take part. Can you do such a thing, Alvin? After ten years is it not time for Posey County to acknowledge that great tragedy?"

"Ah, Eppie, every day I and many other citizens feel the shame of those events. I cannot guarantee you when something will be done, but I can give you my word that I will set up the two trust accounts at Mr. James' private bank. I hope you may forgive me if I proceed slowly on opening up those very volatile emotions. I do not think Posey County is quite ready to face its most shameful episode."

"Sarah and I talked about this. We are aware of the delicate nature of things. That's why we have waited ten years. We know from the news accounts that you are running for governor. We expected to wait longer."

Hovey did not miss the insult intended. On the other hand he was grateful that he would not be pressed to begin the county's process of atonement.

"I will walk Hattie down to see her family this evening. Then we can set up a time for Charles to show us the cemetery. Thank you, Alvin. You are a good man. Do you think you could show me the court records for 1878? I would like to know what happened after we left Posey County."

Hovey felt his stomach tighten and his mouth was dry. "Now, Eppie, you know you won't learn much from those Order Books. They are mainly for judges and lawyers."

"That's okay. I just want to find out about the rape and murder charges and who was brought to justice. I want to show Hattie what happened to her family and their killers. You know, I have never heard that there were any trials." Just as Eppie said this, Parrett and Hattie walked through the door.

"Well, Hattie and I covered every dusty inch of the courthouse. We had fun, didn't we, Hattie?"

Hattie just smiled and nodded her head.

"Eppie, could you and Hattie excuse us a moment? I need to speak with Judge Parrett about a case we are working on."

When Eppie and Hattie stepped out of Parrett's outer chamber Hovey shut the door, but did not notice the transom was open.

"Judge, we may have to lose that 1878 to 1881 Criminal Order Book for awhile. Eppie is still as pushy as she used to be. I am afraid she plans to dig up the entire mess. She wants to see the records."

"Calm down, Alvin; take her down to the basement. She can't do anything with those entries I made unless I authorize their use. Just let her show them to Hattie then when they go back to Ohio we will make sure there is no problem. No matter what she claims she read, without the Order Book, we can recreate history as we think it should be. I will still be the judge until I resign to enter Congress, if I win. Either way, we have time."

Eppie guided Hattie away from the door as she heard the conversation dying down. When Hovey and Parrett came out Parrett said, "I did not have an opportunity to express my sympathies to you for George's death. You will find in the Order Book that Ed Hill was charged with both the original rapes and your husband's murder. He has never been caught, but there have been persistent rumors of sightings in Indian Territory where he may be hiding out as a ranch hand.

"In fact, in my conversations about running for Congress with my friend from Illinois, Congressman William Mc Kendree Springer, Hill's name has come up more than once. Springer wants to open up the vast unused Indian lands for settlement. I agree with him and plan to support his Indian Appropriations Bill if I am elected. It is sound policy based on President Lincoln's 1862 Homestead Act. There is to be a great land run next year if it passes. Many people believe that the soiled doves who were ravaged by the Negroes, also, moved west and made enough money to become respectable."

"Well, as with most power grabs of other's property, I commend Springer for naming the theft in honor of the victims. Perhaps someone should ask the Indians if they want their lands appropriated."

Parrett felt his anger burning his face. Now he remembered Eppie's attempts to get Negroes admitted to white schools and women the right to vote. But before he could retort, Hovey said, "My understanding is that a fair price will be paid for the land. The Indians need money to help them adapt to our society."

"Will the price be as fair as what we paid the French for the Louisiana Purchase? Of course, the true owners got none of that money, so, I guess the Appropriations Act is some improvement. And maybe the Indians prefer their own culture more than an adaptation to white society. Did anyone ask them?"

"Alvin, take them to the records room. I have some work to do. I will join you soon." Parrett knew he was dangerously close to saying things that might hurt his congressional campaign. He needed space from this infuriating female and her young Negro companion. Parrett was so angry he took no note of Eppie's lack of interest in information about her husband's killer.

As Alvin Hovey led Eppie and Hattie down the stairs to the basement he continued to carry the leather valise from which Eppie had produced Sarah's written instructions and the drafts signed by Sarah and Eppie. When she had handed him the case he was surprised at how heavy it was. He asked her about the contents of the valise to take the conversation away from more contentious issues.

"What's in this thing, Eppie? I don't see how you managed it from the steamboat. I should have come on board and helped you with it. What do the gold initials 'I.C.' stand for?"

"I.C. are the initials of Inola Crider. She was someone I knew as a little girl; she died long ago. Hattie shares Inola's last name, but they are not blood relation. This valise is about all that is left of her. Alvin, this is marvelous brick work in these massive arches and supporting columns."

"Yes, one of my soldiers, John Giggy, did this masonry. In fact, he designed and built these wonderful columns that are used for the record room. You may recall that he and I worked together on some of these supports. Here are the records. Some of them date from 1816. Here is the criminal Order Book for 1878 to 1881. The rapes were October 7, 1878 and the last entry concerning those and all the events that they caused was made when Judge Parrett declared the cases closed."

Eppie slowly opened the huge canvas and leather bound volume. She looked first at Judge Parrett's recording of the charges against the seven black men for the rapes of the three prostitutes on Monday, October 7, 1878. Then she found the murder charges against Daniel Harrison, Sr., as returned by the Grand Jury on October 12.

"Alvin, I do not see any charges for the murders of Daniel Harrison, Jr., and John Harrison. You know those occurred before O.C. Thomas, Ed Hayes, Charles Baker and Bill Russell went to Harrison's house. Why weren't there charges against my husband, Bill Combs and Henry Jones?"

Hovey was stunned. He had no idea that Eppie knew about John Harrison's shooting and the particularly ghastly death of Daniel Harrison, Jr. He kept silent as he tried to regain his composure.

"Where's the responsibility for the butchery of Daniel Harrison, Sr.? His bones are probably still right outside this courthouse. Parrett was judge over that too, wasn't he?"

Hovey could feel the governor's office slipping away. Yet he felt a glimmer of hope and relief. Maybe this was what Posey County needed, a fearless eyewitness to 1878 who no longer lived in the county. But before he could respond Eppie screamed at him, "Why were those rape charges still being carried on the books when everyone knew that those boys had been lynched? What kind of cowardly cover-up took place here? People should hang for the slaughter of the Harrison family and the lynchings. What role did you and Parrett play in this tragedy? I am going to take this Order Book to the newspaper office in Evansville."

Hattie cowered behind Eppie as she saw the terrible anger on Hovey's face.

"Eppie, we had no part in those murders. What would you have had us do? Almost every family in Posey County was somehow involved. Would you hang them all? Have you forgotten how strong the Ku Klux Klan was here?

"And what about you and Sarah, the rumors were rampant that the two of you were the start of all of this. Does Hattie know about that or do you want me to tell her?"

Eppie slammed the Order Book shut. "Don't threaten me, Sir!" But the threat worked. Eppie did not want Hattie to hear the whole story. As Eppie could not be sure what Hovey and Parrett knew about Ajax's actions, she did not wish to be too aggressive. There was no statute of limitations on murder.

Eppie opened the valise and drew out the large folio of newspaper clippings that she had brought with her.

"I want to match up these scurrilous accounts and especially the calls for a cover-up with the bloody deeds in this Order Book. I want the truth known now!"

Hovey could sense that he had won the immediate battle. Now he had to figure out a strategy to win the war. He decided to play upon what he correctly surmised were Eppie's greatest weaknesses, her pride and her love for Hattie.

"My dear Eppie, you are, of course, right in every regard. Although neither I nor the Judge is to blame for any of those despicable mob actions, we failed in our duty as guardians of justice. We convinced ourselves we had no choice and that the greater good was to try to atone by public service. Of course, deep down we knew we were just afraid. I have spent every waking moment and many a cruel dream punishing myself for my weakness. I am not asking for forgiveness and fear that God will never grant me peace. But, please believe that I am more ashamed of my cowardice in this catastrophe than I would have been had I turned tail in battle."

Eppie had long wondered what role hers and Sarah's actions had played in the events of 1878. It was easy to blame the mob, law enforcement, the legal community or all of Posey County. But she knew her pride, arrogance and need for a child were significant factors also. She heard Hovey's words; what would be gained by putting Hattie and Ajax through what a full investigation might bring? Maybe for once she should listen to someone else's advice.

"Something must be done. These horrible crimes cannot just be swept under the rug. I want the Judge and you to make these newspaper accounts a part of the court records. Those dead men were slaughtered and everyone knows it. Their lives have to have meant something and so must their deaths. That's why there has to be a public memorial."

"Okay, Eppie. Let me talk with Judge Parrett. If he wins his race for Congress, he will remain judge until the end of this year and still have control of these records. And if I win the governor's race, I will have two months before I take office. At that point, Parrett and I together will have more power and influence. We should be better able to help the county atone if we win, but we cannot win if the voters turn against us. Let me promise you that the news accounts will be added to the Order Book now. As to how and when Judge Parrett and I publish the records and begin the county's expiation of its sins, I am asking that you be patient. After all, it's been ten years already. What is the harm in a few more months or even a year or two? And you can help by having Charles Harrison and his family as well as other coloreds you may know help locate the families who were driven out."

Eppie had no illusions. She knew that she was not likely to ever hear of any exposé of 1878 nor was there likely to be any compensation for victims. On the other hand, Hovey and Parrett could not be sure that Eppie would remain silent for much longer. Also, Hattie would soon be grown and with the assets that Eppie and Sarah were going to bestow upon her, she could take up the fight. As for now, she and Hattie would ask Charles Harrison to show them the Odd Fellows Cemetery early the next day.

"Alvin, I want to take the Order Book with me tonight so that I can properly match up clippings with the Judge's entries. If you allow that, I will bring it back after Hattie and I have selected the plots."

"Judge Parrett may put me in jail, but I will let you take it with you. You know it won't fit entirely in that case. We will exit by the south door on the main level. The old jail is gone now. You are familiar with that old wives' tale about trees dying after they are used for hangings. Well, soon after the murders, our locust trees died. Most of our citizens believe that God killed the trees as an omen that a terrible price would be extracted for our collective sins. It may be true that heavenly retribution awaits us, but the locust trees were killed by the doctor who lives across Walnut Street and just south of the courthouse. He did not like the bushy trees obscuring his view of the courthouse, so he and a doctor friend of his sneaked over at night and bored holes in the base of the trunks. They then poured salt into the bore holes and waited for the trees to die. Our good citizens were already superstitious enough without the lynchings, so the doctor had no trouble getting people to accept his explanation that the dead men killed the trees."

Hovey realized that he was prattling on due to his fear of Eppie's reaction to the cover-up. He knew he had to show confidence so that he would not lose control of the situation. He decided that physical movement was the best way to change the psychological environment.

"Let's hurry past the area of the murders. I can still feel the pain of the victims and their families. My guilt was only after the fact, but my shame never lets me rest."

CHAPTER ONE HUNDRED FOUR

THE RIGHT THING

"DAMN IT, ALVIN. THAT TROUBLE maker is going to take my Order Book straight to the *Evansville Journal*. You know that bastard editor over there has hated Posey County since 1878. Now I am ordering you to go get it back. How could she carry it anyway? It must weigh twenty pounds."

"She put the papers inside the front and back covers and put the book into her valise. Hattie helped her carry it. What alternative did I have? If I hadn't made a Devil's bargain with her, she would have gone directly to the *Journal*. I could tell that she loves that little girl and there is something more I am sure. For some reason she does not want George's murder opened up. If she brings the Order Book back tomorrow, we can dispose of it and all the clippings after she leaves. If she takes the Order Book to the *Journal*, we will charge her with felony theft of government property and you can stop the *Journal* from publishing anything under threat of contempt and a charge of receiving stolen property. However, I am confident that her fear of hurting the child will keep her in line."

"Well, you'd better be right or both of our careers and the reputation of the whole county will be forever besmirched. We will see what tomorrow brings."

Charles Harrison drove the carriage that Eppie had rented up the long hill that rose above the west edge of Mt. Vernon. Eppie was filled with competing emotions as she entered the Negro Odd Fellows Cemetery and gazed southeast across the two miles from Upton Road back to the courthouse.

Although Hattie was only ten years old, Sarah had long ago told her the truth about how she came into the world. Sarah had instructed Eppie to let Hattie pick out hers and Sarah's final resting place. Eppie noted that the Negro cemetery was next to a hog farm. Even in death there was no respite.

Hattie got out of the carriage and walked slowly but without hesitation to an area on the north edge of the carefully tended cemetery where a young locust tree spread its leaves over a small grassy knoll. "This is it, Aunt Eppie. Momma wants us to be here."

When Eppie looked at Charles he was crying. "Eppie, what's left of Daniel be buried there. General Hovey made 'em let me dig up de jailhouse privy after they moved ta da new jail on Mill Street. I's able ta find a bone or two. I used ta try ta keep a board up wit his name on it, but white folks just tore it up. But dat be where's he at. I's able ta move what was left of John's body here too. 'Course, Da was all burned up by dat steam engine. But I's believe Jesus put his sweet soul here wit his fambly.

"What's you want on yore stone, little Hattie? I's mos likely be gone, but we can have Eppie writes it down fo my records."

Hattie repeated what her mother had told her, "Momma does not want her name on the stone. She wants to be buried right where I will be buried. She says she will probably go first so I will be laid beside or on top of her. She wants us to spend eternity together. What she wants on my tombstone is my name, Hattie Crider, and my year of birth, 1878, and just the year I die. Momma was very clear that she did not want the month and day of my birth or my death. She told me that way it would be to her like I had always been alive and would always be alive. She, also, wants a concrete border around it. Mother said she hopes I get married and have children, but even if I do I can still be buried with Mother if I want. She says it will be up to me and whatever I decide will please her."

Charles marked the spot on his hand-drawn plot map and put both Sarah's and Hattie's names on it. "Okay, little niece, I's makes sure ta git it right. I wants to be here too."

When they got back to town Eppie had Charles tie the carriage up at the courthouse and asked him to wait with Hattie as Eppie lifted the valise and heavy Order Book with the articles carefully clipped to the entries that Eppie thought best matched the crimes.

From the bay window in his daughter's home across the street from the courthouse, Alvin Hovey had seen the carriage arrive. Hovey hurried across Walnut Street then on to the east door of the courthouse just as Eppie was struggling to open the double doors while holding onto the valise with the Order Book sticking out of it.

"Let me help you, Eppie. How was your trip to the cemetery? You must not have taken long."

"No, Hattie already knew where she and Sarah should be. It was a little disquieting at first, but then it gave me a sense of comfort and appropriateness. Frances Wright would chastise me for being superstitious, but I felt some healing power in that place. I have completed my work with the Order Book. Is there anything else you need to set up the burial trust or the one for the memorial?"

Hovey took the valise and Order Book and started down the basement stairs. "Aren't you coming, Eppie? I plan to simply put it, as is, back where it belongs."

"Alvin, something happened to me at the cemetery. I somehow know that justice will find Posey County someday. I don't know when or how. I just know those horrible crimes will be acknowledged and atoned for. That is enough for me. I will leave the details to the gods and to you. Goodbye, Alvin."

Hovey knew that he would have to safeguard the Order Book and clippings from what the lawyers called the "dungeon rats", people who rummaged through old court records and often stole, destroyed or altered them for personal reasons. There was no way he could just leave the official court record with this added evidence of Posey County's most shameful episode where relatives or ancestors of the "two or three hundred of the county's best men" could destroy it. His problem was what to tell Parrett and where to hide the Order Book until after he had completed his term as Governor in 1892.

Hovey remembered when John Giggy and he had shared the joy of laying some of the first bricks and stone in this temple of justice, the alcove that they had built where the new-fangled gas furnace was to be installed was dry and free from sunlight. Hovey elected to use wood from the old judge's bench from the 1825 courthouse that had been stored in the maintenance room to seal off the narrow space behind the furnace. The evidence would be safe there until Hovey decided the time was right.

After Eppie had left the Courthouse, Hovey remembered that he still had her valise. But with the possibility of Judge Parrett or someone else coming upon him, Hovey decided to not go after her, it would be apropos to store the means for Posey County's deliverance in a container that belonged to the person most responsible for the expiation.

Hovey placed the large volume into the valise. It covered only half of the book. Then he wedged the case and its contents behind the furnace and shoved the panel of seasoned Posey County golden poplar in front of it. He planned to keep his word to Eppie and reclaim his honor as soon as he could find the right moment and sufficient courage.

He set up the burial trust, but decided to hold the memorial funds in his private savings account until he was ready to speak to his fellow citizens about erecting a monument on the southeast side of the court-house campus.

Hovey made Parrett extremely happy by telling him he had disposed of the Order Book. Parrett asked no more questions. Parrett did win his Congressional race and Hovey became the first and only person from Posey County to be elected governor. He died in office in 1891. He suffered a stroke and at the end could not speak. Long before the onset of his illness he had made out a will leaving everything he owned to Esther. But the other instructions he left for his daughter and Colonel Menzies were painfully scribbled out as he lay dying. They could make no sense of them:

"Trus for mem Monument
Order Book, Giggy alcov
God forgive "

EPILOGUE

THE WEEK THIS BOOK WAS being prepared to go to print, Deputy Sheriff Oscar Cyrus Thomas' name was added to the National Law Enforcement Officers Memorial for officers killed in the line of duty.

Such recognition is certainly proper even after 130 years. Officer Thomas was eulogized and mourned publicly in both Posey and Vanderburgh Counties for weeks immediately after his death in 1878. But honorable service and the ultimate sacrifice in the line of duty is not diminished by time.

However, the seven men who were murdered and the one hundred or so African Americans who were driven from their homes without cause in 1878 deserve recognition as well.

More importantly, the legal system that allowed these outrages to occur, and then covered them up, should not escape the judgment of history.

Perhaps a memorial on the southeast corner of the Posey County courthouse campus where the lynchings occurred and where there may still be portions of Daniel Harrison, Sr.'s, body would be a fitting start.

As for the African American boxer who six years ago in a courtroom packed with uniformed police officers was sentenced to five years in prison after pleading guilty to assaulting a policeman, here is an update. On May 16, 2008, Peg and I attended a boxing match in Evansville where the boxer's adult son, David, had a tough professional bout. The father worked his son's corner. David's *nom de guerre* is "King David"; their entire family has always been devout Christians. The father's professional boxing sobriquet is "The Man"; he is old enough to be familiar with the ubiquitous "Boy".

"Officer" Thomas, the black "Man", and United States Supreme Court "Justice" Thomas, carry the same last name. Perhaps we are coming full circle.

Security for the boxing match was provided by members of the Evansville Police Department who enthusiastically cheered for David as he won a tough fight while his father coached and cared for him.

Printed in the United States
131011LV00012B/52/P